Allegiance

by

Victor Salvatore

Allegiance

The Wild Rose Press, Inc.
PO Box 708
Adams Basin, NY 14410-0708
Visit us at www.thewildrosepress.com

Publishing History
First TWA Edition, 2020
Print ISBN 978-1-5092-3058-7
Digital ISBN 978-1-5092-3059-4

Published in the United States of America

It had only taken two hours, the Marines falling back gladly with no casualties, but thankfully, the people on board had not been able to reach them, their legs gone and their states so deteriorated.

Airlocks sealing, confused captains gladly disconnected from the ships, not knowing they were about to learn firsthand what had happened on board, the thirilian still widly unknown and undetectable by scanners, and now gently filtering through their own ventilation systems.

That one parsec had saved the Shailin system and eight billion people from a nightmare. Communications failing on all channels, a brief cry for help finally came from the third ship in the rescue fleet. "They're everywhere—they've got the whole crew! The captain's gone! They're insane, resistant to weapons, but they still know how to operate the ship and how to... No! Nooooooooooo!"

Heads fell as the screaming started the crewman's firing not enough, as the doors had opened behind him...

The fate befalling the Dren at Crisilis was better, their screams silenced in minutes as an armada of Dren attack ships loyal to the new Maral invaded the seemingly safe system deep in Alliance territory. The Vrail who had been awaiting the arrivals bent on their suffering were vaporised along with them, all ships coming to their rescue wiped out as Maral finally asserted his complete arrival, free now from any possible challengers and unleashed thousands of lightyears outside of anyone's control.

Chapter 1

Valour

The stars hung there in space—an environment so calm, subtle, and serene, but it shattered as weapons blazed across the vision. The Terran vessel pulled up hard, ion fire ripping into its shields; the Dren vessel behind it was preparing for another shot when suddenly it was torn apart in violent brilliance by another Terran entering the fray. Travelling through the inferno, the Terran attack ship broke left to come face to face with Yeris Prime. A huge blue ball of a planet made rich by iridium and trade, though trade was the last thing on anyone's mind as ions and thorans tore through space in front of the planet.

Orders streamed from the starship *Lannan* as its commander Captain Ritter frantically tried to order the battle. Attack ships from both sides opened up on each other, the *Lannan* engaging a Dren destroyer in an effort to help the stricken starship *Valgas* that was now perilously close to the planet. The *Valgas*, battered by the destroyer, attempted an escape pattern as covering fire was laid down. Passing between the *Lannan* and the destroyer, the *Valgas* bridge crew got thrown forward as weapons slammed into their rear. The *Valgas* seemed to reach outward in all directions as she exploded in white light.

Veering up and away from Yeris Prime, the *Lannan* heaved amidst the storm of fire and light. On the opposite side, the explosion slammed into the attack ship *Hordec* so that its crew was thrown from their feet as systems failed—including shields, engines, and weapons one after another. Still carried toward Yeris Prime by the blast, they were for one horrifying moment facing the full might of the Dren destroyer before being carried round the curve of the planet.

"Stabilize this thing!" screamed Captain Maine, and with the same breath: "Report!"

"We're dead in the water; rail is gone and warp engines have failed. Thrusters only!" came the con officer.

Through the sparks and fumes came more replies.

"Navigation is out!" Linch choked out.

"Shields have failed; weapons are offline!" Gray said, struggling to remain calm.

"That destroyer's on an intercept course; we've got about forty seconds!" interrupted the con.

"This is Captain Maine to all vessels. We are disabled and adrift. We need immediate assistance." The request crackled over all channels.

Captain John Fuller on board the *Forestall* could see it all unfolding. In moments, fifty-two people were going to be wiped out in front of his eyes as the Dren destroyer, heavily damaged though it was, bore down on the *Hordec* from around the planet's far side. "*Forestall* to *Lannan*, answering *Hordec*, we are engaging the destroyer."

A voice came back almost instantly—Captain Ritter. "Why have you altered course? I ordered all ships away from Yeris."

"The *Hordec*'s in trouble; they're helpless!" Fuller replied.

"That's none of your concern. You are to re-join the

fleet and draw the destroyer away from Yeris!" Ritter retorted.

"We can't just leave them there—" Fuller never got to finish.

"That's exactly what you're to do. We can't engage the destroyer so close to the planet; the wreckage would rain down on the population below and it would be a disaster," responded Ritter, his voice becoming more stern.

"There's over fifty people on that ship. We can't just leave them there—" Cut off again, Fuller heard an angry Ritter reply:

"You can and you will! They are lost, do you understand? Lost!"

Fuller couldn't believe what he was hearing. Maine was a comrade—a close friend, damn it. Lots of close friends were on that ship....

The channels crackled to life. "This is Captain Maine to starship *Forestall*. Request assistance, acknowledge."

Fuller felt the weight of the world descending on him; the *Hordec* could see the *Forestall* was their only hope and they were asking... no, begging for it. The channel was open between them, and Fuller could feel the terror on the *Hordec* as the panicked voices of the crew reported in on the destroyer rounding Yeris Prime.

"Fifteen seconds till range!" shouted the con.

Fuller was frantic. How could he just stand there and watch them die?

"Eight seconds till range."

How could he leave them?

"Five seconds!"

"They're arming weapons!" shouted Gray.

"Three seconds."

And then Maine screamed, "For God's sake, help us, John!"

"Fire!!!" It was like he'd heard someone else utter the command, not him. Fuller had no sooner opened his mouth than a stream off thorans screamed into the Dren.

Explosions from all over the destroyer blinded the screen from both outside and inside, the volley devastating. The destroyer lurched upward as if in some desperate last bid for survival before being engulfed in a mass of flame.

Fuller looked on in morbid awe as the once invincible vessel imploded into a fiery grave.

His awe was short-lived.

"Fuller... Fuller!" Ritter was incandescent with rage. "What the f... what the fuck have you done?"

What *had* he done? As the explosion melted away, objects glinted in the light—huge objects, debris, the steel bones of the destroyer, and all of it claiming Yeris Prime for its burial ground.

The remaining wreckage had faded as the light from the explosion was lost, but now the slowly tumbling pieces became brighter, brighter than ever... they had reached the atmosphere.

Oblivious below on Yeris Prime inhabitants went about their daily lives.....

"Daddy, are we nearly there yet?" quizzed the child.

Her tired father looked down at her. "Sure, honey," he answered patiently.

"Is Mummy gonna be there?" came another question.

"Sure, hun," he answered. "We've been away a long time, so she'll be right there waiting for you. She's missed you."

The child smiled, reassured, and turned to look at the city below. It was evening, and great skyscrapers rising around them cast their dominant shadows downward as the sun set behind them.

The father smiled and laid his head back against his seat, pleased his daughter was engrossed in the city below and leaving him to rest. Two hours was a long time to be on a shuttle—a hundred and eighty people sitting in two rows of two, all just glad to be almost out of this budget-minded cramped-ness.

His wife would be waiting below, and he smiled, seeing her in his mind.

"Look at the stars, Daddy!"

"That's nice, honey," he replied, tired and still focused on his wife.

"They're so bright."

Bright? It was early evening. Confused, he sluggishly turned, opening his eyes. For a moment, through blurred vision, he saw bright, shining lights approaching….

His vision wasn't blurred. "They're not stars!" he screamed, grabbing his daughter.

Debris smashed into the left side of the shuttle, hurling a dozen seats against the opposite side before they were sucked back through the opening and followed by a dozen more. Depressurising, the shuttle was filled by a deafening howl with screams only faintly heard as people clung to whatever they could.

Still more seats broke free from their mountings, crashing along the length of the shuttle and out through the opening with people and all. Lurching violently to the left, the shuttle spun out of control among the skyscrapers.

"I can't hold it!" screamed the pilot.

Desperately, the co-pilot tried to help, shouting into his mic, "Tower, this is 871, we're losing control—two eight three eight for five, we're going down! Request immediate emergenc—"

"Jesus!"

The co-pilot looked up to see a skyscraper rushing toward them, and he opened his mouth, but...

The shuttle slammed through the glass and people inside were showered with debris, flames streaming in with the shuttle as it charged into the level straight through a wall, glancing off another before crashing halfway through the floor.

Fire engulfed the shuttle, the whole level going ablaze in seconds and leaking plasma, fuelling panic inside as terrified passengers trampled over one another to surge blindly out the opening and into the waiting furnace.

Emerging people screamed with fire consuming them as those choking behind them, still unaware of what was coming, surged toward the opening only for plasma to beat them to it. A wall of flame burst inside, orange turning green as plasma mercilessly devoured its victims, their cries snuffed out in an instant as the whole level exploded out into the city.

A hail of building fell free, glass and fire collapsing on people below as their cries were cut to shreds under the mass of debris. Looking upward, bloody-faced survivors screamed as the world turned black under more falling sections of the once great structure.

Chapter 2

Maynard's Attack

Slamming down the materials so that the noise made the jury jump, Navy prosecutor Maynard lifted his hand from the report he'd forced onto the table. It was the final deliberation; the defence had given theirs, citing Fuller's impeccable record and his Erdial Medal for Valour at Inchelon Pass, as well as his countless selfless actions in the face of certain defeat and the loss of his family, his wife and son, their deaths having come at the hands of the Dren in the Anziel Massacre.

"Fifteen thousand, eight hundred and twelve." Maynard paused, looking down at the report and his voice going soft with regret as he repeated, "Fifteen thousand, eight hundred and twelve souls."

The five admirals watched him intently as he moved slowly across their gaze, head down.

"Lost," Maynard's voice whispered. "Lost, not in some unspeakable act or some battle for survival…." His voice now grew with each word, "But because Captain Fuller decided to risk their lives in one throw of the dice." He turned menacingly, staring at the jury and motioning angrily towards Fuller. "Against direct orders, he fired. *He* fired!" He himself, and without the slightest regard for the consequences!" Maynard's voice was booming now as he continued, "We have heard of the lives saved, how Captain Fuller risked all in a heroic attempt to save the crew of the *Hordec*." His voice dropped sarcastically to a whisper. "Well, I'm sure that'll be of great comfort to the relatives of those he put in harm's way."

Maynard looked down at Fuller on his left as he began moving slowly, turning his eyes to the jury sitting high on his right. "We have heard of his past bravery, oh yes." Maynard spoke purposefully almost with respect, but he didn't falter as he continued, "How time and again he's saved lives against impossible odds; how he's been there for others, selflessly putting himself in danger. Admirable....

"But, is it?" Maynard's voice turned curt as he passed the faces of the jury. "Is it really? Is that what drives him, selflessness? Loyalty to his fellow shipmates? Or is it something else?"

Maynard turned purposefully, the jury now to his left and his face one of concern, of sympathy. "Terrible thing, to lose a loved one. To lose a family, a wife, a child. But they weren't lost, were they?" His voice rose again. "They were killed, murdered by the Dren in the Anziel Massacre."

He turned to face Fuller. "Born of this, we have an officer—an officer who's displayed such selfless heroic acts that, time and again, his name's come up for commendation."

Fuller glared at Maynard, his thoughts clear on his face. How dare he bring his family into this? This pencil-pushing freak, and those like him who he'd fought to protect.

Maynard eased his tone, turning to the jury. "But were they? Were they selfless acts? Heroic acts? Do we have an officer of unprecedented valour?" His voice rose as he asked, "Or do we have an officer fuelled by revenge?"

"I submit to the court that these past two years of

Captain Fuller's life have not been filled by heroic acts, but by blood-crazed rampages undertaken without regard for his ship's crew or anybody else." Maynard threw his voice accusingly. "Time and again, reports show Captain Fuller taking on vessels which have him clearly outclassed and outgunned, fighters' attack ships and cruisers, with him charging into battle at the slightest provocation."

Through gritted teeth, Fuller raged and imagined that he could feel his hands around Maynard's neck; if he could only....

"And then came Yeris Prime."

The planet's name momentarily stunned Fuller as Maynard sent it in his direction, glancing at him.

Maynard turned to the jury again then, gesturing with his hand. "At Yeris Prime, he found a prize, a prize he just couldn't ignore. A destroyer full of Dren troops ready to massacre, ready to murder fifty-two people just like his family, and I submit," Maynard bellowed, "that in an instant of rage-filled memory, Captain Fuller took it upon himself to pass judgement and unleash his hatred without the slightest regard for the consequences!"

Chapter 3

Gratitude

He sat there waiting. Waiting for what he thought they'd already decided—that he, John Fuller, model officer and defender of Terran liberties, winner of the Erdial Medal for Valour, was about to be drawn through the streets in disgrace for his trouble.

Echoing over marble floors, high ceilings, and huge, twin mahogany-doored rooms, the distant tapping of footsteps and soft whispers from the other end of the hallway were all that challenged the silence of this sterile environment. *A pencil-pusher's palace*, Fuller thought. *You'd think with all this expense, they could have found some cushions for these mahogany benches, damn designers.*

He leant back against the wall, which was cold as the vermin that scuttled around this place. This was his reward for his service, for his sacrifice, to be sat amongst this slime, two doors down from the courtroom and awaiting his final humiliation.

The waiting was torture. In any other place, such quiet would have been relaxing, but not here, where his mind was full. *Yeris Prime, the* Hordec, *Ritter, Maynard....* Maynard, that skinny little bastard! He hadn't been there. He lived in this sterile, perfect little place with its rules and regulations, so he'd never been there, never had people's lives in his hands. Who was Maynard to question him? Bringing his family into this, using their memory against him, saying he'd fired out of anger, fired out of hate, fired out of vengeance for their memory…. It was all laughable….wasn't it?

He'd opened fire to save that ship, hadn't he? The *Hordec* was one of theirs, right?

Did he hate the Dren? Had it felt great watching them burn all these years?

Yes.

Yes, damn it! It felt great—those cold-blooded bastards had taken everything from him. He loved watching them go, and that involved anger, hatred, and even vengeance, of course!

But that hadn't been it at Yeris Prime; he hadn't lost his mind and he hadn't forgotten there were people down there or that it would be dangerous. But the *Hordec* had been abandoned; Ritter had left it behind and there'd been people on that ship, good people, helpless people… just like his family.

Maybe Maynard was right, just a bit…. Maybe he had…. No.

Fuller's head was pounding. He tilted it back, closing his eyes before leaning forward and clasping his face in his hands, squeezing his eyes still tighter and breathing heavily as it all raced through his mind.

The vermin's footsteps where barely audible now, just a faint tapping, and he breathed heavy in the cool air trying to clear his mind and concentrate. He was getting there. Funny, he thought, that in all this he could be so calm…. *Tap tap.*

He blocked them out and tried to concentrate.

Tap tap.

Damn vermin!

Tap tap tap.

From among the others, one stood out and came closer. Fuller sighed, still holding his head. *How did they know?* he wondered. How did they know he'd almost been calm, and they could have passed him at any other time, but had decided to pass now.

Well, he wouldn't give them the satisfaction. He wouldn't look up. He'd sit there and let them pass and go back to his calm place.

The footsteps grew louder and louder still, aggravating him as if with intent. Fuller gritted his teeth. They were almost past, he thought, almost past… and then they stopped.

Right in front of him! *This little bastard,* thought Fuller with his hands still clasped round his face, *if he thinks for one second I'm going to….*

"Captain Fuller." The voice was curt.

Fuller did nothing.

"Captain Fuller."

Fuller opened his eyes in his hands, pulled back from them, and looked up. Steel eyes looked down at him from out of a uniform that seemed to fill the hallway, but this was not an admiral—he was a general. What now? It wasn't enough that the Navy had mauled him? It the Marines' turn now? What, had there been a detachment down there or a squad on leave?

"Do you know what day it is?" the voice asked quietly, though it resonated with all the power befitting the rank.

Fuller said nothing.

"Do you know what day it is?"

Fuller sat there silently, motionless under this mountain.

The eyes fixed hard on him, the voice becoming harsh. "Today was my son's twenty-fourth birthday."

Still reeling from the courtroom, Fuller dropped his

head and began to take up what little defence he had left. "Look, you weren't there. We were all they had, and we couldn't just…. I just couldn't stand by and watch them die. The wreckage had a chance of hitting Yeris Prime, yes, and just as much chance of drifting into space. They had no chance, do you understand? No chance at all, so I fired, alright? I'm guilty, guilty! But not of murder and not of negligence. I'm guilty of protecting my own."

"What are you talking about?" the voice growled.

Fuller looked up again, confused.

"Thanks to you, my son saw today; thanks to you, my grandson has a father. Those bureaucratic bastards in there would have seen him dead. They don't know what it means to depend on the man standing next to you. All the Navy does is drop us into the shit and come back to pick up the bodies, and that's why I didn't want my boy joining you pansy-ass bastards!"

Scowling, the man turned away, heading for the courtroom.

Fuller looked after him, bemused. Maybe that was as close to a "thank you" as a general could get. As if reading Fuller's mind, the general stopped upon reaching the courtroom.

Turning, he looked back at Fuller with concern across his face, though it was quickly hidden by a stern look. "No matter what they say in there, you where there for the men standing next to you. You don't belong in the ships, son. Maybe that's something to think about."

Chapter 4

The Best Laid Plans

The airlock opened and Aidin stepped onto Station 172 to be immediately met by a clinical scent like that of a hospital—artificial. The dimly lit corridors were a standard theme among these stations, thinly carpeted in dark grey from floor to ceiling with the dim, neon blue seam lighting the walkways. A blessing that lit the endless warren of connecting corridors, saving them from obscurity.

More and more connections… J4, J3, J2, J1, and finally on to the maglift and up to B1, the galleria. The doors opened to the bustling hub of the station, softly lit in relaxing golden yellow with people from all races and walks of life wandering round the shops and bars. Traders and smugglers, honest and not, made the galleria a hive of activity.

"Aidin!" a voice called over the throng from the other end of the galleria. Aidin tried to see through the crowd, ignoring the shops and bars from left to right as far as the eye could see—all of it swinging round left in a great bend going out of view, as designers had crammed as many places as they could around the confines of the station's hull across B deck. Establishments exchanged people from left to right, blocking his view. A break in the crowd revealed the neon blue glint of the executive maglift dropped down from level A1. It stuck out, official-looking and alien in the mellow light as it waited patiently on the inside curve of the galleria.

"Aidin!" The voice was closer, gaining a foothold above the bustling noise, and from among the crowd came a near seven-foot figure topped with a beaming face.

Captain Aidin reached out his hand to greet the approaching station commander, who also reached out to give him a glancing blow to the shoulder. "You made it!" boomed the colourful Caribbean accent of Captain Leroy Darrant.

Aidin's modesty made him uncomfortable as Darrant drew attention from the crowd, but he did his best to return a difficult smile. "We're heading back to mop up some…."

"Yes, yes, yes, but you must be exhausted from everything! When was the last time you escaped the clutches of that quantum-strained wife of yours? What, five months ago?"

It was a welcome sight, despite the drawn attention. Aidin hadn't seen a soul outside of the Starship *Rheinvar*—his quantum alloy-strained wife, as Darrant had put it—for months.

"She's a hard mistress," sighed Aidin. "But we've got to keep up the pressure; the IAF feels their breaking is imminent. Attacks are becoming less frequent and disorganised, almost desperate."

Them were the last of the Hearack Damervarock—roughly translated to the Hearack Tigran Division—the elite but last surviving unit from the war that had been stranded in the faction's home section of the galaxy Quadrant IL 19 when, five years before, the Genesis Fifteen strike wing had broken through their lines and left the way clear to the wormhole. That was the source of all the anguish. It hadn't always been that way. When the wormhole had first been detected near Fearon Ridge, it had seemed like an opportunity, a gift; it linked directly with Quadrant NM 15 some one hundred and sixty-eight light years away. The potential for new-found raw materials, trade, expansion, and exploration had been unimaginable, made even more so by the reports from the first scouts. They'd spoken of huge systems, bringing back scans of planets and asteroids that had sent the prospecting guild into a frenzy. Tentative steps had been made at first, small settlements and mining complexes established to bring back riches beyond anyone's dreams; and tax free! No-one owned anything in that quadrant; there were no rights, no boundaries, and it had been a boom time until the Dren had showed up.

The Dren were the dominant power in the quadrant, a race born of many millenias advance on themselves their style of living told of by the first Vrail who arrived. The Vrail had arrived on starships and been responsible for the Hearack, the Dren legionnaires' mercenaries: clones of clones who'd been designed to be willing to serve their unseen masters in whatever form was required. Delegations of Hearack led by their disarming Vrail commanders had flitted between starship and starbase alike, charming their way in like movie stars for an almost empiric welcome eventually greeting each arrival as wherever their feet landed mass trade soon followed. It was the same throughout all the factions of IL 19, with even the Irachans' war-like stance seemingly succumbing to the trade offered by this so fortunate of arrivals.

All despite concerns from the Valraich, with the rest of the quadrant's factions ignoring them, blinded by the wealth. The Sariz, the Irachan, the Alliance… all treating them like friends, new-found allies who received all the pomp and ceremony befitting a king. It had seemed so good back then, with trade growing alongside star charts, information, medical cures, and even workforces that were shared. It had all been so right, but then the rumours had started. Ships which strayed too far into Quadrant NM 15 hadn't seemed to come back, and the lists of missing had grown. Militaries from all parts of the IL 19 quadrant had tried to raise the alarm, but no-one had been willing to listen. How could they, when their bellies were full and the riches kept coming? Those in power, the bureaucrats and others, had only been able to see opportunity as they'd languished in their own greed.

Everything had gone unnoticed… the weird interference on the NM 15 side of the wormhole, the increasing size of the Dren transport ships, and the bases springing up on the IL 19 side that were in arm's reach of key sectors. Even the loss of an Alliance starship had been quietly swept aside.

But that had all changed on star date 28.8.527, when a line of freighter pilots had witnessed an Irachan attack ship being pursued by an entire legion of Dren; they'd torn the ship apart, seemingly desperate to stop it entering the wormhole, and they'd succeeded. On fire from stem to stern, the Irachan had voiced warnings on all channels, warning of an invasion, of races deep in NM 15 who were enslaved by the Dren. Listening, the freighter pilots had had no idea that their fate had just been sealed. Pilots spoke of an insane Irachan captain being under fire, almost at the wormhole when he had pulled away charging back through the Dren fleet seemingly toward open space. Surviving crews told of dying screams as the Irachan ship suddenly exploded at a distance of point eight thousand kilometres from the wormhole, and of the last call roared from the captain: "Long live the Empire!"

They hadn't been destroyed by the pursuing ships, but against something, for an instant, a huge black silhouette had become visible in the explosion before vanishing. Pressed for more information, the crews had none; there hadn't been time, as the Dren had immediately turned on them. Of seventy-two freighters, only three had survived.

It had changed nothing right away.

Unimaginable now, after all that's happened, but the leading councils of the factions in IL 19 had tried to cover it up at first. Even when attacks had been launched from inside IL 19, they'd dithered, as if unwilling to believe in it all. It had taken the fear of losing control to jar them into action. That sudden fear had come in the form of Genesis Fifteen, a splinter group of military from all factions in the IL 19 Alliance—Irachan, Valraich, and others—commanders who'd lost confidence in their governments and in their superiors, who'd felt sick of sitting on their hands and finally retaliated on their own. Such was the scale of the group that the faction councils had feared insurrection and hurriedly voiced their support; not that it would have mattered either way, as the people had already been on the group's side. Unable to take command back from the hands of the instigators, the councils had together, now in anguish, supplied food and weapons while skulking in the shadows and trying to re-establish themselves over the military.

Constant fights with the military had come to a head on 28.8.714. when military intelligence had learned of the source of the strange signals on the NM 15 side. The reason the Irachan attack ship had exploded months earlier was that, in an attempt to warn us, they had learned of a cloaked mass of unspeakable power which maintained the entrance to the wormhole on whatever quadrant the Dren had managed to align it with. In an attempt to uncover it, the Irachans had sacrificed themselves for the good of their people. What was worse was that the intelligence divisions of all the factions had sensor data from the three surviving freighters from that day; IN6 and other intelligence branches across the quadrant had known for months before Genesis had found out.

Immediately, accusations of treachery, of selling out people for money, had erupted from the military, who claimed fearful they would destroy it collapsing the entrance to the new found wealth the factions had hushed it up. The factions had, amazingly, agreed… but claimed they had had scientists working for those years to determine how to destroy it, as they did not believe weapons alone would be enough—using the Irachan suicide run as proof of this. They claimed the military wouldn't have listened and would have waded in in a futile attempt, wasting valuable ships and crews. It seemed likely they were right. At each other's throats, the factions had managed to get their findings across to Genesis. They'd turned over sensor data showing complex shielding around the object—a cloaking device—and there'd been countless failed computer simulations running attacks on it. The answer, they claimed, was as old as the Navy itself… fireships. The only way the computers showed a possibility of success was through sending in scores of ships laden with munitions to detonate at a weak spot where shields overlapped around it. A distrusting military had dismissed the plans as rubbish, confident in their weapons because of clashes with the Dren, and they'd refused to listen.

That had all changed on the morning of 28.8.725., when the factions had, in a panic, dropped the cloak of secrecy surrounding their intelligence services and become cooperative with military intel for the first time—some said too cooperative. After the disaster at Yeris Prime, the final Dren stronghold in that area had been overrun, leaving the way clear for one final push to Fearon Ridge and the wormhole.

Maybe if people had known how final that push was going to be, things would have been different. Still reeling from the tragedy at Yeris Prime, Genesis had been readying for a push months down the line when the factions had dropped a bombshell. Despite opposition from distrusting commanders, the situation had become desperate, intelligence reports indicating that a Dren invasion fleet of frightening size was massing on the other side of the wormhole. The factions trying to hold the lines all over the quadrant had sent every available starship to join Genesis Fifteen, but despite this, the situation had been grim. So many had been damaged at Yeris Prime, people called it a suicide mission. In desperation, Genesis had gone over the factions' plan... the fireships. Fearing this was their last chance, they'd grabbed it, and ninety-five freighters laden with a deadly mixture of engine waste and veosene nine had joined the two-hundred-forty-eight vessels already present as they'd turned to fight for their families, for their homes, and even for their species.

A plan had been drawn up whereby, assuming they

managed to punch a hole in the awaiting armada on the other side, the fireships under remote controls would be sent headlong through and on to the cloaked mass holding the wormhole stable. Upon reaching the weak point in in the shield grid, their containment fields would be dropped; it had been claimed that an explosion of that size would be seen from Quadrant IL 19, wormhole or not. And if the remnants of Genesis Fifteen didn't make it back to the wormhole in time, they wouldn't have to worry about the Dren… nothing within a dozen sectors of the blast radius would survive.

On stardate 28.8.731., humanity and the Alliance and Quadrant IL 19 in its entirety had all held their breath as three hundred and forty-three vessels had left to face the Dren and try to wrestle our fate back from the hands of death.

The cost of reaching Fearon Ridge had been horrifying. Outposts near Yeris Prime had relayed the carnage as Genesis Fifteen had slammed into the full might of the Hearack Tigran Division. In minutes, thirty-eight percent of Genesis had been gone, and in a few more minutes, more screams of battle had come from only fifty percent of the fleet. Out of ammo, the Hearack had taken to suicide runs, ramming anything that moved, calling out, "We pledge our lives to the Dren!" By the time Genesis had crashed into the entrance of the wormhole, they'd been down to forty-two percent.

The mission had been completed. That's how the report to the IAF read, glossing over the casualty lists—which was incredible, as they were also complete. No-one had come home.

On the other side that day, the chain reaction in those ships must have set off an explosion far greater than anyone had imagined—something nothing and nobody could have escaped from. The rumour was, that's exactly what the factions had wanted. That they had over-estimated the calculations to make sure of a catastrophic blast yield, securing the collapse of the wormhole to IL 19 and the certainty that the influence of Genesis Fifteen would never be seen again.

What wasn't a rumour was that all sides had suffered a staggering loss; on the Alliance side, the IAF alone had lost thirty-eight percent of its fleet. Subsequent in-fighting and accusations had led to the collapse of the factions' cooperation entirely, leaving the member factions in a state of unstable peace, much like they'd been in before.

The thought of it all weighed heavy on Aidin's mind, the loss, as he momentarily zoned out from Darrant...

"Well, with them almost broken, you can afford to relax a bit, eh?" joked Darrant.

"I don't know about relax, but maybe I'll rest while the *Rheinvar* is refitted; we have to confer with IAF intelligence over the latest plans to locate the Hearack units along the border and—"

"Great idea, and what better way to prepare for your conference than Karack's lounge?" Darrant beamed. "Station 185's much closer to that little skirmish of yours than ours, but it doesn't have our attractions." Darrant laughed. "Why not make the most of their mistake? I'm off duty, so let's pretend for an hour this nonsense is miles away, eh?"

Aidin hesitated, considering the burden on his mind.

Darrant saw the struggle on his brow. "That wasn't a request," he growled sarcastically through a coy smile.

"It's my station, and if you want that quantum-strained wife of yours re-fitted, you'll join me for a drink."

Aidin smiled, took a deep breath, and sighed under the mock pressure. A guffaw from Darrant and a slap on the back sent them off to the den of debauchery that was Karacks. Wading through the crowd was a nightmare; Aidin, used to the sprawling emptiness of a starship's decks, had a hard time dealing with the squeeze around people as they fought through the galleria from one end to to the other. *People here had better hope the fire suppression system works*, he thought, *cause it's all they've got.*

As they continued on, the lighting lowered, going almost dark as they rounded the bend of the hull. Karacks was dimly lit in dark reds and neon green, situated eerily on the outer hull at the end of the walkway, and beyond it was just the bulkhead to separate the galleria and B deck's cargo bay. There was a roar as a Valraich flew through the steel door and onto the galleria, and the roar grew as a huge Irachan appeared—enraged with drink. The Valraich struggled to his feet; he was a skinny man, not much over five feet, and three feet shorter than the mountain approaching him. His protests went unheeded as, grabbing his jacket, the Irachan hoisted him into the air while drawing a huge fist back and…

"What's going on here?" Above the roar of the fight, Darrant's voice had descended like the authority of an angry father.

"Why…" sputtered the Valraich from his lofty position "Why, Captain, so glad you could join us. I was just telling our Irachan friend here that…" he continued cheerfully, pleasantly, as if unaware of his predicament, but such was the Valraich demeanour: they were ever-disarming, a race of congenital liars, never saying anything of consequence and always running a hidden agenda.

"Mr Da Vahr, why is it that, every time we meet, it seems to be under extraordinary circumstances… for a salesman?" Darrant's voice was laced with sarcasm.

"Well, yes, I could see how it could certainly seem that way, but I assure you this is not what it looks like," came back Da Vahr cheerfully, his feet still dangling.

"I will not have my honour questioned by a Valraich worm!" roared the drunk Irachan.

Darrant looked back up at Da Vahr hanging above him now, an amused look on his face requesting an explanation.

"Captain, a misunderstanding. I was merely pointing out that an Irachan warrior….

The sound of drunken commotion filled the walkway, the steel door opening out into the walkway beside them as a flustered little man emerged—clearly oblivious to Darrant as he bounded up to the Irachan.

"You just wrecked half my bar!" he screamed. "The lost revenue alone is a disaster, never mind my furniture! I demand compensation!"

The Irachan's face went from one of disbelief to confusion, and finally to anger as he bared his teeth, scowling and then grabbing the little man by the throat before he roared down at him.

"Stop!" The voice had resounded straight through the scene.

The Irachan turned, still scowling, looking back down the walkway to see a black uniform approaching in the dim light—and the figure was saddled with a scowl which easily matched his own.

"Put him down!" came a growl from the uniform.

With a deep breath, and grudging every inch of the way, the Irachan slowly lowered Da Vahr to the floor. The face atop the uniform continued scowling, raising an eyebrow as he motioned toward the throat of the little man. Nose trembling in frustration, and with teeth grinding, the Irachan drew a deep breath and looked down at his captive. Slowly releasing him, he watched as the little man grabbed his throat. Confidence gone, he looked up in frustration. A guffaw of laughter roared through the walkway as the Irachan leaned back in mirth, appreciating the courage of the little man as he slapped him on the shoulder, sending him flying backward against the bar's door.

The uniform was not amused—that much was obvious as it marched up to the Irachan, face appearing red in the dim light of Karack's and with eyes fixed dead on the Irachan in an apparent battle of stares.

"What's the meaning of this?" growled the uniform.

"That's a good question, Inspector," Darrant commented. "I believe Da Vahr was just about to tell us."

Da Vahr took up his audience like a master chirping comfortably as they turned to him. "Nice to see you, Inspector. Yes, well, as I was just telling the captain here, there's been a misunderstanding; I was just telling the Irachan of people interested in certain cultural aspects of his people when…"

"He wanted information on the Eon 5 campaign!" roared the Irachan, turning toward Da Vahr. "I will not betray my people!"

"Of course, you wouldn't," voiced the inspector gruffly, "There isn't an Irachan warrior alive who'd sacrifice his honour."

The Irachan turned, calming slightly.

"Such people shouldn't belittle themselves in such unworthy establishments," continued the inspector.

"Unworthy!" protested the shocked-looking little barman.

"Yes," returned the inspector—smiling, obviously enjoying the chance to take a swipe at him. "Let's take a walk down to Orens" he continued, motioning behind him with his hand. "Most Irachan I've met seem to prefer it down there; maybe now you know why."

Grunting in acknowledgement, the Irachan threw one more disapproving look at Da Vahr and slowly made off with the inspector.

"That's it!" complained the barman. "Look at this place! Who's going to pay for the damage?" he demanded, throwing his arms at the bar door that was hanging slightly askew. "He turns my bar into a crash scene and you just let him walk away! I suppose next week, when someone burns me to the ground, you'll be just as helpful!"

"Karack, if I were you, I'd file a complaint with the inspector… after the Irachan calms down," Darrant answered, smiling.

"I intend to, don't you worry" exclaimed Karack. "He's a menace! How's a man supposed to earn an honest living around here?" he complained, already walking through the hanging door. "Alright, folks, show's over! I tell you, you won't get excitement like this anywhere else. Jalondra, serve these people, will you…"

"Well, this has been a most interesting evening," chirped Da Vahr, slipping away down the walkway. "We must do it again some time. I—"

"Mr Da Vahr!" cut in Darrant dryly. "Eon 5 has been sealed by the IAF, so I do hope you're not spending your time trying to dredge up classified information from unsuspecting people on my station."

"Certainly not, Captain!" replied Da Vahr cheerfully. "As I said, the Irachan simply misunderstood in his drunken state; you know how they are—only last week, I had one mistake my shop for an airlock and…"

"Yes, I know," Darrant interrupted him, an accusing look crossing his face.

"Drop in and see me anytime, Captain," Da Vahr remarked quickly, escaping round the hull. "I've some wonderful Miralien suits just in, and I think you'll like them…"

"Oh, I will," replied Darrant, obviously amused by Da Vahr as he slipped out of view.

"Colourful place," Aidin commented, smiling.

"Don't let this little incident fool you," Darrant replied, still smiling. "Karack's is the place to go when you want to unwind; everybody living on the station knows that. The rest of the places on the galleria are for, oh, you know, tourists and people not staying too long."

Aidin looked unconvinced as he took another look at the hanging door and dim lighting; the bar looked as if it was trying to hide, and he could only wonder why.

"Ahh, come on inside!" Darrant boomed, throwing an arm round his shoulder as they made their way inside. "You'll be safe from any trouble in here, but as for the women… well, I can't promise you'll be safe from them."

Chapter 5

Sister Calling

Past the door, they made their way down a dark corridor with a muffled din growing stronger as they went—quite befitting the situation, Aidin thought, convinced he was being led into a low-brow cesspit. Voice still booming jovially, Darrant ushered Aidin through a hanging drape to the left, and suddenly Aidin was met by a wave of colour, a virtual carnival greeting him with a huge neon purple bar taking up a corner from the right of the door on, curving all the way over to reach halfway up the adjacent wall. To his left, a maze of seating sat in darkness with all occupants being unseen, while in front, in reds and pinks, a brightly lit stage was adorned with half-naked women providing laid back rock and saxophone music. More came into focus as Aidin's eyes adjusted; ahead to the right, he picked out a spiral staircase near the end of the bar; it sat in darkness, its cover broken only by a small figure coming downward. Ushered forward again by Darrant, Aiden and his friend moved toward the staircase. Pale eyes lit by neon looked out pleasantly from the bar as they passed, unnoticed before; they belonged to more half-clad women tending drinks.

"Captain, glad you decided to come in!" the figure they approached shouted over the music.

"Well, we thought we might as well after you laid on such a good show!" Darrant laughed.

"Ah, ha ha, yes… well, we aim to please!" the figure called back somewhat uncomfortably.

Lights spun above the stage, cresting the figure and revealing him to be the bartender from outside.

"What's it to be? Your usual downstairs!" shouted the bartender.

In the darkness to the right, an eerie green hew ventured tenderly up another spiral staircase leaving it looking like it was hiding Aidin thought.

"No, Karack, we need a place with as few ears as possible. You know what I mean," Darrant replied, his face turning serious.

"Well, upstairs is quite empty this time of day; speak to Shylar and she'll see you right!"

"Will do. Oh, and, Karack, nice landing!" Darrant added, smiling.

"Yeah…." the bartender replied as he left the stairs, clearly embarrassed.

"He's a character, like all Sariz," Darrant supplied. "Come on and I'll tell you all about it!" Darrant shouted, his voice fading some as he climbed the stairs.

Climbing the stairs, Aidin looked out over the stage; to his left, a crimson orgy played out beneath him with bodies writhing to the music, dancing for patrons' enjoyment. *What was next?* he wondered, *a shjell den at the top of the stairs?* The stairs rounded, with light of a different kind creeping down, brighter and bringing a feeling of warmth as they climbed. Rounding the last curve, a deep amber greeted him, his feet meeting a wooden floor. Behind him, the sordid scene from the stage died away, a welcome calm filling the air as he moved on; to his right, a small bar was warmly lit where a bartender quietly served cocktails, while a raised seating area on his left played host to empty chairs surrounded by black walls looking on silently. A brunette woman smiled at Darrant and pointed back into the room as she quietly chatted to a customer. Further in, wood gave way to carpet that was just so black as the walls, the light dimming as they went and the roof growing more shallow as a staircase came into view in front of them. Approaching it, a cavernous space became visible below, and soft jazz brought more welcome calm. Booths lined the walls, the room black but for amber table lamps. Dropping down into the space, fiery red hair appeared in the darkness in front of them.

"Captain Darrant, nice to see you! You're looking well," the woman greeted them, and Aidin noted that she wore a dangerously short green dress that barely held in her assets as she held a tray of empty glasses.

"Hello, Shylar," Darrant returned smoothly. "You're looking as fine as ever."

"Don't know why; Karack's had me in here for the past ten hours."

"Speaking of Karack," Darrant cut in. "He said we might find a quiet place to discuss some business."

"The place is never too busy back here this time of day; don't know why he bothers." She frowned, then added, "Yes, the top booths are all empty—would you like some drinks?"

"No thanks—" Aidin began.

"Yes, we'll have two nardonian brandys," Darrant cut in.

"Sure, I'll bring them right up," Shylar replied, her painted-on smile holding its pose once again as she left.

"What's the matter, old man?" Darrant asked, smiling. "Can't handle the pace?"

Aidin smiled back, shaking his head as Darrant led the way across the room. At the far end, above the other tables, Aidin picked out a platform with yet more patrons sitting in darkness, but stairs soon appeared on either side of the room's edges as they approached the back wall. Climbing the set on the left, Darrant swung into a booth that had been unseen before now, sitting in the left-hand set of built-in leather couches that surrounded a table at their centre. Sitting with his back to the wall, at the entrance to the booth, Aidin was offered a view of the warmly lit booths below, which were empty but for a few people.

"Well, old man," Darrant began, making an Aidin who was fifteen years his junior smirk.

"Outside," Aidin began, "the fight, Da Vahr, this place… you put up with this regularly?"

"Oh that, that's nothing," Darrant returned. "It's not a starship, Aidin. People here want to let off steam from long trips. They're stressed out and want some fun, so sure it can get a little rowdy sometimes, but people are generally happy here."

"Are you?" Aidin asked, as years before Darrant had captained a starship in the Brior sector.

"I've a family now. I have responsibilities and can't go charging around risking life and limb in a starship. Besides, a starship is no place for a family, no matter what the IAF says. How are my kids supposed to learn anything about life while being cooped up in a quantum-strained bubble?" Darrant asked.

Aidin grinned.

"Unlike you, eh?" Darrant laughed. "The *Rheinvar*, top of the line… tell me what's it like having one of only two starships that could cut its way through a moon."

"Useful," Aidin replied, still smiling.

Darrant laughed, rolling back on the couch. "And

the *Trian*, your sister ship; how does our Burge find her—useful, too, eh?"

"Burge has settled a few arguments with her, I've heard," Aidin replied.

"Oh, the excitement! I do miss it. Go anywhere, do anything, report things and do 'em your way." Darrant laughed. "But it's not so bad here—we have Karack's, much to Tiona's objections." Darrant began laughing again.

"How is she?" asked Aidin, enjoying Darrant's mirth.

"Oh, she's fine; says the kids are running her ragged, that I'm on the bridge too much and that she wants someone to sweep her off her feet and take her to a nice planet so she can enjoy sun again."

"A solid relationship then," Aidin joked.

"Yeah, you got it!" laughed Darrant.

"What about 196? Wasn't it better there?" Aidin asked. Two years previously, Darrant had still been the station commander there, and had been for eight years before that; he'd been through it all, as time and again it had been attacked during the war because of its close proximity to the wormhole.

"Better, yes, but busier. That place put twenty years on me," Darrant lamented. "Tiona will tell you it's thirty."

Aidin laughed at his good humour.

"Oh yes, this place has become home; it doesn't have the luxuries of 196, but it's safer."

"Why'd you request the transfer—for safety's sake?" Aidin asked.

"Mainly, yes. After that blasted wormhole collapsed, I wanted to get as far away from Fearon Ridge as possible. Memories, you know?" Darrant replied. "Besides, a top-notch station like that was run with top-notch rules; very stressful."

"And what about this Da Vahr—you know he's trying to find out classified information, and yet you tolerate him?"

"Mr Da Vahr is a bit of a mystery. As Valraichs go, he's as secretive as the rest of them; arrived here two years ago, opened up a trading post, and never left," Darrant offered.

"A trading post?"

"Yeah, it's a front, obviously; he's a spy. He's got to be—no Valraich would be happy toiling his days away in a trading post, but here it does give him access to whoever comes through his doors for whatever stock, and access to influentials to question, and so on. Since his arrival, so many strange programming errors in our logs and communication systems have cropped up... errors that only someone trying to break into our systems could have made. So far, our inspector Mr Hack seems to keep on top of things, but it's only a matter of time before he gets through.

"Oh, I've no proof," Darrant answered Aidin's questioning look. "He wouldn't be much of a Valraich if I had. But I know it's him—I've even given orders not to use the com system to send sensitive information; the man's got me living back in the stone age, sending people around the station with messages!"

"What makes you so certain it's him?" Aidin pressed.

"With all the passwords, trip files, and false data chains, it would take someone very intelligent to go through a system like that and not leave any evidence," answered Darrant. "Hell, half my engineering crews wouldn't know how… no, it would take someone trained very well to hide tracks that well. Someone like a Valraich."

"And, knowing this, you leave him on your station?" Aidin asked, confused.

"Da Vahr has been quite useful in the past—a back channel, if you will, to the Valraich government. How he does it or who he knows, I don't ask, as it would be pointless anyway," Darrant explained. "And if I remove him, I'm quite sure another Valraich would mysteriously arrive and open up another trading post." Darrant laughed. "Besides, our Inspector Hack has him watched like a hawk; if another Valraich took his place, the surveillance would have to begin all over again with trying to learn the new plant's habits. And, to be honest, it's Karack you have to watch!"

"Karack?"

"Don't let him fool you," Darrant answered, nodding. "You know these Salizars; they're born con-men; he's got so many scams going at any one time, there isn't room for anyone else. He's got the place wired, and Hack's forever trying to catch him."

"And does he?" asked Aidin.

"Not as much as he'd like!" laughed Darrant. "It's almost become a game between them—people on the station have even bet on whether or not he's going to get away with various things."

Aidin even felt the confused look on his own face now.

"Oh, he's harmless really—no malice intended; he's just money-hungry, greedy like all Salizars. You see, on a station, you can't rule with an iron grip," Darrant explained. "People will turn away, go elsewhere; you have to give people room to breathe, and that adds character and colour to the place. Besides, Karack makes the best drinks in the quadrant."

Just then, Shylar appeared with their drinks. "There you go, sir," she joked. "Anything else?"

No, thank you, Shylar, but maybe later if you're not busy—" Darrant suggested, his words trailing as he was cut off.

"And after that, the station will be looking for a new captain when Tiona gets through with you!" Shylar laughed as she walked off down the stairs.

Aidin watched her walk downward, his eyes drawn to her thighs as she moved, and Darrant caught his gaze.

"Quite a little quadrant we find ourselves in these days, eh?"

Darrant was almost invisible in the dark across from Aiden, though his personality still beamed out.

"And a busy one," replied Aidin.

"You wouldn't have it any other way!" Darrant laughed.

"I don't know… sometimes, I could have done without the Anseil Cluster," Aidin sighed.

"I heard it was pretty bad out there; they didn't need that after what happened all those years ago. How many?" Darrant asked.

Aidin sighed again. "Eleven."

"Eleven!" Darrant's voice had risen, but now he caught himself. "Eleven starships," Darrant came back quietly. "How can that be after the Fahraren Heights?"

"We don't know," Aidin replied, matching Darrant's lowered volume. "The war is going very badly for the IAF—much worse than is commonly known.

They came at us with some sort of increased yield torpedos and the equivalent of type-sixteen ion arrays, and they sliced through the hulls like they were paper. Any ship that lost its shields was torn apart like a toy."

"They're calling it a war now?" Darrant exclaimed, a shocked look on his face. "What happened to the clean-up operation? How did it escalate after the Heights?"

The Fahraren Heights were a cluster of asteroids laced with tritium and formaldehyde; they lay half a light year from Fearon Ridge and encompassed almost the entire western sector of the Alliance as viewed on Tri mapping. This scene of the largest battle since the war, shielded from sensors by the compounds in the asteroids and the plasma storms deep within a Hearack base, had been found by chance. After losing contact with a scout ship, a deep space mining frigate had moved in to investigate a garbled distress call making it out—but that had been all that made it out. Two days and nineteen starships later—seven lost to plasma storms alone—it had been over, things had gone quiet, and the few Hearack ships that had been out on patrol melted away launching sporadic attacks in later months. Little by little, they'd been hunted down. Things had gotten quiet, everyone thinking it was almost over, but now.... Something had changed, and attacks were increasing, becoming more organised.

"The numbers don't add up," Aidin explained. "There's reports from survivors of raids of large fleets and we can't explain it."

"Another base?" Darrant's query had a worried tone.

"No, there's no way they could have another; it's only been months. They wouldn't have had the time, let alone the materials."

"They are resourceful," Darrant replied, memories of the war clearly troubling him.

"Not this resourceful," Aidin said, laying down a report slate.

Darrant squinted at the slate on the table, its electronic display showing IAF-controlled space, the factions around it, and the latest Hearack attacks—all marked. It didn't make sense. "Why haven't I seen this before?" he asked, shocked by the scale of what was happening.

"It's classified," Aidin answered simply. "*Buried* would be a better term, in fact; the Alliance is worried, and it thinks the people would be more so."

"How could they have gotten so far?" Darrant whispered, staring down at the display.

"The only way…" Aidin paused, "would be if someone's helping them."

Darrant looked all the more shocked. "One of the factions in IL 19? Who?"

"We don't know, but someone's helping them… and something," Aidin paused again, looked down at the table before finishing, "something's coming."

Darrant offered an enquiring look as Aidin raised his head.

"We've captured a Vrail," Aidin answered it.

The Vrail Aidin spoke of were the brains of the Dren armies while the Hearack were the muscle. Genetically modified to serve the Dren as their soldiers, the Hearack took orders from the Vrail, their commanders. Although intelligent in their own right and master tacticians on the battlefield, they were designed as soldiers and lacked the Vrails' cunning. That was an understatement, really, as the Vrail were designed to be masters of deception; though built to be loyal to the Dren, they had every underhanded psychological backstabbing trick at their disposal. Completely disarming, they could charm their way into anything—one minute, you'd be signing over your life savings, and the next, they'd be slitting your throat as you left. One Vrail commanded one legion of Hearack, up to seventy-eight units in all. And upon defeat, the Vrail were designed to execute themselves in order to avoid capture and interrogation. Almost all did, but it was understandable that, with all the devious traits gifted to them, some would turn away from their masters at this point and choose to live, even if the penalty laid down for this was unspeakable.

"And?" Darrant asked.

"He's been… uncooperative"

"What do you mean?" Darrant's face hardened.

Aidin spoke quietly as he went on, "We've been trying to induce his cooperation, but he's been resistant"

Darrant winced, turning away—uncomfortable with what he was hearing.

"We've pumped him full of every chemical combination known to medical science, and I dare say a few that aren't," Aidin continued, "but, we've reached the limit of what our sick bay can do and we need access to a larger facility."

"So, it's not a mistake," Darrant commented, looking at the table, his jovial personality gone. "That's why they sent you here, to be an interrogator."

"I wish there was some other way. Believe me, I don't enjoy this, either." Aidin's tone dropped. "But we need access to tiranolmonosulphate."

"What?" Darrant almost shouted.

Aidin's alarmed expression and glance around the room did nothing to deter a sickened Darrant.

"Tiranolmonosulphate causes blood clots in the brain," Darrant continued angrily, his tone rising and unaffected by Aidin's apparent alarm. "The damage is irreversible; this is not IN6 and I will not stand by and allow murder on my station."

"Darrant, he's probably murdered more people than you and I can count!"

"And that makes it alright for you to commit murder? No! Do you hear me? No!" Darrant raged, his face sickened and his decision unaffected by Aidin's reasoning.

"Darrant!" Aidin returned authoritively, and then, thinking better of it, he lowered his voice as he continued to reason, "Darrant, it's come from the very top of the IAF from IN6; I wish there was some other way, but there's not."

"Then find one!" Darrant growled, glaring at his friend and with his arms spread on either side of the table between them.

Aidin looked away, sighing and putting his hand to his mouth in thought. After a moment, he looked back at a still glaring Darrant. "There isn't time."

"What do you mean?" Darrant demanded.

"What little we did get from him through the drugs has the IAF worried. It has me worried." Aidin looked into the eyes of a still scowling Darrant and spoke as quietly as he could. "Broken pieces, little bits of what he knows… an old friend of ours is returning, but this time they're all coming."

"What does that mean?" Darrant asked.

"We don't know, and the rest was mostly gibberish.

Something about weapons being useless, and that they'll take us from the inside out." Aidin looked down, concern written over his face.

"What? What is it?" Darrant asked.

Aidin looked up again, gnawing his lip nervously as he stared back at Darrant. "I saw him—saw him in our sick bay, Darrant, and he was drugged out of his mind, but…."

"*What?*" Darrant almost whispered.

"I've seen that look before, Leroy, and it was like… like he'd already won. I'm scared, Leroy… and we're out of time."

Darrant rolled back in the couch, turning away with the stress of the decision he had to make showing on his face. "I want to see him," he finally said.

"Leroy, I said we're out of ti—"

"I want to see him!" Darrant insisted. "I'm not going to kill a man without looking into his eyes."

Resigned, Aidin nodded. "He's being transferred to your holding cells as we speak. I—"

Suddenly, they were interrupted as a panicked Karack came rushing up the stairs. "Captain, Ford's downstairs and he needs to talk to you; it's urgent."

"Why couldn't he use the com—"

Karack broke in, "He says it's too sensitive to send, Captain. Please hurry!"

Darrant had never run across 172 in his life, but the look on Karack's face convinced him to do so as he bounded down the stairs and across the room.

Aidin followed his friend down the spiral staircase as Darrant barged through people, drawing attention from customers along the way. Aidin's questions about what lay hidden below were about to be answered as he ran after Darrant, on down the second spiral staircase and into the eerie green of the lower floor. Coming off the staircase, there was little time to take in the sights as betting tables of all kinds flashed past in the green hue. Darrant leapt up a flight of stairs, closely followed by Aidin as they swung to the right and between more tables, on to a bar running the width of the room. Stopping, Darrant looked around in the crowd, and seeing nothing, he'd begun to push his way through when…

"Captain! Captain!" the voice called, its source invisible among the throng of people.

A commotion appeared to their left, with gasps and expletives heard from shocked customers as Ford pushed through from among them, ashen-faced and with his eyes bulging.

"Captain!" the man shouted again, grabbing Darrant by the shoulder and trying to speak as quietly as his nerves would allow him. "It's 196! It's under fire!"

"What?" Darrant demanded.

"The Hearack are all over them; they're being overrun!"

As quickly as they had arrived, they were charging back out through Karack's, people being thrown out of the way as Darrant cleared the staircase and crashed through them. In moments, they were outside Karack's the door all but crashing off the hull as they left.

"When did it start?" Darrant shouted, barging through the crowd as they ran through the galleria.

"Only minutes ago—every available starship's been sent!" Ford called back as they skidded to a stop at the executive maglift.

"Launch the *Rheinvar* and get over there, Aidin. I—

"

"I'm going!" Aidin cut his friend off as he raced toward the maglift he'd arrived on. "I'll communicate on route!"

"Hurry!" Darrant shouted after him as the executive maglift sealed.

Chapter 6

Payback

"Distress call sent on all channels…" Warren was silenced as another explosion rocked the station.

"Report!" Captain Shroeder demanded.

"We've lost the number five shield generator; remaining generators compensating," Warren responded from the docking pit's communications panel, Shroeder standing behind him and staring up at the screen overhead.

Outside of its massive hexagonal centre, the station was lit by plasma fire as the number five generator continued to burn on its mounting near the top of the super structure , illuminating the grey alloy of the quantum-strained hull in an eerie glow. Four more generators spaced equally round the top edge whined feverishly as ion beams tore out from banks behind them, shattering the darkness with streaks of energy. From the top down, the centre column grew wider, being widest at the middle where a huge beam of quantum-strained alloy led out in an arc away from the central structure. Sixteen more arced arms leading away from the beam, complete with docking ports, branched out like great steel arms a thousand meters apart, each one tipped with automatically targeting thoran launchers. The circular launchers spun like turrets tracking their victims from each side of the shafts. As thorans streaked off, their golden colour was matched by more beams of energy from the station's lower banks. From the centre down, the station grew thinner, finishing in a hexagonal superstructure housing the station's reactor cores and a powerful array of energy banks. Nine minutes earlier, a massive steel shaft had led from the centre—twenty thousand metres down to the storage tanks of fuel and other volatiles. Now, though, only a stump remained, impacts from weapons fire on the shields having severed it in the first minutes of the attack, with the tanks now sailing off, safe from the battering the station was under…

Haines frantically manned the defence station, shouting, "Fifty-three Hearack attack ships inbound, five locked up!"

"Fire!"

Thorans shot out in all directions, brilliant golden streaks of fire zeroing off from the station and adjusting height and pitch to match their targets' vectoring as they weaved in between one another as if alive and in a race for glory. Three shot over the lead ship, crashing into the one astern as still more flew over the crippled wreck and into the three ships beyond it. The lead ship, almost ready to begin firing, was denied as the remaining thorans came tearing up under her hull to batter straight through and explode, gutting her with fire.

"Three crippled; two destroyed!" Haines shouted from his station. "Locking targets from the remaining forty-eight; seven of the lead….."

A deafening crash came with weapons slamming into the station, its whole left half glowing blue and shimmering under the straining shields, vibrations thundering throughout the hull from energy that had made it through. People clambered to their feet only to be thrown sideways again as the Hearack continued their murderous assault.

"Report!" Shroeder demanded, gripping the communications panel over Warren in the docking pit as the station shook.

"Moderate damage to shield generators two and three; shields still holding; outer hull breach on decks five through seven!" Mckinlay shouted from the con station.

Shroeder looked directly behind him, at Mckinlay "Status of number five generator?"

"Damage control reports all kinds of electrical problems; it's finished!" Mckinlay shouted back.

"Two more destroyed and moderate damage to five!" shouted Haines.

"Eight more attack fighters approaching!" Allens called from the navigation station "There's something behind them, just coming into sensor range; it… it's huge…."

"What?" Shroeder demanded, still hanging onto the communication panel. When there was no answer, he repeated himself: "What!" he demanded again, glaring at Allens with annoyance at the delay.

"They're…" Allens began, but broke off in shock.

"What? They're what???" Shroeder screamed from his left.

Allens turned to meet him, pale and frightened. "They're huge."

Shroeder looked into his face, seeing it to be one of fear and shock, but Allens had been under fire before—he didn't freeze. He was always….

Realising Allens was useless to this fight, Shroeder left the com panel and stumbled over to Allens with impacts shaking the station, grabbing the corner of the nav panel as he went. He lost balance and stumbled into

Allens. One look down told him everything; the nav panel's left display showed all traffic around the station, and for twenty thousand kilometres out. It was designed to manage traffic and to prevent collisions. But not today—today it displayed a nightmare, a seething mass of fighters vaulting over one another, desperate for a piece of the station. Further out, eight more fighters approached against the dark background of space. Where were the stars? Shroeder wondered in passing as he searched for what Allens had seen, or lost. What was he talking about? Shroeder wondered as vibrations forced him to cling to the panel. There was nothing there, nothing in the lower left or right corners of the display, and nothing in the higher left or right. Nothing in the… nothing in the higher right! Nothing behind the eight ships approaching—not even stars! Shroeder felt the cold realisation of someone being stalked, the growing fear of being cornered. Something was just coming into sensor range, and it was obscured—no, they were obscured, not reading it on sensors till now because the ship was cloaked, but so big it was obscuring the stars behind them!

With a crash, people flew from their stations. "We've lost generator two and three's critical!" Mckinlay screamed.

Another crash.

"The eight incoming have opened up; that makes thirty-nine left; seventeen have moderate damage. Locking up nine of the—" Haines was cut off, lurching under a huge impact.

"Captain, this is the *Blerin*. We're concentrating on the fighters over the number three shield generator," Captain Rawlands broke in over the com channel.

"They're trying to punch their way in!"

Captain Rawlands was in command of the station's attack ship, the *Blerin*, which had left the docking beam just before the battle and had been adding to their firepower, using the *Blerin* to shore up weak spots. From the protection behind the station's massive shields, the *Blerin*—with its weapons matching the station's shield frequencies—had been firing with virtual impunity. Now, however, that was about to change. "Target the ships on the starboard flank!" Rawlands ordered.

"Locked!" returned Edwards, his tactical officer.

"Fire!"

Thorans shot forward, offering a blue halo for an instant as they penetrated the shields, a return of crimson in front of them as the enemy tried to pull away—but their escape was denied as they streaked off, now cones of flame. Their return burst on the outside of the massive shield grid barely registering but for the fiery display.

"The station's shields are holding!" Larez shouted from the *Blerin*'s con.

"Nine more attack ships making a run on the generator!" Preston broke in from the nav station. "They're…" Suddenly, Preston caught sight of something. "What is that?"

Preston's shocked voice drew Rawlands' attention from the other surrounding confusion. "What?" he demanded.

Getting hold of himself, Preston began to report. "There's some sort of huge—no, wait, there's two of them—they're huge, cloaked. They're…."

"They're what?" Rawlands demanded impatiently.

"Some sort of ships," answered Preston. "Massive. They're about a quarter the size of the station… each!"

"On screen!" Rawlands shouted.

The viewscreens display of nine Hearack attack ships suddenly changed, now showing not nine ships, but only one—most of one anyway, for it filled the screen and more.

"It's heading directly for the generator!" shouted Edwards.

"Where's the other one?" Rawlands demanded, wide-eyed.

"Two thousand kilometres behind it," Larez answered. "Its dimensions are the same!"

"Tactical analysis!" Rawlands called out.

Edwards paused for a second, staring down at his displays.

"Edwards!" Rawlands repeated.

"Uhh…" Edwards got a hold of himself. "Reading what looks like seventy-two torpedo launchers and eight ion banks bigger than this ship."

"Alright. Inform the station and target the lead ship." Rawlands tried to hold his nerves, continuing, "Spread our fire across both ships; target their weapons arrays."

"I can't," came back Edwards, visibly shaken.

"What? Why not?" Rawlands demanded.

"The scan was just the first one… the second's not in range yet."

Back on the station damage control teams swarmed like rats desperately trying to repair the stations behind Mckinlay as he shouted "Number three generators fluctuating!"

"Five more destroyed; twenty-seven remaining; eight locked up!" called Haines.

"Fire!"

Thorans shot out from the station then, tearing round the perimeter in an arc to descend on their fleeing targets as if starving for blood. Huge explosions lit up against the station's straining shields, bathing the scene in a calming gold. The calm faded quickly, though, for there was anything but that in the icy blackness of space, from which emerged a chilling sight—a monster of a vessel with its cloaking array dropping, no longer needed. Everything about it was massive, a huge grey form of intersecting triangles. Two falling together and meeting in the centre, drawing to almost a point at the front where they fell inward to a deep, sinister-looking recess. Bristling with hundreds of small lights across its sides, it drew closer—the light from the battle only serving to show more of its monstrous form.

"Twenty-three ships remain!" Haines shouted.

"Generator three's about to go!" Mckinlay called out, smoke appearing around his legs from smouldering circuitry. "Captain!"

Shroeder looked back from the docking control pit, smoke coiling up to his knees as it flowed from smoldering circuitry in the stations around him.

"The new sensor contact that large ship," came Mckinlay.

"What!" Shroeder screamed impatiently.

"They've no shields!" came the reply.

It must be their size, Shroeder thought. *They've sacrificed shielding to cloak because they're too huge to accommodate both that and weapons, leaving them to be just a huge weapons platform.*

"It's coming into range!" Haines announced.

"Hit it with everything you've got!" Shroeder ordered.

In an instant, the station blazed with the firepower of self-targeting thoran turrets spinning, opening up again and again with ions erupting from deep within the station and showering the ship with great beams of golden energy. The sides of the monster were torn to shreds as the beams exposed tens of feet of alloy and vaporised it in seconds, ions tearing great rips in the surface. Molten alloy ejected into space as thorans tore into the hull, craters two stories deep left behind with the ship being hidden for a moment, engulfed in a cloak of fire as incandesecent impurities in the alloy vapourised. On the station's bridge, the crew felt an adrenalin rush of satisfaction upon seeing their horrifying efforts. But it was short-lived, as the monster pushed its way through the flames and emerged like an angry beast with its face scarred and torn into a mass of twisted wreckage, but still coming! A scowling mass of black, carbonised terror, it approached—filling every sensor screen on the station.

"Weapons fully recharged!" Haines screamed.

"Fire!"

Again, the station erupted and the beast was lost in an inferno of energy encompassing everything they had thrown into the fiery mass. Satisfaction came again as they waited for the twisted wreck to limp out in pieces from the flames. But that satisfaction turned instead to horror, all eyes watching as a blackened creature forced aside the inferno. Emerging from the fire, the black mass of twisted steel was no more damaged than the first time, and like a demon it still came forward!

"Weapons almost ready!" Haines gasped.

"Target their—"

Shroeder never finished. He was looking back at Haines, and so he never got to see the horror on screen—

only Haines reaching up to protect his eyes as the bridge filled with brilliant light. The noise was deafening, and all around him people screamed as Shroeder tried to stand, but he couldn't; looking down, he couldn't see his legs beneath the smoke, though he knew they were broken his attempts to stand bringing pain only shock holding most of it back. "Haines! Haines!" Shroeder looked up from the navigation pit through the darkness, a slumped form meeting his eyes over the defence station.

"Generators three and one are gone; shields down to forty percent!" Mckinlay screamed through the darkness from somewhere among the hanging beams and loose cabling. "There's a—"

Mckinlay was silenced as the station rocked with impacts, and Shroeder looked up at the view screen just in time to see the second monstrous starship take up position behind the first. About to order the weapons station to be manned, he was suddenly startled to see masses of brilliant golden colored energy streaming down the sides of the leading starship, running out into space. Choking in the smoke-filled navigation pit, he saw the energy arc back, drawn ravenously into the front of the ship, faster and faster and coursing down the ships' sides and into it. Lying there broken, he watched as the great mouth of the blackened monster sucking in the glowing energy began to darken, going slowly from gold to a menacing amber as if fire were building inside. "Allens, get to the…." The flash forced him to raise his arms as Haines had done, blinded; he could still see it coming from the front of the ship as the impact threw him back. Crashing up against the weapons station, he slumped back down into the docking pit with smoke covering him as the alarms shrieked overhead. Choking and unable to use his limbs, Shroeder struggled, jarring about wildly and panicking under the smoke as he heard the screams and felt the resulting vibrations as people ran past in darkness, unable to see him. With hope gone, and choking his last breaths, he felt two hands grasping his chest with muffled screaming echoing through smoke, and then suddenly there came air as he was pulled up and into the terror of the bridge.

"Sir! Sir!" It was Allens shouting through the darkness, but all Shroeder could do was choke. "We have to get out! Come on!"

Outside, the *Blerin* waited desperately by the crippled station.

"Their shields have failed! Massive damage on all decks! Weapons offline! Larez shouted.

"Three more Hearack ships moving inside the central perimeter—they're cutting her to pieces!" Edwards shouted as the *Blerin* began to shake with impacts for the first time. Shields gone, the unprotected station's central perimeter was breached by five Hearack attack ships veering in under the great quantum-strained beam that secured the docking arms and ports to the station's central living area.

Outnumbered by more than thirty to one, the *Blerin* took more impacts. "Shields down to sixty percent! We've got buckling in the aft quarter!" Edwards shouted.

Rawlands watched in horror as the five invaders began hacking viciously into the helpless station as they now flew around the super structure no shields to prevent them. "Take us into the station and get those bastards!" he ordered, enraged by the carnage. The *Blerin* spun round through a sea of weapons, fire energy beams slicing across incoming beams from all directions. Blazing in front, the station was now a flaming hulk as the *Blerin* bore down on the huge structure, it seeming to rage in defiance with flames leaping up as more weapons crashed through it. The *Blerin* shot under a docking port and broke right as another force of enemy ships closed in behind it.

There was a crash and… "Shields down to forty-three percent!" came Edwards' voice as smoke began to leak into the bridge.

"Where are they?" Rawlands raged.as they tore round after the five ships in front of them the stations central structure now blocking their view as they closed in.

"Half a kilometre in front—we're coming around on them!" answered the helm.

"Edwards, as soon as you get a lock, open up. I want them wasted!" Rawlands ordered.

"Aye, sir!" Edwards answered, his own anger equally apparent.

The ship tore round under another docking arm, the great beam fleeing past them on the left as they closed in.

"Enemy coming into range!" Preston announced.

"Edwards!" was all Rawlands got off as the sterns of two attack ships appeared on the left of the viewscreen. The ship vibrated as thorans screamed out in front, following the same course and narrowly missing the docking arms as they pulled round into the ships. Hulls exploded in front the *Blerin*, unable to evade them flying straight through wreckage their shields straining with impacts.

"Two enemy destroyed!" Edwards said, the struggle

sounding in his voice. "Shields down to thirty-seven percent!"

"Captain, two more enemy moving in behind us!" Larez broke in. "They've—"

Weapons crashed into them as they tore round the station, now becoming the hunted.

"Shields at nineteen percent!" Edwards screamed. "They're rearming!"

Rawlands knew it was over; more than two dozen attack ships and two massive, unknown vessels now stood against them, and they didn't want a surrender. He knew that inside that station, people were going through hell—people burning and suffocating, being crushed and more just like he'd seen in the war. And here his ship was all the station could answer with till the escape pods were rocketed off the station, and answer they would. "Helm, manoeuvre us over and under the arms! Don't make it easy for them; we've gotta give the station as much time to evacuate as we can!"

"Aye!" answered the helm.

The *Blerin* tore over one arm and under another, each time missing them by only tens of feet while travelling at over ninety thousand kilometres an hour. Weapons tore past them on screen, coming from pursuing ships as Edwards continued firing on those in front. Like a great arced track of death, the ship sped over one arm as the Hearack screamed up from under another, weapons launching as the *Blerin* shot under the next to arrive in more weapons fire with the Hearack tearing after them from above. Another explosion in front came just as Edwards landed a shot, debris flying past as they charged through the fires raging out from the station. Suddenly, yet another explosion came from behind as one of the Hearack smashed headlong into an arm.

"Yeah!" Edwards screamed out on the bridge emotion overtaking him. "That leaves two in front and one behind targeting!

"Sir!" Larez screamed out. "They're firing on the escape pods!

Rawlands looked on in horror as the twisted face of the lead Hearack monster, blackened by weapons fire from the station, now rained fire mercilessly on the helpless survivors. Life pods exploded everywhere as great flickering charges of energy came crashing through the battlefield.

"That bastard!" Rawlands cursed. "Larez, scan the—"

"Sir, the Hearack are breaking off their attack; they're heading away!" Preston cut him off.

On screen, Rawlands watched the three Hearack ships move off in the direction of the two huge starships. "Take us away from the docking beam. Come to course 019, mark 0 and keep us between the starships and the station," Rawlands ordered cautiously. "Helm, keep an eye on the rest of those attack figh—"

"Sir!" Preston broke in again. "More fighters are moving off—they're all moving in behind us."

"How many?"

"Nineteen!"

It was finished, but Rawlands wasn't going to abandon the people trying to flee in the pods. "Target the three in front and fire at wi—"

The ship was rocked by impacts as weapons streamed past in all directions, fires breaking out around them as ceiling panels collapsed from above.

"Shields have failed!" Edwards screamed.

"Captain, the three in front are coming around! They're coming back at us!" Larez shouted out.

"Bring us to course—"

"Captain!" screamed Edwards. "The lead starship's ion banks have recharged—its energy readings are off the scale! It's arming!"

Rawlands momentarily forgot their own situation as, on screen, to the right of the approaching ships, the dormant, twisted-faced monster awoke, sending great streams of golden energy coursing down its blackened sides. The energy flowed out in front and arced back like before, Rawlands grimacing as feelings of all kinds racked him—rage, failure, hopelessness, and anger over those he wasn't able to save. "There's people out there in those pods—families who don't stand a chance if we don't help them—so let's show what this uniform means! We're not getting out of this alive, but neither is that twisted-faced bastard! Preston!"

"Sir!" he answered.

"Tie in with Edwards—plot a course into one of its ion banks!"

Gathering his nerves, Preston looked back up at Edwards, the other man giving him a resigned nod as their synchronising began.

"Preston!" Rawlands demanded, still watching the amber jaws of the monster.

"Ready!"

"Engage!"

Inside the blackened monster, the Hearack couldn't see the bravery on the *Blerin* or know the sacrifice coming; to them, it was nothing.

On the *Blerin* bridge, however, the crew sat silently as flames grew around them with the sound of muffled impacts, dignified until the last few kilometres when emotions broke free with their screams, the ship breaking left and spinning over a storm of weapons fire straight down toward the sloping hull of the beastly ship. Hurtling downward at almost two hundred thousand kilometres per hour, the hull rushed up to meet the roar of the crew.

Suddenly, a bright red haze surrounded them—not the haze of the fire of their assured end, but of molecular splice inducer beams transporting and separating their atoms in the last few moments before impact. But this wasn't the pale blue molecular splice inducer beams of the Alliance; these beams were red... they were those of the Hearack.

Chapter 7

Trail of Destruction

It had taken three days, but they'd arrived.

"Mr Evan" Aidin enquired, quietly looking out into the empty mass of stars on the viewscreen.

"Coordinates 317, mark 25, sir. The Fearon System," Evans answered hesitantly from the navigation panel.

Aidin was about to ask an all too disturbing question, but then, thinking better of it, he took a deep breath, his lips pursed as he approached the viewscreen, passing between the nav and con panels with the screen still empty. "Mr Hollin," he addressed his con officer.

"Sir."

"Magnify."

In an instant, all questions were brutally answered— they saw debris, debris as far as the eye could see, blasted out beyond the station's previous position by some godforsaken act. Aidin just stared open-mouthed, the bridge silent behind him with nothing but the gentle system alerts of panels displaying their findings. Aidin watched as huge steel sections of bulkheads and decks drifted gently in front of them, slowly tumbling by as if in some gentle breeze.

The system alerts, however, quite gently brought Aidin back to his responsibilities. "Mr Hollin…" was all he could find to say.

"No life signs," Hollin responded quietly, as if trying not to break a respectful silence for the victims. "Sporadic power readings from various regions, probably loose fuel cells and damaged power units; scans continuing."

"Dispatch a priority one message to IAF command." Aidin paused, looking out at the debris of the once massive station. "Station 196 has been destroyed."

Aidin continued gazing outward almost in awe— they all did, as they'd seen the wreckage of battles before, of starships and even outposts, endless seas of steel and horror, all that waste, but not this… this was something very different. It wasn't wreckage. It was a cemetery.

Over hours the *Rheinvar* moved slowly through the endless expanse of drifting wreckage.

"Anything?" Aidin inquired.

"Nothing yet, sir," replied the science officer, turning back to the science stations with the others endlessly scanning the abyss around them.

The constant system alerts were all the bridge had heard for the past two hours, Aidin feeling like a third wheel as crew members all around him hunted for clues while he wandered between stations, just hoping for answers. He felt useless, watching the science officers follow every detail, feeling almost envious of their work load. The silence was suddenly broken by Steiner, his weapons officer, who stood directly behind him.

"Sir."

Aidin turned to face Lieutenant Commander Steiner, glad someone was finally reporting something.

"Captain, I'm getting strange remnants of something here—something you should see." Steiner had spoken hesitantly, quietly, as if he hadn't wanted anyone else to hear him.

Aidin didn't understand the man's expression as he

moved over to the weapons station. "What have you got?"

"I thought it was nothing… a glitch at first," Steiner replied in near a whisper. "But I'm… well, I'm getting it everywhere, broken down trace elements of…."

"Of what?" Aidin asked as Steiner paused, looking down at the panel hesitantly.

The delay continued a moment longer, and then Steiner looked up. "Of thirilian radiation."

Aidin's eyes widened.

"I've run every system check," Steiner responded to his expression. "There's nothing else that leaves these trace elements."

Aidin knew what the mere mention of thirilian would do among the crew, and took to whispering himself. "Who else knows about this?"

"No one."

"Keep it that way; lock out access to your station," Aidin ordered the man.

Moving past him, Aidin walked round tactical and down toward his council room. "Number 1, you have the bridge." he announced Brenner looking after his agitated Captain as the doors sealed behind him.

Aidin sat down at his desk and tapped out the codes for a secure message to IAF command on the console; this was usually the job of Brenner, but he didn't dare risk anyone else knowing, and in this state of alarm, he addressed errors as he went. He had good reason to feel such alarm. Thirilian had been used in the Anzeil 5 massacre, and it was a terrifying weapon—one without equal. Thirilian radiation, as it was code-named, had never been known before the Dren, never till Anzeil. Anzeil 5 was in the Disis System, one of seven moons orbiting Planet Anzeil and the only one which was habitable by human standards, though so far away. A four-month journey from Earth, but when money was at stake, distance could seem trivial. Anzeil and three of its five moons being laced with precious minerals, and more importantly gravinite, made for a rare find. Gravinite, when purified in its crystal state, was the key to controlling anti-matter reactions at the freezing temperatures needed to contain them. Without any way to process a synthetic substitute for gravinite, and due to its rarity, it had become one of the most expensive commodities ever. When mass concentrations had been found in and around the Disis System, it had been inevitable that a huge colony would emerge there. Attracted by the wealth, miners, traders, entrepreneurs, and all manner of others had come running, along with their families. It hadn't been long before there'd been almost as many people there as in the Terran home system, Anzeil 5 really giving Earth a run for its money with its breath-taking scenery and weather.

Naturally, such wealth had to be protected from the other jealous factions in Quadrant IL 19; it had been said that the garrison there was impenetrable—only the Terran System could rival the firepower—and the forces could take on the entire quadrant if unleashed. It was a fortress. Time and again during the war, the forces had annihilated massive Dren attack wings, which never even managed to break the outer perimeter of the system, three more laying behind that one.

Then came a weapon like no other…

It started like any other battle, ships being torn apart

by long-range hountas platforms, with only a few damaged diehards that got through getting cut down by the outer fleet. Then, it came—a huge ship with no shielding, it was the Hearack's dying gasp sneaking up under a huge cloaking device. Everything they had had been flung into this monster. An ugly beast devoid of any aesthetics; just a hulk of alloy... all their alloy. After smashing through the first two perimeters, it had taken so much damage that it had lost a quarter of its mass, and by the final perimeter, it was crawling forward, defeated. Or so it was thought. It ground to a halt after the last perimeter, on fire from stem to stern... but it was in range of Anzeil 5. Survivors reported the fire being sucked inside with energy of some kind—elements of thirilian. Half the crews were blinded by the first flash, and they never got to see the second or third.

When it was over, Anzeil had only four moons and a charred mass that had used to be a planet. The vessel was finally destroyed by repeated attacks before it had a chance to finish off the rest, but what it had started, thirilian would finish.

Thirilian wasn't even picked up by the bio-scanners; they didn't know what it was, and tens of thousands of survivors were evacuated on all kinds of vessels headed for medical facilities in the Langsdorn System. Armies of medical staff anxiously awaited them, converting building after building into makeshift hospitals on Planet Telsis, spurred on by communications from the fleet of a strange illness breaking out. Nine days later, the fleet arrived on the outskirts of Langsdorn, showing no signs of dropping out of warp and with no communications between them for four days; the IAF garrison on Telsis overrode the fleet's computers and forced them to drop to rail engines. They tried to force communications, to activate viewscreens and computer logs, but got nothing. Theships just drifted slowly forward, closer and closer in complete silence, like a ghost fleet. Fighters sent from Telsis reported no life signs, nothing, their scanners detecting that half the ships didn't have atmospheres and that some even had battle damage, as if they had engaged one another, and several more were missing. With fear escalating, the fleet was halted just inside the Langsdorn System, well away from Telsis; a quarantine was ordered and biohazard teams were brought in—professionals, they'd seen it all, every plague known to man. When air locks were forced open, however, men backed off in terror, and those who ventured inside only lost control of their stomachs and had to be brought out with their bio-suits filled with their last meals. Every ship was the same; bodies looked like they had been set alight, charred from top to bottom, dried blood covering cracks that were still visible in the burnt corpses that had used to be people. All decks were a nightmare of twisted flesh, the bodies not looking human… and, most disturbingly of all, they seemed to have turned on one another. Scanners indicated phasor wounds, head traumas, deep incisions, and even bite marks.

It took days to download the computer logs, and when they were reviewed, hardened chiefs of staff, generals, were left in shock—so much so that access became restricted. But the word was out. The crews had gone insane. Over a period of two days, normal and seemingly healthy survivors had begun to blister everywhere, blood running from every orifice—eyes, ears, and even from under fingernails. IAF officials watched the log reports of doctors as if they were watching a horror movie, seeing video reports from medical bays that spoke of skin beginning to harden as if it were burnt. Video logs showed deep cracks opening in the skin of victims who shrieked in their beds in pain... shrieking because all pain-killers had long been used up. More logs showed blood-soaked bodies lying in corridors—black, bald, cracked open, and shivering uncontrollably as screams filled the air around them. On one victim, video footage moved slowly upward, showing deep tears on the shins, thighs, and torso that were evidently from the victim himself... or herself, as that could no longer be determined. As the footage cleared the neck, gasps were heard in the room from the normally stoic military, everyone covering their mouths as, on screen, a face came into view that was not human; it couldn't be. It was twisted, the mouth pulled up so that the right side joined the eye, the left eye almost shut—stretched across the side of the head—while a honeycomb of holes covered the rest, oozing blackened blood while worm-like protrusions wriggled inside.

There weren't words to describe what it was, though they later found that this had been Lieutenant Moore, a beautiful 28-year-old brunette..

Other logs showed paranoia breaking out among the crews; some accused commanders of being Hearack spies, some of hiding painkillers and antidotes, and others of leading them away from Telsis and into Dren space. By day three, running firefights had begun breaking out on ships as still more faces twisted with creatures fighting through holes in their skin went into a mania, bursting open airlocks, turning on themselves and murdering others. But not just murdering—taking great pleasure in causing unspeakable suffering on one another and laughing gleefully as monstrous victims shrieked in agony. Groups descended on individuals, tearing at their flesh and eating them alive as they screamed beneath them before mouths overflowing with horror, turning on one another.

Similar footage was confiscated, hidden from public scrutiny. Not knowing what had caused the horror, bio-teams were banished to undisclosed moons and held in isolation indefinitely. There were no funerals, and the fleet was destroyed by Shoalar Class battle cruisers based near Telsis, every ship near vaporised for fear of further contamination. At least, that was the official version. Though it remained unknown to all but a few, eight ships were secretly towed away by IN6 to an unknown location where scientists went through body after body, ship after ship. Some three years later, it was uncovered that residual elements trapped in the ships' engine waste had been pieced together, maddeningly, almost re-forming the deadly weapon code-named thirilian. The scientists' irresponsibility in this, thankfully left incomplete, provided enough data to extrapolate that they were dealing with some sort of radiation with an extremely short half-life, of less than forty-eight hours. Unfortunately, the slightest exposure seemed fatal, and data suggested that the very DNA of a person exposed to the substance was ravaged, warped— and the process, once started, seemed unhaltingly aggressive. All further attempts to glean more information failed; key components of the radiation couldn't be found, leading to the belief that they only existed in Quadrant NM 15 and had been brought through the wormhole before it had collapsed.

IN6 claimed to have suspended further research,

thirilian was classed as a meta-genic weapon—the worst known—and was promptly banned with all the others. After a leak brought knowledge of the secret investigation to light IN6 assured its compliance and claimed that all remaining ships and bodies had been disposed of, despite uproar from victims' families citing the short half-life as justification for their return and burial. IN6 claimed that such reservations hadn't reached them in time, through the maze of IAF bureaucracy—really, they ignored them.

With that horror etched on his mind Aidin stared down at the screen…

He looked at the key to begin the transmission, pausing then to glance out the window to his left, into space. He was about to unleash panic of the highest order. What was out there? He wondered. Space stations were massive, the fortresses of their day with huge shielding and uncountable weapons systems able to hold of armadas for days, so what was it that could have cut through them in hours? He glanced back at the console, his reflection in the screen, and squared his shoulders and touched the key.

Alliance command had similar questions and precisely the same concerns as him; indeed, they panicked.

"It's completely gone?" Admiral Chelmski asked, shocked.

"Yes, Admiral, you'd never know the wreckage was a station," answered Aidin.

Chelmski turned away, drawing a deep breath and apparently trying to think through his nerves. Another deep breath, and then… "I don't need to tell you that none of this leaves your council room. Who else knows?"

"Just my tactical officer."

"Make sure it stays that way, Aidin. I don't want a panic on our hands. going through that sector, they're in range of three systems, and we don't have the ships at hand to defend them all," Chelmski said, the strain showing. "Everything we've got is near the Hiiral System; it's the most strategically valuable, but the raids lately don't seem to be strategic. They just seem random, and that leaves Elson and Buenin. I'll have to go through Alliance command, but the shit's really gonna hit the fan. Until then…." Chelmski paused, looking away, apparently unable to think clearly with the news. "Until then, search the area and try to find out where they went, what we're up against, but do not engage—not yet, not till we've…" he paused again, looking down and shaking his head. "Not till we've figured something out. Chelmski out."

The departure was sudden but understandable, as he had to face the whole Alliance Command; apart from the strain of the news, Chelmski's workload was about to explode, and by tomorrow he'd look ten years older.

The doors of the council room split apart to reveal the con just to the right and the nav station further away. As Aidin walked out into the sounding of system alerts, he turned to see an anxious first officer and a tight-lipped tactical officer above and behind him. They were all looking at him, waiting for a glimmer of what had gone on in the council room, but Aidin remained defiant against their gazes walking over to his chair to the right of his first officer Brenner.

"Bad news, Captain?" Brenner inquired, watching the frown across Aidin's face.

"What?" Aidin came out of his train of thought. "Well, it's not good. No, I have the…"

"Captain!" broke in Hollin from the con. "I'm picking up a faint trace of corinine—bearing 048, mark 014; one of the ships may have been damaged in the attack and left venting. It could be a trail, sir."

Finally, thought Aidin, *something*. Corinine was a held-state fuel component used in the Hearack's rail engines, so it made sense that the corinine would be venting from a ship.

"Where does it seem to be heading, Lieutenant?" Aidin asked.

"It starts about five thousand kilometres from the debris field; from the vector I can get on it, it's either heading in the direction of the Elson or Buenin System. But it's fading fast, sir. If we don't start on it soon, it may have dispersed to the point that we won't know where they've continued to."

Aidin couldn't lose this, and he thought quickly. "Mr Steiner, what's in those systems?"

Steiner was already on it, Aidin barely finishing when he came back with an answer: "Elson's fourteen planets are uninhabitable. However, three moons around Elson Four have atmospheres that are just barely breathable, but toxic within days. Elson Two has eight moons, two of them habitable with a huge colony on one, Tirenal, which has a large refining complex. Buenin Two and Three are J5 class and Buenin Two has a small colony, no hard industry."

"And Buenin Two and Three, do they have heavy industry facilities they may need for repair?" Aidin broke in, feeling the need to strain forward like a dog on a leash.

"No, sir," Steiner replied. "It's mainly farmland, but there is a mining complex on one of Buenin's two moons with an orbiting station for ore transports."

Brenner had left his seat and moved over to the con to look over Hollin's shoulder; like Aidin, he couldn't wait to find the assassins. Listening to Steiner and Aidin behind him, a thought occurred to him. "Captain, mining equipment can be used to repair ships. It's not pretty, but all they'd have to do is cannibalise the transports; I've seen it done, during the war."

"Then that's where they'll be," Aidin replied in a quietly determined tone, barely disguising a growl. "Set a course for that system, Mr Evans; they'll never leave!"

The *Rheinvar* came out of warp near the Buenin System, Aiden having decided they'd work all the way in on rail in case their friends tried to make a break for it. They'd never make it if they tried, however; the *Rheinvar* was the flagship of the Alliance, a battleship barely disguised as a science vessel. The *Rheinvar*'s official mission was border deployment, and although this was true, it was just this deployment that always seemed to land her right in the middle of the action. Disputes, fights, wars… she'd seen it all, and so had her sisters, her six proud sisters before her, all meeting a glorious end in a desperate battle for what was right.

She herself was comparatively young, only two years old, but seven on the drawing board, though she'd been speeded up upon her sister's demise—that of *Rheinvar 228-1 F*. *228-1 F* had ended her blistering eight-year reign while holding off a Hearack storm fleet over Mensis Prime. Doomed from the beginning, she'd fought like a lion against impossible odds so that troops could evacuate all they could with a ramshackle fleet of trading vessels and scout ships. The attack on Memsis Prime had been a complete surprise; coming out of the Yale Nebula, the Hearack had been set to wipe out the mining colony there—that was until the *Reclar E*'s captain, one Miles Aidin, had broken away from his orders and veered across two sectors to save people he'd never seen.

It had taken forty minutes—forty minutes for seven Hearack Attack Fighters to stop Aidin's ship. After forty minutes, only three had remained, and still, with no weapons, Captain Aidin had ordered her in front of the escaping fleet to draw their fire, and he'd managed it. The fleeing inhabitants had never gotten to thank half of their rescuers, as five minutes after the last ship had broken into warp, the *Rheinvar* had been smashed with everything the Hearack had. Disabled and almost adrift, Aidin had tried to have her veer round Memsis Prime's perimeter to escape fire, but with shields gone and only barely on thrusters, she'd fallen victim. In her dying gasp, she had saved countless lives as the assault had forced her into the Memsis atmosphere. After eleven years going into her, as many seconds had destroyed her as she'd torn a scar a mile wide through the forests below.

Now, as he and his crew neared the outskirts of the Buenin System, Aidin remembered that moment; without him and that crew, not one person would have survived that fight, and now they were set apart again, alone and far from home.

They'd moved slowly through the system, from Buenin Nine past Buenin Five, constantly watching for their fleeing prey, and were now in range of Buenin Three and Two coming under their sensors' gaze.

"What's in there, Mr Hollin?" Aidin asked.

"I… something's wrong, sir" Hollin answered.

"What do you mean *wrong*?" Brenner asked.

"Buenin Three should be busy with transports; I've met ore traders, sir. They're ruthless managers… as far as they're concerned, if their ships aren't moving, they're losing money, and there's not one in sight. It's like a ghost town over there."

"Captain," Steiner said, "If the Hearack did come here, they wouldn't ask for help."

Aidin knew he was right, and 'ghost town' may have been the best way to put it, because if they had come, that's all there'd be left.

"Mr Hollin, is there anything on long-range scans? Anything at all?" Aidin worried about being jumped while buried so deep in the Buenin System.

"No, sir, nothing," Hollin answered.

Aidin looked across at Brenner, who glanced back with the same concern on his face. This didn't feel right.

"Take us in, Mr Evans," Aidin ordered. "Everyone, report anything unusual, no matter how trivial."

The tension mounted on the bridge as they finally passed Buenin Two, every little system report seized upon by the crew nervously hunting for their quarry. Buenin's moon, Kais, loomed larger on the viewscreen, its side exposed to its sun and casting an eerie, pale blue glow across everything as they began to inch their way through the ore storage vessels and junk littering the ore station. Bits of discarded steel machinery and broken-down ships now surrounded them like an asteroid field as they struck a course almost parallel to the station, along its western flank and inching closer. The station loomed ahead as they carefully avoided each new floating obstacle bathed in the pale blue of Kais with still nothing else to be seen, only silence.

"Still not responding to hails, Captain," Evans reported.

"They should have contacted us before we were anywhere near them. I don't like it, Captain," voiced Brenner

"Mr Hollin, is there any indication of movement inside?" Aidin asked.

"That station's holding all sorts of ore, Captain. I've got readings of naridium, quanesein, aranite, and indications of others; there's so much, I can't penetrate more than a few meters inside with sensors, so I just can't tell," Hollin answered. "But, Captain, there's nine ore transporters docked here, and I've never seen that many in one place in my life. Their engines are cold, sir—no power spikes at all."

"Number one, could you—"

Aidin was cut short as the ship was rocked from behind.

"Hearack attack ship dead astern! It's closing—"

Steiner was silenced as weapons tore up the *Rheinvar*'s spine, coming from the Hearack ship fleeing overhead.

"Ram this crap out of the way and get us out of this field!" Aidin ordered.

The *Rheinvar*'s forward shields blazed like a fireworks display as debris and containers were smashed clear.

"Where is he, Evans?" Brenner demanded, enraged at being jumped.

"020, mark 012, he's powering his engines—he's making a run for it!" Evans replied.

"Where did he come from?" Aidin demanded amid the impacts on the shields.

"He came out from behind ore containers off the stern," Hollin answered as another impact jolted him in his seat. "He must have had his systems powered down and the containers' contents were enough to shield him from our sensors."

"He's gonna need more than that to shield him now!" Brenner growled.

"He's gone to warp!" Evans shouted.

"Track him!" shouted Brenner back.

Aidin saw the way clear ahead as they were subjected to the final jolts from the debris. "Set an intercept course, Mr Evans—maximum warp!"

"Aye, sir," Evans answered.

The blue tinges on the forward shields petered out as the *Rheinvar* broke free from the debris field and shot forward, a blur for an instant before a blinding flash signalled her departure. Behind her lay the ore station and its field of debris and spare parts; the owners would never come to know what malicious vandal had torn the huge path through, costing them so much.

"Where are they, Mr Evans?" Aidin asked.

"Holding steady, course 024, mark 019," Evans answered.

"They're not trying to hide; they're running for something!" Steiner voiced.

"It's not like the Hearack to be scared," Aidin spoke out.

"No," Brenner commented condescendingly, "but their vrail might be a different story."

"Where is their course taking them?" Aidin demanded.

"If they remain on that course for another four minutes, they'll enter the Elson System, sir," Hollin answered.

"A final suicide run on them?" Brenner asked aloud, knowing the Hearack's tactics when faced with defeat.

"No, Number 1, if they were going out for the Dren, they'd have charged us. No, they've worked too hard for that!" Aidin assured him. "They must be waiting for them. Dispatch a message to Admiral Colben. We are in pursuit of the enemy, heading for the Elson System!"

"Then, what's beyond that system? What else could they be heading for?" Brenner asked.

"The Fahraren Heights, sir, or Valraich space," Evans answered worriedly, knowing full well that once there, they'd either have to halt their pursuit in the face of the plasma storms of the Heights or the automated defence systems of the Valraich.

"Can we catch them before they get there?" asked Brenner.

"No, sir," Evans replied. "Whatever damage they took hasn't slowed their engines."

"They must know it's suicide; those plasma storms will tear them apart," Aidin commented. "Unless..." Aidin paused, remembering his conversation with Darrant.

"Unless, Captain?" Brenner prompted.

"Unless it's not the Heights they're heading for."

"Captain, they're dropping out of warp, heading for Tirenal Four. Their—" Evans was cut short.

"Lay in an intercept course and advise IAF command of our situation!" Aidin demanded. "Get us over there, Mr Evans!"

The *Rheinvar* bore down upon Tirenal Four, a planet on the very fringes of Alliance space, coming to the scene of the Hearack laying waste to the defenceless people below. On the bridge, the channels broke open to the sound of Admiral Colben announcing, "We're on route—ETA nine minutes!"

"They're locked!" Steiner shouted.

"Fire all weapons!"

Aidin's call sent a stream of thorans and ions crashing into the enemy vessel.

"They're pulling off round the planet, putting it between them and us," reported Evans.

"Stay on them!" Brenner demanded.

"Where's the rest? Where's their fleet, Mr Hollin?" Aidin called out.

"Nothing on sensors, but—" Hollin was cut short as weapons struck the forward shields.

"But what, Mr Hollin?" Aidin demanded.

"There's some sort of interference—weird signals… I can't—" Another impact silenced Hollin again.

"Captain, shields down to seventy-two percent! Heavy damage in engineering!" Steiner broke in.

"Return fire!" Aidin ordered. "Bring us around behind to course—"

"Captain, they're pulling out!" Evans broke in. "They're making a run for it!"

On screen, the Hearack ship veered away from Tirenal, heading into the distance.

"Engineering to Bridge!" Chief Engineer Danske called in. "We've got plasma conduits blown out on two decks, a coolant leak in engineering, and—" Danske broke off as the ship was rocked by an explosion.

"Chief!" Brenner prompted.

"Make that three decks!" Danske answered, "and we've got micro-fractures along the second intake manifold. Captain, we're at our limit down here."

"How long?" Aidin sighed, watching the glow of the Hearack's orange exhaust grow fainter as it slipped off in front of them.

"We're looking at an hour, an hour and a half down here; we're—"

"You've got thirty minutes, Danske," Aidin cut him off.

A barely disguised sigh came over the com system. "Yes, sir," Danske acknowledged.

The bridge crew watched the other ship as they slipped away, their damage thwarting their pursuit.

"Mr Hollins," Aidin began.

"Sir?"

"Follow them on sensors, relay our condition to the fleet, and—" Aidin didn't get to finish.

"Sir, they're gone!" Evans shouted.

"What do you mean they're gone?" Brenner demanded.

"They just vanished from sensors! They just... disappeared," Evans replied.

"Gone to warp?" Aidin inquired.

"No, sir, they just vanished," Evans repeated.

"Some sort of cloaking technology?" wondered Aidin aloud.

The only cloaking technology they knew of came from the Hearack; factions in Quadrant IL 19 had dabbled with limited success for decades, but it hadn't been till the war that the full horror of cloaking technology had been unveiled. Hearack starships had begun to appear without warning around that time, destroying whole colonies before they had any chance to respond; it was said that a few more cloaked ships could have turned the war. Wrecked starships from various battles had revealed why there were so few, however; the equipment necessary was enormous, taking almost three quarters of a ship's internal space to install. Apart from these ships being able to carry only a limited amount of troops and supplies on top of such technology, the cost of running these things seemed staggering. Estimates for running a starship cloaked with this equipment amounted to cutting a starship's range on one fuel load by eighty-two percent! It was understandable why enthusiasm was low regarding the relevant research; apart from the cost, if these things fell into any one faction in IL 19, the balance of power would be unfavourable for those without it. It was no surprise then that the data gathered had become classified by IN6 and then mysteriously vanished not long after the wormhole had collapsed, and with it any further progress on cloaking technology—officially, anyway.

"Something we haven't seen since the war," Brenner started. "Maybe…" Brenner suddenly stopped as the bridge erupted with system reports and alarms.

On screen in the distance, a massive explosion shot downward in a funnel of flame.

"Mr Hollin! What are we looking at?" Aidin demanded.

"Vitrium composites, eraldihite alloys. Sir, it's them—it's the Hearack ship, or what's left of them," came back a confused Hollin as he scoured the incoming data.

"How can they have disappeared and then exploded without reason? What' going on!" a frustrated Brenner demanded.

"Number 1," Aidin called, raising his hand calmly. "Mr Hollin, what's happening?"

Hollin clearly struggled to give an answer. "There's no ships in the area, no spatial anomalies."

"A core breach, then?" Aidin asked.

"No... no, sir," returned Hollin. "The data just doesn't support it; we'd have detected it beginning to go, sir. It... it just exploded!" continued Hollin, knowing his answer wasn't good enough.

"And the rest of their fleet?" Aidin asked.

"Nothing on sensors, sir," Hollin reported, obviously feeling more useless with each question.

"Mr Evans, was there any sign of—"

Aidin was silenced as a damaged plasma conduit blew out on deck five, the ship convulsing in response and throwing the crew from their feet. Steiner grabbed his station in an effort to keep standing causing a scream to ring out from deep within the ship as he struck the weapons controls accidentally.

"Steiner!" Brenner shouted.

On screen, thorans tore off harmlessly into empty space in front of them.

"I'm sorry, sir, an accident!" returned Steiner, embarrassed as Brenner frowned at him.

"That's alright. It happens," Aidin assured him. "Bridge to Engineering—Danske, what's going on?"

"Damaged conduits have blown out on deck five, Captain," Danske answered. "Sir, half an hour's just unrealistic with this kind of damage."

"Mr Danske, your best estimate!" demanded a now

frustrated Aidin, abandoning his calm façade.

"Sir, we need at least two hours. I've got teams spread across eight decks."

"Mr Danske—"

Aidin broke off as the bridge erupted with system alerts. Wheeling round, he saw a fireball far in the distance, built from the detonating thorans, and for an instant a massive, deep green object became visible before disappearing with the dying flames.

Now, more confusion forced a silence over the bridge.

"Mr Hollin?" Aidin voiced quietly.

"Unclear, sir," Hollin began. "They've hit something."

"What?" Aidin asked.

"I don't know, sir," Hollin answered, more frustrated at his lack of answers. "But…"

"But what?" Aidin asked, sharing his frustration.

"Based on the readings before it vanished, sir, it's…"

"It's what?" Aidin pressed.

"It's huge," reported Hollin, "and it's heading toward us."

An eerie chill crept over the bridge crew as they looked into the empty vastness on screen, knowing that, hidden within it, a massive shape was now descending on them.

Aidin's mind raced. He'd just watched a Hearack attack ship destroyed in seconds in front of him, and the power needed to do that was….

"Let's get the hell out of here!" Aidin commanded. "Mr Evans, bring us around one-eighty and set a course; any heading, Mr Hollin…"

On the bridge, Aidin continued to bark orders over the flurry of activity as the huge hulk of quantum-strained alloy that was the *Rheinvar* forced herself round on all thrusters.

"One-eighty answered," reported Evans. "Setting course 258-mark-185."

"Now, Mr Evans!" ordered Aidin. "Engage."

Outside, the *Rheinvar*'s engine manifolds began to surge a brilliant blue, brighter and brighter until, suddenly, a wash of green light appeared, grabbing for the *Rheinvar* in the instant she burst forward.

Cries filled the bridge as a massive jolt threw the crew from their feet, and all over the ship, the broken bodies of crew filled the decks as they slumped down from the walls.

Pinned down, Aidin screamed, "What's going on?"

Desperately trying to push up from his panel to report, Lieutenant Hollin wheezed, "Inertial dampers have failed—something grabbed for us. I…."

The *Rheinvar* barrelled through space at warp speed, out of control with people inside pinned down and fighting for breath against the centrifugal forces, the ship trying to squeeze their lungs flat.

Suddenly, the com channel came on overhead. "Danske to Bridge… we've… ah—"

Cut off by the forces pushing on him, it was soon clear what he was trying to say as the computer broadcast it throughout the ship: "Warning—warp core breach in progress! Core breach in eighty seconds!"

"Bridge to Enginee… ah… Mr Dans—" Aidin desperately tried to call Engineering as crew members crawled to their stations.

"Captain… we can't… it's gonna—" came a

desperate attempt at a reply from Danske.

Overhead, the only clear voice onboard came from the computer reporting in, "Warp core breach in fifty seconds!"

Aidin knew what he was hearing, or at least he hoped he did as he summoned every last ounce of strength to make the call required. "Bridge… Bridge to all decks: Abandon ship!"

The *Rheinvar* corkscrewed through space as people inside of it crawled for escape pods. Splintering apart, hard points broke free from the ship, and here and there escape pods began to jettison from among the wreckage, some of them being torn open immediately with others spinning off uncontrollably at warp speeds.

"Warning: twenty seconds till core breach!"

Inside, the crew were flattened against walls and floors, hearing the computer taunt them as a few more pods released.

"Warning: ten seconds till core breach!"

Pod doors slammed shut, the poor remaining souls onboard hearing escape thrusters vibrating off the hull as they broke away.

A few more, a few more… and then it happened.

For those left in Engineering, it was instantaneous, the core walls bursting open and brilliant white energy spewing out. No walls, quantum-strained or otherwise, could hold back the wave of energy as it melted through the ship like paper. Still held down, the crew felt the ominous explosion and were treated to a few more seconds of terrifying life before it was upon them.

Outside in space, those pods able to see clearly, for the briefest of seconds, watched their ship, their home, light up with more brilliance than they'd ever seen and, with one final send-off, shatter like glass spraying out steel energy and memories to the dark void behind them.

Chapter 8

Family

Rawlands woke with a start, calm for only a second before flailing round in utter darkness, panicking amidst the waking fear and staggering right till a wall met him. Grabbing at nothing, he slid down smooth steel to the floor, reaching out and struggling like an animal wounded before finding the corner of his darkened cell. How long had he been out this time after his latest bout of interrogation?

He couldn't know it, but the two weeks he thought he'd spent there had been a mere four days. Days he'd spent wishing he knew what had happened to his crew, his family….

The door opened, splitting apart with its sharp clang of steel and hydraulics startling Rawlands before he was bathed with the dim amber light of the corridor outside.

"You will come with us." The guards motioned for him.

Rawlands rose to his feet slowly, walking out as the guards gestured him to the right, two following behind him with one leading him, some distance in front. The corridors reminded him of a station—dark, still as if underground, but not grey with neon blue… they were black, black everywhere, and even a black carpet met black-panelled walls which in turn met black ceiling. Along the floor where panel met carpet running the full length of each corridor, a thin strip of amber light on both sides gently lit the darkness, giving away the joins between panels. It was gothic, almost medieval, like a modern day fortress… only more sinister still.

After some time, they began to approach a door, Rawlands taking a deep breath and preparing for what lay inside.

The doors opening caught Rawlands off-guard; the scene, the room, was warmly lit, welcoming in soft reds coming from candles flickering calmly. Entering ahead of him, the guard motioned him to the left, Rawlands' eyes turning to face a large dining table where a Vrail sat on the opposite side from him.

"Do come in," the Vrail began warmly. "I trust you have been treated well. Please sit—you must be hungry."

Rawlands took a seat directly opposite the Vrail commander. It was surreal, to be three feet from the enemy in a warmly lit room, candles gently reflecting off silverware. The Vrail motioned to the guards and the domes of the silver platters were lifted away to reveal a feast. The warm scent of finely cooked meat wafted over Rawlands, and with his body not having eaten in almost fourteen hours, he salivated openly.

"Please!" The Vrail motioned a welcome, picking up his cutlery, and Rawlands remembered his training—to eat whenever possible, aware that to survive lengthy interrogation, the body must have fuel. Such lessons weren't needed to help him begin dining.

The Vrail looked pleased, and followed suit. "This must be quite overwhelming, Mr Rawlands," began the Vrail. "My name is Maral, and—"

"My crew?" Rawlands cut in, his mouth full.

"Let me assure you," Maral spoke softly, "your crew have been taken care of."

"My family?"

"Your family…" Maral paused, taking another

mouthful of food. "You will be with your family very soon," he assured Rawlands, meeting his anxious glance. "That is, of course, if you're prepared to cooperate, as there's been far too much bloodshed already, Captain, and there need be no more. You see, we are not the monsters you've been led to believe; simply speaking, we are at war as you are, and with the same strains and responsibilities placed upon us."

Maral paused, sipping wine as Rawlands ate quickly, wondering if it was a trick, thinking that shortly the food would be snatched away and telling himself to eat as much as possible before that happened. Maral noticed his eating, the speed, and he smiled as if understanding Rawlands' strategy. "Yes, it's quite a dish the chef provided; I've never eaten it myself, but the chef tried very hard to find something palatable. I'm afraid we've little experience with your cuisine."

"It's good," answered Rawlands quietly, sipping down wine.

"Yes, it was your crew who put us onto it," continued Maral, clearly pleased that their efforts at dinner were appreciated. Raising his hand, he motioned to the guards behind Rawlands as he added, "Please have some more. We have much to discuss."

Maral was completely disarming, so that Rawlands felt strangely at ease as the domed silver platters of extra portions were placed in front of them over their almost empty plates. From behind the guards who'd been serving the meal, another guard appeared and gained Maral's attention with his approach, the polite meal's mood suddenly broken as Maral shot an evil look at the intruder.

"Sir," the guard spoke with soft respect, "Chef

reports there will be a short delay in dessert."

Rawlands watched as his polite host's eyes blazed over his clenched jaw before he uttered, "Tell him... not to worry."

Rigid with tension, he reached for his wine, and sipping from it, he looked up from his glass again. "Captain, I can respect your rank, your loyalty, your will for your kind, but what price will you pay for this? Mr Rawlands, we are at war, and as such, we have the pressures of those demands to meet. Before your ship's untimely destruction, we managed to download some of its files as its shields failed; unfortunately, they seem to be protected by some form of carrier coding. We must have access to these files, Mr Rawlands. We must."

Rawlands felt his gut fall under Maral's stare, and he tried not to show his dismay, but knew it was futile.

Maral grimaced, looking to the right and taking a deep breath as he began again. "Captain, we must have access by any means, but I'd rather it did not come to that. You see, you are going to have to betray a side, Mr Rawlands; on one side is your people, and on the other your family. But it's not a question of betrayal for you, Captain, more a question of what you can live with. You see, whether we have the positions of your ships and defences or not makes very little difference, as we'll find them anyway. It's simply a matter of time. But it would be much easier with your files, for both our sides. Captain, I can guarantee you we are going to win, and the less lives lost, the better. We are merciful rulers, I assure you. Can you live with letting down a few anonymous faces who would have you sacrifice your family so they may selfishly protect themselves at your expense? Can you look at the photos or the graves of your family, knowing you could have prevented it, Mr Rawlands? You have a duty, yes, and you have honour to uphold, but surely, surely it is to your family that this duty comes first." Maral paused, staring at Rawlands, his look one of sorrow and of genuine regret practised many times before now on such beings as this guest crumbling before him. "Unfortunately, despite all the training, despite all the vestige of honour, it always comes down to this." He feigned a look away before coming back, and adding, "What are you prepared to live with?"

Rawlands tried to hold his calm at the question, even with terror engulfing him. He thought of his family, and he thought of everything else. "If we were cooperative, what, eh…." he stammered, trying to play for time as he gathered his thoughts.

"You would receive fair treatment and be assured a decent standard of living in the new order for this quadrant," Maral assured him.

"And my crew?"

Maral seemed to become impatient, but answered, "Well… you see, your crew were less than cooperative."

Rawlands, though stony-faced, felt his eyes being pushed back down, losing the fight against an all-powerful Maral, but just then the door opened and dessert was rolled in behind him. "What do you mean?" he asked quietly.

"They did not provide…" Maral began, and then he re-started, "Perhaps it is time for this entree." He motioned toward the platters of extra helpings on the table.

A shaken Rawlands thought about his next move, grateful for the time as a guard reached in front of him to move dishes around and place a new one upon the table.

He looked down after the guard's hand as it grasped a silver platter, and he saw his reflection look back. If he could only… and then his thoughts left him as the guard lifted the platter's cover. Rawlands watched his reflection lift away to reveal his first officer's face beneath it.

Frozen in shock, he stared and then felt his insides convulse, throwing up his meal over the table and trying to rise, but finding himself only forced back down to face the platter. Rawlands screamed in anguish, vomiting as his head was pushed toward the platter, toward Edwards, by Maral crashing round behind him.

"We must have access, Mr Rawlands!"

Rawlands felt Maral release him, finally, but was still screaming as he threw himself away from the table, vomiting everywhere as he collapsed convulsing on the floor.

"We will get what we need from your family," came Maral's voice behind him. "I can only hope they'll be more forthcoming…"

"N-n-n-no. N-no! It's 235787939834554239 Eral 5275 Beta 97."

Smiling gently, Maral turned away for the door.

"Hey! Hey! My family! You said—hey, stop!"

Pausing, Maral turned, raising his head arrogantly so that his eyes fell on a snivelling Rawlands. "I told you you'd be with them soon," he crowed, swivelling his eyes to the guard next to the dessert tray.

The platters were lifted as Maral turned away, the doors closing on a screaming creature as the guards moved in on him.

"Download the files immediately!" Maral ordered his viceral.outside the interrogation room "And inform personnel," he growled, "that we're going to need a new chef."

Chapter 9

Impression

The sand stung his face. Wincing, he closed his eyes as he walked from the APC he'd arrived in. *What a place*, he thought. Five years on, the war was still hurting, and here came another. He laughed at himself as he walked toward the base commander. He had no right to complain—it could have been worse, a lot worse. They'd let him walk, and sure, they'd taken his ship, his career, but they'd let him serve out his twenty... to Ritter's dismay. Laughing again, he remembered Ritter's face when no objection had been made to Marine General Briar's request to have him transferred to a second-rate Marine platoon on Fearon Ridge, solving the problem for the other admirals who'd been hesitant over his continued presence in the navy. He'd risen in his time; in five years, he'd made captain... again. After numerous clashes, with reports coming back of his influence, he'd even been transferred to a decent division—commanding Unit 57. They weren't perfect, far from it, but that suited him down to the ground; tired of bureaucratic crap and superiors, he felt at home, almost comfortable, though that wasn't the case for some around him. There wasn't the most appreciation for his presence or fast progress, as his story was out, and it wasn't just Yeris—there were those who took objection to his quick rise through the ranks of the Marine core. They didn't like a bird captain in their ranks and they didn't like him having the ear of high-up navy officials like General Briar, either. Yeah, he was almost comfortable, thought Fuller.

Right now, though, comfort was the last thing anyone on this dust-laden rock felt. Gorsearan 4 was a waste ball at the outer edge of Maires Drift, but within striking distance of three Alliance outposts; passing ships had reported anomalous readings when passing near the planet, suggesting a possible Hearack base. A staging point to build up troops and supply ships with equipment and manpower—that's how they worked these days. They never attacked in ones or twos anymore; it was always in overwhelming waves released after their build-up. This time, though, they'd been spotted, their power readings caught on sensors, and they were never going to leave this place. Fuller relished that development, at least.

"Captain Fuller," Commander Holsen greeted him, his English accent proper and making itself stand out among them as Fuller arrived. "I was just telling Major Norren how we need another scout team."

"Sir," acknowledged Fuller.

"Yes, it seems we've left a gap, a remote possibility… really, it's hardly worth bothering about, but we have to be sure. There's a system of small passes, deep gouges to be precise, in the mountainous regions in Sector 4-19. Understandable why command overlooked it; it's virtually impassable with anything other than a rel track, but we… well, I'd like to be sure."

"Yes, sir," Fuller acknowledged again, Holsen's thoroughness impressing him. He'd heard stories about him. He wasn't popular among the men, maybe because he was of British decent among a mostly decent American unit, or maybe because he was such a stickler for regulation—who knew?—but Fuller liked him. He was an outsider like him, which might explain it. Just then, a column of armoured personnel carriers caught Fuller's attention as Holsen continued on discussing the situation with Norren; half-listening, Fuller watched the carriers come down from the hills above the perimeter fence in the distance. Fuller found it hard to concentrate on Holsen as the carriers headed along the road behind him and outside the base. Disappearing below the fence, they followed the road round its sharp left turn before appearing shortly thereafter at the checkpoint entrance.

"I was going to siphon off some of the men from one of our sixteen units already searching for them, but Major Norren tells me your platoon that's scheduled to arrive shortly was a dedicated recon unit on Fearon Ridge," Holsen added.

"Yes, sir, they were," Fuller replied as carriers rumbled past on the makeshift dirt road on their left, heading on from the checkpoint and sending fumes out to interrupt the smell of steak wafting over from the mess tent further over on the other side.

"Frightful place. Don't know how you stood it."

That was an understatement, thought Fuller, remembering the bitter conditions they'd faced as he viewed the mess tent diners sitting casually outside in the sunlight.

"It's not where I'd vacation, sir," Fuller agreed.

"Indeed," Holsen commented.

More vehicles entered the base, rumbling on past.

"Captain Fuller, we have never met, and I have no previous experience of your unit," Holsen began. "Therefore, I hope you don't take these remarks as derogatory, but I do so hope you have the very best men in this man's army, for it is imperative that we find the

Hearack before they find us. Long-range satellite reconnaissance showed an impressive concentration of troops and materials here; however, on arrival, we've found nothing. It's bad enough they can defract, but to manage to hide such a mountain of equipment is, frankly, unnerving," Holsen said, the defracting he spoke of being the Hearacks' ability to bend light around their figures using some sort of chrysalic device not yet understood by the Alliance—which, in conjunction with their battle suit computers, made them invisible when still and a mere blur when moving. "We can't have them appearing without warning, Captain Fuller I... I hesitate to say this, but we're simply not ready; why the IAF dropped us here in such a fashion and so sparingly is quite beyond me."

"You won't find better men anywhere, sir," Fuller assured him.

"The IAF has much ground to cover, sir, so perhaps there simply wasn't time to plug all the holes as efficiently as they'd like," came what appeared to be a more than defensive Norren behind him.

"Yes, well, it only takes one hole to sink a ship, Major," returned Holsen sharply.

Just then, the deep rumble of another armoured personnel carrier caught Fuller's attention, the sound turning him to see the familiar sight of his unit's war-scarred transport cresting the brow of the hill amidst the dropping sun. With Holsen and Norren engaged in a dispute over the IAF's efficiency, he distanced himself from them and watched his unit come down the hill.

Inside the carrier a normal aggitation played out...

"Oh, come on!" Fulkes protested.

"You're driving," Carson replied.

In the cramped APC, this latest feud was all Brice needed; finishing paperwork, he tried to ignore it.

"It's been four hours and you ain't done nothin' but sit on your ass; I've been driving this crate from the start and you're the one who gets coffee! Come on!" Fulkes argued.

"Just keep your eyes on the road, little man; that's where they need to be," Carson answered, to the sniggering approval of the unit.

"Now, that last one had nothin' to do with me—that guy knew damn well I was comin'!" Fulkes defended himself. "Now, come on, man, give me some coffee."

"Look, you is a dangerous—"

"Just give the man some coffee!" Brice snapped, unable to stand the bickering.

Carson looked back behind him to face his huge, nerve-wracked black sergeant's stare, the look all that was needed for him to soon find himself reluctantly pouring a cup. A final look back at a glaring Brice, and he reached over. "Here you go, little man, I hope—"

A rock slammed under the right tire, sending a jolt through the carrier so that coffee spilled over Fulkes' extended hand.

"Aaaaaaaaaaaaaaaaaaarrrrrr... shit!" Fulkes screamed, grabbing his scalded hand with his other.

Fuller watched them dip below the fence and out of sight; shifting his gaze to the right, he waited for them to appear at the checkpoint. It was quiet, the sun long since having gone dipping behind the hills, leaving a golden glow and his envy at the view the guards had from the entrance.

The fence exploded to the left of the checkpoint then, wood flying everywhere as a sixteen-ton carrier came barrelling through into the compound, the men having their dinner looking up to see an armoured monster tearing towards them. Tables flew amid panicked yells as men ran in all directions, Fuller only able to watch.

"SSSShit!!!" Fulkes screamed with the mess tent approaching, both his feet slamming on the brakes.

Outside, a huge bang signalled the carrier's emergency brakes slamming on the wheels that locked up as it grinded toward the mess tent, gauging a channel in the ground so that dust went flying everywhere. Cutlery crashed with drinks spilling everywhere as it smashed its way through the tables, stopping inches from the tent and the staff inside. Shouts began to fill the air with diners' shock giving way to anger as they moved in on the carrier, Holsen standing with his mouth open as he watched the vehicles side door wind up, shouts dimming as it went.

"What the fuck did you do now?" Carson's voice carried over to Fuller as he emerged out of the carrier, Fulkes right behind him.

"I didn't do shit! Your dumb ass burned me with the coffee!" Fulkes answered.

"My dumb ass, huh? You crash twice in two hours and you're calling my ass dumb," Carson hit back as Brice, Rians, and Copeland emerged behind them.

Amidst the arguing, the angry mob approached unnoticed with an overweight sergeant at its helm.

"Who was driving?" screamed the huge black

sergeant over the shouting crowd.

"I was!" Fulkes shouted back, paying nearly no interest while still raging with Carson.

The sergeant moved in on Fulkes, all of six-foot-something and not a stone under twenty-five as he kept looking down on his ten-stone opponent.

"You spilled my fuckin dinner!"

"Yeah, well, looking at you, I did you a favour!"

The sergeant screamed aloud as he grabbed Fulkes by the shirt.

But a big right hand came in from Brice and he was on his ass. Then, fists waved and kicks flew with the crowd surging in over the shouting and screaming.

Across the way, Fuller—with Holsen and Norren behind him—closed his eyes, took a deep breath, and lowered his head into his hand.

Chapter 10

Recon

"Fulkes. Fulkes!" Brice shouted, but no answer came. "Mother fu... fuck is he at?" Brice muttered to himself while mapping coordinates on his chart.

"Aaaaaahhhhhhhhh!"

"You mother fu—come 'ere!" Brice demanded, struggling to reach a laughing Fulkes from the harness of the rel track a light weight tubular roll cage with engine and wheels used for scouting. "Stop fuckin' around and get in this piece of shit—we got a fuck load more to cover and we don't need none of your foolin', you got that?"

"Aw, come on, Sarge, jus a lil humour," defended a bored Fulkes as he climbed into the driver's section in front of Brice.

"A little humour, my ass; we got that prick Etrick ridin' the cap's ass, and if we screw up, he'll repor—Ugghhh!" Brice almost choked as the rel track burst forward. Winded, Brice barely recovered enough to grab Fulkes' collar. "What the fuck are you doing?"

"Hearack!!!!!"

Brice turned to see a fortress of steel charging toward them. "Aaaaaaaaaiiiiiiiiiieee!!!!!!" His screams left meeting the steel wall roaring up to meet him slowing within inches of the rel track bumper as Fulkes desperately pulled away. "Get the fuck out of here! Go—get on! Go, go!" he screamed, striking Fulkes' helmet in front.

"Call it in!" Fulkes screamed back.

"Two-eight-one from seventeen, we got—" his transmission was cut off in a scream, Fulkes tearing up an incline to the left of the chasm as the Hearack broke by to their right, leaving Fulkes pushing the vehicle to the absolute limit.

Tires roared as the rel track cleared the top of the ridge, crashing down on the other side and tearing down the hill as Brice screamed into his mic. "Two-eight-one Hearack scout patrol in sector 14… Aaaaahhhhh"

The slope gone, an iron monster appeared to their right, Brice watching as it swung in to narrowly miss them with its left wing, the right even closer as it crashed into the wall of rock beside them.

The rel track sprinted in front as, behind them, one side of the chasm was torn open by a steel rage crashing headlong through the rock behind them. "Two-eight-one from seventeen!" Brice signalled as they cleared the chasm, sandwiched between wider cliffs as the sound of an ear-piercing charge increased behind them. "Hearack scout party on—" Brice was silenced as a deafening crack launched over them, his head crashing off the side of the rel track with Fulkes veering right through a cloud of dirt, a crater left by a plasma charge passing on their left. A shriek drew eyes behind them to an unleashing plasma array, Brice being partially blinded in the flash as his head smashed off the other side of the rel track, Fulkes tearing to the left through another cloud with the next attack almost reaching them.

Realising they were under their guns, Brice rattled Fulkes' head again. "Slow down, for Christ's sake, slow down!!!"

Revs dropping, Fulkes tried to hold the line with Brice trying the mic as another deafening crack missed them by inches. Disappearing into a cloud of dirt, Brice felt the rel track collapse into a crater, its suspension crashing as they tore up the other side, coming over another crack, then another, a tear to the right, to the left, and to the….

Lost in the impact, wheels screamed as they went over, arms and necks flailing helplessly against seat and panel with each flip jarring them till finally they broke through the dust, skidding to a halt on their side. A choking Brice gathered his senses, coming to with blurred vision while hanging helplessly in his harness amid the steel frame, his thoughts slow and battered, only vaguely aware of what was happening as he tried in vain to reach forward to Fulkes. A sudden roar forced him to look up, though, from where he was cradled in his harness. The noise came from inside a dust cloud fifty yards away. His thoughts were slow; they had come from there, and there was a… suddenly, a swirling in the centre of the cloud brought deafening noise, Brice's mind clearing to the realisation that the the cloud was tearing open to show a Hearack T49 bursting through and coming up on the helpless men. Brice opened his mouth to shout, but was denied the chance as weapons fire screamed overhead, the T49's front exploding in a mass of flame and weapons fire continuing as it erupted, throwing itself in all directions. Brice got his chance to scream then as a huge, burning section of armour flew forward, momentarily singing his hair as it crashed behind them, throwing them again like a toy as a blaze of armoured plating and fire took their place. Flipping end over end, a fully wakened Brice felt each bone crushing smash against the tubular cage he was trapped in, landing amid the backdrop of carnage and coming to rest right side up.

Momentarily dazed, Brice's nerves got the better of him with feeling trapped in the harness, and he began to panic, straining violently and screaming like a mad man as a groaning driver came to with the inferno raging behind him. A groggy Fulkes, unaware of what had happened, could barely make out figures running toward them through a haze of heat and smoke; behind them, three huge and standing shapes were obscured in the distance.

"Get me out of this fucking thing! Get me out of this fucking…. Heeeelllllllp!" screamed a hysterical Brice.

Head already pounding, Fulkes was treated to more unwelcome knocks with his head banging off the back of his seat as Brice jarred the rel track back and forth in a desperate bid to escape.

"Get me out of this fuckin' thing! Get me outa this fuckin' thing!"

continued a nerve-shot Brice.

"Hang on, buddy, we got ya—" Cut short, their rescuers were treated to more tirades.

"Get me out of this fuckin' thing!" Brice roared.

Head pounding, Fulkes winced in pain as he felt the thuds and bangs of the kicking and screaming Brice being wrestled from the seat behind what was left of the rel track, his tirades continuing uncontrollably.

"Get the fuck off me!" screamed Brice, wrestling free from his rescuers and shoving one sprawling to the ground, gesturing to the other two as he made off screaming before whirling round amidst confused looks, heading straight for Fulkes. "Are you alright? Hey! Are you alright? Answer me, you fuck!" Brice screamed, grabbing Fulkes by the jacket and shaking him.

"Ughhh, yeah," Fulkes spluttered in response amid the shaking as the three soldiers tried to pull the hysterical form away from him.

"Get the fuck—I told you, get the fuck off me!" Brice roared again, throwing one soldier aside and barging through the other two. "I've had it! I've had it with this fucking place! It's a fucking.... It's a..... Aaaaaaarrrrrgghh!"

Coughing and spluttering, Fulkes strained, adding to his struggle for air and unable to help laughing at the near-postal Brice screaming on amid the confusion of the soldiers.

Three kilometres away, an ecstatic Holsen received the news and responded, "Indeed, you're sure? Excellent."

Outside the base command tent, a familiar scene was unfolding as Captain Fuller and Captain Etrick exchanged their usual pleasantries.

"They sent your squad, driving?" Etrick asked, frowning condescendingly.

"Yes, they sent my squad," Fuller answered, an equally artificial expression on his face.

"I'm sure they'll do very well," Etrick continued. "Their record speaks for itself."

Sniggers flowed freely as Etrick's remarks registered with his unit behind him, drawing Fuller's irritated expression, but his response was cut short.

"Captain Fuller!" General Holsen's wall of strictness showed cracks as he approached from the command tent, beaming. "Captain, we've received news from Sector D14; lead elements of a Hearack scout party have been found, and the net's closing. Now we know where to look, it shouldn't be too long."

"My men, how—" a concerned Fuller was cut off.

"Your men," Holsen echoed, beaming. "They've been through a bit of a scrape, but Captain Vogts reports they're a pair of the toughest mother fu… well, you get the idea' they were saved by three of Vogts's compliment of 8 trans. It seems they got there just in time, but I understand it was you who insisted they be transferred with your division from the ridge."

"Yes, against some resistance from our divisional commander at the time," Fuller replied, remembering how, during the engagements at Fearon Ridge, he'd been transferred to command his present unit, which was one of many under Etrick's command. Thereafter, time and again, he'd fought with Etrick over unsound decisions and unnecessary risks; it had been two months of misery culminating in a situation Fuller couldn't believe.

Fighting from moon to moon along the ridge, fleet command had transported them to each one until Hearack attack fighters had begun showing up in ever increasing numbers. The IAF had immediately transferred in several starships to bolster the fleet and put all Marines it included under one Captain George E Ritter. It wouldn't have been so bad—Fuller's squad had been one of hundreds, virtually invisible among the units—but of course, Ritter had had to liase regularly with the four unit commanders, one of them being Etrick. It hadn't taken long for them to discover their mutual grievances with Fuller, and things had then just gone from bad to worse as each one of his decisions had been blocked or questioned in some manner. Finally, on leaving the ridge some months later for Gorsearan 4, Fuller had requested Captain Vogts and his compliment of eleven 8 trans be transferred in order to aid the search for the elusive Hearack, reports of the terrain and his own experience convincing him of the value of the aging vehicles. The huge, wheeled trans assault vehicles were faster than the new but much heavier K27 Lores Tanks, which with their tracks were slower, but with Fuller having barely escaped death time and time again in the 8 trans, he knew speed was everything. Once again, Fuller had been sidelined on that request, but this time, feeling his squad was being endangered by Ritter and Etrick's petty feud with him, he'd snapped. He'd never done it before or since, but one message to General Briar, and Vogts and the 8 trans had been sent away the same day. Ritter and Etrick's rage at being pushed aside was another story—it didn't go anywhere, staying with them instead, and it appeared every time they dealt with Fuller.

"Ah yes, Captain Ritter, marvelous fellow; shame he's in fleet command!" Holsen quipped sarcastically.

"The K27s weren't far behind," Etrick said in defence, annoyed with the swipe at Ritter.

"Yes, but that was hardly of any use, was it?" responded Holsen curtly. "In any case, with the situation appearing to be in hand, I'm transferring your unit to Sector 3F.

"3F?" Etrick echoed despairingly.

"Yes, I understand elements of your unit were mired down in clashes before leaving their last posting, and with this latest performance, I think a less demanding environment is only right for a while," continued Holsen as Etrick looked accusingly at Fuller, realising his units latest efforts were being rewarded with this granting of respite for them all which would keep the rest of the units under his command, including his own, out of the action in a useless boring sector used to rest and rearm.To

Etrik's dismay he listened to Holsen confirm his fears. "3F is at the western-most point of the perimeter surrounded by ridges, far from 14D; should be just what the doctor ordered—General Norren has your orders." Turning back toward the command tent, and to Etrick's annoyance, Holsen passed Fuller and adopted a quietly respectful tone, voicing a simple, "Captain."

Chapter 11

The Battle

Around the camp, they had barely started to deploy equipment, but people were bustling back and forth by the command tent as, inside, Marine Captain Etrick monitored each section's progress.

The radio crackled to life: "Fuller to Etrick, come in."

"Captain Etrick," the radio operator answered abruptly, "is very busy."

"Well, tell him," the voice came back, "to get on the horn or the only thing he'll be busy doing is picking up the pieces when his little deck of cards collapses around his ears."

The staff in the tent looked up with irritation at Fuller's voice, but among them was one person whose look was far more than irritated—it was a look of loathing, and it was carried right across the tent by Etrick as he reached down and grabbed the microphone. "What do you want now?" Etrick demanded barely disguising his sarcasm.

"What I want is what was supposed to be here two hours ago," Fuller responded, with his voice rising all the higher, the more he spoke. "We're wide open up here."

Etrick looked round behind him through the tent doorway and on up the seventy-foot ridge in the distance; it was two hundred yards away, and Fuller was just over top of it on the other side, but that wasn't far enough.

"Wide open," Etrick repeated. "Well, let's see here," he began, looking down at a report. "Four emplacements dug in, one battery of IN28s with sensors uplinked and established, three A317s complete with ammo trains and—"

"And no fucking bodies!" Fuller broke in. "We've got twenty-three people up here, including me."

"Well, I'm sure if you're having problems, Captain, one of the other twenty-two will be able to show you what to do," Etrick sneered.

"And when we're overrun because you've got three units down there holding hands, what then?"

"Look, I don't have time to babysit—"

"Babysit! *Babysit!*" Fuller lost it, ranting, "We're up here with the only triple-A you've got and you're letting our asses hang in the breeze! What, are you fucking blind or…."

Sitting in the ammo pit of the A317 with Walsch, Rians listened to the argument in the tent on his left and smiled as he heard Fuller exchange expletives with Etrick far below him. Picking up his binoculars, he listened to Walsch liase through the 317 handset with Hal, who was sitting in the 317 above them, and through the com link to Merrin in the centre and then Henric further down as he tied them into the radar guidance system that was safely buried halfway behind them. Each 317 crew consisted of the gunner inside it, the control officer, the loading supervisor, and two loaders—all of them reporting progress back to Walsch as their ammo trains could be heard grinding into position. Now fully loaded, the 317s were impressive, with their great steel spires pointing skyward, huge two hundred and six millimetre barrels coupled with matter and anti-matter mortars scanning the air. Attached to them from below, in each ammo pit, three escalating train-ways stood poised to deliver their deadly cargo. On the left, forty-eight-litre nitroalergian canisters awaited their call, and in the centre train, MA type-seven mortars sat one after another, exposed, while to their right 2871 standard explosive-tipped rounds sat in load boxes. But the sky was clear, with nothing, not even birds, to be seen… and that was understandable.

Amidst the chatter, Rians looked up over the ridge of his ammo pit, lifting his binoculars as he scanned across the sparse clumps of high grass on the bowl-like hill. He looked out to the forward ridge two hundred yards in front of them, snaking its way diagonally right down the gentle slope of the hillside. First, almost directly in front of them, he saw the backs of Aitkins and Mitch, and fifty yards down to their right were Stratten and Calaway; another fifty yards down, Shouler and Danick could be seen, and another fifty yards on but a little closer in were Peters and Bren… all of them scanning out in front of them from behind their sandbag emplacements like Rians. The forward emplacements had a better view over the ridge were he couldn't see each looking for the slightest shimmer indicating a moving Hearack defracted in their suits. Rians winced as the sun dropping down behind him to his right caught his eye, still listening to the chatter as a gentle breeze began blowing up the hill. Leaving Peters and Bren, slowly, he scanned back up along the ridge, seeing its thin clumps of tall grass rippling in the wind behind Danick as he moved up. Continuing on, he suddenly realised he'd missed Shouler, but upon moving back down the hill, he felt still more confusion. Danick was gone, too. He tensed as the hairs on the back of his neck raised—where were they?

Nervously, he scanned their position, trying to figure out why they'd ducked out of sight with his mind quickening as he debated whether or not to raise the alarm. Tensing his grip on the binoculars, Rians desperately scanned the nearby terrain, zooming in on the emplacement with the grass gently rippling in front, waves of wind passing through as he... something caught his eye—a break in the waves, again, and ten feet closer! "Hearack!!!" he screamed.

Rifle fire exploding above his voice, Rians laced the grass with fire in an instant, wishing he hadn't Hearack exploding forward from the grass, their defraction dropping as they charged behind the lines in seconds. Caught in a crossfire, the emplacements began to take casualties almost immediately despite the fire from the ammo pits behind them. Below the ridge, base camp was suddenly engaged in a desperate battle for survival as Hearack swarmed out of the western hills. The ground shook on the ridge from the 317's thumping away coordinates for mortar fire, commanders streaming instructions into gunners' headsets and trying to hold the Hearack off the base far below.

"They're through our lines! We need reinforcements now!" screamed Fuller over the battle.

"We're fighting off a whole fucking regiment down here!" Etrick screamed back from the command tent.

"So are we, and we need help now!"

"You'll have to handle it. We—" Etrick was silenced by a deathly howl coming from Hearack Shar fighters tearing out from the western hills overhead. Bodies flew from positions in the base camp as the fighters opened up, and on the ridge, the Isan missile system kept tracking from the uplink; it whined round automatically. An ear-piecing rush sounded out and the ammo pits were swamped in dust, an Isan shooting up over the ridge. Troops at the eastern end of the base fired hopelessly as the two Shar fighters came tearing toward them when suddenly a stream of smoke from the right brought an Isan slamming into its target. Explosions sounded overhead, offering a moment of joy for the troops that was ripped away by the second fighter bursting through falling wreckage and dropping incendiaries. Howls ringing out over the eastern hills, the base exploded in a bath of flames. Perimeter gone, more defractions failed with the Hearack battle suits unable to keep up the with the changes as they charged in from the eastern hills, tearing through the destroyed flank as shaken commanders desperately called for mortar fire to halt the wave.

Up on the ridge, huge thumps echoed over the weapons fire as the 317 gunners laid down mortars for the frantic commanders below. Stratten was down, and Calaway was next; seconds later, it was Mitch, emplacements being overrun with tracers flying from the ammo pits. More casualties came fast—the control officer in the central pit, a loader in the lower—and while returning fire, the control officer in the lower pit turned to his supervisor to relay a message from Walsh, halfway through a blue flash, and a headless supervisor fell away.

His position untenable, Fuller flung himself headlong into the top pit as his command tent was raked with fire. Still relaying messages back and forth with those below, he was interrupted by a familiar thump from behind… mortars!

"Incoming!" Rians screamed out, ducking with the others.

Explosions sent dirt flying from craters behind the pits, more explosions following them till suddenly, with a crack of steel, fire swamped the hillside and rushed over pits even as the men huddled inside. Subsiding fire revealed an awful sight—the Isan missile system lay wrecked, overturned beside some twisted wreckage... the uplink. Communication gone, the 317's mortars could no longer be directed, but there was little time to dwell on that with Hearack storming through emplacements in front. Tracers erupted again from the pits while enemy mortars continued to fall around the soldiers. Ripping off his headset, Fuller grabbed the com piece from the back of the 317 in front of him, communication still being active. Fuller keyed it, screaming over the noise: "Get the mortars behind the emplacements—get the mortars!"

Hydraulic whines joined the crescendo of noise as the huge 317s turned to redirect their barrels on the Hearack mortar teams behind the emplacements. Inside the 317s, the gunners right feet fell down on their pedals, swinging their barrels right and adjusting elevation by pushing and pulling on their twin-handed firing arms before pulling back on the double-triggers under their indexes. Firing desperately, the men in the ammo pits momentarily lost aim with each firing of the 317s, their huge recoils shaking the ground. Again and again, mortars fell beyond the emplacements, forcing Aitkins to take cover with each blast. With no way, to aim the gunners dropped fire everywhere, hoping for a strike. Over the firefight, the mortars kept returning over and over again, being exchanged constantly until suddenly there was an explosion in front of the emplacements. The Hearack team was finally hit, but not before one final return. Whistling overhead, it crashed behind the central ammo pit and the crew was showered with shrapnel as they were hurled to the ground. Only two of the three would rise, but to a horrifying scene; the ammo train was hit.

Fuller grabbed his headset, hoping they would find some way to uplink from below, but everyone below was frantic; there wasn't time.

Below, in the command tent, orders were flying back and forth when suddenly the tent was shredded through, leaving the commanders visible to the western perimeter, still ordering tracers that tore between them—two falling where they'd stood, the others drenched with blood as they went. Hemmed in by the ridge two hundred yards south and the stores fifty yards north, commanders squatted down and continued barking orders as tracers flew from east and west. Over it all, a howl cavitated through the air, the remaining Shar screaming in from the east with dirt flying as it opened up on marines and dead alike, before howling off west from the attack Covered in blood, Etrick desperately tried to raise Fuller.

"We need mortars! Alpha seven, Alpha three!"

Suddenly, the barracks and stores exploded, silencing Etrick as the returning Shar tore off to the east.

"Where's my goddamned air cover?" Etrick screamed.

Above on the ridge, a cut-off Fuller looked out across the hillside. They kept coming… they just kept coming. How long could he hold them? he wondered. For every ten they dropped, another fifteen would appear. Looking on amidst the weapons fire, he watched the distance as the last two emplacements under his command fought for their lives—Aitkins alone and exhausted in the top emplacement, Peters and Bren in the lower one and further back, fighting a losing battle against a sea of Hearack. How could he hold them? Fuller wondered. How? But the answer was simple. He couldn't—not unless... not unless they could drop the 317s. Sure, they were a firebase to support the troops below, but with communication gone, they were just hanging there.

The battle raged on as Fuller thought... if communication was established with those below, they would need... but then, if it wasn't, his men would die as he waited, and even if it was, these men were depending on him. If it was found out that he had dropped the barrels in the heat of a battle.... Just then, Fuller watched Aitkins' chest explode, blood burning black from the wound as he went screaming backward.

He'd seen enough.

Grabbing the 317 handset, Fuller screamed into the com piece, "Drop the fucking barrels—waist the motherfuckers!"

No movement; the three gunners sat poised in their seats, though they had been ordered to...

"Now!!!!!"

Ears almost burst by Fuller's cry, they slammed their sticks forward and flicked up the weapons switches above their right thumbs. Below them, in the top ammo pit, Fuller heard the whining hydraulics confirming his order as, in front of him on the rear left of the 317, the mortar arm light switched from red to green and the 2871 went from green to red with an answering jolt from the ammo train. Tracers flew forward from men in pits, ion charges returning from the Hearack who were throwing themselves forward against the falling barrels of the

317s. Peters and Bren ducked for cover as Hearack surged around their raised emplacement, wide-eyed pit crews watching a wall of killers surge toward them….

They were twenty feet from reaching their targets, and the pit crews' fire couldn't hold them when suddenly high-pitched whining came from the 317 barrels bursting into spin, and with a rush of coolant coming from exhausts…

Fuller's com link crackled: "Ready!"

"Fire!"

Eight-foot flames shot from barrels as an army of red-eyed monsters burst like balloons, explosive rounds tearing through their grey ranks so that arms, legs, and heads went flying back only to be shredded again as they went, their cries unheard above the deafening thunder of the barrels.

Still adding what fire they could, pit crews were deafened as the top pit—with Fuller, Rians, and Walsh—disappeared under a steel coffin clanging by overhead so that they had to duck, the jolting drive train signalling 2871 arming lights from green to red as another box loaded up, thunder resuming. Hardly up, they were ducking again with another clang sending a spent nitroalergian canister out to the left from the 317 above, so that it fell into the pit below. Barrels thundered as the gunners inside watched lines of rounds deplete from right to left in the bottom right of their visors, firepower unloading on the enemy. One line dropped to the next five lines below, another level taking over as four levels signalled ejection on a clang of empty shell casings. A jolt of rearming had red meeting green with the round count illuminating again and dropping as nitroalergian percentages fluttered across to the right, desperately trying to cool the barrels.

Bodies flew, torn apart over a sea of blood with thunder tearing past Peters and Bren, who huddled in their emplacement with rounds ripping by overhead. Desperately, the centre gunner tried to hold back the tide, watching wide-eyed as endless troops poured forward. Feet manoeuvring on pedals, left to right. he watched the sickening sight of bodies being shredded to the clang of empty round casings, jolts of reloading giving way to more blood up in front.

In the central pit, canister after canister of empty 2871 rounds crashed out over the drive train time and again until suddenly the alarms screamed out with alerts flashing: *OVERHEAT! OVERHEAT!* Unaware of the damage behind him and screaming into his mic, the central gunner watched through the green tint of his visor as a sea of Hearack surged in toward him, bars rising from the left lower side and going from grcen to amber as alarms raged in his helmet. *"Get some fucking nitro up here!"*

Below, in the pit, the two remaining men struggled—trying to wrestle a canister of nitroalrgian from the shattered aft train. Collapsing to the ground, one almost fell under its massive bulk as they were left with seven metres to drag it to the barely functioning forward train. Inside, in front of a nerve-shot gunner, alarms screamed over the thundering barrel.

"Where's my fucking coolant?"

Collapsing, feet slipping in the loose clay, they desperately tried to haul the cylinder to the train with thunder continuing overhead, the gunner watching bars rise from yellow to red and flash in the visor as bodies rushed forward, rounds streaming as alarms grew louder.

"Come on, come on!" came the gunner's cries. "Get it up here!"

He couldn't stop, even with the bars rising; he just couldn't stop—they kept coming, from everywhere, they just kept coming. Over the orange flame from the barrel, he watched the red eyes come in row after row, feeling every round and every shake as he…

It was instant. The orange flame rushed back as the barrel gave way. Aflame for an instant, the gunner screamed before being carried up in the wreckage of the 317 exploding skywards, taking along the Hearack in front and the pit crew behind it.

The blast wave forced each remaining gunner against the side of his seat as their pit crews were hurled to the ground, saved only by the cushions of swirling dust above them, trapped under the raging carpet of fire. Exchanges had stopped on both sides, all concussed from the blast with the men struggling in ammo pits battered down, blanketed by dust and coughing on the silent battlefield, fighting for air. The gentle sound of light weapons fire filtering through from Etrick's struggle far on the other side made no sense. No sense, that was, until, with a huge whine and a deafening bang, the ground shook violently as the 317 above Fuller opened up.

More shaking came then, but of a different type as a voice burst into his ear even as hands began pulling him to his feet. *"Come On!"* It was Rians.

Looking over the pit ridge to the right of their 317, Fuller watched as the massive machines mercilessly cut down the remaining waves of Hearack, watching them fall wounded and screaming in pain… almost feeling sorry for them for a moment.

Far below, under Etrick's orders, men clambered up a hill on the western side, dragging surface to air munitions in a desperate attempt to deal with the remaining Shar. Nearing the top, a soul-wrenching howl came from behind, and for a split second, faces turned to see steel talons descending as a burst of weapons fire buried them into the hill.

"Fuller! What the fuck's going on up there?" Etrick screamed, enraged over seeing his men fall and ready to launch into another tirade when a sudden sound caught his attention, making him key off the handset and look out over the western hills. The mechanical howl began to echo over the valley then, seemingly indiscriminate, but Etrick—like anyone who'd been seasoned on a battlefield—knew when something was coming for him. Bloodied and seething, he glared at the hills raging under the sound, and then it came... clearing the hills in seconds, it burst out of the dropping sun, coming clear at the command tent, Etrick only able to throw his rage. On the hills behind him, amid fluid filling lungs, a bloody arm reached through the grass and fell on a keypad with a rush of air sending a white-trailing reply to the victim's attacker. The dark howl coming at Etrick was suddenly fought for dominance by a streaking pursuer catching up and slamming into the Shar from the rear. Weapons fire flew harmlessly skyward as it wrenched upward, breaking apart from the impact as troops cheered from below before running for cover as the Shar came flailing down in a mass of fire. Everything they had didn't cut it, though, with a final few falling victim and being buried under their winged foe, tons of armour exploding on impact as, far behind it on a lonely hill, a bloodied arm fell loosely to the ground.

The last ranks tore sickeningly open, pained faces spinning backward, the bloody masses unrecognisable as they landed. 317s kept firing, barrels spinning as spikes of earth shot tens of feet into the air with rounds raking the surface from gunners who were unable to stop their nerves taking over. The sounds kept coming—kept coming in their ears and growing louder, more audible, as their senses came round.

"Ease ire!"

"Cease ire!"

"Cease Fire!" Fuller's voice finally got through, the barrels firing for a few seconds more before giving way to the whining turbines as they lost their power amidst barrels winding slowly down.

It was quiet, smoke from mortars and smouldering remains drifting gently across the hillside and passing between the two remaining 317s, their gentle hum overlaying the graveyard they'd created with nitroalrgian filtering up from their coolant holes. A ghostly sight lay in front of them, eerily quiet as Fuller peered over the ammo pit with the others, suspicious and waiting for the next wave, but nothing came. For Fuller, suspicion quickly gave way to concern as he scanned the top emplacement. Aitkins hadn't made it. Stomach dropping, Fuller sighed, cringing—he'd failed them. He hadn't dropped the barrels in time, and they'd all… suddenly, faint cries began to come over the smouldering hillside, and still clutching weapons, soldiers strained over the ammo pits. Wind whisked up smoke in places here and there, dull figures appearing and disappearing in the distance; finally, there was a clearing, and Peters and Bren were in it. Lying at the bottom of their emplacement, struggling and screaming, but they were alive, thought Fuller as he experienced a strange joy at their cries.

Bren screamed unintelligibly, covered in blood as Peters desperately tried to pull him backward; visible were two bones of a waving stump that had once been an arm, sending him further into shock.

"Hang on, I'm gonna get you..."

"Help me, motherfucker, oh God, help me!"

"We'll fix you real good, we just gotta—" Peters was silenced as a roar deafened the pair.

Looking up, they saw rotating steel appear overhead and Peters joined his voice with Bren's screams under the collapsing tracks the Hearack lights on the vehicle the last thing they saw. The screams were silenced in an instant, the Hearack 86 assault tank smashing down so that their blood was hidden in the swirl of dirt as it roared out of the ditch, eyes fixed on the lower 317. The gunner in the lower only saw a flash as he was rammed back against his seat, pinned in by the shock wave as the shot missed by inches.

"Get it!" was all Fuller could say.

Turbines burst into life as the top 317 swung down, its shot coming in only just behind the lowers with the 86 exploding, becoming hidden in a mass of flame, and then another shot from the upper, the lower, the upper, all only adding to the fireball blanketing the creature.

The gunners sweated in their seats, the lower watching... hoping, but....

Bursting through the firestorm enraged, it came on as, inside, orders were barked over the Hearack, the commander calling to his gunner and driver below him as he watched through his headset, glaring as his blue target visor setting fluctuated on the 317, the guns' red targeting setting coming in to match and overlapping his scream "HASHAR!"

Crashing into the driver, the shell broke through the 317, taking most of it back over the ammo pit and leaving the wreckage to crash down on the pit crew below. Above, the last 317 fired again and again, the shots having no effect as the 86 growled forward, climbing with its right barrel turning to meet it. In the pit, the crew watched shot after shot explode harmlessly on its hull as the gunner frantically struck. Barrel almost on him, his nerves betrayed his aim as he shot under its belly, shattering the ground. The 86's tracks whined feverishly, losing their grip as the earth fell away—rolling it back over with the crew still inside screaming as it fell to the bottom.

Rolling again and again through the final twenty feet, the 48 came to rest on its side with its engine still running, the crew laying broken inside. Staring down through the visor, he knew it was a fluke, and that if he hadn't…. A shot suddenly flashed by his head, and another, then another, crashing above his seating column so that the plasma rounds ignited the seating fabric, dropping it burning behind his neck. Struggling with it, the gunner felt the shots keep coming as his neck was scorched leaving himenraged as he used his helmet sight to range out over the hill below to see the attacker, a lone Hearack firing. Running for his position, just crossing the line two hundred yards from the first 317's wreckage, the gunner stared for a moment in disbelief—surrounded by his armoured fortress, squinting at the insane figure through his visor. Another shot struck his canopy shield in front harmlessly, and then another, another—above him, the seating took a hit, dropping incandescent fibres to his neck once more, his patience expiring. With a whining rush, the turbines signalled his intent as he slammed the left pedal and forced his firing arm forward and to the right. The massive bulk of the 317's aft section swung back to the right, the remaining sunlight peering into the ammo pit as its front barrel, with trilaser bearing down, became visible for a second through the smoke falling out onto its hapless victim. Another shot, and then another; a coolant rush, an ear-piercing shriek, and the barrel opened up. The ground in front shot for tens of feet in a deadly curtain before impacting its helpless target. Amid a shower of earth, the body exploded backwards, spraying up a quiet mist that turned heavy in the dirt spiralling off with a remaining arm.

Watching from above, the gunner viewed a sickening sight; it was the first time he'd seen what he'd been doing—the first time he'd seen his weapon go against an individual. As he looked down to the right, the dropping sun glinted against his helmet. Heart heavy, he looked down at the wetness that remained of his victim strewn on the ground. With him staring out over the hill, the reality of the surroundings became evident as pit crew and gunner alike looked out at the dark mass of blood which had gone unnoticed before. All over the slope, steam rose from round-savaged carcasses and unrecognisable remains, the whole hillside lying hot with death, its soil held down fast with blood.

Staring blankly at the carnage with the others, the gunner fixed his eyes on the scene below with the rhythmic hum of the 317 only adding to his trance. Looking down and to the right with the others, he saw the steam rise across the hillside, flickering off his helmet in the sun as he stared at his work, shock growing with adrenalin ebbing away. It started slowly, creeping in—guilt, creeping in as the nitroalrgian hissed through the barrels' vent holes, and creeping in all the more as he stared at the carnage. The remains everywhere, the rising steam flickering on his helmet from all over the slope…. He didn't notice as the guilt took hold, and didn't notice the flicker change, become more uniform and repeat again and again, growing, emerging in the distance through the glare. On the inside of his helmet, his subconscious finally alerted him with that gut-wrenching feeling. Slowly realising an image like an insect crept over the right side of his visor, his mind suddenly cleared… *Tracks!*

In the distance, the crash signalled the huge tracks clearing the ridge, smashing down in a cloud of dust that roared forward immediately on the 317 in the distance. Fuller didn't get the words out before the gunner rammed down hard on his right pedal, and with a straining whine, the huge barrel began to come left, lifting as the gunner pulled back on the firing lever. From the pit, the three men watched in horror as a similar struggle played out in the approaching 86, its barrel swinging right to allow it to climb the hillside and now coming left, slowly, bearing toward them.

"Come on," murmured the gunner nervously, watching the opposing barrel turning. "Come on, come on!" He began to panic.

From the pit, Fuller watched with the others, looking back and forth between the barrels as the hydraulic whine strained above—back and forth, back and forth. "He's not gonna make it," Fuller worried aloud, unsure even as he watched.

Hydraulics whined as nerves strained, the 48's engine heard true as it came through the smoke, and finally it was clear....

"He's not gonna make it!" Fuller shouted. "He's not gonna make it! Get outta here!" Ramming a hand against Rians' shoulder to make his intention clear, Fuller jumped up, pulling himself over the pit's ridge and then, with the others, running down the hill. Scaling the 317, Fuller grabbed the canopy, screaming at the gunner to leave. Dropping the firing lever, the gunner struggled with his harness, panic thwarting his escape.

"Come On!" Fuller screamed, reaching in over the canopy and grabbing for the release. The harness bursting open, Fuller pulled at him hurriedly, helping him from the seat. Clearing the cockpit, the gunner's feet clipped the canopy and sent them tumbling to the ground. "Get Up!" Fuller shouted, pulling at him as they rose staggering to a run, passing the ammo pit with Fuller in the lead when suddenly the shot rang out....

The ground lit up in front of Fuller as he ran, the sound bringing the heat he knew accompanied the blast wave. It crashed into his back, lifting him from the ground before beginning to wrap itself around him with arms and a head... it wasn't the blast wave—it was a body, the gunner! Fuller for a second felt the blood ooze from the gunner's mouth, down his neck, the heat growing behind him; unknown to him, the gunner's back was strewn with steel daggers of shrapnel that he himself had been saved from due to his human shield.

The crash down was barely felt as Fuller was forced forward under the wave of heat, his shield wrenched away as he tumbled down, seeing for a second the ridge line approach....

In an instant, he was falling, tumbling and striking the ridge wall with the ground approaching fast, fear never getting a hold on him as a final smash to the ribs signalled freefall. Crashing down on the canyon floor, he felt the snap as his ankle went. Howling out in pain, he flailed helplessly against the sand-strewn ground between two rock faces. Suddenly, his screams were joined by more as the blue sheen of plasma rounds tore by overhead; struggling in pain, Fuller saw two figures approaching in the distance and firing through the gloom. Amidst the pain, he reached for his rifle, but it lay just inches out of range to his side and his attempt was blocked further by pain. Desperately trying to reach through the agony, he saw shots tear by overhead as the figures came, Fuller turning to see his attackers as he stretched out… their shots lowering, almost on him, the heat from the plasma close and passing inches above him. Looking at his end, he saw the blood red eyes came into view, locking with his as he watched one take aim and braced for the….

Suddenly, the two tore open, blood bursting from wounds with their bodies being forced to the rock face, plasma rounds flying aimlessly as they slid to the ground.

Shock taking the pain from him, Fuller watched wide-eyed as another figure appeared from the right through another canyon opening onto his, and watched as he turned, firing back where he'd come for. Immediately, the figure was surrounded by plasma rounds as they screamed past him, forcing him to the ground and slamming into the rock face behind him. Outgunned, the figure rose from its crouch and came running toward Fuller—closer, clearer, as voices grew behind him. *Rians.*

"Let's go!" he screamed, grabbing Fuller's arm and hauling him up almost without stopping, barely giving him time to clutch for his rifle before forcing him forward so that he stumbled through the pain with Rians' arm round his shoulder. Stumbling forward, they didn't get far, Fuller collapsing in pain only to be hauled right back up despite his cries, Rians forcing him through the narrow canyon. Arm over arm, they struggled forward, breaking out of the walls to a flat rocky plateau in front. Clearing the canyon, plasma rounds followed them with air crackling as they missed. Twenty yards clear, Fuller collapsed in pain to the loose stony ground.

"Come on!" screamed Rians, pulling with two hands and barely able to hold his rifle. "Get up! Come on!" *Trees*, thought Rians, *they had to get to the trees*. They were only thirty yards away, and he'd have to pull him. They had to make it…. Plasma rounds flew nearer as he struggled to pull Fuller up, shadows appearing on the canyon walls behind them with their pursuers gaining ground. "Come on!"

With Fuller crying out with every step, Rians virtually dragged him the last ten yards. Fuller, looking back at the canyon, felt a shudder as Rians jammed his boot into the ground, bringing them to a dead halt. Turning, Fuller's eyes fell on a forty-foot drop—loose rock tumbling down to the trees below as they stood precariously on the edge of a cliff. More rounds came, more accurate, as suddenly Hearack cleared the canyon behind them and Rians watched, struggling with Fuller at the edge of the drop. Forced down under fire, they collapsed to the right behind a small outcropping of rocky ground that barely covered their black combat fatigues, which stuck out like beacons against the light grey surroundings. Backs to the drop, they returned fire from their squatted positions with Rians on the left as Fuller did his best with one leg out, struggling in the loose ground and trying to grip the edge of the drop. Hearack bodies began to fill the plateau ahead of them, dropping as they cleared the canyon… dropping, but still coming, storming out of the canyon with weapons blazing. Plasma passed between them, over them, and struck the ground in front of them, scorching the grey earth black with each strike. Pulling back and forth behind their cover, they couldn't hold them; for every one they dropped, two more moved forward, and they could see their eyes, blood red, using bodies for cover as they approached. A shot narrowly missed Rians, forcing him down as it crackled past, and past Fuller, too, bright blue rounds leaving his vision blurred. Head raising up, Rians fired back as Fuller tried to aim, levelling through his blurred sight and about to fire when the ground suddenly gave way under his good leg. Calling out, he slipped back, Rians managing to grab him—only to be pulled up out of cover by the weight. Exposed and with his right hand holding Fuller, Rians turned to see red eyes meet his from behind the barrel of a rifle; his aiming was too late, the flash searing forward. Plasma slicing past Rians, he let out a yelp as he felt the rip over his chest, the shot glancing past Fuller, who felt his hand released as they went over.

Rolling, smashing off the cliff wall, Fuller was soon scratched by trees as he entered the foliage, crashing off the remainder of the cliff before smashing down, back-first, to the forest floor. He was in agony, screaming aloud with pain racking his body, when there was a crash beside him that came with screams to silence his own pain.

Fuller looked over wide-eyed to see a creature flailing helplessly on its back, its whole chest pussing up, bubbling over as steam rose with the shrieks of its owner. In shock, Fuller watched him grab at his chest, only to shriek louder and throw his arms away, continuing to flail wildly while under the dark canopy of the trees they'd fallen through. Shielded from view, Rians' shrieking was soon joined by similar sounds, plasma bursts falling like rain through the cover of brush and trees alike that were going up in flames around them. A casualty himself, Fuller grabbed his shrieking comrade's uniform by the collar and, joining his cries, pulled with everything he had—pushing with his good foot and slowly moving the two men on their backs as plasma showered down around them. Above them on the ridge, over a dozen Hearack stood firing blindly into the canopy below, guided by Rians' screams even as Fuller kept dragging him through the forest below. Among the trees, darkness had given way to fire, bark and foliage going up like tinder with aimless charges bringing down flaming branches and debris around the soldiers. As the firestorm took hold, the intensity of crackling foliage and crashing debris almost drowned out the screaming Rians, Fuller pulling him through the inferno. Escape routes became blocked one after another as branches fell ahead of each attempt, Fuller choking badly and looking around with Rians gripped by the collar, heat searing their exposed skin. Fighting through the smoke, Fuller caught sight of a clearing and made the best progress he could, hauling the screaming victim beside him. Hair singed and with fire scalding him still, he caught sight of rocks as tears began streaming from his eyes, obscuring his way. With the blur nearing, Fuller began to feel shale—small rocks digging into him as he struggled forward with fire raging behind him; he wrestled them from its grasp. Pulling on his back, Fuller felt the air to be cooler ahead, and felt earth giving way to rock, tearing at his skin as he pulled them forward. Glancing ahead of them, with Rians kicking and screaming in his grasp, his blurred vision made out a shape, dark, close... a cave! Pulling Rians with everything he had left, he felt loose rocks fall away from them, each push bringing blood streaming from his hands that were growing more and more torn on the rock.

Rians agony forced him on still as he dragged him, kicking and screaming, into the cave. Over the mouth of the cave, the cooling was immediate, their scorched skin finding relief as they moved deeper inside it. Less so for Rians, however; for him nothing of his injuries changed as the crackling fire was left behind and Fuller heard the full horror of his comrade's bone-chilling screams. They didn't stop—didn't falter for a second—echoing around the cave as Fuller pulled them deeper into the blackness. Deep enough in, Fuller let Rians go, feeling him thrash from side to side in the darkness with the smell of burning flesh growing overpowering. Lying on his back, struggling with his ankle, Fuller aimed for the cave roof thirty feet in front of them and opened up his weapon. Exploding rounds quickly shattered the roof, firing drowning out the ground's rumbling as it destabilized, collapsing in so that falling rocks quickly blocked out the backdrop of fire. Fuller closed his eyes in the darkness, rocks falling close in front of them and vibrations running through the ground; he expected each one to crush them. He could feel them dropping in close, but all fell short, the rumbling eventually subsiding and sealing them in.

Coughing in the thick, dust-laden air, Fuller searched for flares in one of the many pockets of his combats. Rians had been screaming for nearly two minutes without rest now; the sound cut through Fuller as he tore at the Velcro on his right leg, fumbling in the darkness. Two cylinders coming to hand, he broke the cap off one and hurled it forward with his eyes hurting as the bright pink crackled onto the rocks. A pinkish hue lit the cavern eerily, only revealing the horror beside him as the still screaming Rians gyrated, clutching and releasing his steaming chest. Fumbling with the Velcro on his left leg next, Fuller brought out a small, stainless steel canister, a slice of glass cutting through its centre revealing the sight of quarenal inside. When he reached toward Rians, though, it was knocked clear out of his hands and off behind him with Rians' uncontrollable thrashing. Unable to stand the screaming, Fuller called out in pain as his ankle bore weight with his reach across Rians' to break open the Velcro on his left leg and grab his own quarenal. Suffering blows to the head and neck, and fearing he'd lose this one, as well, he just managed to jam it into the man's exposed midsection. A high-pitched alert signalled success as the contents hissed in. Blows quickly subsided as a wide-eyed Rians grabbed for the cylinder with both hands, his screaming abruptly stopping. Rians, in shock and choking for breath, left Fuller feeling the strain of his hands over his as he released pressure on the cylinder, hoping to save some of the precious contents. A squawking burst of sound, a tightening of the grip, and Rians' wild eyes made him jam it back down, its hissing continuing as it forced its way in. His patient began to breathe easier then, shaking less, and taking bigger and longer gasps as Fuller looked on. Slowly, he released his grip, and for a moment Fuller thought he saw a smile as he fell back, his head striking down onto the cave floor. Pulling back with the cylinder, Fuller looked at it through the pinkish hue flickering between them; the green, flowing light was out and the red standing on. Through the glass channel running the length of the cylinder, Fuller saw the precious liquid lapping at the bottom; it was only an eighth full. That aside, Fuller quickly wondered about the outside; had they been seen? Were the Hearack out there? How were they going to get out when….

Suddenly, laughing sounded out loud, and Fuller lowered the cylinder from his sight, revealing Rians' behind his open, steaming chest with his head back and laughing. It got louder almost surreal as Fuller struggled to understand his ailing friend, putting a hand on his shoulder and asking the ridiculous, "Are you alright, Rians?"

Rians' head suddenly sprang up, wild eyes meeting his, and there was a second of silence before he was off again, hysterical—throwing his head back and almost crying with laughter.

The drugs in mind, Fuller watched as Rians fought for control, his head shaking and laughter finally lowering to intermittent bursts he looked back at Fuller in glee. "Alright? Alright? Yeah, I'm fine!" he assured Fuller, looking down at the gelified, steaming mass of his midsection. "I'm fine, but Carla's gonna kill me when she sees this uniform!" And he was off again, head rolling back in hysterics.

Fuller fought back a smile at the humour; he knew

how bad he was, and it wasn't funny. Time passing, Rians fought for control again, trying to talk through the laughter. "Ca…. Ca—aha—Cap, you gotta try this… shit! If I'd have known about this at Eldridge's party that time, well, shit… aha, ha… ha." More laughter sounded, but Rians fought back faster this time. "Captain?"

"Yeah, I'm here." Fuller leant over as Rians fought to lift his neck.

"How much is left, because I… I ha—I don't want to feel that again."

"There's only a little in this one, but that other canister's back there and it shouldn't take much to keep you where you are now," Fuller assured him. "We can keep you like this for days."

"Days!" Rians laughed back, struggling for air as he swallowed. "Shit… I'm almost glad I got hit!" He laughed on, more controlled now than at first, smiling up at Fuller and trying to make light of it all as the two lay behind the sealed entrance up front.

With them wheezing and coughing despite the drugs, the smell of burning flesh filled the air as Rians began to drift, babbling relentlessly and then breaking into song.

Fuller tried to interrupt his mania as he lay shaking his head from side to side, singing at the roof. "Rians… Rians…." There was no answer, and the last thing Fuller was going to do was raise his voice at this sorry state, so he persevered until finally the singing stopped and Rians turned his head to look at him, his lost expression saying it all; the man barely remembered who he was.

Trying to coax him round, Fuller continued, "Rians, what about Walsch? Do you remember Walsch?"

"Walsch?" Rians looked lost.

"Yeah, Walsch, in the ammo pit. Remember?" Fuller questioned him.

"Ammo pit… yeah, oh fuck, yeah… we… we slid down right into them…. Hi… heh hi—they were already round… they'd been… been coming round that canyon on us, and we…" Rians struggled. "We ran right into them, and he…"

"Take your time, man" Fuller told him.

"He… he didn't make it… he… I'm sorry."

"Hey, that's alright, man, you rest now. You're here," Fuller said.

Rians managed a bare smile as his head slid back, his mind entering who only knew where.

Fuller lost track of time once the flare went out; he didn't light the space anymore and couldn't see his watch. It felt like days, but at least the screaming had stopped.

Fuller was suddenly woken from a sleep by a crash…

Rocks began to fall in the void in front of them, each crash to the ground making the air thicker as dust stirred up. Still staring into darkness, Fuller clutched his rifle, aiming not by sight but by sound at whoever it was grinding through.

Suddenly, a shaft of light that was hurtful to the eyes came through, and then another, rocks falling beside light surging into the cave with fresh air striking the men for the first time in what Fuller guessed to be days. Head pounding from the light, Fuller squinted into it, aiming at the noise of some mechanical beast filling the cave and coming into view for a second, blocking out the light behind it... but still only a blur to the squinting Fuller. The growling engine dropped to idle, the machine grinding to a halt as if spotting them—as if alive and staring in. Then, in a roar, it hauled backward, showering the men with the painful light and disappearing from view, leaving them to choke in the dust with loose rocks continuing to fall. Fuller listened as, outside, the engine dropped low and moved away, cutting out some way off and leaving him with the sound of his breath and thick dust swirling around, invading with the sunlight. It was warm to the skin, welcome after the chill in the cave, but there was little time to enjoy it with voices approaching. Injured and with cold senses that were dulled and disorientated, Fuller couldn't tell what they were; he couldn't make out words, just sounds, and so he instilled his faith in his waiting rifle, hoping. He heard rocks crushed underfoot outside, his eyes adjusting on the shattered entrance through his aiming sights with Rians silent by his side for the first time. Figures appeared and fell away, dark against the light and unwilling to come forward, distrusting—like the broken men inside. Only their shadows ventured in, coming and going as they positioned themselves near the entrance. It unnerved Fuller as he lay there, finger on the trigger with all the poise that his exhaustion would allow.

Silence.

It all grew still, unnaturally so with each side unwilling to make the first move, and then it came.

"Alliance forces! Identify yourselves or we'll be forced to clear!"

Clear. Clear meant they would frag the place.

"57th! We're elements of 23rd core!" shouted back an anxious Fuller, not wanting the cave painted with his body. A gentle shuffling of rocks could be heard as shadows moved in on the walls, eyes still squinting into the light as figures gingerly appeared in the entrance—the advantage theirs as Fuller lay with his rifle on the ground beside him.

Two figures came down slowly, crouched and with their rifles trained. "Identify yourselves!" demanded the lead figure.

"Captain Fuller and Lieutenant Rians, Unit 57!" Fuller called back to the veiled approachers.

"Fuller?" came back an almost instant response, barely hiding surprise that quickly turned to disdain as straightening figures called back through the entrance, "Tell Etrick we've found our big heroes!"

Outside, a bedraggled Etrick stood against the hood of the emplacement dozer, tired and bloody like the rest of the soldiers around him; all day, they'd been following up sensor data showing bio readings all around the battlefield. Fifty yards in front of him, from up the small incline, one of his men now came running down the loose shale and over to their position in the charred remains of the forest.

"What?" Etrick exclaimed, listening to the report.

"It's Fuller, sir, and one of his men, badly hurt," the soldier explained.

"No," growled Etrick. "He's not even begun to hurt yet."

Barely finishing his sentence, he saw a wreck of a figure appearing in the distance, lurching through the entrance to the cave with his arm over the shoulder of a reluctant Marine. Fixing the figure with a scowl, Etrick hadn't a scrap of sympathy as he watched Fuller's pained expression twisting with each step as he struggled down the loose shale. Even when Fuller got closer, and could see the scowl, Etrick didn't flinch; he wanted him to see it—he hated his guts.

"Well, well, well," Etrick fired the opening barrage. "Do you want your medals now or should we wait for the honours ceremony?"

The bullshit sniggers from the men around Etrick didn't phase Fuller as he lurched the last few yards, Rians on his mind. "Enough with the bullshit. I've got a wounded man back there!"

"Then he's a lucky one," retorted Etrick, unconcerned.

"What?" Fuller demanded, incensed at the ignorance.

"I said he's a lucky one," returned Etrick, slumped idly against the dozer. "Lucky to have survived around you, as I've got twelve hundred that didn't."

"What are you talking about?" Fuller shouted.

"I'm talking about the twelve hundred people that ain't goin' home because you couldn't hold that shitty little hill!" screamed Etrick, leaving his sarcastic tone behind as he stood off the dozer.

"That's my fault?" exclaimed Fuller. "I warned you for two hours, but you wouldn't send me shit because you were too busy shining a seat with your ass!"

"Well," replied Etrick, adopting his usual sneering attitude and expression as he came almost nose to nose with Fuller, "you can try and sell that to the judge advocate. That's right, the word's already out; you're the butcher of Gorsearan."

The smile on the end of it was all it took, exhaustion disappearing, Fuller felt the snapping cartilage of

Etrick's nose under his knuckles. Sprawling back against the dozer, Etrick had barely landed when another right hand smashed into the side of his head—Fuller launching himself at him. Enraged to have this happen in front of his men, Etrick struggled off the hood and grabbed for Fuller as he raised another right hand. But his injuries hadn't disappeared, his sudden yelp confirming that much and his right hand never landing; he collapsed backward instead as Etrick forced him onto his broken ankle and down to the ground.

There was no real struggle Fuller could offer; doubled over in pain, he took blow after blow as Etrick rained them down, screaming from above. It got dark quickly this time, much quicker than usual, and for Fuller the pain was gone… he was unconscious.

"Aaaaarrrrgghh! Let me go, you fuck!" raged Etrick, kicking at the lifeless Fuller as his men dragged him off.

"He's out!" shouted one of the soldiers as they struggled to hold Etrick off. "Sir, he's out!"

"I know that, you fucking idiot, I'm not blind!" Etrick screamed, struggling like a mad man.

Rians had gotten to watch it all supported by two of Etricks' men as he'd been half-dragged down to the scene.

"Let me go!" shouted Etrick, calming slightly and no longer kicking out. "Get the fuck off!" he ordered the men, shrugging off the last arms to leave him glaring at their owners. Looking down at Fuller, he raged behind his ashen face, unable to finish the job and breathing heavily as he stood over him, barely on the side of control. Still focused on Fuller, he became aware of the people approaching on his left and turned to see them with blood streaming from his shattered nose. The shock of seeing Rians' open chest between two of his men caught him off-guard, though; he was about to offer help when he was cut short by Rians bursting into laughter.

"Well, that's the last beauty contest you'll ever win! The Cap really fucked you up, man!" Rians managed to get out before howling into his face.

In an instant, the anger was back, boiling, and transferred from Fuller to Rians; grabbing for a rifle near the dozer, Etrick spun round, aiming for the laughter. He felt the rifle wrenched upwards just as bodies slammed into him, his men wrestling him from the brink—they were used to his temper. The shouts and struggles only added to Rians' drug-fuelled hilarity as his keepers carried him off.

Still struggling, Etrick could only glare after him as he was held back by his men. As if sensing it, Rians looked back over his shoulder with glee, shouting, "See you later, beautiful! Sweetheart! Sugar!"

Chapter 12

Lost Souls

Faces where bloodied, and could be seen even in the dark of the escape pod that was pierced only by the faint glow of the distress beacon strobing over the sound of broken bodies groaning on the floor. Aidin knew they hadn't made it, not all of them, and he felt that feeling which no one but a ship's captain could understand... the feeling of responsibility and failing at it, lives lost as proof. He was glad of the darkness, glad no one could see him; he felt ashamed, guilty. This was the second time he'd lost a ship—a flagship, even.

For three days, Aidin sat with the guilt, sitting with th.e others and their pain with rations and hope dwindling—unlike the smell, as the smell of eight people locked in a steel tomb floating alone in the vastness of space only got stronger.

They didn't know it yet, but they had it easy...

Point three one of a lightyear away the crew of the Starship *Arnhem* were patrolling near the Fahraren Heights over a light year away from the massive hunt for the Hearack, they were bored... it wasn't to last.

Like many other starships in remote parts of Alliance space, they were a bare minimum, a skeletal force on the fringes of the Alliance perimeter guarding the back door while every other vessel available chased glory in the Drift. Each ship in this depleted force moved alone and silent through space, their crews reluctant with knowing they'd missed their chance, or so it seemed…

"Sir, there's something on short range sensors," reported the con officer Lieutenant Martin.

"Short range?" Captain Grant repeated.

"Yes, sir," replied Martin. "It just appeared with a barrage of strange signals."

"Why didn't we detect it earlier?" Grant asked.

"Unknown, sir," Martin replied.

"Analysis, Mr Waite," Grant said.

"It could be a ship," Waite replied. "Quite small, about the size of an attack ship."

"Put it on screen," Grant ordered, standing from his chair as small system alerts came from the tactical station above and behind him, the object brought to screen.

A small, dim point of light appeared, far off in the stars atop the right of the screen in front of him.

"Magnify!" Grant ordered.

In an instant, the small point of light almost fillcd the screen, metallic with a faint green tinge; it appeared smooth, but for some deep angular cuts which apparently gouged deep inside.

"What is it, wreckage?" Grant asked, walking toward the forward stations.

"Sensors aren't picking up any other ships or debris for two parsecs," replied Waite. "And the computer is unable to identify the signals."

"Then what is it?" Grant asked aloud, looking at the strange form onscreen.

"Sir, this is strange," Waite voiced, studying his data. "The object appears to have only two dimensions."

"What?" Grant questioned, his face squinting.

"Only two dimensions," Waite repeated. "It has length and width, but no depth… no depth at all."

"How can we see gouges in the surface, yet the surface has no mass?" Grant asked.

"We shouldn't be able to, sir," replied Waite, looking at his data. "I'm at a loss to explain it, sir."

"But there it is," Grant mused. "What's going on, Hannigan?" he asked next, turning round from the con to the tactical station behind him.

"There's no power signatures, nothing that can be construed as weaponry," replied Hannigan.

Grant turned back, staring for a moment. "Mr Waite, take us closer; easy, though—not too fast."

Slowly, the object grew larger on screen, filling more and more of it as they moved closer.

"Anything?" Grant asked.

"No, sir," Martin replied, shaking his head as he looked at the information on his panel. It didn't make sense, that it was just hanging there in space with no depth to it at all.

System alerts around the bridge ran off feverishly as all but the captain were engrossed in their data—so engrossed that no one saw the edges of the object begin to blur as they approached. No one but him. Thinking his eyes were tired, he said nothing for a moment, his mind wrapped in with everything else. Why would the edges blur? Memories of the past began to filter through his thoughts. Memories of the war, of the Anzeil Massacre and other horrors. If only they'd have known they were coming that day; if only… then maybe they could have stopped it, but how could they have when the Hearack had brought in technology they didn't understand? Through that damn wormhole, they'd brought terror unseen, those bastard starships that were invisi…. Suddenly, it dawned on him—they were looking at a cloaked ship!

"All engines back full!" shouted Grant, startling the crew and garnering confused looks as all he got back. "It's a cloaked ship! Full reverse!" he demanded, shattering their confusion.

Confusion was soon lost, the crew throwing themselves into action, realising that if it was a cloaked ship, then the starship-sized portion on screen was only part of a monster lying behind it.

Martin had barely touched the helm panel when the bridge erupted in alarms, their engines throwing themselves into reverse as Waite saw his navigation display fill with huge mountains of alloy. Looking up at the viewscreen, he watched, stunned with the others as the shape onscreen began to grow into a vast wall of green alloy. Appearing out of the darkness, it expanded faster and faster, completely blocking any path in front of them and beginning to curve at each edge—in toward them!

"Bring us around one-eighty!" Grant ordered. "Get us outta here!"

At full reverse, the *Arnhem*'s massive steel bulk wheeled round to see two huge, hex-shaped ships decloaking far in front of it.

They didn't move, and the helmsman seemed frozen as Grant looked on from behind, incensed at the delay. He barrelled over to the helm. "What are you waiting for? Take us away from them!"

"I don't know which direction to go in—it's all around us," answered Martin, looking at his displays. "Every time I set a course, it decloaks right in front of us; it's massive—it's already eight thousand kilometres long!"

"What?" Grant uttered in disbelief, confused as to why he hadn't set a course through the two ships on screen. *Eight thousand kilometres*, he thought. What was he talking about? The ships approaching ahead were huge, but not more than a couple of hundred kilometres across. "Come on!" Grant shouted. "Set a course before they get here and close us off!"

"They're already here!" Martin tried to explain, clearly panicked.

"What are you taking about?" raged down Grant.

A pale Martin turned to meet the anger. "They're all part of the same ship… it's decloaking all around us!"

Rage turned to fear as Grant finally understood, and looking down, he saw the helm displays full for thousands of kilometres in each direction… five huge hex shapes connected to a massive bulk over and around them with a giant tail of steel running back for thousands of kilometres into the darkness, growing all the time as it decloaked, surrounding them—when suddenly movement caught his eye from above.

Looking up, he watched as two huge roads of steely green materialised out of the darkness on screen, reaching far ahead and connecting to the approaching shapes, disappearing off the top of the screen overhead.

Coming to, the crew veered desperately to port, the massive steel hull continuing to decloak around them, only to find five steel roads with the deep gouges in their surface contracting as they bent in toward them, bringing the huge hex shapes in at their tips. Closer in, the hex shapes tipping each steel road were like the end of great, rotating arms wheeling round and bringing in five massive, circular recesses in an x-like pattern to bear, each recess having four smaller ones surrounding it.

Frozen for a second in awe, they saw the dark, steely green of the hexes suddenly illuminating twenty-five recesses bursting into blazing green.

"Bring us around and get us outta here!" Grant screamed.

Green eyes watched the *Arnhem* wheel round at full rail, the crew finding clear space under the miles of dark hull around them. With the ship bursting forward, strange alloy passed above the panicked vessel, green recessed eyes beginning to diminish behind them when suddenly one flared up.

There were screams as the crew were flung forward, the ship brought to a dead halt in an instant. Astern, a beam of light from one of the hexes held the *Arnhem* fast as four smaller recesses around it turned an angry red. Struggling to their feet, the crew saw the first flash of red energy from the recesses round the tractoring green centre. Panic on board was eclipsed by streams of red energy coming again and again, the ship being sliced apart—rail exhausts, engines, and decks ten, twelve, and fourteen seared off in seconds—twenty-four other green eyes watching as it happened.

Helpless, the remaining crew stumbled through smoke and flames, fires raging on all decks and dying bodies littering the smashed corridors with people falling as fumes overcame them, toxins swirling all around. Amidst the panic, vibrations suddenly stopped as the hex ceased its attack with one final shudder signalling its tractor release, the green hue melting away. Cries of anguish now dominated the crippled ship, survivors bearing a new terror over crewmates and loved ones who were transported from their very arms by some sort of molecular inducer beams, leaving them alone to their burning end. Those left behind joined the screaming, echoing their voices through the red tomb while trapped under bulkheads and shattered decks. Others trapped near viewing ports by their broken bodies saw the very stars above them disappear as, unseen, a dark vale descended around them till only the twinkling of clear space below them was visible. In the panic, no one realised the huge ship was descending over them till a sea of fire appeared between them and the stars below… a force field.

Victims were silenced by the crash from above, all resistance torn from the ship with the remaining decks collapsing on the lucky as survivors watched the burning lake beneath the ship rise up to meet them. Plasma fire surged in through every corridor, integrity fields collapsing—overpowered as the ship was forced down by the unseen vessel above.

Outside, in the calm of space, no evidence of the horror was seen as the massive ship recloaked around it, claiming the terror for itself. Instead, outside, the stars twinkled gently in the calm stillness of space, interrupted only for a second by a huge column of fire dissipating in the distance.

Chapter 13

When It Rains

"You mean it'll never heal?" Fuller looked at the doctor in shock.

He'd been at Rians' side all the way back from Gorsearan 4, telling him not to worry, and that when they got to Station 185's medical infirmary, everything would be fine, but it wasn't. He'd done his best to keep Rians' mind on other things in the transport's medical bay, and he must have tried to talk about every damn thing there was to keep him from looking down at the holplast holding in his chest as it oozed beneath. Lying full of quarenal, Rians hadn't even noticed the people with missing legs, the people looking at him shocked even though they themselves had only half a face! His chest was seared through by the plasma burst, seared black so badly that every time it tried to heal, it cracked open all over again. His skin was breaking down, held together only by the holplast, and there wasn't a damn thing anyone could do; they just kept filling him with more quarenal and, all the while, Fuller'd been telling him everything was going to be all right... but it wasn't.

The doctor looked at Fuller, pursing his lips uncomfortably before turning back to Rians, who was sitting up on the infirmary bed but still heavily drugged. "Mr Rians," he began quietly, "you've been hit by a type seven plasma range. The damage this range causes DNA is irreparable."

Rians felt himself swallowing hard as he listened to the doctor, the dim blue light of the recovery wing doing nothing to calm him.

"Fortunately," the doctor continued, "it was a glancing blow slicing past you instead of striking directly, leaving your organs undamaged. Your tissue, though, is another matter. The penetration was not deep; in fact, it only penetrated a short distance into your tissue, leaving the DNA—although moderately damaged—still with some stable qualities."

"You mean I'm gonna be all right?" Rians reached hopefully.

"What I mean is that you won't get any worse," answered the doctor.

"What does that mean, Doc?" asked a concerned Fuller, mindful of Rians' barely coherent state.

Looking between them, the doctor tried not to appear negative as he took another breath. "Mr Rians." He paused. "Your chest will never heal."

Rians looked away, rolling his eyes as he sat on the bed; drugged though he was, he knew full well what it looked like down there. Fuller may have tried to shelter him, but he'd seen the faces of those in the ship's infirmary. What about Carla? What would she think? What about….

The doctor continued, "Although your body will form new skin over time, it will be extremely weak. Your body has lost certain DNA coding—coding necessary to maintain the strong bonds between the atoms of your skin in the chest region. Your body may learn to cope over time, but any large or fast physical exertion will tear the skin as though it were paper. I'm sorry. We have drugs that will assist with its elasticity, but…"

"And will I always look…" Rians broke off, unsure what to say and tentatively fearful of the answer, thinking of his chest remaining this seared sight.

"No," the doctor reassured him quickly, as if pouncing on some positive light. "The lesions will diminish over time; they will always be there, rough, but your skin colour will return."

"What about the telamear regenerators?" Fuller asked hopefully.

Swallowing at being posed the question, the doctor took a professional stance. "We did absolutely everything we could with them in theater, but they—"

"You mean you've already used them?" Fuller cut in, shocked, and realising too late that Rians was seeing him try to play down his reaction after-the-fact.

"Heh," said Rians quietly, bringing Fuller's head back to focus on him. "That's alright, at least I'm here. I'm gonna see 'em, right?" he asked, smiling genuinely as he thought of his family.

"Yeah," Fuller answered, gathering himself quickly, forcing a smile and overdoing a nod as he tried to share the good feeling.

"Now, I know this has been a terrifying ordeal, gentlemen, but the best thing for you now, Mr Rians, is rest," the doctor said as he withdrew slightly, motioning with his hand to Fuller as he left the recovery wing.

Fuller nodded after him, and levelled the same look at Rians with all the encouragement he could pretend as he followed the doctor out.

"John, don't tell them!" Rians called after him, stopping Fuller before the door. "I mean, tell 'em I'm alright... just...."

"You got it." Fuller nodded, looking back with his hand on the door and watching Rians feign a smile, his own fading as soon as he made it through the door.

Alliance Station 185—modern, spacious, with every luxury and vice imaginable, centred between the two demilitarised zones that separated the Alliance from Irachan and Valraich territories in a way that set it up as the entry point for any ship crossing over. Crossing over or smuggling, in fact, as freighters from thousands of sectors crossed paths here along with their passengers. Cadets joining the Alliance dreamed of this place, and worked all their lives hoping to find a post here to slip in through the back door, and here Fuller and his unit walked straight in through the front... but it wasn't for the luxury. It was for the courtroom.

The station had everything. Food, bars, clubs, and all that went with them, including the nearest courtroom to Gorsearan 4—one that was never quiet with this place being what it was. The Alliance wanted to know right away what had happened, and they weren't going to wait till Fuller and his men got home; they'd waited for the injured to leave the infirmary, though... waited a whole day.

In the courtroom after that one day...

"You mean to say you hadn't arranged sufficient manpower to defend what was in fact the regiment's only surface to air defence?" asked the prosecution lawyer, stopping in an over-dramatic stance.

Trying not to take the bait, Fuller attempted to stay calm as he sat to the left and a little below three generals and two admirals in the levy box while the prosecution paraded between him and all present in the room. Ritter and Etrick sat in front of him on the left, and Rians sat a way's over on the right with their defence team while various notaries and onlookers sat behind them in the back rows. Ritter was there as a star witness after having picked up various ships and transports from the battlefield with the Langan, and seeing for himself the aftermath and the injured. From the word *go*, his little buddy boy Etrick had thrown all the blame squarely at Fuller. Poisoned with hate for Fuller, it hadn't taken much persuading from Etrick for him to come along and try to tighten the noose. No such luck for Fuller and Rians; when Holsen had split them from Brice and the rest on Gorsearan 4, it had meant those folks willing to speak for Fuller and Rians had had to wait in line with the rest for the transports while Fuller had made it off with Rians and the injured in priority. Now, the people who could speak for their characters were five days out, and so they were on their own.

"Captain Etrick had two units sitting idle for four hours…" Fuller began.

"And in four hours, you didn't think to ask for them?" broke in the lawyer, a certain advocate prosecutor Morris.

"I asked!" Fuller almost shouted. "I asked for hours, but his damn staff ignored me just like he—"

"Ignored you?" Morris cut in.

"Yeah, he ignored me!" Fuller retorted, angered at being cut off.

"It couldn't be, perhaps, that with so many responsibilities, they simply overlooked your situation?" Morris returned. "It couldn't be they were relying on officers in charge of each element to adequately deal with that element's needs?"

Here he went again. It had been like this for three days; they hadn't wasted any time. A day after Rians had been able to walk comfortably, the hearing had started… they wanted to lay the blame where it fell, and do it fast. There'd been constant rebuffs by Fuller's defence, constant attacks by fleet prosecution high on lies and half-truths provided by Etrick, and thousands of others injured and wanting someone to blame. Over and over again, Fuller's defence team had argued against the mountain of circumstantial crap from hundreds of so-called witnesses, but there was so much of it—complete with statements from thousands more—and as for Etrick, he was a born liar. Threatened with contempt of court, Fuller's eruptions of rage and outbursts at his lies had only served to make him look worse, especially after the fight outside the cave. Naturally, Fuller's defence drew up the strongest case they could and would have called Fuller's witnesses, they said, but they'd all been killed, all except for Rians… but they'd written him off, too, claiming his testimony was untrustworthy due to his drug-induced state at the time. Instead, Rians, on this final day of deliberations, sat with the defence after having been picked apart throughout the day by the prosecution, leaving him angry even as Fuller was pulled to the witness stand one last time.

"No," said Fuller.

"No?" repeated Morris.

"No! No. No. No!" Fuller shouted. "How many times am I going to have to say it? That prick Etrick left us in the shit and we all paid for it!"

"Surely, you don't expect us to believe a decorated commander was negligent when thousands of witness statements suggest the blame lies with you," rebuffed the prosecution.

"Look, I told you I spoke to Etrick's staff, who were

ordered to tell me Etrick was too busy to even listen to—"

"Oh yes," Fuller was cut off as the prosecutor paraded to his right in front of the generals. "Those staff who were conveniently killed in a Shar attack, their statements lost with them."

"Convenient!" raged Fuller, standing. "Those men died because that bastard doesn't give a fuck about the men around him!" he screamed, pointing at Etrick. "All he cares about is his position in—"

"Captain Fuller, you will take your seat!" demanded one of the generals seated higher to his right.

"And he couldn't give a fuck who lives or dies!" continued Fuller, not even hearing the general. "All as long as he gets his control fix at everyone else's expense!"

"Here we go again," countered the lawyer, gesturing in front of the generals with a look of contempt on his face as he eyed Fuller. "Slandering my client's good name—no evidence or substance to speak of, just wild claims and unfounded accusations." He easily switched his practiced look to one of disapproval as he led the court's opinion. "Mr Fuller, people are dead, lives have been shattered... don't you know how serious this is? Don't you care?"

That was it. Fuller lost it. Charged with such crap, he barged out of the witness stand and down the three short steps to the floor, the generals protesting behind him. The watching prosecution team shouted out, coming to their feet as he barged across and in front of them. Their lawyer's controlled expression was gone now, as he was standing frozen and wide-eyed as a seasoned Marine descended on him. His prissy-assed legal mouth couldn't save him as, body trembling, he reached out a hand in trying to calm the approaching rage. The hand did nothing, though, as a red-faced Fuller ploughed through him, throwing him aside and descending instead on a confused Rians who was sitting among the defence. Grabbing Rians from the other side of the table and offering no explanation, Fuller hauled him to his feet and, with a sharp rip, tore his shirt apart. A pained yelp from Rians heightened the shock of the courtroom, Rians almost falling over as he grabbed Fuller for support from the other side of the table.

"I'm sorry!" Fuller whispered in his ear, and then, assisting him, he slowly stood him up. Gasps were heard from the jury as the full extent of Rians' injuries was revealed, complete with running wounds, his chest torn open anew by the sharp grab from Fuller. "Don't I know how serious this is?" Fuller glared down at the lawyer on the floor. "Don't I care!" he screamed up at the jury. "I watched men, good men under my command, torn apart because that fuck left us wide open, and you bastards ask me if I care!!!"

The stunned jury didn't know where to look and were too shocked to put up an objection, Fuller taking over. "I care, alright! And so did everyone else on that hill who fought to help those below us down there, and for what? So their names could be dragged through the shit, their families lied to by a bunch of pricks who weren't even there and who are now more interested in finding someone to blame than finding the truth! Oh, I care!" Fuller shouted, fixing the jury hard with a stare. "It's just a shame you don't."

The deliberation had taken almost sixteen hours, and the verdict was a surprise to everyone—even Fuller. *Not guilty*. But it didn't lay the blame on Etrick, either, instead going for the pussy approach in citing battle stress and logistical overload as the culprit,. Battle stress huh? If it hadn't been for those boys on that hill, none of those ungrateful pricks would have made it out alive, thought Fuller. And with the gossip around the station and other things he'd heard that week, there was a part of him that wished they hadn't. He wasn't ashamed of that, either. Why should he be? They just didn't deserve it. Anyway his unit been reassigned to Aurin 2, and it was going to take another five days for Brice and the others to get transport from Gorsearan 4, the decision having been made to evacuate the planet, what with transports left in short supply. What a surprise. Five days on 185, Fuller thought, smiling; he wasn't going to waste them....

On the opposite side of the station...

A weary captain rode a maglift alone down 185 in silence—the first time he'd heard it since arriving. It was ironic that they'd gone through the worst and ended up in such a place for their troubles. Aidin had barely been able to look at his surviving crew when he'd met them in the docking area. After the debriefing and hearing, he'd just wanted to get away from it all, and away from them. He felt responsible, guilty, and the worst of it was that they didn't even know what had happened since even their sensor logs had been lost. The looks from the admirals in the hearing had said it all when he'd tried to explain the fact of a green shape appearing and vanishing, their frustration understandable when the press for more had brought nothing. Frustration or not,

Aidin had been assigned to ferry troops to a desolate outpost; the job was beneath him, but given the circumstances, he hadn't objected. He just wondered what kind of ship he'd be given to complete his embarrassment.

His system was shocked when the maglift doors opened. During the debriefing, all Aidin had wanted to do was get out of that little room—it was too much like an escape pod. He'd wanted to be out among the buzz of people, but now, faced with the hive of activity on 185's main galleria, he found it overwhelming. He wasn't a drinker, but this was different; he'd been in space most of his life and never given it a second thought, but the pod had changed things. For the first time, he seemed to feel how far away from home he was. In the pod, all the injured and their families had only been able to talk about their children; it had made Aidin feel lost, as he had none. He had a blistering career, and a record like no other, but it had come at a price—he'd had no time for romance, no time to make something work long-term. And he'd never missed that. There'd always been another report, another problem, another mission far away, but the pod had made it all look small, fruitless, and now he needed something to take the edge off.

There were happy smiles everywhere as he made his way through the galleria's purple haze, its matching carpet a quarter mile long and enhanced by the lighting above while the best food and goods for two light years were strung along its left wall, with windows into space on the right. But Aidin wasn't here for shopping, and was glad when he slipped down the walkway on the far right to reach the music below. Walking down the purple carpet gave way to neon red as the windows were left behind above to be replaced by solid walls, a myriad of pubs and clubs lining both sides as far as the eye could see, whereas the leftward sweeping bend of the station hid still others out of sight ahead. Almost immediately, Aidin had to fight his way down the walkway into the writhing crowd, thousands cramped into the narrow corridor, fighting for space and air—all pushing in different directions as the music pounded overhead. Above, people had looked at Aidin, and he'd seen them out of the corner of his eye; a bit of a celebrity wherever he went, he was usually secretly pleased about it, but not this time. The word of the *Rheinvar* was out, and he just wanted to melt away from it. Between the walls, thirty feet of floor space bustled with weary traders, travellers, and merchants. Prostitutes, fugitives, and underworld factions added to the melee that was usually avoided by Aidin, but right now he felt as guilty as them. Fighting his way through the throng, he noticed voices straining to be heard as each bar's music fought for dominance over the others. Faces became visible for a second, only to slide away into the neon red like those behind them as here and there shady deals went on between groups huddled against corridor walls. Bright neons flashed on each side, bars' facades vying for attention against their red surroundings. Aidin, clutching his pockets, moved deeper inside. Passing each bar, Aidin felt thumping music with the accompanying din of voices flood through and into the corridor only to fade behind subsequent bars in front of him that took their turn to assault his senses. In his frame of mind, each one was less appealing than the last… neon purples, greens, and blues all fighting their way out into the red corridor with drunken people under their light.

He'd come so far down now, struggling through so many people while being buffeted and bumped in the stifling atmosphere all the while, air getting harder to breathe as irritation grew with angered, drunken mobs colliding as they passed. The thought of turning round and trying to push all the way back through the space was too much; it had been a quarter mile, at least, and each bar was as loud as the last with the ever-present ticket touts trying to pull him in as he passed. He was about to give up when something happened as he passed the translucent blue on his left—there was no sound! It was the best advertisement Aidin could think of as he pushed left through the last few stragglers of the crowd and in through the door. Arriving inside, the relief he felt was instant; the sense of the assaulting music outside was left behind and Aidin was only too glad when the door shut, almost snuffing out the sounds completely. There was music here, soft jazz, but it wasn't loud… it was just here, quiet, non-intrusive, and it didn't seem to attract many customers. The place was perfect. Dark, too, darker than the corridor, with a translucent blue bar beckoning in the distance with its light centring on the bar, only barely reaching Aidin and filtering out other spaces, leaving both sides of the room serenely hidden. Slowly approaching the bar, Aidin made out chairs and tables on each side through the darkness, with occasional silhouettes of people sitting quietly—soft jazz for company.

Arriving at the bar, Aidin glanced over the gantry at countless bottles of alcohol, all of them a translucent blue under the lights. Here and there, individuals sat anonymously around the bar while, to his right, a break with tradition saw a customer chatting to the barmaid.

Not wanting to interrupt, Aidin felt content to wait, listening to the music and undisturbed by its softness as he took a seat at the bar. Relaxing in the calm, Aidin slowly became aware of a red tinge emanating from the darkness behind the gantry and to its left, his eyes becoming accustomed to the bar's light.

"See anything you like?" came a purr.

The voice made Aidin start; he hadn't noticed the barmaid approach. Standing in front of him, he saw that the lights gave a blue sheen through her long brunette hair, her striking looks throwing him for a moment. "Em, harelin… light, no ren," he managed, gathering himself as the barmaid turned for the drink while smiling at her effect on him. Her back turned to him, Aidin smiled, too, sheepishly at her influence on him. A moment of weakness, he thought, since he was old enough to be her father.

"Here you go," she said, coming back with the drink and still smiling, obviously pleased with herself. "That's 28."

28 credits, thought Aidin as he handed over his mat card; this might have become the number-one station for shore leave, but you certainly paid for it. Taking a sip while the barmaid ran his card, Aidin revelled in the sharp spirit. He hadn't tasted real alcohol in months, the taste so striking against the synthetic imitation aboard ship.

"There you go," purred the barmaid, still smiling as she handed back his card. "Will there be anything else?"

"Thank you, no," replied Aidin, feigning a smile but becoming irritated by her smugness, and taking heart in the running of the station as she moved back to her conversation, hips swaying for all the attention she could gather. Aidin smiled after her just as smugly as he let his gaze drift back to the bar, realising she was just eye candy—like most of the women on the station, she was simply here for male enjoyment. The feminist committees a decade back had petitioned the Alliance time after time over what they saw as exploitation of their fellow women. The captain of 185 had been worse than Darrant, Aidin thought, smiling quietly to himself. Every high-ranking official, from admirals to generals and attaches to ambassadors, had sampled the delights of this place at one time or another, with the head runner here a certain Captain Seamus Lafferty. He had so many connections, he could almost run the Alliance single-handed. That, though, wasn't his style; an Irishman of good standing, he'd found times of grace around himself his true calling in life, and it was enviable. The feminists had pressured Alliance officials to assemble committee after committee to look into what they called immoral exploitation of womanhood, but every time the committees had come, it had been the same. Seamus knew most of the members anyway, and any he didn't were soon singing his praises all the way back to Alliance Command once he'd…. well, shown them around his little station for a week.

Aidin laughed to himself a little as he attracted the barmaid's attention for another drink, feeling less like the one being used for attention as she swiped his card.

"Is that everything?" She smiled, handing it back.

"Yes, thanks," Aidin replied, taking the card and then continuing in the same breath, "Could you tell me what that is back there?" he asked, motioning toward the red glow with his head.

The barmaid followed his gaze. "You mean the

down club?" she asked, turning back to him. "Oh, it's a little club we have here—another bar and music; the atmosphere's a little heavier."

"Thanks," said Aidin, the mystery solved.

"Sure." The barmaid smiled, walking back to her conversation with an air that was beginning to get to him.

He enjoyed his drink, taking every sip like it was his last with the calm, anonymous atmosphere soothing his mind. It stayed that way for the next couple of drinks, gradually, though, with the onset of euphoria, Seamus' little place began to get to him. He'd stopped asking himself about the *Rheinvar*, if he could have done anything differently and so on; no one else cared about things like that here, so why should he? His curiosity over the red glow further back steadily grew, too, and with his eyes being caught drifting to the barmaid's figure again, he decided this quiet venture had yielded all it could. Rising up, he caught the barmaid's glance—unhappy at the loss of attention, and with Aidin now smiling smugly. Her bar trap was not his own.

Disappearing into the darkness, the gentle companionship offered by soft jazz began to receive competition as Aidin passed through a gap in the thick curtain wall. Darkness turned to reds as he went, music meeting him the second he was through. It was more upbeat, but he was feeling that now, and the people filing past with women or wine didn't bother him anymore. Indeed, moments later, led by a trail of perfume and laughter, he found himself moving off to the left of the curtain and going deeper into the club, eventually sitting among the laughter in the middle of a large seating area. Alone at his table, he wasn't noticed as people near him vied for attention, camouflaging his presence with their drunken mirth leaving him free to take in his surroundings. His veiled entrance now hidden in folds of curtain thirty yards behind him and somewhere to the right left him in the middle of a throng of tables. Aidin's gaze right was met by darkness as the deep red of the club's lights failed to push all the way back to what he assumed was a wall. Behind him, beyond a ten-yard gap, another hive of tables could be seen, some twenty yards across like his own seating area, and there sounded out more drunken laughter from the seating curving round right to the far end. Looking left, Aidin was met by a huge bar some ten yards off, which ran the length of his seating area and past the gap, and on parallel with the next seating area behind him; it was staffed by tens of scantily clad barmaids who were made even more alluring by the deep red lighting over the bar. The bar's length was one thing, but the breadth wasn't far off it, a central island in its middle housing the gantry in a huge, rectangular column that was see-through in the centre with the bottles and their optics held on by crystal mountings. As barmaids moved back and forth among them, Aidin caught glimpses through the gaps in the gantry of what looked like a huge dance floor beyond it, seeing it through the people standing at the other side of the bar. It was hard to tell from where he sat, but the dance floor seemed to be forty yards long, running the full width of the club with a raised stage area with four half-naked women dancing suggestively as a band played behind them. The dancing people on the floor, the band, and the people near the bar contrasted darkly against the deep reds of the club, giving the impression of sleaze and debauchery. Aidin laughed to himself, out loud but unheard in the noise of the club. No wonder

Darrant wasn't allowed to come here anymore if this was what the barmaid next door called a little heavier; the other clubs must be downright orgies.

Smiling as he enjoyed his drink, Aidin watched as men chased after women and vice versa, making him wish he was ten years younger. If only he didn't have his reputation to think of in the Alliance; still, maybe he didn't... who would ever know, he thought, as he'd come in down the corridor from the galleria outside and been here for an hour, and still not seen a face he knew. His own crew were in here or places like it next door, and he'd not seen hide nor hair of them, either, so who would know? He laughed again. Still enjoying his drink, looking out over the scene, conversation at the table on his left began to catch his attention; it stood out out among the laughter around him because it had none... just serious faces that were unhappy over something.

"What do you mean they said no?" Brice asked in disbelief, the dark shadows of red glancing round him in the pounding, curtain-walled club.

"They said his injuries weren't serious enough to warrant discharge, that the insurance wouldn't cover him or his family," replied Fuller, unaware that a starship captain was listening on his right.

"Not serious enough!" Brice retorted, his nerves fraying as usual and not helped by his drinking. "The man's chest's held together by threads! When does insurance cover you, when your head comes off?"

"Heh, Brice, come on, man!" Fuller responded, making a face at his insensitivity with Rians and the rest of the unit sitting around the table.

"I'm sorry, brother," said Brice, taking Fuller's lead

and apologising to Rians. "It's just wrong, man, it's all wrong."

"Yeah," replied Rians. "They could have done much worse, though."

"Tried to!" Fuller put in. "That fucking Etrick," he said, shaking his head.

"Trial was tough, huh?" Carson asked, imagining what it had been like.

"Yeah," replied Fuller, sighing. "You're lucky you were delayed and didn't get here a couple of days sooner or you would have watched him and Ritter try and fry us." A silence ensued as Fuller thought how lucky they'd been, and then, noticing the mood descending quickly, he changed the subject. "Anyway! We can bother about that later—we're not shipping out for two days, so let's enjoy 'em!" he laughed.

"Yeah, like you haven't already been enjoying them before we arrived!" Carson accused as the table laughed on.

"When in Rome!" Fuller defended himself to the sound of more laughter.

"Have you seen the sweets walkin' around here?" Carson asked, looking over and surveying the bar.

"Yeah, you better have a good look," returned Fulkes. "With your lines, that's as close as you're gonna get!"

Brice choked on his drink as he watched Carson's head spin back to meet Fulkes.

"Aha, is that right?" retorted Carson. "Is this the same grinnin' fool who got flung out of a whorehouse on Spanis?"

"Yeah, but at least I got some!" Fulkes laughed back with the table's support.

"Yeah, cause she probably didn't feel you slippin' in, little man," Carson retorted, the weight of the laughter getting to him.

"Now, play nice now," laughed Fuller at their latest display. "Out here, we're all gonna get some, right?" he suggested, raising his glass.

"Damn straight!" replied Brice, raising his glass with the others.

"Fulkes, isn't it about time you got them in?" asked Fuller, talking about the drinks.

"Sure, Cap!" Fulkes smiled, getting up for the bar. "Don't worry, Carson," he said over his shoulder as he went. "I'm sure there'll be some blind desperate around here somewhere!"

Carson glared after him as he turned away, narrowly missing someone before making for the bar.

"Smartass little pri—" started Carson as Fulkes left.

"Heh, you two'll have plenty of time to argue later. Let's just enjoy this place while we can, huh?" Fuller cut in, receiving a reluctant nod from Carson that ended the other man's comments. "Yeah, and you'll have no time for arguing soon; just wait till you taste some!" continued Fuller, the table laughing on.

Aidin began to lose interest as the table next to him stopped talking shop and reverted to the pleasures of 185 like all of the other conversations around him; instead, his attention drifted to the stage as the scene became more enticing, the dancers professionals at attracting attention. He was at peace finally—maybe it was the drinks and maybe it was the anonymity of his surroundings, but he didn't care. This was the first time since the pod that he'd felt rest from the guilt and responsibility. It was ironic that, in such noise, he could find peace. It was great, too, but it wasn't to last.

Words from the table on his left began to filter through again, as one of its members, Fulkes, had begun chatting to a woman occupying the table near him.

"So, you come all the way out here to this place and he just leaves you sittin' alone? Now, that's not right—he obviously doesn't know what he's got in a fine woman like you. He…" rolled on a well-practised Fulkes.

His words were getting through, but annoyingly so, breaking Aidin's peace as he tried to concentrate on what was going on across the stage even against the flirting continuing beside him.

"Ah, you should kick him into touch, or better yet, leave him behind—he obviously doesn't know how to party, and a good looking woman like you should be having fun, shouldn't you?" Fulkes continued his rant, returning the smiles from his amused quarry and not noticing a large figure appearing to his right, returning with friends from the bar. "He don't sound too good for you," continued Fulkes to the woman, not realising her missing boyfriend now stood at six-foot-four beside him, listening. "What kind of a dick leaves his woman all—"

"A dick!" roared a voice above Fulkes, making him start. Aidin, too, was jarred from his trance by the burst of aggression. "The only dick around here is you! How about I pull you outta that seat and we'll see who's a dick?"

"Well, look," began Fulkes, relaxing in his seat and calmly regaining his composure as he turned back to the woman. "All that outward aggression is obviously hiding something, making up for some shortfall in other areas."

Fulkes smiled, now turning back to the boyfriend. "Anything you wanna tell us, champ? You know, there's operations that can help little guys like you…"

Fulkes never got to finish as the boozed-up hands dropped their drinks to the floor, closing on his shirt and hauling him clear out of his seat. "You're gonna need more than an operation, you little prick!!!"

Picking up Fulkes, though, only served to make it easier for him to drive his foot into the man's groin. Pain came through the boyfriend's roar as he winced, legs almost buckling as he smashed Fulkes with a right hand, sending drinks flying with his crash into the table behind him. With him lying among the glass and broken table, exclamations came from its former occupants who were now standing above him. Aidin listened as they were quickly answered in Fulkes' usual style, sparking another brawl as Fuller and the rest became busy with the boyfriend and his entourage that was now crashing through tables of their own.

Fulkes' mouth had gotten him in trouble; despite his size, though, his training stood him well as he fought off three different men, but with a fourth and fifth, he was soon overwhelmed. Bruised and bloody, he hung on well, but with no help coming, his injuries mounted and his smart comments ceased under the weight of numbers. Outnumbered and fading, he seemed resigned to the infirmary when suddenly another fist entered the fray. Two more brawlers fell into tables behind him, sparking more fights as the fresh pair of arms broke in on Fulkes' side. Between exchanges of blows, Fulkes caught sight of his help, which was wearing a captain's uniform. Fulkes had no idea he'd been fighting alongside the head of the IAF flagship… Aidin.

Aidin had always been for the underdog, and watching the unfair match-up, he hadn't been able to stand by and let them gang up on him, whoever he was; the trouble was, the place had erupted. Music was drowned out as glasses flew, smashing among shouts and cries with the club degenerating into a wrestling ring, drunken servicemen and vagrants alike kicking and punching through one another like sworn enemies. Minutes passed with no let-up, staff fleeing as the bar was smashed to bits, the club in near darkness and only the translucent blue from the adjoining bar offering any light through the curtain wall. With no end in sight, people blindly punched anyone in the darkness, the violence threatening to spread out to the adjoining corridor when suddenly high-pitched noises accompanied by brief red flashes began.

Not noticing at first, the noise suddenly came in Aidin's direction along with the searing sensation of heat from inside his body. Almost going down, he knew it was a del 10. Managing to glance over at the curtain wall, he saw a row of dark figures now standing between them and the translucent blue of next door. He'd thought he was immune, thinking that because of who he was, but in the dark, the station security couldn't see a rank or face; they just fired at everyone. Faces of pain emerged in the darkness among the bright flashes, inexperience telling as they went down from their first hits. Egos were saved from their fall, the light fading from each strike with faces hidden before they crashed to the ground. Aidin could feel the thumps through the floor as bodies fell near him, and he tried to walk to the guards, but they weren't interested. Suddenly, another searing pain from inside joined semi-blindness as he went down with the ranks below, silently passing out on his way down.

Chapter 14

Old Friends

Reluctantly, the security chief glared at Aidin through the tenwork grade glass, round proof virtually bomb proof with its mixture of tensile strength enhancing elements and the sand super-cooled in manufacturing, which made it virtually impregnable… but it couldn't stop his stare.

The intercom channels opened in the cell the voice leaving Aidin confused as his first officer had already been down and was off somewhere on station 185 busy in the process of arranging his release, could he have been that quick?

"Hello?"

The voice was familiar, but the transmission was bad.

"Hello, Aidin. Hello."

Then, suddenly it dawned—"Darrant!" Aidin uttered,moving to stare at the panel on the wall. "How'd you get through here?" was all he could manage stunned at how Darrant had managed to arrange communication from his station all the way to station 185 and down through the security to his cell wall.

"Well, I used to run that little station, remember? Seamus and I go way back; if I could, I'd introduce you to him, but that's not why I called." Darrant seemed uneasy, as if he had something troubling to tell him.

"Is everything alright?" asked Aidin.

Darrant paused, and then sighed. "I couldn't stop them. You know how they just come in and take over;

there's nothing you can do."

It was guilt he was seeing, but guilt for nothing, Aidin thought, after what they'd done to him. Aidin could never figure out why Darrant never let these debriefings of enemy troops go on onboard his station, or why he cared, but a lecture wasn't what he wanted.

"What about our guest?" Aidin asked.

"Our guest," repeated Darrant, a feigned laugh barely disguising his discomfort at the subject. "IN6 left two days ago, and from what I hear… well, there's not much left."

"They got what they wanted, then?" Aidin asked.

"I don't think so," Darrant replied. "Our Mr Hack says they weren't exactly jumping for joy when they left; perhaps…" Darrant sighed. "Perhaps that explains the Vrail's condition."

"You haven't seen him?" Aidin had sounded surprised.

"No, Hack explained—." began Darrant despondently, his mind elsewhere.

"You know he might be able to help, Darrant."

"Help us!" Darrant laughed. "After what we've done to him."

"None of this makes any sense to anyone in Alliance Command; every time we try and guess where they'll strike next, we end up way south of the mark and people die," Aidin said seriously.

"And he's gonna help us figure it all out just out of the kindness of his heart." Darrant laughed again, half hiding his discomfort with the word heart being associated with a Vrail ridiculous.

"I know you don't like it, Darrant," replied Aidin, "but if you glean even the slightest hint about what's going on out there, it would save a lot of official letters going to families, you know."

There was a long pause, and then Darrant replied reluctantly, "Yeah, I know, but he's not gonna help us."

"No," agreed Aidin. "Not willingly."

"What do you mean?" Darrant asked.

"We could trick him," answered Aidin.

"Trick a Vrail?" voiced Darrant. "What did they give you in that infirmary?"

"Look," Aidin said, brushing aside Darrant's sarcasm. "You know how they love to brag about how superior they are; maybe news of 196 being destroyed will fill him with pride, and he might even brag about who this amazing commander is. After all, force didn't work on him, did it?"

Another pause came as Darrant held back over the last statement, barely answering. "No, it didn't."

"Look, Darrant, I know it's tough for you, but it could make all the difference to a lot of men out there—men with families, you know, but do what you think is right. Contact me if you come up with anything. We're headed to Aurin 2, and I'll check with you as soon as I can," Aidin said, making a gesture that he was signing off.

"Yeah," replied Darrant half-heartedly as he flicked off the channels.

Slumping back into his chair, he thought about it. If it worked and they tricked the Vrail into naming names, it might help second-guess whoever was out there. *Huh*, Darrant thought, *trick a Vrail*. Right. He'd know what they wanted before they'd even sat down, and there was another problem… he'd have to see him.

Sighing, he stared out of the window in his office,

watching the stars twinkling brightly outside; it was quite a distraction, his office only dimly lit—almost dark and silent, oh so silent. He'd gotten used to it like this, and it made him feel safe; during the war, he'd been captured during a botched raid on a Hearack weapons plant. Taken to a secure facility, he'd spent almost nine months there with… with the others; he could still hear them screaming, day and night—screams had echoed through that place. The clunk of steel doors being opened, the scuffle as another was dragged out, and then… then, the screaming. He could still see it all: the machines, the instruments, and the blood. It had been random, too; they'd look through the bars into the dark inside and just pick someone—sometimes they wouldn't even ask any questions. The only thing you could do was sit quietly, still in the darkness, hoping their eye would pass over you… till the next time.

Darrant shrugged off the memories before they got too deep, too painful; he didn't like what had happened, and he'd let the same thing happen on his station. He felt bad, really bad; was it because he could have prevented it? Was it because he should have tried? How could he face the Vrail after letting that happen? Darrant's breathing was shallow, uneasy as he sat alone in the gloom, his thoughts drifting to all those who had never come out of there. He had to face him, he thought; if he didn't, more of their boys would go to these places, and he'd have to live with that.

It was a long walk for Darrant and his team to where the Vrail was being held…

"Ah!" half-gasped the dying Vrail at Darrant's

entry. "Come to see your superiors' good work."

Darrant stepped inside with Mr Hack and Da Vahr, the door closing behind him on two stone-faced security officers outside. The Vrail sat on the left of the long elliptical table, a little off-centre at the far end and clearly suffering, his body shaking in the bright light of the room as he gazed vacantly out the oval-shaped window behind the table. Darrant had decided to show no feeling, no mercy of any kind, as he walked purposefully down the right-hand side of the table. Stepping quietly over warm, tan carpeting flanked by varnished wooden walls on each side, indentations housing small ornamentations, he tried to appear strong, unfazed by the Vrail's suffering in case the prisoner was watching as he passed on the opposite side of the table... and he was.

The interrogation had already begun, but not the Vrail's—Darrant's. Shaking and pathetic, the Vrail's attention seemed to be lost on the two carpeted steps leading up to the plush landing in front of the window, the wooden walls giving way to soft cream at the steps and arcing round to meet the window. But it wasn't. His eyes facing the window took no notice of the stars, themselves masters of interrogation—his clear, yellow-tinged and ice-like eyes were gathering every facet of Darrant's face. Every muscle change, colour, bead of sweat, and pupil dilation... even the way he walked; all were monitored constantly with the Vrail looking for a weakness, for a way in. Darrant hadn't even sat down, and he'd found it.

Try as he might, it had slipped out.

The Vrail saw the expression of pity in his eyes, if only for a second, and it was enough. Now he could manoeuvre—he had an oar to grind a way forward to gain control, and that, of course, was what it was all about. In Darrant's thinking, it was common decency, humanity, but in the Vrail's, it was stupidity brought on by weakness of mind, and it had lost Darrant the interrogation before he'd even started.

Taking the head of the table with the oval window now behind him, Darrant pulled his seat in, splitting reports and schedules in front of himself while still trying to appear indifferent to the suffering one sitting on his right. On his left his team sat down facing the Vrail, Hack fared better, with interrogation being almost a daily occurrence to him; he was unshaken when taking his seat leaving Da Vahr taking the next seat down in from Hack, leaving him directly opposite the Vrail. Darrant continued shuffling reports as the sound of moving seats subsided, leaving an awkward silence. Darrant tried to figure out the coldest expression for his opening, but it wasn't in his nature; his own past suffering had left him tired as memories, of the weapons plant came flooding back, and he tried to hide it in the shuffling, but....

"It's alright, Captain," said the Vrail quietly, his gaze seemingly still fixed outside. "It's alright to be uncomfortable, to feel pity... isn't that regarded as a strength in your society?" he continued, already trying to steer proceedings.

"Not in mine, it's not," answered Da Vahr sharply from the other side of the table, with a stare still encompassing that ever-present smile but not friendly; this time, it was evil.

"Hmmm," the Vrail murmured, almost laughing as he struggled. "A Valraich."

"Yes," confirmed Da Vahr, his grey paste-like skin almost matching the Vrail's.

"I suppose this doesn't affect you, as your race is more than comfortable with proceedings such as these," continued the Vrail.

"More than comfortable," agreed Da Vahr, leaning toward the table, his enthusiasm sickening Darrant.

"Gentlemen," began Darrant, "let's not fall back on petty squabbles. We have a lot to get through."

"In that case may, I request the lights be lowered? I'd find it much easier to concentrate without them," the Vrail requested.

"No," came a sharp answer from Hack, used to interrogation and realising immediately that the Vrail was trying to lead them in his own direction.

"Oh, I'm sorry," apologised the Vrail. "I thought you were in charge here."

"Rather a pathetic attempt to begin a rift between us, is it not?" answered Da Vahr, recognising what he was trying to do.

"Hmph!" laughed the Vrail. "You Valraiches, I suppose, would notice pathetic manipulation; you've built an empire on it." Suddenly, the Vrail broke into a coughing fit brought on by the laugh, clearly in pain with blood spurting from his mouth suddenly and running down the left side of his face and out of sight as he began convulsing, struggling for air with his nerves fighting for control.

"I would have thought by now that you'd realised that pity wasn't a commodity found in abundance here for you," countered a wide-eyed Da Vahr, clearly amused by the suffering before him.

"A Valraich, and your head of security," muttered the Vrail as he wheezed for breath, knowing he didn't have to say anymore, that his belief in Darrant's ability to interrogate was clearly stated in his appraisal of the help he'd brought.

"You see a lot for someone looking out of a window," said Darrant, irritated at the Vrail's swipe.

The Vrail turned his eyes lazily to meet his and began moving, turning around in his seat and revealing a bloodbath behind him. The whole right-hand side of his neck and head was awash with tissue and blood, fresh, the tan seating almost black with dead leakage and his right arm hanging hopelessly to his side. "Is that better?" struggled the Vrail, easily reading Darrant's shock—his attempts to hide it useless. "I'm afraid all the suffering has already been inflicted by your superiors," the Vrail crowed.

"Oh, but we can always find some more," Da Vahr assured him.

And so it went on, two hours of their best efforts, with the Vrail swatting them away each time like he was dealing with amateurs.

The Vrail smiled after Da Vahr as he followed Hack out, Da Vahr not hiding the fact that he was upset at not being able to intensify the questioning. Darrant didn't even bother looking back—what was the point? The Vrail felt him to be the most ridiculous of the trio anyway, and that had shown all the way through, with the interrogation turning into nothing more than a blunting of egos.

"You weren't able to find him, were you?" asked the Vrail just before the door closed.

Darrant stopped in the doorway, looking back. "What?"

"I said, you weren't able to find him, were you?" the Vrail repeated, struggling in pain and looking out the window again. "He seems to know exactly how to avoid you, as if he knows your patterns well." The Vrail coughed, shifting in the chair. "If he knows how to avoid you so well, and his attacks were along a path two parsecs from 196, I wonder why he would risk coming all that way, why he would risk such detection."

Darrant grimaced in the doorway, his patience for games gone and saying nothing.

"It was so foolish of their commander to run those risks, so pointless... useless... unless...." the Vrail struggled visibly, turning quiet for breath.

"Unless what!" demanded Darrant finally, with no sympathy for his struggles.

"Unless he had a score to settle...." came the Vrail's response as he turned to meet Darrant with an evil look, watching his expression betray a frightening realisation at his words. "That wasn't such a long interrogation after all, was it?"

Darrant didn't answer, the door sealing behind him with no instruction given to the guards outside as he barged into people while making his way to ops, moving faster as his mind became coated in fear at the thought accosting him.

Chapter 15

Risen

Looking outward, Aidin was stopped by the hum of the force field, hearing what was going on, but it was clear that the head of security was upset with the station commander's news. From his position on one of the matt grey benches lining the wall, Aidin looked across the breadth of the grey-floored, rectangular cell with the others as punishing white lights bore down. To the uninitiated, it would have seemed that they could all just walk out into the corridor before them, through the open space in front, but the light blue line running the length of the floor and the walls around it hinted otherwise.

Aidin watched the outside as the head of security gave increasingly frustrated exchanges to a terminal against the right wall, twenty yards down the grey corridor and just past two more seemingly open spaces on each side, their own blue lines vibrating brightly. The exchange seemed to reach its peak as the security head became exasperated, trapped between his authority being challenged and his respect for the station commander. The cramped cell remained in still silence as all eyes watched the drama in front of them, unable to hear for the hum of their cell—everything being clear just the same from the body language. The meeting reaching its climax, the station commander on the screen threw his arms aside, the head of security's head falling in a grimace. The grimace was quickly joined by frustration, the loss of control telling as he took the blow, trying to hide his expression over the station commander's words.

Try as he might to hide it from his celled guests, the reason for his frustration became clear as they read the station commander's lips onscreen through the forcefields. "We need everyone we can get…" They were to be released.

Another warren of tunnels came. He was getting sick of looking at them, these stations all being alike. How did Darrant stand it? he wondered, and then he quickly checked himself, thinking of the wounded and those worse, without the luxury of being wounded. He didn't even have time to freshen up; while half of those who'd been in the holding cells went straight back to the clubs, the other half had had enough and crammed into maglifts, limping back to their quarters—Aidin among them, though he wasn't to make it.

Exiting on E level and moving three corridors over, he passed through the grey and neon blue only to turn a corner and find two security officers waiting at his door, their pristine black uniforms contrasting with his own, torn and stained—all but a burned ruin after the securities crowd control efforts in the club. No rest… after a short dispute, Aidin tired and, running out of enthusiasm for the drama, gave in to the station commander's insistence and was escorted by his dogs all the way back up to the galleria and on to the executive maglift.

Exiting the mag on the main bridge, he found that this one was just a copy of Darrant's station and the late 196; they were all the same, like they'd been moulded in a factory with even the same iron grating walkway running from the maglift to the stairs and up to the commander's office. Motioned forward by the security, Aidin passed behind the con station on his right and then the defence station as he looked down into the docking control pit; the communication and navigation panels were busily directing shipping. Leaving the walkway, their metal-sounding footsteps were replaced by soft thuds as they made their way up the several grey-carpeted steps to the similarly coloured doors that broke apart at their approach.

Captain Seamus Lafferty started from behind his desk on the far side of the room, his expression evident even ten yards away from them. "Well, come on in—don't just stand there, man," Seamus said, his Irish accent almost a song to Aidin, who wasn't used to the sound. "Thank you, lads, that'll be all." He motioned to the security, who nodded and promptly disappeared, the doors appearing from the hull and sealing behind them. "Bloody doors," grumbled Seamus. "You'd think with the price of these bloody stations that they could have put a bell or window on them so you could see people coming. I just don't know…."

Aidin moved slowly toward the seat on the other side and to the left of Seamus' desk, tired but still taking in the office and comparing it to Darrant's, searching for any remote difference. There was the large oval window behind the commander's desk, the same black marble desk and grey seating matching the grey wall to wall carpeting, and extra seating on either side of the room, all of ten yards across. The same small black marble tables were here for conferencing, but they were all to one side, as if unused; Seamus must do his conferencing elsewhere. Aidin almost laughed at the similarities. Of course, there were the ferns, dotted around the office in corners and with smaller ones on the tables; it was the IAF's attempt at staving off the drab cost-cutting interiors, as they did bring a little civility. The only thing different here was the light being much brighter than that found in Darrant's office—Aidin had never understood why he kept it so low. The office was the same, Aidin thought, almost disappointed—the same, save for a large standing item that looked like an elegantly sealed bookcase on the left of the window against the wall.

"Ah!" Seamus exclaimed, catching his gaze as Aidin sat down. "My ornamentation," he said, rising from his seat and blocking Aidin's view as he opened the bookcase. "I've always said these bloody rooms need some lighting up."

Aidin was a little confused, but the man's meaning was soon clear as Aidin heard ice chinking into glasses, his discovery that the bookcase was a drinks cabinet confirmed when it came into view as Seamus left it open, moving back to his seat ferrying a bottle of Harelin light. Aidin's brief look at the elegant glasses held in the cabinet with fine spirits and wines was interrupted when Seamus sat down, placing the bottle and glasses gently on the left of the table before getting comfortable and pouring. Aidin squinted suspiciously at the bottle of Harelin. How did he…

"Security footage," said Seamus, answering the question on Aidin's face. "Not bad in the bar," he said, smiling and putting one of the glasses in front of Aidin before pouring his own. "Took two Del hits to put you down," he said, laughing. "Who says you can't handle it when you're old?" he continued, laughing aloud again.

Aidin looked at the Harelin in his hand, uneasy at drinking it but not wanting to offend Seamus.

"Ah, laddy, don't worry now," Seamus assured him. "You're not on duty and I'm up to my eyeballs in alcohol suppressants, so let's join the rest of this place. Why should all them bastards underneath us do all the sinnin', eh?"

Accepting the glass, Aidin began, "Why have—"

"Why have I asked you here?" Seamus interrupted him.

"Yes, why have you asked me here, Captain Lafferty?"

"Oh, call me Seamus, please, I've never been one for all that official nonsense," he replied, sipping the Harelin. "It's not me that's hauled you in here in half a uniform, laddy, it's Alliance Command. They have a little job for you—a sensitive one."

"A sensitive one?" Aidin echoed.

"Yes," replied Seamus. "That's why I asked you to come here, so I could tell you personally and hand you the orders myself; it's a bit of a rescue mission, you see, and I didn't want to tell you over the intercom or risk anyone seeing the orders if I sent them to you."

"Security seems to be a problem on these stations," Aidin remarked.

"What?" Seamus questioned him.

"Oh, it's nothing," Aidin assured him, realising he'd spoken out loud. "I've just heard of station commanders being reluctant to use their intercoms, that's all."

"Aye, the smart ones," replied Seamus with a wry smile as he raised a glass. "Anyway," he continued, "you know the Alliance is stretched far and wide trying to find the bloody Hearack?"

"Yes, I've heard," Aidin replied.

"Aye, but maybe you've not heard how badly," said Seamus, leaning over the table and lowering his voice as if someone might hear them.

"What do you mean?" Aidin asked.

"You were in that pod for a while, lad, so let me bring you up to speed," answered Seamus, still quietly. "We can't find them, the Hearack, and it doesn't make any sense. They're not working along any discernible route toward any objective we can see. They just seem to be attacking at random, going after weak outposts which are poorly defended... strategically useless colonies. That's why they're so difficult to find. As soon as we surround one system and establish perimeters, they appear again in another, attacking weak, useless targets I tell you, they're dragging us to the very limits of the Valraich and Irachan borders.

"They're pulling our fleet away from the Alliance interior," Aidin remarked, knowing the conclusion was obvious.

"Aye, that they are," Seamus agreed. "But we don't know why a fleet big enough to take on an Alliance station isn't doing some serious damage to the IAF interior. Wasting resources and time on the outskirts makes no sense, especially with them coming in already for Station 196—why didn't they keep going? Why pull back after that?"

"Are there any reports of any trouble elsewhere?" Aidin asked.

"No, nothing," Seamus answered. "Everything is normal in the Alliance; it's bloody quiet, as usual, and been that way for months apart from Maires Drift."

"We've only known about those two cloaked ships they have and the increased fleet size for a few weeks, since the last communications from 196," Aidin mused. "Maybe they've been attacking light targets to keep us busy, to stop searches for their construction facilities;

maybe they didn't have the strength before…."

"Well, we know they have it now," Seamus cut in. "But they're still not using it and we know they're not cowards. In the war, if they were cornered, if it was over, they'd attack the nearest thing and go out in a blaze of glory; for the Dren, that means… well, you've seen it, right?" He motioned to Aidin. "Ever since that bloody wormhole collapsed, we've had fewer and fewer sporadic attacks on innocents—the last gasps of a group of murderous bastards hell-bent on doing as much damage as possible before we get a grip of them."

"But that's not happening now?" Aidin questioned, prying for what the other man knew.

"No," replied Seamus, pausing. "We haven't had any sporadic attacks since 196 went up three weeks ago." Seamus looked at Aidin in deadly seriousness. "No more wasted ammo; no more wasted time. Only that bloody phantom fleet out there—it keeps turning up just out of reach, and all we can do is chase after the distress calls, but by the time we get there, they're gone. So far, you could fit all the survivors we've found in this room."

"Survivors?" Aidin asked, surprised.

"Yes," Seamus said quietly. "I hear they're quarantined, put in stasis, and then… then, nobody knows what happens to them or where they go."

"I haven't heard any of this—how did you?" Aidin asked.

"I heard," returned Seamus, a stonewalling look on his face.

"When the attacks were sporadic, did you ever hear of any survivors without a starship getting there in time?" Aidin queried.

"No," Seamus replied. "And I never heard of any

accounts of them being scared off by approaching ships, either, if they thought like they had nothing to lose in a battle, if they thought they were beaten, they'd go on killing on outposts right up until ships arrived and destroyed them.

"But they're not doing that now?" Aidin asked.

"No, they're not," replied Seamus.

"Then, that means…."

"That means they think they can win!" Seamus broke in loudly, frustrated.

"The two cloaked ships, the increased fighters, they must have shipyards, facilities again; they must have—" Aidin was cut off again.

"I tell ya, they don't!" Seamus argued, frustrated and taking his head in his hands, then taking a breath and looking Aidin straight in the eye, beginning again quietly. "I tell ya, lad, they don't. Not the Ferancs Array; not the Shairin; not ships and not sensors and not bloody spies or smugglers—none of them have seen or heard a thing for months. There's been no build-up, no facilities adopted, and that means…" Seamus paused, Aidin's look requesting an answer. "That means they're not building them in Alliance space, and since any of the other factions would destroy them as soon as look at them, that means one of them is sheltering them, helping them."

"Is there any indication which?" Aidin was cut off again by Seamus's lack of patience.

"No, no, but suspicions abound from Alliance Command—conversations I've had, you know, with high-ranking friends who pass through on occasion; they're worried, Aidin," Seamus said, taking a sip of his drink. "Worried," he repeated, as if for emphasis.

"Who do they think it is?" asked Aidin, adopting a quiet tone like Seamus' at the seriousness of his question.

Seamus paused, looking away and gathering himself before glancing back. "The Valraich."

"It can't be!" Aidin returned, nevertheless remembering how, at the start of the war, they'd helped the Hearack... but switched sides partway through after pressure from the other factions. "They wouldn't. The Irachans wouldn't wait this time; there'd be no words." Aidin was referring to the near miss experienced when the factions' unity against the Dren had almost disintegrated, the Irachans already having had an inherent hatred of the Valraiches and almost taking matters into their own hands. "No delegation would stop them if they got wind of it; they'd sweep through Valraich space like it was the 22nd century, and all the factions would be destabilised. We'd all end up at war."

Seamus nodded his agreement. "I know, but you know as well as anyone what Valraich are like... if they think there's the smallest chance of gaining a better foothold among the factions, they'll shack up with anyone." Seamus grimaced. "It all adds up, don't you see? They're attacking all along the Irachan border, as far away from Valraich territory as possible—like you said, drawing our strength further away from our centre. At the same time, we mass more and more ships along the border looking for that fleet, it prompts a response from the Irachans on the other side to match our build-up... it's becoming a bloody powder keg, Aidin. just a spark that's all it will take, a spark."

"Then they could be trying to start a war with us first, to weaken us perhaps," Aidin voiced.

"Maybe," answered Seamus. "Every time you study

it with the ship assignments and concentrations, you come up with all kinds of scenarios."

"Has there been any contact with the Valraich Committee?" Aidin asked.

"And if the Irachans intercepted such contact, with our ships along their border?" Seamus posed clearly. "In the meantime, every crew and ship is either hunting down that Hearack fleet or on patrol—we've never been spread so thin. All non-essential personnel and settlements are being pulled back deeper into Alliance space in an attempt to limit the attacks on far-off outposts and stations. The most likely targets are already covered, but there's still backwaters."

"Why do I get the feeling we're about to clean toilets?" Aidin asked.

"Look, I know it's not the job for a flagship crew," Seamus began, cementing Aidin's feeling. "But right now, you're in the right area and times are tough."

"What area?" Aidin asked.

"Aurin 2 in Maires Drift is being evacuated," Seamus explained. "Sure, it's lightyears away from 196, but ships patrolling near the area have reported strange sensor readings and unknown signals, intermittent."

"What kind of signals? Before we were attacked—" Aidin's explanation was cut off.

"Could be cloaked ships, could be damper units already on Aurin 2 shielding whole bloody regiments; we haven't had the ships to monitor everywhere for weeks now. I tell you, we're spread thin, man. Look, this mission is sensitive," Seamus said gravely. "The Irachans are making a lot of noise and I can't blame them; we're massing ships along their border, pulling vulnerable outposts out of their reach… it doesn't look good."

"It doesn't," Aidin agreed, dropping the issue about the signals till later.

"The plan is to give the Hearack less to go after and then pull back behind that line in a tighter arrangement, away from the Irachan border," Seamus explained.

"A fire break," Aidin commented.

"Aye," Seamus confirmed. "Hopefully, it'll do two things—starve out the Hearack and defuse the tension with the Irachans."

"And we're to assist by evacuating Aurin 2," said Aidin, getting an understanding.

"Not exactly," Seamus began, to Aidin's confusion. "Your job is to deliver troops to Aurin 2; they'll help guard the infirmary till a troop ship or settlement carrier becomes available—right now, they're all assigned."

"So, why don't we just begin evacuating it?" Aidin pressed.

"A, we don't have a ship big enough because they've crammed so many patients into the place over the last few months, and B, because we've no way to escort it right now," answered Seamus.

"Why, what's going on?" Aidin's voice had raised in frustration. "Half the fleet's out there, so surely, they can spare a ship—"

Seamus raised his hand gently, prompting Aidin to calm. "That's the reason I didn't want to use the intercom or risk sending you your orders. An Irachan delegation is on Noiren 2. On the far side of the drift near the Soanaar border. They were engaged in trade negotiations with a Soanaarin delegation when this broke out."

"Trade negotiations?" Aidin repeated with a frown. "Noiren 2 is a scum hole full of pirates."

"That may be," began Seamus "but Command is placing the highest priority on escorting them safely to the garrison on Station 177 at Telarin 5, where the Irachans will send a fleet to take them the short ways across the border. That's why our fleet's so busy; they're to pick theirs up and escort them, and so are you: After dropping off a detachment of Marines to bolster the defences on Aurin 2, you're to rendezvous with the fleet under a Captain Ritter. It's imperative that the Marine deployment goes unnoticed, as we're already pulling back from Maires Drift; if the Irachans detected us deploying troops in that area, they'd take it as a sign war was imminent. Apart from that, I don't have to tell you how important the safe transfer of that Irachan delegation is, Aidin. Our peace with the Irachans is on a shaky nail as it is, and they still believe we were part of the Genesis Fifteen disaster. If anything was to happen to that delegation, with all the pressure at the moment...."

Aidin nodded. "Then, why don't they send their escort fleet all the way in there themselves?"

"Sure," Seamus commented sarcastically. "Why don't we tell them we can't handle it, that we've a near disaster on our hands. Huh, we'd be a laughing stock, and we're still not completely sure that the suspicion is right about the Valraich. It just looks that way; it could be one of the other factions... hell, it could be the Irachans themselves. It would explain why we can't find them if they keep jumping over the Irachan border, and would side us against the Valraich for them. Not that they'd have the brains for that. In either case, the less enemy ships we have deep in our territory, the better; no, we escort the delegation to Telarin 5, and that keeps the Irachan fleet near our borders.

"Aren't you getting a little paranoid?" Aidin asked. "It's not in the Irachan nature to do something like that; they'd consider it dishonour."

"Really?" Seamus responded dryly. "Well, that's nice, but I'm not about to risk the safety of this quadrant on the hinge that Irachan honour would rule them out of suspicion, and there's still the matter of 196; it doesn't fit."

"Doesn't fit?" Aidin echoed.

"No," answered Seamus. "Why risk coming that far into Alliance space and using such resources, and then pull back and head in the other direction? The only people that benefit strategically from Station 196 being missing is the Irachans—they could march right across the border deep into Alliance territory unopposed now."

"But..." mused Aidin.

"Yes, yes, yes, their honour," remarked Seamus, sighing. "I hope you're right, Aidin, I really do, because I don't think the heat's even here yet."

"What do you mean?" Aidin asked.

"I don't have all the answers, Aidin, but your ship, the *Rheinvar*... before it was—" Seamus paused, "...lost, something appeared, cloaked like those two ships. It made a grab at you, you said before...."

Aidin looked up, surprised. "That report hasn't been released yet—how did you know?" He paused. "Does every high-ranking IAF official pass through here?"

"You work hard, you gotta play hard, right?" Seamus asked, laughing out loud and then in the same breath turning deadly serious. "The signals, Aidin."

"What do you mean?" Aidin demanded.

"The signals, man, in your report—you said you detected strange signals just before something grabbed at the ship," Seamus pushed.

"Yes, but we weren't able to decipher them," answered Aidin. "Just after the Hearack ship exploded, we saw a disturbance in space… a green haze ahead, and when we turned to pull away, the signals began. Command thinks we ran into some kind of anomaly, perhaps a spatial rift."

"A spatial rift!" Seamus mocked.

"It's happened before," Aidin pointed out.

"And the signals?" Seamus questioned, pointing directly to the problem with this explanation.

"Could have been interference on our channels from the anomaly; we don't know. We weren't able to decipher them, so perhaps they were just interference and there was nothing to decipher," Aidin tried to explain it.

Seamus looked back at him steadily. "196 couldn't decipher them, either."

"What…" Aidin started.

"People have told me that, in some of the last communications with 196, they reported strange signals, unrecognisable ones," Seamus replied. "That's two sets of unrecognisable signals at either end of Alliance space, one at the Valraich border near the Fahraren Heights and one at 196 near Maires Drift. I don't believe it was an anomaly, Aidin."

"What people?" he asked.

"People," said Seamus staunchly. "Don't you see, I bet those damn signals are one and the same—not an anomaly and not interference, but communications. They must be, and from what I hear, a sample was caught in a communication from 196."

"There's no progress at all in decrypting it?" Aidin

questioned.

"Supposedly, they're being analysed, but so far they can't be decrypted; our computers have never seen anything like it," Seamus replied. "Some still believe it's nothing but static caught and polarised."

"Why hasn't the fleet been informed of the possibility?" Aidin asked.

"What do you want them to do?" Seamus demanded gruffly. "Admit to the fleet, to the people, that they have no answers? That they're overstretched and something's brewing, huh? There'd be a mass panic."

"Then what are they doing?" Aidin asked.

"Only thing they can do; keep watching, listening, for anything," replied Seamus.

"Then why not send a fleet to the Valraich border? We could spread them out, set up an enclosed sensor grid; we—" Aidin was cut short.

"Aidin, I'm not exaggerating when I say we have no ships." Seamus sounded strained as he added, "We've recommissioned retired hulks; even freighters have been commandeered to find the enemy along the drift... the place is a bloody war zone."

"How many of our ships are concentrated there?" Aidin asked.

"Too many," Seamus assured him. "That's why the Irachans are so twitchy and why I'm concerned we're spread so thin across the rest of the Alliance; we're trying to hold back a reserve, but they raid every other day, so what else can we do?"

"Well, what about some of these freighters? Just to look along the Valraich border and the Fahraren system where our sensors aren't strong?" Aidin suggested.

"Where?" asked Seamus. "The area's huge, and

from your report, it's a cloaked ship. Besides, thousands are dying along the Drift each day; if we try and pull off any ships to search, it will cause an outcry. There'd be murder."

"So, we just sit and wait?"

Seamus looked at him dryly. "I'd say your little encounter gave us a valuable warning; you were never meant to see that Hearack ship explode, and you were certainly never meant to get away. Every sensor grid's been charged and every long-range array has been trained on that area."

"We didn't sense anything before," Aidin reminded him.

"But we weren't looking before," Seamus replied. "A ship that big, big enough to grab at a starship with a tractor, might be able to hide out on the outskirts of Alliance space where sensors barely reach and interference from the Heights causes problems. But cloaked or not, when it begins to come closer and away from the Heights, into the stronger bandwidths of our sensors, we'll find it."

"Then what?" asked Aidin.

"Then we'll see," Seamus answered simply. "My guess is that a plan is already there to swing the whole fleet round like a big right hand, and believe me, laddy, that's a big right hand! In the meantime, you're to get underway as soon as possible to deliver that complement of Marines, then make your rendezvous with Ritter and the escort fleet."

"So, what have we got for the job?" Aidin inquired, sipping down the last of his Harelin.

"Well…." Seamus took a deep breath as he replied, "Look, the 185 shipyards were emptied last month, but the ships in the adjacent repair docks were—"

"You're not serious!" Aidin cut in, barely getting his drink down.

"Look, like I said, times are tough, lad," Seamus repeated.

"You want us to salvage some scrapheap from the wreckers' yard?" asked Aidin, still astonished.

"No, no," Seamus assured him. "The scrapyard was picked clean a few days ago."

Aidin relaxed somewhat.

"No, I've secured authorisation for you to charter any suitable ship that passes through 185 for—"

"You want a top Alliance crew to beg for a ride?" Aidin cut in, shocked all over again.

"Look, like I said—" Seamus began.

"We'll be a laughing stock!" Aidin voiced, alarmed.

"Look, Aidin!" Seamus shouted before stopping himself, calming somewhat and remembering that he wasn't talking to some junior officer. "Aidin, you've just sat and listened to the kind of trouble we're in, and you've seen the brief. I'm telling you, laddy, we're in it deep here, so don't make any more for us to be dealing with; now, it's just this once, eh…?"

Aidin sighed, looking away before nodding reluctantly.

"One more thing," Seamus said. "A few of your buddies you were detained with from the little scuffle at the bar are to be in on this one."

"The Marines in the cell, Fuller and the others, they're part of the detachment?" Aidin asked.

"Aye, they are," Seamus confirmed. "But I want to put you wide to the situation. Look, Aidin, that unit's got a reputation, you know… it keeps getting attention for all the wrong reasons, and their files are full of all kinds of insubordination and reprimands."

"So I heard; just about everyone's shit on them," Aidin returned, thinking of his own brushes with superiors over the years.

"Aye, well, it might be with good reason," replied Seamus. "They've never been charged as a unit, but they've been accused of some pretty serious stuff, you know?"

"They seemed alright to me," Aidin commented.

"Aye, maybe, but I'd keep well away from them. Aidin, trouble always seems to come their way," Seamus explained.

Aidin pulled a face, clearly doubting the accusations.

"Alright, Captain," Seamus said respectfully, seeing the expression along with Aidin's seniority. "But think about this… you'd only been around them ten minutes and you were in a holding cell; if it wasn't for the pressure on the Alliance right now, you might not have gotten out so easily."

Aidin looked at him squarely, not happy with the man's opinion of them, but realised he was only trying to warn him off and nodded respectfully as he rose to leave, saying, "I'll keep that in mind, Captain," as he offered his hand.

Seamus nodded back, shaking his hand. "Mind how you go, lad, and if you can make it back here in a few months, it will be worth your while." Seamus smiled. "We've a hell of a celebration planned for some high-ranking friends of mine coming by."

Smiling back as Seamus went into a bout of laughter, the two men broke company, Aidin lifting his orders from the table and making his way out, having found that a ship was now his priority.

It took Aidin almost an hour to find Brenner, who was under the galleria in one of the bars with some of the crew. Aidin was thankful he wasn't too far down the noise-crammed corridor, as the day's events had finished him. After an explanation which was devoid of any details explaining his appearance, Aidin informed Brenner of the situation and of their need for a ship. Brenner responded just like Aidin had in Seamus's office at the news, but after Aidin informed him somewhat of the situation, and seeing his captain's tired expression, Brenner quickly hid his reservations behind a scowl at the floor.

"The crew is pretty spread out, but I'll round them up, given some time, sir," Brenner assured him.

"No, no," Aidin replied, having to shout over the din that was still annoying him. "The crew's been through a lot lately. They need this, and you're in the right location anyway for traders and smugglers, so I don't see why you can't mix business with pleasure. Besides, this place with its noise and drunkards is perfect to ask around quietly." Aidin looked around the bar's cliental, who were similarly half-naked to what he'd seen before, just like the other places on the station. "I have to turn in. Meet me tomorrow afternoon in the Eurian Bistro on the galleria; I hear they make quite a breakfast there, and it looks like you're going to need it," Aidin said, smiling.

Brenner returned the smile, watching his captain disappear through the door with his own night now a little more complicated. Looking back, though, at the lack of clothing on the dancers around him, he didn't think it would be too much of a problem.

Leaving the maglift the next day, Aidin exited onto the galleria where maintenance personnel were still clearing wreckage from the night before. All around him, half-eaten food and litter lay among God knew what under tables and chairs, the relaxing purple hue of the galleria now changed to bright blue and doing nothing to disguise the onslaught from the night before. Walking through the clean-up operation, he felt that the quiet was fantastic; on his left, bistros and eateries slid past as Aidin began to follow the gentle bend of the station round to the right. No more invasive sounds, no more screaming inebriates... just the gentle lights of eateries with a mixture of modern cafes and classic wooden facades beckoning weary travellers in as, on the right, massive rectangular windows gave views of the stars outside. Faces passed on Aidin's left, tired and gaunt, with their attempts at dragging themselves up for breakfast not helping at all as they retreated back to their quarters, hoping for recovery before the next night's carnage which was guaranteed by 185.

Arriving at a quaint little bistro, he noticed there were no neon lights or desperate advertising marking the entrance; instead, the spot boasted just a few potted plants around a wooden façade which hinted at Earth's French styling within. The two large windows on each side showed a warm atmosphere inside, doing more to beckon Aidin onward as he pushed the wooden door aside. Making his way in, he found that it was everything he'd come to expect from a Eurian bistro their race chipped out completely with technology causing some to long for their agricultural based past, this longing showing through in much of their architectural tastes. Wooden floors and walls with green velvet in places mixed with cream ceilings giving a relaxing feeling immediately, the warm lighting being all the more soothing. Tables on either side of the door were occupied by gentle conversation while a bar just a little further on to the left offered menus and drinks. Beyond the bar, three steps led up to a seating area that was warmly lit and had a longer bar to its right, the conversation there sounding equally relaxing. Aidin's pause had prompted service, and now a waitress in black and green leaving the bar on his right was soon asking if he'd like a table. Answering with enthusiasm, Aidin was led up the steps through the conversations and past double French doors to an even larger wooden-floored seating area beyond it. Lit lighter still, it had fifty tables lining each wall, now black in colour with their v-shape arrangements looking on to the far side of the room, where a pond offered gentle sounds of falling water, its descent obscured by lush foliage and small trees. But for the small rockery offsetting the atmosphere, the centre of the room was clear, leaving the feeling of space to continue almost thirty feet overhead as a huge, curving window followed the station's hull up from behind the pond, showing stars twinkling in the distance. Led to the left wall near the pond, Aidin was shown to a table for four, and he asked for some light coffee before being left a menu, the waitress leaving him to his thoughts. Soon, he guessed, things would get a lot busier.

Brenner looked tired when he arrived, but Aidin didn't mind, knowing full well that the crew needed leave. Still, he couldn't hide his disappointment upon learning that the search for a ship was not going well.

Brenner ran Aidin through the search, the turning faces, and the various people pulling away—more interested in 185's offers than his. About to suggest following up with a run on the miners, Aidin was interrupted by some more weary travellers as Fuller and Fulkes having run into some of Aidin's crew the night before. were led in by the staff.

"Look, it's just me and the boys." Fulkes fidgeted awkwardly at the side of the table. "Well, we'd like to say thanks, and I, eh… I'd like to say thanks," he finished, struggling. Things like this were difficult for him, particularly with Fuller standing beside him.

"That's alright, Mr Fulkes," Aidin replied, smiling. "I'm sure one day you'll help us out, too."

"Mr Fulkes," Fulkes repeated, laughing at the politeness. "Well, eh… yeah, you can count on that, Cap. I, eh… I mean, sir."

Aidin nodded in reply as the two turned to leave them to their breakfast, before turning back to Brenner. "We still need to find a ship. There was definitely no luck at the trading lodges?"

"No." Brenner shook his head. "Something about incidents in the past."

"Incidents?" Aidin echoed.

"Yes, sir, it seems cloak and dagger missions, what with the Alliance saying it was bartering a ship for one reason and then it turning out to be for a different reason, with the ship and owner not coming back… it has them, well, reluctant, sir," Brenner replied.

"I see," said Aidin, sighing disappointedly.

"Eh, sir," voiced Fulkes, overhearing them as they'd been leaving.

"Yes, Mr Fulkes," Aidin said, still sporting a

stressed expression.

"Well, me and the boys were in the armoury, you know, getting our ammo replaced for this gig, and, well, we got to foolin' around… and, eh…" Fulkes paused, a disapproving look from Fuller setting him straight. "Em, I got to foolin' around, you know, past their machining rooms, and eh… they've got a ship down there in the R-and-D lab.

Aidin looked back at Brenner, the stress lifting and smiles creeping in as they turned back to Fulkes with smiles in place. "Is that so, Mr Fulkes?" Aidin replied, standing and stepping closer to Fulkes to avoid talking to loudly among the other tables "Tell me, where exactly is this… lab?"

Several levels below…

Now walking briskly down the corridor toward the armoury, Aidin's presence seemed to have upset a white lab-coated technician whom he'd asked for directions to the armoury. Flanked by Brenner, Fuller had insisted on directing them with Fulkes leading the way , the technician now seemingly desperate as they walked, trying to convince them they were wasting their time.

"I'm telling you, the ship's a wreck; it's a research model put together with parts of other wrecks. I'm telling you, it won't be suitable!" the technician chirped from Aidin's right, starting a little run now and then to keep up.

"I appreciate your concern," Aidin repeated, "but we must see it; it's imperative we find a ship, and if there's the smallest chance it can do, then it must be pressed into service," he added, unsure as to why there was such resistance at his request.

"Look, the ship is designated 151; it's not even commissioned anymore; it had to be hauled here by breakers from a crash site!"

Aidin looked at Brenner before squinting at Fulkes.

"What I saw down there was no wreck," Fulkes assured him as they continued round a bend and along the corridor to the armoury. The grey walls and carpeted floors of the station had long since given way to white marble floors and blinding, white-panelled walls associated with station science and armoury decks. With the technician protesting every inch of the way, they made their way into the same blinding white surroundings of the armoury, the line rooms and class demos playing audience as the men continued unabated. Further on, they passed the machine rooms with technicians looking up from their white marble workstations to the passing strangers, their white-coated comrade's objections drawing attention.

In front of them, a stainless-steel airlock loomed as they passed through the last machine room, the technician becoming irate. "It's simply out of the question!" he screamed finally, stepping out in front of them and throwing his arms across their path as they arrived.

Brenner looked at the scrawny technician in front of them, the man's whining voice having cut through him all the way down to the armoury, and now he stood blocking their path telling him what to do. Turning, Brenner met Fuller's similar expression... the technician's time was up.

In a similarly blinding lab, more technicians who were oblivious to the melee outside sat hunched over marble white workstations. Adjusting light yielding equipment causing reflections of themselves to be thrown onto four large, rectangular windows spaced evenly along the right of the room. The peace inside was suddenly shattered as, startled, the folks inside looked left up several steps to see their colleague bundled through the braking airlock and collapsing as he slid across the landing at the top, two burly servicemen—Brenner and Fuller—following him through.

Up almost immediately, the technician launched himself at his aggressors with a tirade of abuse, wheeling his finger like a weapon as his two facilitators towered over him and desperately tried to hold back their tempers. Their efforts fading fast, the screaming labrat was seconds from disaster when....

"What's the meaning of this!?!" The voice was older, experienced, and clearly carrying authority as its demand stopped Brenner And Fuller just in time, their years of services' training taking over seeking out the holder. "I said, what's the meaning of this?" the voice came again, unseen for a second till its taller-statured source, complete with lab coat, emerged from behind the rest of the technicians, leaving their camouflage behind as he came forward glaring at the new arrivals. Brenner watched as the older man began climbing the stairs, carrying all the anger of a raging father. "I asked a question," he growled, his next outburst cresting the last step with him to the landing.

"They just burst in, Director!" uttered the labrat, his voice still shaking irately.

"I can see that," remarked the director dryly, glaring at the servicemen.

"I tried to stop them, but they wouldn't listen,"

continued the labrat.

"Really," the director uttered quietly, his glare at Brenner and Fuller not relenting for a second. "Gentlemen," he began quietly, "that airlock is there for a reason; behind it in here, we are dealing with delicate and potentially explosive materials." His glare deepened. "So, kindly tell me why you've endangered my staff and half the fucking machine rooms!" he screamed suddenly, Brenner and Fuller jolting at the burst of aggression.

The two servicemen's confident stance had gone, their assured control of the situation evaporating. They were lost for words under the director's fury. Unable to offer anything but uncomfortable expressions, they stood now like children under the director's rage.

"My god," came an astonished tone from outside the airlock behind them.

Eyes turned to Aidin, who was still in the machine room, his stare fixed through the airlock on something just visible halfway across the third window on the other side of the room from the landing. Turning to see what had his captain transfixed, Brenner was struck immediately by the same sight, his words taken away by part of a hull that was suspended in space behind the windows to the outside.

As if in synchronisation, Brenner and Aidin began to make for the stairs, open-mouthed, immediately prompting a response from the labrat still facing them. "No!" he screamed, moving for Brenner. "You can't go in there! You don't have clearance!"

"It's alright," said the director quietly, raising an arm in front of the irate technician blocking Brenner's path.

"But…" the technician tried again, jarring his head

to one side over the director's shoulder after Brenner.

"It's alright now!" the director said firmly, Aidin passing behind him joining Brenner on the stairs, the director's tone lowering further as he saw the anguish on the technician's face. "It's alright, son…"

For a second, Brenner and Aidin stopped in awe as the fourth window came into view at the top of the stairs, revealing more of a familiar hull outside in the R-and-D bay beyond the windows. Still gaping, the men moved down the stairs, their eyes fixed through the windows with the technicians moving aside as they passed the workstations. Halting beside the third window, Brenner and Aidin stood lost to the sight ahead of them, the bow of the ship outside now in full view, its identification visible:

IAF RHEINVAR 228 - 1F

"How…" Brenner uttered finally, unable to take in what he was seeing.

Outside, the rail exhausts of small shuttles and drones moved back and forth past the ship, some huddled in small groups and with sparks flying from their efforts, the flickering of repairs casting shadows across the bow. Sealed in behind the bay doors, the ship sat mostly in darkness, faint spotlights piercing the gloom and revealing small steel parasites tending to its needs.

Transfixed on activities outside, the director's approach barely registered. "So, someone's finally come to take her away from us," he said thoughtfully, staring out of the window with the men. "Well, I suppose if it had to be someone…" he offered, turning, though his smile didn't quite hide his regret.

"How?" Aidin repeated Brenner's earlier question.

The director sighed, laughing a little. "Come on." he motioned to the glass window of his office near the back of the room. "We have a lot to talk about, hmm?"

There wasn't much in the way of furniture in the office, and there certainly weren't drinks like in Seamus'—just a modern glass desk with black wooden legs, a black leather seat sitting behind it and two smaller ones in front with two additional ones against the right wall. Following the director inside, Aidin let the old-fashioned glass door swing through ninety degrees on a hinge to close behind them, becoming part of the glass wall separating the office from the lab outside. As the director took a seat behind the desk, he pressed a button, making the men start spinning round as a noise sounded the entry of more old-fashioned furniture. Grey drapes appeared from the left wall, slowly running right over the length of the glass and turning as they went, blocking out the observant faces of the labcoats beyond the office.

"Don't worry, gentlemen," the director reassured them. "A quaint design, but quite safe."

The office boasted grey carpeting, black walls where there wasn't glass, and a black ceiling, the only consolation in the drabness being the lighting emanating from an uplighter in the floor behind the director, the room dimly lit and a welcome break from the lab's whiteness. Fuller and Fulkes brought seats from the right wall sitting off Brenner's right while Aidin, sitting to Brenner's left, demanded to know why the ship had been concealed from everyone when it was common knowledge among the station personnel that a ship was required for urgent purposes.

Over the next twenty minutes, the men sat in silence,

the director telling them of their past—which was now resurrected a short distance through the wall on their left. Fuller and Fulkes, slightly bemused, realised it was something important among these circles, and sat respectfully quiet, coming to realise as the director went on what this random ship Fulkes had stumbled upon really meant.

The director told of how various salvage companies had tendered for the tractor lifting off Mensis Prime, but without being able to agree over costs with Alliance Command which was still at war leaving salvage a low priority. Weeks had gone by with other, more important matters clouding the subject until a passing vessel posing as a mining frigate had been caught attempting a little salvage operation of its own, headed by three Valraichs.

The obvious danger highlighted, Command had focused its efforts and, ignoring bureaucratic complaints of cost, chosen a company at random—ordering the wreckage lifted from the planet and its sensitive equipment secured. Again, the war had gotten in the way and, although the wreck had been tractored up into free space, no ships could be spared to escort it the vast distance to the nearest IAF garrison. Instead, the company had been ordered to tow it to the nearest facility that could house it with relative security till it could be moved to a more suitable location for disassembly, the nearest facility being 185. The wreckage had been berthed in the 185 shipyards quietly, no special security procedures implemented to disguise the fact that what looked like a mangled hulk was an Alliance flagship.

"But the war dragged on," continued the director. "There just wasn't time to deal with it, and over a period of months, it was slowly pushed to the corner of one of the shipyard's perimeters and eventually forgotten… by most. The ship had carved out a bit of a reputation in its time, though," he said, smiling at Aidin. "A fact not lost on the technicians here; they barely get a chance to see the improvements on systems they design on paper in real life, and certainly don't get near starships, so when a test bed was needed for new designs… well…." The director motioned aimlessly with his hand. "It was done quietly; what was left was brought into the dock, doors were sealed, and work began. The station commander was more than helpful, and with the shipyards being so big here, over time, we got to salvage just about everything we needed to put her back together. Oh, she's far from perfect; wiring's missing on nine decks and life support doesn't work on five, but with parts from a recently wrecked starship, we were able to fix the lower hull." The director looked past the men, a proud shine in his eyes as he gazed at the blinds as if seeing through them. "They're amazing," he said, obviously talking about his staff. "It's taken years, but that ship out there is ready to fly even if it is running on a mismatch of parts."

"He knew there was a ship down here?" Aidin asked, referring to Seamus and astonished that the *Rheinvar Mark 6* had been allowed to sit in a hangar all these years.

"He knew we had a ship to experiment on, allowing us to provide good results with new systems," replied the director vaguely.

"Did he know which ship?" Aidin pressed.

"He didn't ask," came the reply.

"Uhhgggghhh! This place!" Aidin shook his head, taking it in his hands at the ridiculous lack of communication.

"Anyway, he's forever got his hands full," the director pointed out.

"Yeah, we saw that in a club last night," Fuller broke his silence.

The director grimaced, looking away. "Look, these people of mine found something special, took it in, treated it like their own... and they brought it back to life. Don't be too hard on them, Captain," he said, catching Aidin's look of disapproval. "They've broken their backs over her for years; even ironed out those little bumps you left in her." He smiled "There's a lot of heart and soul that's been put into her."

"There was a lot of heart and soul already in her," Brenner retorted.

"I know," the director answered, raising his hand and nodding agreeably. "We always knew this day would come, that no matter how hard we tried to keep it quiet, someday someone would come and take her away." He paused. "Never imagined it would be you, though." He smiled, and added, "It's just hard for them letting go, you know?"

"Oh, we know," Aidin replied, finally returning the smile.

Chapter 16

Cut from the Same Cord

Out for their final night on 185, the men quickly stopped as an inconsolable woman with a concerned party around her almost barged into them when they'd been making their way out of a bar on the group's right, the group escorting her being oblivious to all around them with their concern for the woman's grief.

Now, though, none of the concerned group could understand what she was seeing—they could only see what was happening on the outside.

Earlier, though, it had been a very different scene for the woman...

She'd been in a function bar reserved for the crew of an attack ship her son among them, celebrating their last night with friends and family. But something was very different about this night, felt only by her as she left the galleria and began descending into the corridor with her husband. For all the heat and stuffiness, the lower she went, the colder it grew.

All through her life, she had been plagued with visions, and in this modern time of starships and warp engines, people with these unexplained "illnesses" were treated as cranks or as having brain disfunctions. They were forced to hide their condition or risk being hit by a plethora of mind-altering drugs; what was to happen that night would make this woman wish she had them.

The strange feelings had started as they had made their way to the celebration…

The crowd was light as she and her husband descended the ramp, leaving the galleria's purple lights behind for the reds of the corridor below as the air became thicker. Moving down was easy, with only a light crowd meandering through; they'd made sure of that by coming early, the woman having no stomach for heaving throngs of people. A short way down the corridor, the couple came to a wooden bar on their left, its old-time look spoiled only by two small neon signs advertising beer above the door. The husband had quickly grown tired of the heat, which was thick with shared breath, and the woman, too, felt more than willing to leave the corridor as she kept her unsettling feelings quiet from him.

Reaching out, the woman's arm suddenly tensed at the first touch of the door, fear engulfing her and drawing his attention. Having been together with her for years now, he knew the look, but asked anyway—her casual attempt to brush it aside doing nothing to convince him it was nothing as she insisted on going in, ignoring the feeling of foreboding as she opened the door.

A welcome atmosphere greeted them as they ventured inside, and a small, wooden-walled hallway led them through an open doorway into a long, warmly lit bar. Through the doorway on the left, set back several feet away into the wall, an old-style varnished mahogany bar ran the length of the room, complete with varnished gantry and facias. A dirty blonde, wooden floor played host to people celebrating merrily, some of them standing at tables built into supporting pillars which were evenly spaced in front of the bar and others laughing in groups further out. Half a dozen tables with four chairs each lined the right wall, one occupied at the top while another open doorway to its left led through to a similarly warmly lit wooden-floored room, a huge rectangular table waiting at its centre and already set.

Looking over the bar with her husband at her side, familiar faces in the forty or so-aged crowd began to appear, the woman quickly forgetting her experience at the entrance.

"Mom!" a voice broke out from behind the groups of people along the middle of the room. "Mom! Dad!" it came again.

All other feelings fell away, the woman beaming with pride as a tall, handsome-faced young man who looked sharp in his Alliance uniform came through the throng.

"How are you guys?" he asked, joyously hugging his smiling mother before offering his other had to his father, still holding his mom with one arm and repeating, "How've you been?"

"Great, son," his father said, shaking his hand firmly, having to hold in his pride and not having his wife's luxury of going to pieces. "It was a hell of a flight, but you've had it worse, I suppose," he joked.

"Oh, don't listen to him, John, the flight was fine," his mother assured him, beaming.

"Yeah, apart from the food, huh?" John laughed.

"You're not wrong there; that was awful," replied his dad. "Luckily for me, I've been eating your mom's cooking for years, so I was fine."

"George!" his wife laughed, delivering a playful slap to his chest.

"Well, don't worry about that," John said. "We've got this big table back here in the other room—by the time you leave here, you won't need to eat for a month."

"Yeah, I saw that on the way in," said his father. "It looks—"

"Newmyer! Hey, Newmyer, will you get your dumb ass back here? Kaytlins wants to... oh, wow, eh... Mrs Newmyer. Sir, I, eh..." the beer-merry friend had been suddenly cut short upon seeing Newmyer's parents, feeling embarrassed by his behaviour. "Sorry, guys, I didn't know you were—"

"That's alright," Newmyer's father assured him. "Don't mind us. You enjoy yourself, son, or should I call you Lieutenant Morton now?" He laughed.

"No!" laughed back Morton. "Scott will do, and don't worry, sir, we're gonna have fun, alright."

Fun they should be having; it had taken four years to get where they were. Transferred from mundane duties aboard small transport vessels in remote sectors, they had secured promotion and places on one of the most powerful attack ships in the Alliance and had been serving on it now for almost three months. The attack ships, though small, were the stepping stone to serving aboard the real deal, the deep space starships were all the action was, and this ship, this *Hordec*, was their ticket to them.

"Hey, come on over and meet some friends of ours," Newmyer said, motioning them forward and smiling.

"Sure, son," his father agreed, beginning the walk toward the back of the bar with his son.

Morton tried to follow, but was quickly held back by Newmyer's mother taking hold of his arm, slowing him from following the other two. "Who's Kaytlin?" she asked, smiling.

Moving through the groups of people, Newmyer's mother held onto Morton's arm with each group of people passing aside in front of them till finally, with the last group moving, laughter and smiles greeted them. Newmyer's father stood joking with his son, accompanied by seven of the relatively new friends he'd made on the *Hordec*.

Over the next hour, drinks flowed and laughter rang out as Newmyer's mother met Kaytlin among the seven—a pretty brunette science officer her son had been dating for almost a month. Kaytlin's friend Louisa introduced Newmyer's mother to her boyfriend Curtis, as well as his friends Philips and Blair, all of them being in engineering like her son, only specialising in damage control. The engineering theme continued, Newmyer's mother in her element as she was introduced to two more engineers—Sloan and the hulking Mannan—who'd met her son when he'd transferred to their ship three months previously. The laughter continued for over an hour, drinks passing and Newmyer's mother so happy for her son in his newly found friendships; it was all one big happy family.

"Well, guys, I gotta go," Curtis announced over the latest joke.

"Oh, come on, you can't leave! We haven't even eaten yet," Louisa tried to reason with him. "Morton's just gone to the bar for drinks."

"I know, I know," Curtis said, going on to defend himself, "but I gotta be up at 0400 to realign the new engine strains."

"Oh, to hell with them! Just say you did and hide the new ones! Who's gonna know?" Mannan asked, laughing.

"Yeah, right," laughed Curtis, walking away down the hallway to the door through the near-empty floor, most people now occupying tables on his left. "Nice to meet you, Mr and Mrs Newmyer—I'll try to keep an eye on that son of yours!" he called over his shoulder as he reached for the door.

"You do that!" shouted Newmyer's mother after him. "He snuck a girlfriend into his life without even telling me, and he—" She stopped instantly as Curtis opened the door and she saw an explosion rushing in to take him off his feet. And then it was gone, the light from the corridor fading as the door closed quietly behind him, but the feeling of dread stayed with Newmyer's mother. Suddenly consumed with cold, she tried to turn right to her husband, but caught sight of Morton instead; he was screaming, shaking in pain and stuck to the bar rail... he... he was laughing, joking with the barmaid, his painful expression gone.

Suddenly thrust into shock, the dread she felt was overpowering, cries being masked by music before grew to screams behind her. Shaken, the bar grew dark as she spun round to witness half-scorched, screaming victims behind the tables, nurses running between them. Newmyer's mother froze as half-burnt human monsters reached out for help, faces wide-eyed and racked with pain, beer spilled over tables turned to blood streaming down table legs to the floor and clotting between bodies as it made its way toward her. Burned almost beyond recognition. Shock wracked Newmyer's mother as she suddenly realised what she was seeing... they were all in Alliance uniforms.

"Martha!"

Newmyer's mother spun round sharply at the hand on her shoulder startled, by her husband's call; in an instant, the dread vanished. The bar was no longer dark, but instead warm with light and music, the cries gone. She looked back over the tables—there was nothing... no blood, no bodies, just people laughing and singing like before.

"Martha, what's...?" Her husband never got to finish as she spun round to meet him, panic-stricken upon realising what she'd been seeing.

"He can't get on that ship! He can't! He can't go! He can't!" she stammered, grabbing her husband's chest and shaking him as she buried her head against him.

"What's wrong? What do you mean?" her husband demanded, holding her close and hiding her from those behind them as he spoke quietly into her ear.

"He can't go!" she repeated more loudly, raising her head sharply with fear emblazoned in her eyes.

"What do you mean? Why?" her husband asked, trying to calm her. "It's just nerves—don't worry, it's natural to be worried with him going away, but he'll be fine. He..."

Nails digging through her husband's shirt, she was barely listening with her state of mania growing when, over his shoulder among her son's group of friends she saw Philips smoking leaning against the wall, holding a lighter for Blair. Blair lent toward the lighter as it struck gently, cupping his hands and sucking the flame to his cigarette, the light making their faces glow red.... Suddenly, they burst into flames, fire searing through their screaming faces as their skin melted away. Jarred by what she was seeing, she tried to look away, closing her eyes; the screaming stopped, leaving Philips and

Blair smiling happily when her eyes returned to them. Her inhale, quivering she tried to look away to the left, still gripping her husband in fear, it seemingly passing for a second. Looking at the rest of the group—Mannan in the middle laughing heartily at Kaytlin with her son on his left, his head rolling back as he held his drink among them—she saw the rest of them laughing, too, Louisa tapping Mannan on the shoulder to continue the mirth, Mannan turning right to hear her, and... Newmyer's father suddenly felt his wife breathe in, her gasp of shock quickly followed by the pain of her nails as she witnessed the light from behind Mannan through sears in his face.

"Martha!"

The voice shocked her, forcing her to look at her husband. Gazing back over his shoulder, she saw there was nothing; her son's friends stood laughing in their group with Philips and Blair smoking, Mannan laughing on with not a care in the world. The stress was too much; the vision coupled with the knowledge that her son wouldn't desert his ship on the strength of her warnings and that no one would listen broke her as she fell into her husband's arms sobbing.

With her unable to contain her emotion, the sound soon drew attention and Newmyer left his confused friends to find out why his mother had become so upset. Martha could only listen to her family speak as she remained huddled against her husband, sobbing over what she'd seen. She listened as her son asked what was going on, and listened to her husband explaining it was the illness, that she didn't want him to go and that she thought something bad was going to happen.

She barely heard their muffled exchange of

concerns, distraught and putting up no resistance as she was passed from father to son.

"Mom... Mom," her son's kind voice whispered from above her. "Mom, it's gonna be alright. Mom... Mom, look at me."

She looked up, ashen-faced and timid as her son held her, telling her everything was going to be alright. His was a warm face full of love, honesty—a face any mother would be proud of—but then she saw him, saw him in his eyes falling toward her, a face of terror screaming as his arms flailed helplessly as he came....

The next day Aidin sat among a maintenance crew on a shuttle...

Arguments with the research teams quelled by the director and Seamus, the gentle clunk of steel hulls signalled that the shuttle had grappled against one of the *Rheinvar*'s docking ports. The only obstacle now remaining between Aidin and his past was the airlock in front of him.

Standing with a handful of station maintenance men, he felt almost hesitant as one of them reached for the panel to the left. A clunking of steel mechanisms shuddered through the hull as the steel doors broke apart in front of him, cooler air flooding into the shuttle from the ship as if it were greeting its former captain.

"E deck," Aidin voiced, looking down the long, black-carpeted corridor walls and the ceilings that were panelled in cream, numerous corridors breaking off to the left and right. Like all other decks, it was indistinguishable from the others but to a few who had called her home. The station maintenance crew working on her for years had long since lost their appreciation for the famed ship, but recognised the nostalgia in Aidin's eyes and naturally hung back, waiting for him to board first. The walls were plain, with standardised panels as far as the eye could see, but not to Aidin as he took his first step. The firm, carpeted deck-plates seemed to welcome him immediately as he wandered aimlessly to the first junction, memories flooding back. Lost in the past, he didn't even hear the maintenance crew approach, only being jarred from his thoughts when the last of them brushed past him, laden with tools and disappearing down a corridor to the right as he headed to engineering. Emotions abound, Aidin lifted his hand to the panelled wall as if afraid to touch, his brush across it only bringing more memories. *I'm an hour in front of the rest of the crew*, he thought, taking a breath as he moved off down the corridor to the left. He'd never had the ship to himself before, and in heading for the bridge, he resolved not to waste a moment.

The hour seemed to fly past, though before his rush of crew arrived, he'd walked out onto the bridge from the maglift, with the weapons station at its rear immediately greeting him. Its steel form arced down on each side before cutting back from both sides toward the maglift, tapering down to the floor and protecting whoever occupied it in a steel cocoon. Below it,, on the other side the black leather seats for the first officer, captain, and engineering relay—when present—lay all in line and abreast of one another, set into the front of the steel casement that made up the weapons station. An old design surrounded again by black carpeting and cream panels, whereas modern ship designs—unlike the *Rheinvar*—favoured the first officer and engineer being spread away from the captain in case panels exploding under weapons fire took out the whole command at once. Claims of better progress without the captain being able to look over their shoulders had also been made, but Aidin didn't buy it. Many times, they'd scraped through a problem only because they'd been situated so close together and been able to work in tandem with split-second timing, which could be accomplished with this set-up with no need for shouting across the bridge. No, this was the way to do it, Aidin thought, with everyone facing forward to the viewscreen and able to see what was going on and react instead of facing a wall or panel.

The room, rectangular at the back, swung round at each end, running down the sloping walkways on both sides of the weapons station to the main floor. The walls continued on to a smaller, concave wall in front, the viewscreen curving along it and giving the feeling of depth when turned on. Just back from the viewscreen, the con and nav stations sat side by side just like on stations in a recess partway into the floor. Steel casements overhanging at the back blocked any view of the occupants and were designed to protect the command behind them from any debris, should their panels explode during battle. The casements also doubled as their own protection from the weapons station behind them.

Aidin had already walked around the room's teardrop structure, been in the Captain's council room through the door to the left of the con station and in the conference room through the door to the right of the nav station, memories from each returning as he had. He'd even tried the science stations on the right wall, seated in a similar casement arrangement to the side of the weapons station, but to no avail; his attempts to access them had been met with blank screens and no friendly acknowledgments. The old girl was still asleep, he'd thought. Unlike the rest of the ship, though, the bridge was spotless—no dust, no stained carpeting, no visible damage... a far cry from the twisted mess of blood and glass Aidin remembered. The labrats really had put a lot of work into her, he'd realized, looking around and deciding right then that it wouldn't be for nothing.

"Sir!" the shrill voice jolted Aidin from the daydream of wandering the bridge alone. "Lighting's been established along decks eight through fifteen, life support on one through seven has been stabilised," reported the engineer.

"And deck 5?" Aidin asked.

"It's a real mess, Captain. The deeper into the ship we go, we're finding parts used from eight different classes of ship and another three kinds we're not even sure of. We're looking at weeks to get her ready, sir," replied the engineer.

"Thank you, Lieutenant," Aidin said. "But most repairs will have to wait; we don't have time. All effort is to be directed toward the shields, weapons, and power transfer conduits—as soon as they're above seventy percent, we're on our way. The rest will have to be handled on route with the main emphasis on the shuttle bays; we need them by the time we reach Aurin 2 for our troop drop."

"Aye, sir," acknowledged the engineer, moving off with his orders through the hive of engineers, their black Alliance uniforms tipped with two blue azure stripes running down to a point on the outside of their left forearms. This easily identified them as they lay in and around every bridge panel among the split drums of niran optic cable, feverishly refitting her and bringing her back to life. The engineer making his way through them was almost at the maglift door when it split open, its passenger's rank making him salute. His salute dropping, he boarded the lift as Brenner emerged to run the gauntlet of engineers, his black uniform having thin gold lines running from his neck across his shoulder and down, tapering out just above his elbow along with the gold and black-lined insignia emblem of the Alliance cresting the left of his chest. The only other indications of seniority were the three thin gold strikes on the left of the collar; one strike more, and the uniform would have been that of a captain. Bodies half sticking out of panels and units didn't even notice him pass, their wrestling inside given away as their legs and feet strained for grip on the carpeted floors.

Passing carefully through the last of them, Brenner arrived from the left walkway to greet the captain. "The reports from the fuel assemblies and loading stations, sir," Brenner said, handing a display handset to Aidin.

"And the infirmary?" Aidin asked.

"It's still a mess." Brenner paused, glancing around the bridge to the engineers crawling around on the floor like rats among the cabling. "They're thinking at least eighteen hours, and that's if the cirvo beds ever arrive."

Aidin sighed, looking at the handset with the pressure of time and logistics mounting on him.

"There is one other thing, sir," Brenner added.

"Yes?" Aidin asked, still going through the handset.

"It's the Marine detachment, sir," Brenner began to explain.

"What now?" Aidin sighed, looking up from the

handset half-expecting to hear that one of the units in the detachment they were transporting had started another fight in the ship's lounge or a fire in some off-limits area.

"No, sir, it's nothing like that," Brenner replied. "It's just one of the units, sir—their the ones…" Brenner paused, looking for the right words, "held with you, sir," he said finally.

Aidin looked away, his face awash with discomfort and embarrassment. "Fuller."

"Yes, sir," Brenner confirmed. "He wants to speak with you; says it's urgent… his… eh" Brenner paused again as he tried to find a way of conveying his disapproval of his captain's new friends. "He's getting in the way, sir, being insistent on seeing you."

Aidin thought for a moment, realising the Marines were unused to the rigidity in the naval structure of the Alliance and perhaps requiring leniency with their behaviour—their being cooped up on what for them must be a steel prison. "Very well," agreed Aidin finally. "But not until we're underway; we can't afford any more distractions. And, Number 1?"

"Sir?"

"See that they're kept out of the mess hall at night; I really can't abide another fit of tantrums from the ship's catering," Aidin said with a tired face.

"Yes, sir," Brenner acknowledged, pleased that his efforts to highlight the problems being caused not only by Fuller's unit but also by the other Marine units on board had gotten through.

Two days later, the *Rheinvar* was on its way. Brenner had almost felt sorry for the labrats as they'd backed the *Rheinvar* out of the R-and-D bay, the great shadow of the ship rolling over their faces pressed hopelessly against the windows in the lab adjoining the director's office. Almost, but not quite—he didn't have time, as the ship could move and throw a decent punch, but the amount of repairs still to be carried out was ridiculous. Danske, the *Rheinvar*'s chief engineer, hadn't even had time to glance at the experimental, enhanced magnetic ioniser array which the labrats had painstakingly tried to mate unsuccessfully with the ship's own standard arrays. Instead, it just remained welded to the bottom of the hull, mere inertial baggage as he wrestled with the engines, the original standard weapons systems, and the power transfer units… all of them fused or fried from their last encounter together. It was the same everywhere on all decks and at all stations; everyone was repairing, stowing, and reporting; it was chaos all round with enough stress for all. But none more so than for Brenner, as every couple of hours, a new report would come in—a complaint or a demand or a plea. *"Marines are stealing from the mess hall again." "Marines have started a fire in the armoury." "Marines are running down E deck naked!"* And on and on.

He was at his wits' end.

Later as the captain approached the ship's lounge…

The doors moved aside for Aidin, splitting slowly and almost in a welcoming fashion as he moved inside, their mahogany faces closing quietly behind him as he let out a long sigh of relaxation, exhaling for the first time in sixteen hours, it seemed. He paused for a time, resting on the bar to his right and taking in the ship's lounge once more; the crew had done well refurbishing it. No doubt, the crew members who'd survived the crash on Mensis Prime had toiled with the task more in a state of appreciation for being home than having work, wrapped in memories like him and trying to capture some of the past. Brenner had questioned the relevance due to more important things, as he'd seen it needing to be done. But Aidin had known, known that if the crew was expected to break their backs working, they'd need a place to relax, to enjoy themselves and wind down, so once they'd shipped out, he'd put it on a priority as high as life support and power transfer. What a job, they'd done, he thought upon looking out across the room's dark beige carpeting, forty yards over to four massive rectangular bay windows that ran almost floor to ceiling, set in walls lined with black suede stars streaking past outside as the ship ploughed forward toward Aurin 2.

The fourth window on the right was a little obscured from Aidin's perspective as he looked up the passageway from the corner of the bar. The obscuring came from a large booth sitting three steps high off the ground, carpet flowing up the stairs into and around it while a black oval table sat in its centre surrounded by a semi-circle of seating built into the booth. At this time of the morning, the booth sat empty—a carpeted island alone on one side of the room while, on the other side, a second booth shared the emptiness from the other side of the bay windows. Out just beyond them, the carpeting continued on to a single step leading up to a viewing platform five yards deep and running the breadth of the room, gently curving back on each side to meet the walls shared by booths. The second booth on the left side of the room didn't sit alone, though, having more booths adjoined to it. The booths ran the length of the room along the left wall toward the windows, all three steps high and sharing the same fine beige coat. Below them, on the floor in the middle of the room, black tables and matching chairs sat silently waiting for occupants, one walkway dividing them from the booths along the left wall and another on the opposite side running from the island booth to the corner of the bar where Aidin stood.

"A drink, sir?" a voice asked politely.

"Eh, yes—Harelin, please," Aidin answered, shaken from his musings as the barman made off down the bar which curved in from the wall past Aidin and straight back ten yards into the small room off the main floor. Inside the smaller room, the decor was much the same with a few black tables and chairs nestling inside of it, complimenting the bar's simple but elegant marble design with a gentle, terracotta light mounted on the wall opposite and lifting the effect fully. Aidin had never agreed with the cream ceiling throughout this area, but this soft lighting from the mounting in the smaller room and those along the left wall of the lounge above the booths made for a relaxing hue which blended perfectly with the colours elsewhere.

"Your drink, sir," said the bartender, returning.

"Thank you," Aidin replied, caught less off-guard this time as the barman made off, leaving him in peace with his thoughts.

Aidin thought quite a bit more as he enjoyed the drink alone in the warmth of the lounge, the next shift now on and the rest of the crew sound asleep. Memories came flooding back as the smell of fabrics around him filled his lungs, unlocking past thoughts both good and bad, warm and irregretable all aside from those final hours on the ship. Then, this place had been crushed almost unrecognisably, he thought, running his hand over the chairs to his left as he made for the viewing platform beyond the booths.

Arriving there, he found that it was silent, peaceful stars streaking by as he sipped on his drink; at times, it was hard to believe they were at war again. It just didn't feel right.

"Hell of a view, huh?"

The voice was familiar. There was no startling turn, though, the Harelin already soothing down his nerves. Turning to the left, he was more curious than anything else to see who the voice belonged to. His curiosity was answered fully as he saw that the voice came not from behind him, but from a familiar face slouched down at the back of the booth just off the window. He hadn't seen the figure on the way in, the booth hiding him away, but a man like him rarely forgot a voice... especially that of an old cell mate. "Yes, quite a view," Aidin agreed, smiling back at a tired-looking Rians. "Shouldn't you be lighting a fire somewhere? Or crashing a shuttle through my walls?" continued Aidin, referring to the antics of Rians' comrades more than those of the man himself.

"Nah." Rians smiled, his eyes almost closing with tiredness. "That's Fulkes' job," he added, laughing a little to himself.

"And your job tonight?"

Rians sighed, his eyes coming to rest on the table in front of him and his smile fading. "My job is to figure out if I've done the right thing."

Aidin looked on for only a moment before deciding to join him, moving for the other side of the booth; his calm reflection was gone now anyway. Sitting down, Aidin took the view of the lounge from this other direction, sipping a little as the stars streaked past unseen behind him. "Something troubling you, Rians?" he asked without looking at him, leaving his eyes to gaze over the lounge.

A long pause ensued before a strained voice began, "It wasn't before, when we were shipping out and all, but, ah…"

"Now you're not busy," Aidin finished for him. "And you have time to think."

"Yeah," replied Rians quietly, apparently unsure of how to talk to a virtual stranger, but knowing it was an older man in front of him—the kind that hadn't been on the shuttle from the dock.

"It's family?" Aidin asked, recognising the look.

Rians looked up, surprised. "How could you guess that? I mean, the word is that you don't…"

"No, no, that's right, I don't have a family; at least not on board or back on Earth, save distant cousins and the like." Aidin paused as he found himself opening an old wound. "No, I recognise the look from the crew. You know, there are times when it comes up."

"Ah." Rians smiled, his eyes dropping as he nodded his head.

"Yours is back home?" Aidin asked.

"Yeah." Rians lifted his head with a hard smile on his face. "Earth… things are a little out of whack right now, though; you know marriage, it… eh." Rians looked down again, forgetting Aidin wasn't married and starting to run on. "When you get married, you think it's alright now; you know you're there, you're gonna build up this thing together and be happy, and it's like that for a while." He paused in his memories. "And then a kid comes along and you change… you know, everything. Everything becomes clear—what's important, what's not. You get more serious, and maybe that's where it all goes wrong."

"Goes wrong?" Aidin asked.

"Yeah, it… eh, it becomes almost like a job at that point, a job to come home to," replied Rians, his eyes still lowered. "Your wife's there, but she's not… you know. It's not the same; it's different, and gets harder. Kids, though—I mean, they're the greatest thing in the world, they're the only job that's worth it, right? The only one you don't mind not getting paid for." Rians smiled. "You never think about it? Never been married?"

"I never…" Aidin paused, memories swaying him, "had the time. I, eh, this career, you don't notice the years going by, and it takes so much from you, it…."

"Oh man, I'm sorry. I didn't know." Rians apologized. "So never married eh?" he repeated realising he couldn't do any more damage.

"No. A couple of times, it came quite close, but… no." Aidin looked around the ship at its walls, almost regretfully; he'd spent all his life fighting for his position in the Alliance, and it had cost him dearly and he knew it. Every Christmas, every Easter… every conversation like this one compounded the empty part of his life that he so wished he'd filled. If only he'd known back then how much this position was really worth when compared to what all those around him took for granted. "There just wasn't time," he added simply.

There was a long pause as both men dealt with the stress the conversation was bringing. "A shame," Rians said finally. "But at least you don't have to miss 'em, or have to worry about 'em being driven nuts all the time by you not being there."

"Yeah," Aidin replied, him now the one who was

looking aimlessly across the room with a forced smile.

Silence came again for a while, Rians knowing he was feeling low. "Still, at least you've got Brenner for company."

Aidin looked back at the other man, unsure whether or not to laugh.

"And that cook… a great guy—real friendly at night," Rians continued as Aidin began to laugh. "I suppose, in a way, you've got a family right here, and they're as messed up as any family I've ever seen."

The two men laughed at the thought of it, conversation continuing on for almost an hour more over old battles than old flames, Aidin introducing Rians to Harelin and describing how the best came from a bar in Earth's New Providence South, which was situated on what used to be the western coast of Africa. Rians returning with his disbelief that Aidin had never seen the Cranelin Falls torn through what had used to be the eastern coast of North America when the Canary Islands had fallen into the sea, causing tsunamis and ultimately the quake.

A lot more Harelin flowed that morning, the barman amused at the noise in the bar being there so early and bearing sole witness to his captain getting drunk at such an hour. It finally finished, though, both men limping away back to their cabins, having gained new respect for each other's peers and swearing to sort out what they'd missed regarding Harelin and the Falls when the war came to an end.

Sleeping through the day Aidin later came onto the night shift rotation…

That very night, though, Brenner–unlike Aidin—wasn't so happy around the Marines; another day of pulling them apart and clearing up after them had left him seething, as he now had to escort some of them to meet the captain. It was the last thing he needed as he headed to the ship's lounge to find them.

"So, how long would it take you to squeeze into one of those uniforms anyway?" Fulkes smiled as the science officer over the table began to smile back at him, finally bending to his charms in the lounge. Across from her, it was a different story, though, as her friend in the same black and turquoise-sleeved uniform maintained her disapproval, her expression leaving no guesses as to her thoughts.

"He's at it again," Carson complained, sitting at a table further back on a raised, carpeted platform to the right with the rest of the unit. "All he had to do was bring drinks back from the bar. Shit, he couldn't even do that right."

"Yeah, but he might bring back a little something that goes down easier," Copeland said, a laugh of approval erupting from Brice at the other side of the table.

Fuller, too, tried hard not to choke on his drink as Brice rocked the booth with laughing to his left while Rians, Copeland, and Carson sat laughing on his right, spaced round the circular booth with their glasses empty on the table in front of them.

"We gotta get to that Aidin guy soon cause this latest attempt at a plan is all wrong," Fuller continued with the earlier conversation, dropping the mood a bit.

"I'm sure he'll listen; he's been around and been in

a lotta bad ones," Rians said. "And he seems alright," he repeated again, having said the same thing earlier when telling them about the drinks they'd shared in the early hours of the morning.

"Yeah, if we can get past that erand boy of his," Brice said, referring to Brenner.

As if on cue, the lounge doors split open and the very obstacle to their audience with Aidin came through, his contempt for the Marines written all over his face as he stared disapprovingly at the drunken rabble. With an expression that hid nothing, he took a deep breath and walked reluctantly down the right of the room, searching for Fuller with the knowledge that, the sooner he got him away from these morons, the better his patience would hold.

Just then, two female science officers—both gasping in disgust—sprang up from the far side of a table on Brenner's left, so that when he was almost past them, his path was suddenly blocked by a chair pushed back by a short Marine as he stood up to offer a few more crass words. But it was his previous offerings that had the women seething, and with this latest suggestion, he was suddenly awash with alcohol, his former partner throwing her drink over him.

Eyes clearing, though stinging with drink, he could make out only a blur in front of him. But any doubts as to what he was seeing were quickly answered as a thunderous slap filled the lounge, it being met by whoops of laughter as Marines fell over their tables in hilarity. The two women stormed out, leaving buckling Marines and the ever-grinning face of Fulkes to look after them, his quiet guffaw of satisfaction joined by hurls of appraise from his audience. No appraisal came from behind him, though, and Fulkes' eyes cleared to an awareness of a tall figure standing close by. Turning, smile in place, Fulkes looked up to see a first officer standing six-foot-two with a stained uniform having been caught in the crossfire that was topped with a look far from hilarity. Glaring at Fulkes through clenched teeth, words weren't needed with his face saying everything. Fulkes' smile quickly dropped as Brenner glared on for a few more seconds. Message conveyed, Brenner dropped his eyes to the chair that was still blocking his path, then back to Fulkes as the room fell quiet. Fulkes, after a time, gingerly pulled the seat away as Brenner followed him with his gaze before moving on while his temper still allowed him to. Calls and jeers over Fulkes' obedience sounded out from drunken Marines, but were similarly silenced by Brenner's scowl as he approached Fuller's table.

"Mr Fuller," Brenner growled with the most grudging respect. "The captain would like to see you… now!"

The walk to the maglift was completely silent, with Brenner in front and Fuller and Rians following close behind, both of them able to hear the soft footsteps of their companions as they sank into the plush, dark carpets. The lift opening ahead of him, Brenner barely noticed the ensign's salute as he left, instead just moving inside and turning round to face the doors, waiting for his guests to step in and determined to get it all over with as quickly as possible. Fuller and Rians moved into the lift, the same black carpeting greeting them along its oval floor; the walls displayed the same cream panelling like everywhere else on the ship. Rians was sick of it, and looking up as he entered behind Fuller, he half-begged in his mind to see something different, but the ceiling was the same as in every other lift he'd been in… cream, again. Brilliant white light spewed from a circular slit running the circumference of the lift, coming from who knew what was buried behind it. Cascading down the walls, the light filled the lift with the same clinical light, nauseating and artificial, that offered the same feel as the corridors of the ship. Rians was in good company in thinking this, as Fuller, like everyone else, was sick of the ship—it was just one big lab to them, none of them wishing to stay.

Doors closing, Brenner hadn't even looked at them, just throwing his attention to the new panel halfway up the wall and searching among the tens of small black buttons, their edges silhouetted red against their blackened glass facades. Frustrated, he grew agitated over being unable to find the bridge option, the new control set-up throwing him just as it had done several times over the past few days. Only, now it was happening in front of Fuller and Rians, and so it left him angry, embarrassed… he just wanted to be rid of them.

The men behind him could sense something was wrong, and not because they hadn't moved; they could feel it via the atmosphere in the lift. Fuller looked at Rians, then at Brenner's back, thinking of offering help before he thought better of it, realising Brenner would think they were laughing at him. No, putting up with the dark atmosphere was a far better option. Finally, sweating in frustration, Brenner jabbed at one of the buttons, and a gentle movement and whining followed the move, leaving him relieved as he took a step back— still refusing to lay his eyes on the men behind him and to his right.

It was intolerable to Fuller. "So, how's things getting on?" he probed with the question, using it as if they were in battle and sending the first man—this question—over the ridge.

"Alright," came the response, Brenner slightly turning his head but stopping short of eye contact.

"Yeah, good, good," Fuller remarked. "We'll be off soon, too... a few days, I hear, and then we can get out from under your feet. Let you get on with your next mission."

"Yeah, a few days." Brenner almost sighed, showing signs of loosening up, relieved that the constant calls for help and security were almost over and that the zoo would soon close.

The lift was almost there, but Fuller couldn't help it; he had to keep going. "So, how long did it take you to cut the 37th out of that shuttle once they'd crashed it through the bay wall into the corridor?"

Brenner turned fully this time, looking Fuller squarely in the eye. Fuller couldn't help it; and the smile creeping onto his face was infectious, Brenner feeling the hilarity of it all and almost laughing aloud, but pulling away instead, choosing to grimace instead and rolling his eyes as the two Marines behind him laughed openly at the situation.

"Well, at least it wasn't Fulkes this time," Rians commented, still laughing.

"Yeah, that's the first thing I said when I heard," Fuller added with a guffaw. "Where's Fulkes!"

The laughter continued, Brenner still finding it hard to join in.

"Ah, come on, Commander," Fuller said, happy the ice was somewhat broken. "At least you'll have some great stories at parties, eh?"

Brenner finally smiled at that, closing his eyes and nodding his head as he let out a sigh, beaten by the absurdity of it all.

When the lift doors opened, it was Rians who took in the bridge, feeding his curiosity about the nerve centre of the ship. Fuller, though, barely noticed as they moved toward the council room—his mind on other things.

"Captain Fuller, sir," Brenner called as they entered the room.

Rians quickly took in the room as the doors slid closed behind him, a rectangular shape running length-ways to an angled workstation that was black with shaded top glass set off-centre and to the left at one end. Behind it, Aidin rose to his feet, revealing a chair swivelling still as he left it, it being the same colour as the line of seating built into the left wall—and, unlike the desk, contrasting sharply with the black carpet. Cream walls and ceiling were darker than elsewhere on the ship, and adequately lit from up-lighters at each end of the left wall. A simple room built for business and not pleasure, the only comforts being the standard potted fern plants which the Alliance designers were so fond of—here, placed in the right corner. The last decoration was the two-foot-wide and almost floor to ceiling window set in the right wall near the door.

"Captain Fuller, Lieutenant Rians," Aidin said, smiling and offering his hand. "Sorry about the wait, but at least it wasn't spent in a cell this time."

"No, it was a bit more comfortable." Fuller smiled, shaking his hand.

"So, I understand you have problems with the Alliance set-up on Aurin 2," Aidin commented, gliding over any more pleasantries.

"Not with the drop, sir," Rians replied.

"No with the lack of surveillance and orbital cover," Fuller cut in. "After we're dropped, the *Rheinvar* just leaves, right?"

"Yes, we have matters that require attention elsewhere," Aidin answered casually, belaying the seriousness of the situation.

"Attention elsewhere," Fuller repeated, screwing up his face. "Aidin, you've got a hospital down there with wounded men, and all they've got is a handful of Marines slung this way on a second-hand thought from those morons in command."

"You were all they believed they could send," Aidin replied.

"All they could…" Fuller shook his head in frustration, searching for a display handset in his pocket. "Have you seen the pattern they've taken through the drift?" he asked, angling it for Aidin.

Aidin glanced at it for a second, seeing it mirroring their information. "Yes, I've seen it, completely random and never hitting one system without passing by three or four others… completely random."

"It's not random at all!" Fuller almost shouted. "They pass any half-defended system and go straight for the vulnerable ones."

"Command's aware of that, Mr Fuller, they're not blind, but maybe if you take a look at what's near Aurin 2, you'll better appreciate the situation," Brenner moved in to defend his captain over Fuller's outburst.

"*Appreciate*," repeated Fuller, unable to believe the stonewalling.

"Yes, appreciate! Appreciate the fact that there's a

dozen mineral complexes, three starbases, a refit yard, and only a half-dozen starships in this area to cover them," Brenner continued.

"Maybe you're not listening," Fuller retorted. "They're not going to attack an outpost with defences."

"Is that right?" Brenner asked sarcastically.

"That's right!" Fuller shouted, feeling as if he was in a courtroom again. "What these clowns at Command can't see is plain to us on the ground; the Hearack aren't here on a campaign. They're drawing our forces away from our centre." He turned back to Aidin. "We're being pulled apart, spread thin while they conserve their strength for some kind of offensive."

"Command isn't blind to the situation, Mr Fuller, but there are things happening further out that aren't common knowledge; it's the influence of this that's having the—" Aidin was cut off as he tried to reassure Fuller without divulging what he knew.

"There are things happening here! People are dying here! And unless someone breaks free of this bureaucratic bullshit and acts on what he sees, it's not gonna change!" Fuller shouted, feeling the argument slipping away. "What's so damn important that you can't hang back here for a couple of days?"

"We have duties elsewhere," Aidin repeated. "People who need us out there in—"

"You have people that need you here!" Fuller shouted in desperation. "Isn't that what you Navy boys are supposed to swear to? To protect the people, the Alliance, the peace? That means nothing, huh? All bullshit, so you can swan around in fancy uniforms!"

"That's enough!" Brenner screamed. "We've been nothing but courteous and helpful to you people, and all you've done is thrown it back in our faces!"

"You people! You people!" Fuller shouted back at Brenner, facing him. "So you make distinctions between people, huh? We Marines aren't as good as you Navy boys? Those people down there aren't as good as whoever it is you've gotta go see, either, huh?"

"You know damn well that's not true!" Brenner shouted, nose to nose with Fuller now. "We're stretched to the damn limit up here and your bullshit doesn't help!"

"Doesn't help!" Fuller echoed, glaring back at Brenner. "Who's gonna help those poor bastards down there when you leave them there to die!"

Brenner tried to respond, but didn't get the chance as Fuller brushed past him, storming out of the room in rage at their blindness, the doors sealing after him on the gentle system reports of the bridge—leaving them in the council room with the atmosphere grown only darker.

"What's the matter with him?" Brenner voiced angrily. "Can't he see we're stretched to the limit here? What the hell does he think the answer's going to be, making a request like that?"

"He's trying to protect his family," Rians answered quietly..

"I thought his family were killed in the Anzeil Massacre," Brenner replied.

"They were," Rians answered with a disapproving look, making his way to the doors that began sliding open at his approach. Almost through, though, he stopped, turning back to Aidin. "He's trying to protect the only family he's got, and I thought you'd understand that… but I guess not."

Aidin watched Rians disappear through the doors, his words striking hard as they sealed behind him.

Chapter 17

Blind Charge

"If we pick 'em up far enough out, we'll be able to put up a good defence," Copeland said.

"We better, cause we can't expect any help from them," Fuller said, his face one of disgust as he watched the shuttle rise through the clouds.

"Shame… they seemed alright for a while," Rians said.

The scouting patrols had been out all night… again. Aurin 2 was an arid, rocky place, a dustbowl by day set under a baking sun and a cool, silent and ghostly place at night, when shadows stalked in the pale blue under the three moons above.

Aurin 2, stripped clean of its mineral wealth, was little more than a supply depot now, storing surplus ore from other bodies in the sector and providing the main medical complex for the region. Most of the ore had been transported away due to the recent Hearack activity in neighbouring sectors, but this was considered only precautionary—nice they were so cautious with the ore, too. It had been a great moral boost for the patients left behind.

Nestled against the back of a rock face with natural ridges on each side, the complex stood defended only by a run-down mortar cannon which had been installed during the war atop two huge blast gates laying four hundred yards from its entrance and strewn between the ridges. The two eighty-foot-wide blast gates, one hundred and twenty feet tall were machined into the ridges each side and had been installed just before the peak of the mining operations there, and installed because just beyond them lay the corilium and syntharit mines. The ore from these mines could be frighteningly unstable under the heat of the sun; enough concentrations going off together magnified each other, throwing out a blast wave big enough to make most starship captains envious. Despite efforts to ensure adequate cooling, facilities ran continuously and breakdowns would occur occasionally, though they were usually fixed quickly enough to avoid catastrophe. It seemed a wise precaution, then, to protect the medical facility and staff there, and it was; it would have been better, though, if they'd done it earlier and prevented the tragedy of '72. Still, they'd done it eventually; had to, really, since rebuilding the medical facility had cost a fortune.

Out of the hundred and fifty Marines, most were busy preparing patients for evacuation on the transports due in two days, leaving only seventy-nine Marines on patrols. Fanning out, now eighty kilometres from the medical facility, they'd found nothing—no sign of Hearack anywhere. Each patrol had hooked round for twenty kilometres in a wide arc in an effort to cover more ground and they were now coming back on themselves toward the facility. This night was like all the rest—cold, monotonous, and boring—but with the cresting of the next ridge bathed in blue moonlight, all that was about to change for one patrol.

"Shit! Get down!" Fuller hissed, dropping to the ground.

Behind him, Rians and Copeland crawled slowly up the loose shale to his position. The two men peered gingerly over the ridge at what had Fuller rattled. Hearack!

"There's not very many of them," Rians whispered, surveying the site below. "Where's the rest?"

"I don't know," Fuller replied quietly, looking through visual enhancers. "There's three T49 APCs, two below and one off in the background, and there's a lot of activity around the two below us." He watched as Hearack moved around, carrying objects that glinted in the moonlight. Fuller looked hard. "What are they arming with?" he whispered, stretching his enhancers out past Rians to the squad's resident engineer, hoping he could make sense of it.

Copeland watched intently, zooming in on the pale blue scene far below as Hearack continued to move back and forth.

"Copeland!" Fuller whispered.

"It's not weapons," replied Copeland.

"Then what are they doing?" Fuller asked.

"The things they're carrying around look like… bits of machinery, spare parts maybe; I don't think they're arming. I think they're damaged—it looks like a makeshift repair station down there," Copeland whispered scanning the site. Below, the two T49s sat side by side facing the hill they were peering over, and Hearack moved in and out carrying machinery to and from what looked like a large workbench set up in front of the T49s. Further back in the distance, another T49 sat alone in the gloom, surrounded by equipment. Visual enhancers passing back over the activity at the tables…Hearack engineers, Copeland thought… he'd only ever seen soldiers, and on that thought, he began to pick out sentries, one a little way off from each side of the two APCs below them and one off to the right of the APC in the distance.

Small rocks were peppered over the men below as Fuller, Rians, and Copeland quietly shifted back down the ridge on their stomachs. Looking to the approaching men for answers, Brice winced as his eyes were filled with dust. "What's going on?" he asked quietly.

"Hearack over the ridge," answered Fuller. "They've got three T49s down there; looks like some sort of repair depot."

"I wouldn't even go as far as that, Captain," Copeland whispered. "Not enough equipment—they might have broken down and called out for help. It's probably why they're not bothering with the 49 in the distance; there's probably nothing wrong with it. Could be it's a repair rig sent out to recover."

"Not enough guards for a depot, either," Rians commented. "I counted only three."

"Yeah, three," Copeland agreed.

"If they had to drive here, the main force must be far off; otherwise, they'd just tow it in," whispered Fuller. "Is communication still jammed?"

"Yeah," Rians answered.

"Now we know why," Carson voiced hoarsely. "There must be a base somewhere in front with a damping field; no wonder no one could find them."

"You said there were three guards. What were the rest doing?" Brice asked.

"Looks like there's another five engineers," Copeland answered.

"Engineers?" Brice echoed, as curious as Copeland was.

"Yeah," Copeland replied.

"But we don't know how many are in the T49s," Rians cut in.

"If they had more guards, they wouldn't be in the APCs; they'd be out on watch," Fuller said.

"What do you want to do?" Brice asked.

"One of those 49s would be handy if we have to find out what's out there; one of them could have maps, plans, anything inside," Fuller said.

"Yeah, and they've got ground radar," Copeland whispered. "You can see the nodes on top of them in front of the plasma arrays."

"That would show us what's out there," Rians said.

"If we start a firefight, whoever's out there might hear it," Carson commented, clearly concerned.

"If they had to drive here, I reckon they're way off," Fuller said. "But we can't have any of them defracting and getting away; if we hit 'em, we gotta wipe 'em out in one go."

"And the 49s," added Copeland. "If any of them get inside and seal the doors, we've had it—those plasma arrays will roast us."

"Yeah, assuming there's no one in them now," Rians said.

"I think it's worth the risk," Fuller said. "If we get one of those 49s with the ground radar, we can avoid their patrols and we'll be home free; without it…."

"Then how do we do it?" Brice growled enthusiastically.

"Rians," Fuller began, "you circle round to the right; work your way to a position above that single guard in the distance. Carson, you and Fulkes work your way round to the left and take a position as close to that 49 in the distance as cover will allow your free to fire we'll open up when we hear it. The rest of us will take up a position on this ridge. Now, look," Fuller added, looking round at everyone. "Carson and Fulkes are gonna start firing on that guard in the distance then run for that far off 49; Rians, when you hear their shots, you waste that guard because he'll turn away from you to see whats going on and then we'll open up on the other one and the engineering detail. You two—" Fuller pointed at Carson and Fulkes, "you throw yourselves into that APC and waste anyone inside before they get a chance to seal the door. And listen," he whispered more loudly, looking at Brice and Copeland, "when we open up, I want frag grenades launched through the doors of those APCs."

"You got it," Copeland replied, clutching the grenade launcher mounted under his rifle.

"Again, we've only got one shot at this," Fuller said, reinforcing the gravity of the situation before turning to Carson and Fulkes. "When you get inside that 49, you figure out how to work it quick; that plasma array might be all we've got if they get those doors sealed on the others."

"You got it," Fulkes replied.

"Alright, everybody clear?" Fuller asked, looking around at nodding faces. "Alright, Rians, you first. Remember to hold fire till you hear the first shots. Go."

Rians headed off around the ridge carefully, his footsteps diminishing in the distance even as Fuller kept thinking about the plan, and about the Hearack below. If just one got away, they would be.... Well, there was no time for that worry now.

"Carson, Fulkes, go," Fuller hissed, their footsteps acknowledging him as they disappeared round to the left. Turning now, Fuller looked at Brice and Copeland. "We can't miss. I'll take the guard to the left and launch a frag grenade into the left APC. Copeland, you take the guard to the right and frag the other APC. Brice, I don't want any of the rest of them to make it to any one of those vehicles."

"They won't," came a definite reply.

"Alright, let's go." Fuller motioned the men on and began to quietly crawl up the ridge, Brice and Copeland on his right.

Fuller crested the ridge on his stomach, drawing his gunsight over the pool of engineers working on something lying on the table in front of the APCs, and then brought his weapon's sight to rest on the guard who was busy scanning the ridge to the left. The gentle sound of shale being disturbed as Brice slowly crawled into position beside him ceased, signalling they were ready. Fuller couldn't see Carson and Fulkes moving behind the ridge on the left, nor could he see Rians slowly moving into position atop the smaller ridge to the right. Instead, his open eye was fixed dead on his target—an apt choice of words. Fuller watched the guard, his grey skin against the pale blue of the night visible through his sight; the guard moved his head now and then, scanning… scanning everywhere but above and to his left. He was so clear, Fuller thought, feeling he was right beside him. *Why can't he feel the sight on the of his head?* he wondered, practically believing he could reach out and touch him. Lying on the ridge, there was time to think, and time to worry; he hoped Rians was in position, he hoped Carson and Fulkes would make it, and he hoped that the doors wouldn't seal, as well as that—time was up!

A crack shattered the night in the distance, the flash

in Fuller's gunsight sending the guard reeling backward as Brice erupted, silencing them all. Cranking the grenade launcher, Fuller levelled his sight on his APC's door—a jolt and a resounding thump sent a grenade straight in. Seconds later, an explosion drowned out the weapons fire, night turning to day as a stream of fire burst from the door and forced heads down as the blast wave rippled over the shale. Heads were up and sights targeted as night rushed back to claim its realm, fire and light consumed under its pale blue grip. Nerves on edge, sights swept erratically back and forth as shale peppered down from above. With the rush of the assault, the second explosion hadn't even been noticed, timed perfectly with the first. Nerves calming, the men watched as small fires surrounded the APCs, flames licking hungrily out of Fuller's and Copeland's targets confirming success. After the sudden violence, things fell silent, allowing them time for a careful scan of the bodies the guard Rians had been assigned lying face down in the shale.

Soon after this final scan, Fuller felt relief as they made their way down, guns drawn on the first APC sitting to the left of Copeland's. *We'll approach the side of the first APC, using it as cover from the other*, Fuller thought, *and secure it and then move round to the second*. Fuller began to feel excitement through the relief, and when he was down the slope and half way across the ground to the first APC, he was almost euphoric at the success—and then the door slammed shut on the second APC.

"Shit!" Fuller hissed, crouching down lower as he moved with the others and trying to stay out of sight of the second APC, ducking behind the first as they finished hurrying over the remaining ground. Coming down clear, they'd crossed the ground in seconds and slamming against the first APC's steel side, Fuller and Copeland on the left of its door with Brice on the right. Using hand signals, Fuller ordered Brice on his mark to go in first, to the left, and Copeland to go in to the right, signalling that he would follow. Raising his arm slowly, the confirming look he offered sent adrenalin flooding as he dropped his hand.

Brice burst in to the left, slamming into the right wall as Copeland tore past and into the back of the vehicle, Fuller right behind him. A second passed, and another…. Nothing. Nothing so far, but it was dark at the back and they couldn't see to the end. Fuller looked over his shoulder to see Brice shaking his head. Turning back, Fuller took aim and dropped a hand on Copeland's shoulder, both men moving slowly along the left wall and each taking his sector. Nothing greeted them but containers, parts, debris, all passing slowly by as they made their way back with the stench of charred material all but overpowering. Out of the dim light coming through from behind them, the murky blackness finally relented to a welcoming sight—the rear bulkhead. This vehicle was clear… one more to go.

Cautiously, they left the APC, sweeping right along its armoured hull while shielded from the second APC's line of sight. Crouching to a stop near the nose of the thing, Fuller knew what they were about to go up against; he'd seen the plasma cannon in action on Maires Drift. The array mounted on the roof of the 49 APC was designed to melt through armour inches thick, and it was waiting for them on its swivel mount. At least it would be quick.

With Copeland and Brice behind him, he held back his hand, signalling for them to hold as he slowly peered round further and further. The other APC's nose came slowly into view, scorched black from the attack. A little further on came the door, sealed, and Fuller drew breath; gingerly, he leant forward searching for the tip of the array—further, further, there! The sight forced Fuller back, his nerves rattled; the array was facing straight forward, not at them. Fuller slowly looked out again, more confident and taking more in. Silent, it just sat there, sealed, a blackened hulk. Still crouching, Fuller moved forward around the nose, motioning for the others to follow. All three nervously took in the view, sizing it up; it just sat there, a flame-charred monster with the silence continuing—whoever was inside wasn't making the first move. Crouching low over the ground, they carefully approached, keeping tight with their weapons aimed. Just ten feet from the door now, moving footstep by footstep as they kept a sharp eye on the array, getting halfway there and….

Suddenly, the door slid open. Freezing, crouching lower, they were open and without cover. With a slam, it was closed again, and their fingers poised on triggers. With a sudden whine, it slid open in front of them, no one in the doorway, though Fuller could make out a blackened interior just…. A clang of armour on armour sounded out and the door was closed again. Fuller squinted, confused. What was going on? As he tried to figure it out, the door suddenly opened again. It lay open in front of them, not a sound coming from within. Waiting for the last rush from inside, they were ready; whoever it was wasn't coming out alive.

But nothing happened… there was just the stillness

of the night passing between them.

Uncomfortable with their position, Fuller signalled the two men to the left as he moved to the right, their weapons focused as they moved slowly and came to rest against the hull on each side of the doorway. For the first time, they noticed their breath was just visible in the still blue around them, as from inside there was nothing—no rush, no movement, not a sound. They'd wait no longer. Fuller signalled to the men that he'd go in first, heading for the driver's position, and they'd follow behind heading for the rear. Again, a nod of understanding started the adrenalin flowing through a maze of nerves already pushed to their limits. Eyes fixed, Fuller rushed through the door and... clang! The light vanished as the door slammed shut behind him; throwing himself back against it, he frantically searched for his trappers. He couldn't see a thing and his head spun from left to right, panicked and trying to silence even his breathing as he listened for them... but there wasn't a sound. After a while, the faint glow from the driver's compartment up front caught his attention, barely filtering through the treated visor port—a pale blue luminescence from outside doing its best to join him and giving a point of focus in the darkness.

He remained still a while, not wanting to give away his position in the darkness and instead listening... but nothing came to him. He couldn't just sit there, he thought, hiding; after a while, he gathered his nerves and crept forward with his heart thumping. Suddenly, he realised he stood on an arm, and a few steps later he was sure it was a leg he stood on. Now close to the front as he was, the driver's view port was just ahead of him on the left; gently offering a soothing blue, but doing nothing for Fuller as the light revealed the front to be clear... he'd come the wrong way. The man inside this vehicle was behind him; he had to be.

A cold sweat broke out as he began to feel eyes on him, and tightening his grip on his weapon, he imagined a scope on the back of his head... the tables had turned. Fuller made up his mind that he wasn't going out like the guard he'd dropped; he was going to crouch as he spun and, even if he didn't make it, a lucky shot might take the bastard with him. His eyes began to adjust slightly in the faint light, and he imagined he was silhouetted from the back as one big human target. He steadied himself in his last moments, preparing to lunge round and feeling his breathing heighten as he gripped his weapon and, in one final push, he... suddenly, a red glow to his right flared; it was a Hearack in the darkness. Blinded by muzzle flashes, the sound of deafening thunder sounded out as his body took over on instinct, emptying everything he had into the figure. The light disappeared, but still he fired into the darkness, rounds ricocheting from all directions off of armour and equipment as they crashed into every surface trying to find a way out. Finger jammed on the trigger under nerves, Fuller heard a whisp of a sound by his ear as a round flew past; throwing himself back near the driver's position, his trigger held.

Fuller froze then, deathly still and with his weapon held back against the other side where darkness protected his foe. Nothing but silence; no movement. Fuller strained against the darkness, but it held solid—giving nothing away. After a time, his heightened nerves subsided, his iron grip on his weapon relaxing. He'd gotten him. He must have, Fuller thought; if he hadn't, he'd have known about it by now, right? Fuller knew he couldn't hide in the darkness forever, and so, gathering his nerves, he began to move. Suddenly, a red light appeared in front of him. The sound of the door opening to his right was eclipsed by a grotesque figure appearing in front of him, Fuller falling back to the wall and pulling the trigger... *CLICK*. No ammo left.

The light suddenly disappeared and a resounding slam came from his right; Fuller was locked in with it, and it knew where he was!

Fuller's breath shook as he prepared for the thing he'd seen to lunge out of the darkness. *Why hadn't he reloaded?* he thought to himself. *You stupid bast.... Red light!* Fuller never even heard the door open as the monster appeared again; instinctively, he raised his useless weapon, but the light shut off again as the sound of the door came cavitating through the vehicle.

Fuller frowned in the darkness. What was it waiting for? What the fu—his thought was cut off as the light appeared again. This time, less panicked, he picked up more of the scene; there was a small red square on a panel, the light slowly creeping out and revealing a hand resting over it, and the ghoulish owner was lurched over the rest of the panel. Fuller looked at the monster and felt like an ass—it was a dead body, dead from the moment he'd fragged the APC and all but unrecognisable with its injuries, intermittently opening and closing the door as it lay over a control panel. A dead body, and it had fooled him!

"Captain!" came a hoarse whisper as Brice carefully made his way inside.

"Over here," answered Fuller loudly, lifting the clammy hand of the body from the panel.

"You got him," Brice congratulated him upon arriving on the scene.

"Nah," Fuller replied, smiling with relief. "He got me."

They'd done it. They'd nailed themselves some wheels and, more importantly, the ground radar installed in the APCs. It was just as well, too, as Fuller Brice and Copeland joined the others in the undamaged APC, sitting alone.

"Sometimes, luck's on your side." Carson beamed 'as they entered.

"Not if this radar screens anything to go by," Copeland said, looking worriedly at the panel in front of him.

"What do you mean?" Fuller asked.

"Captain, if this thing's right, it looks like a whole fucking regiment's out there," replied Copeland, concerned.

"Any activity near us?" Fuller asked.

"No," Copeland answered. "But we've wandered right inside their perimeter. Looking at this, I don't know how we're alive… just damn luck they didn't notice us. Looks like a big concentration of activity eight miles north of here; probably a base and multiple patrols a ways out, east and west of that position. Other than that, we're all alone out here, so going back the way we came would be suicide."

"Well, at least that gives us some time to figure out how these damn things work," Fuller commented. "Fulkes, any luck on that?"

"We've figured out main power and various system panels, but interpreting them is a problem. They're all in Dren, so its trial and error, Captain—pushing buttons and seeing what they do.

"Try not to push any buttons belonging to that plasma array when we're outside," Rians commented.

"Yeah," Copeland agreed nervously as he studied the radar screen.

Just then, a deep rumble forced the men to steady themselves as vibrations through the hull signalled the engine starting.

"Way to go, little man!" Carson shouted, standing beside Fulkes in the driver's seat. "That's why you's the driver, baby!"

"Not bad, Fulkes," Fuller said, joining them. "Can you move us any?"

"There doesn't seem to be any throttle controls to speak of—just buttons," Fulkes replied, looking at the multitude of buttons on what was obviously the steering column.

"Well, I didn't say you was a great driver," Carson quipped.

Fuller frowned at Carson as he moved closer, peering over Fulkes' shoulder. "Well—"

The vehicle lurched forward, forcing everyone to grab hold of something—all except Carson, who fell back to the floor.

"You alright?" Fuller asked, holding the back of the driver's seat and trying not to laugh as Carson struggled up from the floor behind him.

"What'd I tell ya!" shouted Carson as he struggled to pull on his helmet. "Mother fucker's the worst driver goin'!"

Fuller turned back amid the laughter behind him. "What'd you do there?" he asked.

"This one seems to increase…" Fulkes began.

"Eh, Fulkes," Fuller began, pointing at the two APCs getting bigger on the screen ahead.

"Shit!" Fulkes shouted, frantically tapping the buttons around the starter, a sudden shift and diminishing growl giving out as the engine slowed, though Fulkes was unsure which button had done it. Standing and watching, Fuller noticed a huge steel arm to his right gently dropping as Fulkes slowed them, finally figuring on the use of a slot of three raised buttons.

Catching his gaze, Fulkes frowned at the arm, shouting, "That must be the accelerator differential—it's huge!"

"Take us around and bring us to a stop just behind the other two," Fuller said.

"Right," Fulkes acknowledged, watching his progress through the screen.

After taking stock of their situation, they began checking over the equipment lying nearby— most of it being unfamiliar. While a few Hearack phase rifles were gathered up, more studying was done on the radar information, which didn't paint a great picture. With that, they found that the other two APCs were all but lost, and the second, Fuller's, had been near totalled. He'd aimed well with the grenade, finishing it off in dealing with his phantom inside. The other, Copeland's, was in better shape, though its accelerator differential wouldn't lift electronically so to change out of first gear wasn't possible, as Copeland figured out, it seeming that this was the problem the workers had been attending to.

"We can't change it?" Fuller asked.

"The other one was inside when you guys fragged it; it looks pretty beat up—especially the linkage cables—and that's what's wrong with the one in it already," Copeland replied, looking over the scorched differential on the floor.

"Shit," Fuller commented. "It would have been handy to have two of 'em."

"You still could," Copeland said.

"What do you mean?" Fuller asked.

"The differential itself's alright; it's just the linkage cables that're the problem," replied Copeland. "We can lift the arm manually from inside to force it into higher gears but it would take a few of us to do it."

"Well, it's an idea, but I reckon we'd better just stick with the undamaged one," Fuller said.

The undamaged recovery APC now parked behind the other was having trouble of its own, though, as inside of it two figures stared over small shapes on a screen—3 yellow triangles and multiple waves around them offsetting square references and elliptical patterns.

"I'm telling you it's a con radar," Fulkes insisted, arguing with Carson over what seemed like a small con station.

"Little man, you have trouble pushin' pedals—how you supposed to know what it is?" Carson retorted, motioning his head at the screen.

"I know what your mama is," Fulkes replied from the right side of the vehicle behind the driver's position, struggling to pull down another panel full of controls which seemed to be jammed, but were partially recessed into the ceiling above what appeared to be the communication officer's seat.

"Yeah, you keep talkin', fool, and I'll let you know something, alright." Carson struggled on Fulkes' right, reaching up for other side of the panel which he couldn't get down. "Watch it, man, come on," he grumbled, pulling the panel free so that dust came, falling between them as their eyes met Carson wincing condescendingly at Fulkes' frame. "Fuck you get into the Marines with those arms?" he asked.

"Fuck you get laid with that face?" retorted Fulkes, Carson instantly making a grab for him as he did the same with...

"Alright, cut the bullshit!" the booming voice surged through the 49, its owner right behind it with a face full of rage. Brice's face glared out at them half his angry expression obscured with dirt and dust, but it didn't matter—both men huddled back against the panels all the same as he came charging through the vehicle, about as angry as they'd ever seen him.

"I don't care about your mama and I don't care about your arms!" he raged, almost nose to nose with the cringing subordinates. "But you will if you don't know how to work this thing in twenty minutes, cause you'll never see 'em again!"

No more words came; instead, Brice just stared ahead, seething as if unwilling to go any further for fear of losing it, and the men just looking back at him—just looking, though, as they didn't dare to stare. About to try to say something more, Brice finally just pulled away, clanging through the 49 and booting aside debris as he went, making for the door before he did any more damage.

Outside, people knew not to talk to him. Even from outside the steel hull of the 49, they'd heard him, and so they just watched as he ambled off a ways from the group in front of the APCs, breathing hard as he sat down near a small dune to file through maps he'd drawn from his fatigues.

A few minutes later, straightened out but devoid of the Brice's pressure, lights suddenly blinked on in the undamaged 49's its console responding as Fulkes tried a previously untested set of buttons.

"Oh, look at that!" Carson exclaimed, genuinely excited as the panel they'd pulled down suddenly lit up above them. "Little man found the on switch."

The three panels below them showed no change from left to right; what Fulkes claimed to be a radar screen still showed its elliptical patterns and three triangles while the other two panels showed the ion array status and what looked like engine stats. Above, Fulkes' supposed radar screen was mirrored by another identical screen with four others to its right, which hadn't yet been turned on by the hapless two.

"Heah heah!" exclaimed Carson as he got the next screen above them working, it displaying what appeared to be more engine stats.

"Hey, stop screwin' around!" Fulkes stood up in protest as Carson began fiddling with buttons and dials to his right under the three screens beside him, a further screen in the five above coming on as he did so.

"Sit down, bitch." Carson pushed away his hands as he continued to meddle. "Sarge's gonna be back in five. You really wanna tell him we ain't got it yet?"

Fulkes frowned, weighing up the idea in his head, when suddenly the triangle on the radar screen furthest back from the other two went red, Carson laughing as the engine stats on a screen above them came to life unnoticed.

Outside, Brice looked up in confusion with

Copeland from his maps as, a little way off, Copelands 49 suddenly came to life, its running lights beaming as it stared the men down.

"What about this one here?" Fulkes asked, intuitively pushing a button with a symbol that looked familiar.

Outside, a hail of dust and gravel burst up as the Copelands 49 tore forward, Brice and Copeland instantly running to get out of the way as it grinded toward them.

"Huh, look, that red triangle's movin'!" Carson exclaimed. "What about this dial here?" He wriggled an indented, circular control back and forth, it seeming to affect the red triangle's path on the screen.

Outside, Copeland ran right and then left as the huge 49 seemed to try to follow him, changing course erratically before finally moving past him—seemingly more interested in an irate sergeant fleeing for his life. Left or right, it didn't seem to matter as the 49 turned with him, his screams appearing to be attracting it before, in desperation, he threw himself aside at a right angle, the machine surging past him but still pulling right as it ploughed headlong into a dune, burying itself halfway in.

Inside the undamaged APC, shielded from the engine noise, the button-pushing pair felt the tremor of the Copeland's 49 slamming into the dune, the red triangle on screen coming to an abrupt halt and now flashing as an alert rang out.

Looking at each other, the realisation came to them at the same time. "Shit!" they cried out, nearly as one, and with that they began clambering back down the APC for the door, the realisation of what they'd been doing now dawning on them.

"This is the best yet!" Carson's voice came through the dust as they opened the APC's door. "Crashed the fucking thing and you weren't even in it!"

"What? You were steering it!" Fulkes replied.

"Steering, my ass—you had the accelerator!" Carson retorted.

"How am I supposed to see through the fucking walls?" Fulkes shouted.

"Wouldn't make any difference if you could!" returned Carson.

"That's a crock of…." Fulkes cut himself short as the dust began to lift, revealing a dishevelled and wheezing sergeant not far off from where they stood.

Standing side by side, Carson And Fulkes made eye contact through the dust, a raging Brice looking back at them. For a moment, there was silence as the two men stood frozen under Brice's confused look.

"Run?" Carson asked.

"…Yeah," agreed Fulkes.

Breaking to the right, they heard a roar behind them as Brice came stumbling after them.

Fuller and Rians watched from the doorway of the nearby wrecked 49 that hadn't moved.

"Well, at least we're figuring out how they work," Rians commented as Carson and Fulkes ran past the back of the 49.

"Yeah…" Fuller said thoughtfully.

"Aaaaarrrrgghh!!!!!" came a screaming Brice, shattering Fuller's train of thought as he went tearing past the front of the wreck after his two subordinates.

Forty minutes later, sitting on the passenger seats in the damaged 49, the men quietly discussed the situation. With rations running low, Copeland drank from one of the last protein sachets before passing it to Brice. Sipping some, Brice next passed it to Carson, who tried to take it, but found it held fast. Still holding on, he turned with a questioning look to the holder. His questioning was answered fully by Brice's expression, Brice holding the thing for a while longer to make his point as they looked at one another. Happy the message was through, Brice reluctantly released his grip, Carson turning quickly away and still sensing his glare, tilting his head back with the sachet as Fuller and Rians entered the 49 to his left.

Standing in front of them, Fuller began, "We've come up with something that might just work."

Carson turned to his left, tapping Fulkes on the shoulder to pass the sachet and feeling happy for an excuse to look away from Brice.

"What we think is…." Fuller stopped, squinting at Fulkes as he turned to Carson for the sachet, revealing a black eye. Fuller looked over at Brice, noticing a satisfied expression looking back. Rolling his eyes, Fuller sighed before beginning again. "We can't make it around them; the 49s' radars are picking up mass patrols all over the place, so we'd never make it, but we could make it to the base."

"They don't seem to stop approaching vehicles till they reach the main gate," continued Rians. "And—"

"Sir," Copeland cut in. "What good does that do us?"

"All we need to do is get to the base and then we can make a run for it," Rians answered.

"How do we pass around it if we're going up to the main gate?" Copeland questioned.

"We're not passing around it," Fuller explained. "We're going straight through it."

"What?" Carson gasped.

"The patrols are heavy on each side, east and west, but they're minimal in front," Rians replied. "We'd take around eighteen hours to make it back trying to avoid them, maybe a day, and we might not have a day. We need to get out from under this damping field and warn the others, and from the look of activity on that radar screen, there isn't much time. Cutting through the base, we could be out from under this field in as little as two hours, and the base itself doesn't seem to be heavily guarded for its size."

"Yeah, cause bases always contain mobile ST20s; you'd have to be crazy to go anywhere near it," Brice said.

"Yeah." Fuller smiled. "You would."

Brice sighed, looking away and shaking his head at what he was hearing; he'd seen what ST20s could do during the war—they were massive, inductive plasma cannons capable of hitting targets in low orbit and bringing them down. Lowered to ground level, they made deadly field artillery weapons, and what made it worse was that they were mounted on tracked crawlers, so they could move.

"We can ride right up to the gate without suspicion in one of these," Rians pointed out, looking around the 49.

"And then?" Copeland asked, bemused.

"Then we floor it," Fuller answered happily, still smiling.

"We won't get a hundred yards!" Brice uttered in disbelief at the plan.

"Well," said Fuller, walking over to Fulkes and smiling positively, "that's up to him."

Brice looked down the line of seats at the two of them grinning back at him. "Oh fuck," he muttered, dropping his head into his hands.

"Oh, and that's not the best part!" Fuller chirped. "Rians is gonna make you all feel better and tell you the rest of the plan." He beamed down at the faces staring back at him from the seats.

It took an hour. An hour to hash out the plan among everyone and, at the end of it, was anyone feeling better? The only ones smiling where Fuller and Fulkes.

"We're gonna die," Brice said, sitting up in the passenger seat nearest the door.

"Way to be positive, Sarge!" Fulkes shouted from the driver's seat to his left.

Brice turned and looked at the back of Fulkes' head as the man began to bring the 49 online; they were putting their lives in his hands. Fuck.

The engine growled into life in the afternoon sun, and rolling forward, the tires spewed out sand behind them as if ejecting a cloud as the vehicle moved. Inside, Fulkes steered the metallic giant as Rians, Carson, and Copeland struggled to lift the accelerator differential. Behind them on the right side sat Fuller in the oversized seat meant for a Hearack communications officer, monitoring not only com traffic but also the weapons and radar panels which were only barely within his reach. Brice sat in the seat on the opposite wall, holding on as the 49 rumbled over uneven terrain—his worries keeping him company, given there was nothing else for him to do.

"Dum dum dum, de dum... dum dum, dum de dum... dum dum dum di..."

"Hey, Fulkes, would you shut up? I'm trying to be

nervous here," Rians complained, standing with Copeland and Carson, the accelerator differential splitting them.

"What?" Fulkes asked. "I'm bored—there's nothing in front of us but desert and rocks," he said, his humming ceasing for the moment.

"Is that why we haven't hit anything for a while?" Carson quipped sarcastically, Copeland only smiling.

"You don't have to worry about hitting something," muttered Brice from his seat on the left. "We get near that base, we'll be hitting something, alright…. Can't believe I'm gonna buy it in this tin can," he grumbled to himself.

"Could be worse," Fulkes said. "Least we'll go together."

"Sure, that makes it alright then," Carson retorted sarcastically. "I'll make sure they put that on your tombstone; it's okay because he went with friends." He grimaced. "How about you, you alright with that?" he shot the quick question at Copeland, trying to hide his own growing discomfort over the situation.

"No, man." Copeland frowned, but didn't go against continuing the macabre subject. "I want a jazz band at my funeral with everybody smiling…."

"Smilin'?" Carson cut in, an astonished look on his face as he glanced over at Rians and back. "You realise at this funeral that you'll be dead, right? What the hell has anyone got to be smiling about at a funeral?" Carson's bewildered look remained as Copeland shook his head, dropping away laughing at Carson's expression.

"What about you, Lieutenant?" Carson turned back to Rians, his look now one of disturbed confusion, "You like anybody to be smilin' at your funeral?"

"…No," Rians finally said, and laughed a little at Carson's confused state.

"No!" repeated Carson, glad everybody was amused over his discomfort.

"No, I'd want something quieter," he continued, laughing. "Maybe something on the edge of a hill overlooking the sea."

"Overlooking the sea, huh?" Carson echoed in thought.

"Yeah," Rians answered, drifting into memory. "There's a place like that back home… used to dance there with Carla at sunset—fall into the wheat fields, and… you know."

"Yeah," Carson said, smiling and not questioning anymore, instead turning the spotlight away to Fuller. "And you, Cap? You been pretty quiet sitting back there."

"Yeah, well…" Fuller muttered from his seat, still blindly fiddling with consoles he didn't really understand. "Been a little busy here. I'm… gettin' nowhere. Eh, what do I want? Eh… guess I—"

"Anybody want to hear what I want?" Brice cut in, his voice a little bit strangled. "Huh? Anyone? I want everyone to stop talkin' about dyin', like it's gonna happen…"

"But, Sarge, you said…"

"It doesn't matter what I said," Brice continued over Fulkes, his nerves fraying. "We ain't got no time for this silly talk."

"Sarge, we got ages—there's miles…"

"No, we don't!" Brice shouted back, the rest of them finally realising he was close to another burst of fraid nerves.. "Now, look at this man over here—he's on the edge!" Brice said as he pointed at a becalmed Fuller. "He's been tryin' to figure out those damn panels since we left! Now, if you all got so much time on your hands, why don't you get back there and help 'im before he loses it?" Brice glared on at the now silent subordinates, none of them wanting to trigger his next stage of anger.

"Thank you, Brice, that'd be a big help over here," Fuller said calmly, trying to ease the situation as Brice rested back into his seat, looking aimlessly over Fulkes' shoulder at the instruments up front.

"Got ages, my ass," Brice grumbled.

Forty minutes later, things felt tight with the base getting ever nearer.

"How we lookin'?" Fuller asked.

"I can't see shit for this dust," answered Fulkes.

"We're just about right… no enemy vehicles in the area," Fuller replied.

"This differential's a bitch," Copeland called out, straining with the other two.

"It's good for you, baby—puts hairs on your chest!" Carson returned.

"How far?" Fulkes asked.

"Just under two kilometres," Fuller answered. "We're still behind this ridge, but the last two hundred metres are gonna leave us wide open."

"You reckon we'll get through the gate alright, Fulkes?" Fuller called out over the rumbling engine.

"Don't you worry, sir, it's just a pissy wire fence. I'll have us through there before they know what happened!" Fulkes shouted back.

"It's just a pissy wire fence cause what's inside don't need protecting," grumbled Brice.

"Ah, we'll fly through, Sarge," Fulkes reassured him.

"Yeah, just make sure that when we get out the other side, we're not on our roof," cracked Carson to the sniggering of the others.

"What about the base? What's it look like?" Rians asked.

"There's too much activity to make much sense of what's inside," Fuller replied as blue blips and shapes flashed over his terrain map on the screen. "I can't pin anything down."

"Great," Brice grumbled.

"Any sign of ST20s?" Copeland asked, squinting back at the radar panel to Fuller's right.

"It's just too busy to tell in there," Fuller answered, shaking his head amid the drone of the engine.

"How about the flanks?" Carson shouted, the weight of the differential telling in his voice.

"The patrols are still a ways off, east and west," Fuller shouted back. "The closest one is five kilometres out, east."

"Looks like the door's open!" Rians voiced happily.

"Yeah, just listen for it slamming shut when we're through," muttered Brice.

"Heads up!" shouted Fuller. "We're rounding the ridge with two hundred yards to go. Fulkes, come left thirty degrees." Fuller watched as the ridge fell away to the left on his visual display over the radar screen. "Good, good, another thirty… steady, steady… again, Fulkes, another thirty." Fuller watched as the 49's front camera view on screen, above him among the five pull-down stations, showing the gate coming into focus with a blur of a guard on its right. "A hundred yards to go…

fifty yards. The guard's motioning toward us."

"Alright, throttle back the engine," Fuller instructed. "Everybody, look sharp."

The steady drone of the engine lowered along with the vibrations as Copeland, Rians, and Carson lowered the differential, feigning their compliance for the guard.

"He's walking toward us; twenty yards," Fuller said.

"Alright, this is it!" Fuller shouted, the faces around him turning deadly serious. "I'll see you on the other side, gentlemen…." Fuller watched the guard on the screen above him, close in, and saw his expression suddenly change, his eyes widening as he began to see… "Floor it!" Fuller yelled

The guard's arrogant walk toward the APC had stopped, his eyes widening as the steel beast roared into life and began charging forward. The guard thrown aside, the gate came next with the 49 slamming forward so that the gate wrapped round its face before being torn from the ground—posts and all sliding down to be trampled underneath the six-wheeled monster.

The vehicle tearing into the base, sporadic weapons fire began to strike the APC here and there with Hearack coming to; a quarter way through the base, tents began passing on their left, the APC's tires leaving a massive dust cloud for two hundred yards behind it and tearing up the loose, arid ground.

"There's huge concentrations of movement up ahead!" shouted Fuller as they began to near the centre. Watching on screen, they saw that, beyond the tents, the base was a hive of activity, and they didn't have long before they found out why. As the last tent approached on their left, their cover was about to be lost. "Alright, here it comes!" Fuller shouted.

With them clearing the last tent, a hail of plasma fire slammed into the APC, lights smashing and armour scorching as hundreds of charges flew into the nose, fire erupting up and along the roof as they went.

The ion array took a hit, tearing it from its mount and sending it barrelling backwards to disappear into the dust behind them. As Fulkes tried to hold the APC straight, there was a crash against the front, Copeland thrown into the roof and coming down out cold, leaving only two men on the differential.

"Brice!" screamed Carson, straining under the falling arm.

Brice leapt forward, jamming his weight under the arm with Fulkes desperately trying to hold their course as he heard the three straining beside him.

"Come on!" screamed Fuller, looking at the radar. "We've got to move faster!"

Flames streamed from the mauled 49 surging through the middle of the base, Hearack firing relentlessly as they were forced aside.

"Fulkes, left twenty degrees!" Fuller shouted.

"How far?" Rians screamed at his breaking point with the differential.

"We're over halfway; hang on—" Fuller didn't finish as, on screen, a large blue blip appeared ahead, moving behind tents and making to cut them off. Fuller could see its size, and knew there was only one thing it could be.... "ST20 ahead!"

Moving out from the tents, a massive mobile platform crawled out in front of the approaching vehicle, coming to a halt ahead; explosive bolts secured it to the ground with a high-pitched whine of hydraulics signalling the massive barrel lowering.

Concentrating on the radar, Fuller shouted, "Come on, we're losing ground!" Just then, the viewscreen above caught his attention, his eyes widening as the huge ST20 barrel fell ahead of them. "Jesus! Fulkes, hard left!"

Explosive bolts almost ripped from the ground as the ST20 unleashed on the 49, its target vanishing in a wall of flames and shrouded for an instant before bursting through, unrecognisable from before.

With the APC careening forward in a bath of flames, the gunner took aim at the flailing beast, the men's eyes bulged as they watched on screen the second shot ring out—in a direct hit! These weapons were supposed to bring down orbiting ships, and despite the recoil, the gunner saw the fire blast outward as the front caved in under the impact, pitching up as the fire twisted inside; the APC was on its side in moments. Still skidding forward, it tore up a great gouge as it came, throwing up even more dust as it was pulled slowly left by the ground, all under the gunner's watchful eye. Coming to a near halt, flames on the side roared from the gaping hull, ferociously consuming anything they could as the blanketing dust cloud blocked out activity behind the APC, which lay roasting fifty yards short of freedom.

Satisfied, the gunner released his controls, happy enough that they were burning inside the wreckage as he unbuckled his harness, the inferno raging on in front of him. Molten alloy burst aloud as flames continued to rage inside the hull's steel, melting under the roar of fire. Suddenly, though, there was another roar that sounded out louder over the flames—the roar of an engine….

With a crash, the wreck burst sideways as a second 49 came charging out of the dust cloud. Caught in his harness, the gunner grabbed for the controls, but the looming giant already blocked out the scene behind it. His screams weren't heard as the thundering beast smashed into the ST20, crushing him under its six wheels and veering up over the steel grave to maul him into the twisting metal. Tearing out of the wreckage the 49 crashed forward, smashing into the ground debris flying everywhere from the smashed cannon behind it. Inside, roars of triumph deafened the smiling Fulkes. his neck jarring back and forth as a still straining Brice, Rians, and Carson fought to rap their knuckles off his head, shaking him from all directions.

Chapter 18

True Colours

The machinery of war rumbled back and forth everywhere, units setting up positions unhurriedly— unaware of what lay nearby. Night having fallen once again, the ground was saturated in the ghostly pale blue laid down by the moons far above, watching the defensive scene and lines being arranged in front of the infirmary compound, its blast doors lying open.

A hundred yards forward of the doors lay the first line of emplacements, dug in as much as possible into the stone-laden ground; the ten fell back in an almost semi-circular pattern from the first two closest to the doors. In front of them, the ground sloped up by fifteen degrees to the second line that was a hundred yards in front of them and in the same circled-back arrangement, with visibility blocked in places by small hills. From here on, the ground sloped gently up by about five degrees before flattening out and leading a hundred yards off to the third line of twelve emplacements that could be seen circling back like the others. All lines were hemmed in by the ridges on both sides, giving excellent cover but making commanders in the first and second lines nervous with only being able to see straight ahead up sloping ground. Only the third line, set at the mouth of the last ridges, had an unobscured view of the ghostly plateau out in front. It wasn't much, either, but with two aging K27 Lores tanks and an artillery piece hurriedly set up on top of the hinge of the right blast door, they were all that stood in front of the infirmary. Behind them, through the blast doors, the compound was a four-hundred-yard, flat length of ground lying open between the ridges, with the twinkling lights of the infirmary at the far end where patients—helpless and otherwise—were being hurriedly prepared for evacuation, the impending danger felt by the staff intensifying by the hour.

The feeling was also felt by Marine Captain Mendez as he surveyed the defences under his command in front of him, based from his command tent set out just behind and to the left of the first line. He tried to shrug it off, to forget what it could mean, but he'd felt it before many times before. Call it a sixth sense, intuition, or what you would, but he'd learnt to trust it…. Something was coming.

His train of thought didn't last long, though, as his gaze across the lines was interrupted by a disturbance in front of the fifth emplacement of the second line. Minutes later, muted gestures and muffled anger could be heard coming up from the first line as seven black silhouettes filtered between emplacements four and five, their compliments returned by irate Marines on either side as they moved toward the command tent. Soon enough, there came more anger, but this time from Mendez as he opened up on the lieutenant escorting the men. "I thought I ordered, as of twenty-two hundred, that no one was to pass through the lines!" The escort didn't get to answer, his attempt lost under the drone of the K27 passing left of the front of the first line amid Mendez's continuing rage. "What are you, deaf? What if you'd been run over by one of those bastards!" screamed Mendez, pointing at the 27 as it rumbled on into formation with its partner.

"I'm sorry, sir, but—" the lieutenant tried to explain.

"Sorry! Sorry! Sorry doesn't quite cut it, soldier; when I give an order, I expect it to be followed, for Christ's sake! What if one of those emplacements had opened up? Did you even stop to think about that?"

"Sir, yes, sir, but these men were just picked up from their scouting patrol ten clicks northwest of here driving a Hearack T49!" voiced the lieutenant. "That damping field's still blocking communications, so we had to cross it; it seemed urgent that you—"

"What?" A voice approaching in the shadows halted the lieutenant. "What was so damn important that you had to cross my lines?" the voice continued as they watched a tall, lean shadow emerge from the darkness behind them and to the left. It was Commander Hayward. "Well, son? Why did you just get yourself a court-martial!" He glared at the lieutenant.

"Sir, these men—"

"These men!" Hayward repeated, cutting him off and staring at Fuller. "These men have done nothing but screw up since they got here; these men who—"

"Sir, they—" the lieutenant's attempt to explain was cut off yet again, not by words, but by the scowl of Hayward as he spun round at him.

"When I'm talking, you don't!" Hayward screamed above the noise around them. "When I'm—"

"If you'd get your head outta your ass, you'd hear what he's trying to say!" Fuller burst in. "There's a whole fucking regiment on its way! They can't be more than a few clicks out, and they—"

"Really!" Hayward retorted. "We've got a dozen veteran recon teams out there, and you're the only ones who've seen any sign of them, huh? The only thing worse than your mouth is your imagination, Fuller—the scopes are clear and there's no com traffic—"

"There's no traffic because it's being jammed, you moron!" Fuller shouted back at him.

"We've analysed that as interference from this rock's high mineral content; you're chasing mere scout teams of minor force. Anything bigger would have been detected from orbit, so you're chasing shadows, Fuller!" Mendez replied.

"And that T49 we arrived in—was that a fucking shadow? What kind of scout team would have one of them?" Fuller screamed.

The arguing developed into mayhem, each man trying to force his point over the shouts of troops and rumblings of K27s till finally one man backed out, and then another, till finally only Hayward was left for a second voicing his all before abruptly stopping, the atmosphere catching his attention. No shouts, nothing… the lines had gone quiet, and people looked down the lines as far as their eyes would take them, trying to see the third… but only the idling of the 27s on one side were left to challenge the stillness.

Confused looks went back and forth—nervous, unsure, expecting at any moment for the false alarm to be given, as had happened so many times throughout the night. But it didn't come. Instead, an eerie sound began to filter through to the first line, through the calm around them. A quiet pulsing sound, unrecognisable with the distance involved, sounded out around them, the confusion remaining till suddenly shouts began to direct marines' attention accordingly, with ears not eyes giving the updates as, out in front, the second line had become a throng of activity. Marines could be seen arming weapons and pulling in tight as it became all too clear what the sound was… the third line's proximity sensors!

The sound at the third line wasn't quiet at all—now it was more like a pulsing shriek from the tripods out in front of them, painful to the ears and polarising their attention on the horizon as they frantically searched for the enemy. Sweat-soaked, adrenalin-laden eyes scoured the ground in front through aiming sights—straining, willing themselves to see the shimmer of the suits before they came too close, but there was nothing, nothing….

Eyes continued searching into the night, ruthlessly scanning but to no avail as the shrieking alarms pulsed in the ears of every soul facing the invisible threat ahead. Two minutes went by, palms sweating on rifles with the pulse now throbbing through ears. Adrenaline ebbing away, soldiers felt sweat trickle down their necks, their hearts pounding as the sensor screams did more damage to morale than any enemy could now that fear had descended. More minutes passed till finally the sensors reset, the sudden cut-out of noise forcing men to jolt on their rifles with the silence being just as nerve-wracking and their eyes still scanning into the darkness.

Thoughts raced with sweat as minds tried to reason. Had it been some animal? Had the Hearack moved up even though their suits were still out of visual range, and stopped? Were they right in front of them, frozen so that sensors wouldn't arm? Whatever the answer was, eyes didn't flinch, instead continuing their battle with the darkness, challenging the silence out ahead.

Suddenly, the whole plateau was illuminated in front of the third line, shadows leaping up ridge walls with proximity sensors screaming as plasma rounds tore out of the darkness in front. Half the emplacements on the third fell instantly to a swarm of blue energy, leaving the rest in horror as waves of Hearack burst from the darkness, suits failing at the speed of their approach. Over the deafening noise, the second line tried to pour on support from behind, but within seconds, the enemy had closed on the third. Distinguishing friend from foe had become impossible, so the second line could only watch as sharp glints in the night indicated bayonets and hand to hand combat—positions being overrun.

Watching wasn't an option for the third, as those left were quickly swamped, rifles useless as enemy shot dead were simply used as shields by those behind them, carried the last few yards and then hurled into emplacements to block any line of sight before arms eight times stronger than the defenders' reached around the dead, searching for human flesh. Marines across the third line heard screams of men turn to gargling panic as not knife nor blade but hands and teeth closed mercilessly on weaker throats.

From the second line, shadows leapt across the plateau—savage in front, but only for a second as their makers burst from emplacements, grey skin and red eyes surging out of the mist. Plasma charges flew in all directions to be answered by rifles from the second, Hearack crashing to the ground in waves, their plasma sent skyward from dying hands, their own following simply surging over their suffering eyes and bodies fixed on the second line.

Again, as before, the next line laid on support, the first throwing everything it had into a desperate bid to help their comrades, but they were soon unable to tell friend from foe with the cries ahead signalling more hand to hand combat. In the fifth pit, amid the screams, a Marine aimed over his dead partner, firing his last shot into the chest of a grotesque form emerging from the darkness—his rifle jolting to a stop as his target slumped down, chest torn open as he dropped. But he never made it to the ground— suddenly, he was rising, surging awkwardly forward with his head slumped to one side and roaring as he came. The Marine instinctively raised his bayonet, realising too late his mistake as the carcass came crashing into his pit, his bayonet piercing through and jamming into the body as it took him to the ground. The roars came, too, but from behind, monstrous hands appearing from around the body and grabbing for the Marine, his screams joining the others when he found himself unable to raise his sidearm.

"We gotta pull back!" Fuller shouted at Hayward as they watched waves of the enemy descend on the second.

"We have to keep them from the door!" Hayward staunchly argued, ignoring the impending disaster and unwilling to accept Fuller's warning as the 27s began opening up from the left of the first.

"We're gonna be overrun! We have to pull back behind the doors and hold them there till—" Fuller was silenced as a huge enemy salvo came through the mist, crashing into a 27 and leaving it floundering as its right track was torn off. Its drive gone, it was left aflame on its right side, a virtual bullseye in the night that was confirmed seconds later when a huge charge slammed into the hapless 27, blinding those around it. Channels crackled from the remaining Lores as it pulled off left into the mist, reaching for the darkness as its partner burned furiously behind it.

"Multiple enemy vehicles, four hundred yards and closing—pulling to cover behind the... INCOMING!"

The ridge line to the left exploded, rocks flying

everywhere with the 27 becoming visible for a second through a curtain of flame before disappearing in the inferno, channels falling dead.

Second and third down had cost the Hearack dearly, the plateau now being filled with mist and smoke from plasma fire, the unbroken waves of enemy now small groups cut to pieces by the first... mere stragglers now coming through the night. Blood couldn't be seen in the mist—just outlines piling up and still jerking from nerves, arma-tipped rounds exploding in flesh and tearing off arms and legs so that cries went unheard as the first rained hell on anything that moved.

"Hayward, we gotta pull back!" Fuller screamed, struggling to his side with rifle barrels bursting all around them.

"We can—" Hayward tried to shout back, his stubborn arrogance gone with weapons fire cutting him off.

"We gotta pull back now!" screamed Fuller, sensing the indecision in his face.

But Hayward's instinct was to argue, to keep the reins of power at all times, his expression suddenly turning back to one of disdain. "We can't just pull ba—"

Hayward was silenced as a massive charge tore out of the darkness, its huge sender illuminated for an instant coming through the lines before allying with darkness once again, lost while its plasma charge screamed overhead, crashing into a ridge line behind. There were no more arguments, no more doubt as Marines started a fighting retreat, ordered through their headsets to fall back as a massive shape appeared, rumbling over the second line to widening eyes as it let loose another charge, revealing itself and sending half a dozen men spiralling to their deaths. Panic gripped Marines as it rumbled forward faster, unhindered by the second line's efforts and instead spraying the ground in its path with energy, the light from its ion array revealing the T49 and more of its kind in the distance, all en route. Energy smashed up off the ground from the array, tearing in all ways so that troops began throwing themselves right and left for cover as the huge machine swung right, bearing down on the helpless figures. With it almost upon them, they could only watch as the huge ion array above redirected toward them, swinging right, its engine deafening, when suddenly a blackened hulk came surging out of the shadows and slammed head-on against the armour, both exploding instantly. Already on the ground, Marines felt the blast wave pass over them, tearing outward to steal away more life with fire erupting from its source as their Lores saviour, visible through the wreckage, disappeared, consumed by the blaze with the 49.

Dazed men tried to fall back, dragging bodies both wounded and dead along with them, but the daze was short-lived, plasma charges erupting from their right so that faces turned in horror to a mass of shimmering down the ridge line to their right, failing suits bringing more enemy out of the darkness.

The Hearack had managed it; they'd done the impossible, making their way over what had been assumed to be an impassible ridge, men now paying for this arrogance.

Plasma charges seared in from the right, ripping into their flank, Marines carrying wounded becoming victims themselves as still more charges came from in front with the remnants of the Hearacks' initial assault now reaching the first line. Dragging a wounded man himself, Fuller looked left for his unit only to see a Marine carrying a wounded comrade have his chest go up like a flare, plasma taking him down along with any hope of rescue for the man he'd been carrying. Headsets raged with screams of the dying as they desperately pulled back, trying to crouch on open ground with plasma charges coming in from all directions, air cracking as it passed. Those reaching the towering blast doors crowded in on either side, offering what support they could and forced to watch as wounded tried to limp after them, their faces appearing from the darkness only to be cut down en masse.

"Where's Hayward? Where's Hayward?" Mendez could be heard shouting, but no answer came—there was nothing to be said as wide eyes watched the silhouettes of Hearack appear behind the last few men who were alive, surging toward them. Looking from the left door, Mendez knew what had to be done; there was no time for anything else. There simply wasn't time. "Seal the doors!" he heard himself yelling, barely able to watch as the huge coffin lids began to creak shut on his men. Grinding together, the huge steel forms began to close the gap on the faces outside, garnering horrified looks as they realised what was happening. All but cut down, a sole Marine dragging his shattered comrade through the bodies emerged in the distance, screaming for more time, but all Mendez could do was mouth the words, "I'm sorry," to the anguished face he'd condemned. Watching the space grow smaller between the closing doors, he saw the struggling Marine suddenly being struck down by a charge from the right, sending him reeling out of sight with his injured comrade crashing to the ground, face wrenching in pain. The doors almost closed, Mendez watched the helpless figure try to crawl forward, his cries of pain drowned out by the silhouettes appearing through the smoke behind him.

Hayward didn't have to see their putrid red eyes glinting in the fires, nor watch as one descended on the victim, but he thought he had to, that it was the least he could do, to look into the man's eyes as the bayonet went through his back....

With the doors just inches from sealing, there was a flash on the horizon, the view lost to closing steel with questions answered as to what it was an instant later, the crash behind the left door telling them well enough that all remaining men had been seared with flame as fire spewed through the gap. Flaming bodies rolled in agony as the doors slammed shut finally, the fire having illuminated the scene as the round's remaining energy had been forced upward, appearing angry at the denial of the great doors.

With the fireball diminishing thirty feet higher, the light gave way to the ghostly blue bodies writhing in flames, rolled over the ground by themselves and others—those few officers left still desperately trying to bring order to the chaos.

Shouting the names of his superiors, Mendez quickly realised that no further answers would come as he pushed from the right side of the blast doors to the left, trying to order men across the plateau to positions near the infirmary. Muffled crashes and the heaving groans from the doors gave away the Hearacks' determination to break through, flames occasionally reaching over the top from the other side. He couldn't understand even as he moved, couldn't understand as he screamed into the ears of men trying to push past him to scale the ridges. Rifles could be heard from above, sporadically firing from Marines already up there but drowned out every few seconds as the mortar went off, now focused on the ground instead of skyward. It was madness, completely against their planning; they were trying to hold a static position against a mechanised enemy when they should have been pulling back and spreading into new positions. He couldn't understand it; he couldn't… And then a figure in the distance provided all the answers: Fuller.

As Fuller approached, battling through floundering Marines, he watched him direct men up the ridges.

"Move up further to the left; don't give them only one group to worry about!" Fuller shouted over the noise at the shaken Marines. "Take care of the infantry and keep them off the mortar cannon's back—let him deal with the armour…."

"What the hell are you doing?" Mendez screamed, arriving behind him.

Fuller looked round before spinning back to the Marines. "Go!" he shouted at the men already making for the ridge as he turned back to Mendez.

Livid as he was, Mendez's rage did the talking. "What the fuck are you doing?" he screamed into Fuller's face before motioning men down.

"Stay where you are!" screamed Fuller, the men pausing… unsure as a different battle erupted below them. "I'm doing what you and that asshole Hayward should have done hours ago!"

"You're gonna get us all killed! They're bringing up more armour out there; these doors won't hold for shit, so we gotta pull back!" Mendez insisted.

"Pull back to where? We don't have anywhere to pull back to! You lost that option out there!" Fuller roared, pointing over the doors.

"I didn't lose shit!" screamed Mendez over the firing above. "The only thing lost is your mind—you're gonna get us all killed! You should have stayed in the Navy with your nancy boys—"

In an instant, arms grabbed for one another, eyes fixed and the start of new fight began when… suddenly a crash jolted any further thought from them, the vibration through the ground almost bringing them down as a huge fireball crept up over the door, this one even larger than the first. This time, the fireball was accompanied by an ear-piercing creak of metal on metal, men watching as a fifty-foot section of door slid off with the edges still glowing as it crashed to the ground, coming to rest against the remains of the right door.

"Oh my God, they've brought up an ST20," uttered Fuller, staring through the gap.

The glowing edges of the gaping hole cast shadows on Marines who were now fleeing, it now being obvious the position couldn't be held. Wounded and concussed, the men began a disorganised rally across the plateau with Fuller and Rians waiting for the last to come from the ridges, following on as they made it down.

Outside the gates in the distance the last targeting information needed was spread across the ST20's load screen as it zeroed in on the hinge of the left door, with a shot ringing out so that the recoil almost broke it free from its mounting.

Inside, fleeing survivors witnessed a huge section of steel sheer off and catapult into the air behind them as the remains of the doors, still barely joined in the middle, groaned on, shielding their escape. The tremor through the ground signalled the section landing as they ran, the shattered wrecks of doors behind them now becoming perforated as, again and again, weapons fire began burrowing through the steel from the other side with Hearack weapons pounding them into submission.

Soldiers running on, eyes looked back to see red areas begin to spew molten metal, holes appearing as rounds came through again and again till finally... Crashing through, the first vehicle smashed the steel apart, fire clearing off a mauled 49 as it veered right, more barrelling through behind it so that the doors were ripped apart by the armour pouring in. Angry headlights now pierced the ghostly blue, searching for their prey with the running men's path suddenly lit up like daylight as they fell. Behind them, searing plasma now surged forward from a staggered line of chasing armour, men flung into the air as flames engulfed them with others' hands outstretched for the infirmary enclosure, never making it and instead being torn away by the horror behind them. Those inside the small enclosure in front of the infirmary could only watch from each side of the walled entrance, those who were foolishly trying to fire being ripped away as plasma seared through inside. Panic driving men apart, some of them scaled the ridges on each side of the infirmary, looking down into the plateau that was now full of Hearack armour driving forward and halfway across the open ground thundering toward the helpless inside the facility. As plasma tore yet more victims away from the enclosure's entrance, beaten eyes looked out, awaiting their turn, the armour charging in in front of them, the next wave sure to...

Suddenly, the blue night was shattered by a scream deafening all noise before it, men reaching for their ears only to change direction for their eyes as a gold shimmer tore at their retinas, slamming into the ground before them. Those not blinded were able to open their eyes on a towering column of energy reaching up, grasping for air as it sent out a wave of destruction below, the enemy lost from sight in a sea of fire from a blast wave racing toward the infirmary. Those with any sight left pulled the blind to the ground as a wall of dirt and flame tore over the plateau toward them. Involuntary screams came from Marines and patients alike as the deep rumble descended around them. The heat was felt first, and then the howl of debris and energy came as the wave surged through the enclosure, sucking men from the ground and tearing others from the ridges before slamming headlong into the infirmary. Screams were silenced as glass flew inward, shattering over walls and patients and pulling them from the floors to hurl them against the tiles, the building's foundations shaking to the core.

Slowly, screams began to be heard again, the moans of patients and others coming as the deep rumbling subsided, the wave passing and dissipating further on, leaving only destruction behind it. Out in front of the infirmary, those lucky enough to have held fast began to rise as best they could, though there weren't many—only a few who'd found refuge against the rock on each side of the enclosure came stumbling out dazed and confused. Atop the ridges on each side, a similar story played out, it being known only too well by those surviving. The blinding light of the wave had tried to push through their closed eyelids as they'd struggled to hold to the rock, feeling bodies lift from among them—those of the ones who couldn't hold on. Opening their eyes, they already knew most were gone, and they weren't proved wrong as just a few struggled in the debris around them.

Fuller checked around him frantically for Rians, blackened faces looking back with no words heard as ears rung on, people immobile from shock. Finally, the eyes he sought looked back at him, Fuller half-falling to his knees beside him and shaking his shoulder in an attempt to check him. Rians just looked back as if he didn't recognise him, but he had looked; he was alive. Sitting for a second, Fuller struggled for breath as muffled calls began to be heard, survivors struggling to their feet below. Mind clearing, Fuller thought of them coming, the Hearack, and he rolled left onto his thigh and looked back up the ridge; half-crawling, he struggled the ten yards to the top where two Marines stood—gaunt, confused, staring blankly down the other side. Crawling the last bit of space, Fuller struggled to his feet with pain appearing as the shock began to fade, looking at the others; he got no reply to his stare, and instead they kept looking down as if they were statues held in place. Struggling, with a limp beginning from wounds to his leg, Fuller soon knew why; below, there was nothing… no Hearack, no vehicles, no ground—just a massive crater with heat billowing from scorched earth as the plateau wept smoke from a gaping wound. A hundred yards out, where there'd been enemy before, and been machines of war, there lay a smoking ruin, hundreds of small fires and embers lying around a crater that was almost as wide as the plateau with smoke hiding its depth below.

Shock still preventing thought, minds were unable to find answers to what they were seeing, men standing still with stares that brought no clarity, eyes vacant while scanning the destruction below. Ears barely registered the hum still ringing from before, but finally bodies recognised what minds could not. Fear filled those who were standing as they began to struggle, looking around as the hum could now be felt pulsating through the air. Those still with weapons tried to reach for them, only to find their arms broken, even such injuries as this having gone unnoticed before. Looks all around brought more fear as the sound intensified, echoing off the ridge walls and drawing still more panic. Suddenly, Fuller's face was cut; the sting had come from his Marine crest, torn up from his uniform and drawn across his cheek and away. Similar scenes played out all around him, with panicked cries emerging as steel filaments and wreckage began to lift from the ground, weapons also being torn from their holders by some unseen magnetic force. The pulsating increasing, what was happening suddenly became clear as a blinding light burst from over the ridge behind the infirmary; eyes were shielded by hands and at first peered out in panic, but that panic turned to mania, cheers going up all around Fuller as the exhausts of an Alliance ship cleared the ridge. Soon, Fuller also was among those cheering as he saw the insignia designated along the bow…

IAF RHIENVAR 228 - 1F

They were alright, after all, he thought as he watched the huge hull of the starship pull up through the clouds and fade off out of sight.

Shuttles ferried survivors back and forth in relays

Aidin arriving on one…

"Engine trouble?" Fuller wheezed hoarsely, smiling at Aidin from among the medics in the triage centre that was now hastily being repaired in front of the wrecked infirmary, Rians and the rest of the unit all around him, also having survived.

"Yes, we've had problems with it ever since leaving 185; seems the technicians there haven't gotten it quite right. Danske found some problems that forced us to stop and ensure the safety of the ship," Aidin continued, Fuller not believing a word of it. "While we were making repairs, we picked up the increased activity on Aurin 2 through sensors, so it's lucky Danske and his staff are as good as they are, or we might not have made it back here in time."

Fuller looked at Aidin straight, both men having the beginnings of the same wry smile on their faces. "Technicians, huh?" Fuller asked. "What about those other matters elsewhere, about the rest of the fleet?"

"I don't know," Aidin answered, looking skyward with his smile fading. "I just don't know."

Chapter 19

The Ghosts of Yeris

Ships desperately tried to hold the line, a mismatch of order and damaged vessels struggling on.

"Conway to any and all vessels, this is the *Holstadt*. We are under fire from multiple hostiles need immediate assistance—respond." The silence was shameful; the attack ship *Holstadt* had become separated. While escorting the delegation through the Dren Fleet, they had engaged an attack wing on the coalition's flank to prevent disaster and were now entangled in a bitter battle for survival.

"*Holstadt* to all vessels, respond," came another desperate hail over the channels with the sound of weapons fire and wounded in the background.

Suddenly, another voice broke over the channels, "*Hordec* to *Langan*, request permission to engage."

A frayed Ritter responded, "Negative, *Hordec*, maintain formation."

"*Holstadt* to fleet, taking heavy damage; attempting to reach a nebula engaged with seven—repeat, seven– we're in…"

Maine listened as the memories of Yeris came flooding back, the panicked voices of the *Holstadt*'s crew merging with the memories of his own… the fear on board, the strain in the captain's voice as he tried to remain a figure of strength for the crew. He'd been there, and he remembered the feeling of helplessness, of abandonment….

"Conway to fleet, engines are failing; we're losing

helm control, attempting to…"

Desperate, Maine tried to reason with Ritter. "We can't just leave them there; we've got to—"

"You've got to hold the line like everyone else!"

"But we could reach them."

Ritter was incensed, the fleet hearing Maine questioning his authority. "We're carrying the whole Irachan delegation; you've got some of their council onboard!"

There were no delegates on the *Holstadt*, so Ritter was leaving them and Maine knew it, even with memories from Yeris racing through his mind, deafening him with the panic, the screams, all of it mixing with the cries from the *Holstadt* till he couldn't tell the difference anymore.

"Ritter, I can't just leave them!"

"You listen to me!" Ritter roared. "You hold the line, do you hear me? Hold the line! Mainc… Maine…. Maine!!!"

No answer came; among the fleet, the *Hordec* fell silent, the channels bristling with the sound of weapons fire as the *Holstadt* was battered behind them. Helpless cries echoed through the lines, crews freezing to the sound of the screams of dying comrades as they filled space around them.

"Mayday, mayday! *Holstadt* to fleet, we are disabled and adrift, shields are failing. Mayday, mayday!"

Through shrieking alarms, crews listened to the desperate calls for help, voices fighting to be heard above muffled impacts and weapons fire as they reported in.

"Shields are buckling; auxiliary power's failed!"

"Two more Hearack coming down the port side!"

"They're firing again!"

"Brace for impact…."

The deafening crash resounded through the shamed fleet, crews frozen under Ritter's hand, when suddenly more cries filled the channels.

These were the cries of frantic captains trying to steer clear of mayhem erupting in the tightly packed formation.

"What's he doing?"

"Full starboard!"

"Wheel right!"

Ritter heard the commotion, as well, demanding, "Punch the fleet up on screen!"

Chaos appeared before him. The lines of brilliant blue rail exhausts behind the *Langan* were a mess, ships veering dangerously in all directions with exclamations from more and more ships joining the channels.

Ritter looked on in disbelief when suddenly, through the centre, came the culprit… the *Hordec*!

Knifing between two starships and narrowly missing a third, she tore out through the top of the lines.

"Maine! Maine!!!" Ritter's rage could be heard above the already deafening channels as the *Hordec* charged back toward the *Holstadt*.

"Shut him off!" Maine barked.

Far behind the fleet the Holstadt continued being battered to pieces…

The explosion knocked Conway from his feet again as he tried to reach the helm under shuddering impacts. Shoving the slumped body of his helmsman off the panel, he demanded, "Report!"

Through the smoke and noise, what was left of the bridge crew came back.

"Shields are gone!"

"Weapons are out!"

"Two Hearack aft, coming in; five more in front!"

Conway stared at the smashed panel below him, the instruments illegible; the crew were waiting, but waiting for what? He could feel the crew—terrified, looking to him for an answer, but what could he tell them? The ship was lost, the fleet was gone, and the Hearack would destroy any life pods that were launched. What could he do?

Weapons crashed into the hull, the helm panel exploding and taking a faceless Conway backward in a hail of shrapnel. His thinking days were over.

Her shields down, the *Holstadt* was torn into by raging weapons, fire raging on all of her decks. No more orders were necessary, as those inside struggled through the smoke-filled corridors amid the horror of dismembered remains, the impacts unrelenting....

Decks collapsed on screaming victims, the deafening crash of falling beams above the weapons fire coming along with raging flames as helpless crew were treated to an all too bone-chilling sound... the ear-piercing shriek of coolant rushing from the core!

The *Holstadt* was finished, and the crew fought for breath in the inferno as two Hearack vessels moved in for the slaughter, descending like wolves with crippled survivors watching through windows as they unleashed everything they had.

Hearack weapons ignited in space, a wall of fiery light and hell descending on screams, eyes watching it all come on. Smashing into the ship, the wall of light turned blue, shimmering, the two ships overshooting the *Holstadt* with thorans screaming after them, one exploding as weapons crashed under its rear—shockwaves rushing back toward the *Holstadt* and bursting again in more shimmering blue. Crew members looked on in shock, unable to figure out why it was all happening, when suddenly a deafening roar came overhead—the *Hordec* had arrived, shields extended and weapons blazing!

"How long?" Maine shouted.

"One minute, forty seconds!" replied the transporter room.

"We gotta hold out long enough to get them onboard—draw their fire!" Maine instructed.

"Aye, sir," Gray acknowledged, "three ships comin' hard; two more to port!"

"Target the lead ship!"

"Locked up!"

"Fire!"

The *Hordec* blazed, weapons raining down on the lead ship so that it exploded, already having become weak from the fight with the *Holstadt*, as two others which had been hidden in the aftermath charged out, opening up.

"Manoeuvring thrusters; track the—" Maine's voice was cut off by weapons tearing into the forward shields. "Report!"

"Forward shields down to sixty-two percent; port and starboard down to eighty!" shouted a nervous Brent.

"Rotate shield generators—equalize them!" Maine ordered.

Brent frantically tapped the helm panel, equalizing

as instructed, but behind him came a shout from Gray: "Two more aft, locking us up!"

"Fire!" screamed Maine.

Thorans shot out in front in an angry yellow, turning in an instant and screaming back over the *Hordec* toward the approaching ships.

"Direct hit—they're still coming…" Gray was cut short, lurching over his weapons panel with salvos tearing into the rear, the deafening crash giving way to steel howls onscreen with ships shooting overhead, disappearing in the distance.

"Report!" Maine roared over the noise.

"Ions are out, thorans reloading!"

"Shields down to forty-eight percent; number two generators damaged…"

"The other two are coming in fast from ten o'clock!" interrupted the con.

"Ready thoran dispersal, pattern beta— "

The *Hordec* had lost its shine; grazed and torn, its shield generators whined feverishly with trying to shore up the damage. In the infirmary, blood-soaked walls went unnoticed as survivors arrived directly, materialising in wrenching agony as staff shouted frantically over their screams. Dr Fahren desperately tried to handle swelling numbers… *"20 cc's, Halpsidine; Williams, seal that artery!"* More victims came in; the beds were full, people materialising on the floor.

The bridge was filling with smoke, as well, flames appearing on stations behind Gray as plasma seals failed.

"Thorans away; direct hit on their—"

"Incoming!"

A deafening crash sent sparks showering the bridge,

panels blowing out. "Report!"

"Heavy damage to power conduits on deck five; life support failing on eight through ten!" Brent was visibly shaken. "Shields down to forty-two percent, Captain, we've gotta get outta here!"

"Hold your shields!" came back a determined reply. "Damage control teams to deck five!"

"Hostiles comin' in twelve o'clock low!" Gray hollered over Maine's voice.

"Fire at will!" Maine roared.

Thorans blazed out of the *Hordec*, streaking out on screen in front with a terrific explosion coming in the distance, signifying the lead ship collapsing in a mass of flame that flashed angry red as ion fire tore through from the following ship.

"Hostiles, eight o'clock low!" Gray screamed as two more ships bore down, silhouetted against the brilliant blood dark nebula sprawling like a sunset behind them.

"Damage control teams approaching section— aaaaarrrgghhhh!"

Screams filled the bridge as the outer hull burst inwards, the team sliced to pieces and sucked out into space.

"Outer hull breach on deck five!" Brent shouted. "Shields down to twenty-eight percent, port shields failing!"

"Transporter room, report!" Maine demanded.

"We need forty seconds."

The infirmary was a blood bath filled with screaming monsters, lasers slashing into flesh as staff desperately cut away searing shrapnel. Williams took aim with a sorin scalpel at the steaming mass on a victim's neck, just about to pull the trigger when the room was rocked by an explosion. The patient screamed, the laser tearing through his face as Williams lost his balance.

Fahren was incensed. "Captain, you've gotta get us outta here!"

Suddenly, screams filled the room as beds flew into the air with patients, weapons crashing under the hull.

"Shields down to nineteen percent; port shields critical!" Brent was losing it. "Captain!"

"Hold your shields!"

"Hostile two o'clock low!" Gray shouted.

"Hit him with everything you've got!" Maine ordered.

The *Hordec* erupted, blazing yellow as thorans shot out at the approaching ship. An angry response of blazing red appeared before crashing thorans tore the ship apart.

"Target destroyed—hostiles coming around course two-five—" Gray was silenced as the response slammed into the hull, an almighty explosion rocking the *Hordec* as its number two generator exploded.

"Port shields have failed!" Brent screamed.

"We've lost navigation!"

"Remaining shields at fifteen percent!" announced an irate Brent.

"Four ships approaching ten o'clock high!" sounded the con.

"We've gotta pull out!" Brent shouted.

"You will hold your shields."

"Hostiles fully armed!"

"Captain, we have to go!" Brent screamed.

"Hold your shields!" Maine demanded.

"Transporter room to bridge, we've got them!"

"Manouvering thrusters, position us port on to the *Holstadt* and use her as a shield!" Maine ordered.

The four Hearack bore down on the *Hordec* as it manoeuvred behind the crippled *Holstadt*, weapons erupting from them. In an instant, the *Holstadt* was annihilated, whole decks exploding into space as weapons tore into the exposed ship. On the *Hordec*, the crew watched in horror as the crimson glow off the screen on their port signalled the *Holstadt* being ripped apart when suddenly a crash threw everyone from their feet.

"Report!" Maine demanded.

"The *Holstadt*'s been forced into our port side from the Hearack attack!" Sanderson shouted from the con.

"Torpedos are jammed; they're offline!" Gray shouted.

"Damage control teams to torpedo room!"

"Engine room, we need more power to the shields!" Maine shouted.

"We've dumped in the core; we're already running at a hundred and fifteen percent!" screamed Franklin.

"Then get me a hundred and twenty!"

"I can't maintain that kind of containment pressure!" His words were drowned out in an explosion as Franklin looked up in horror to see coolant rushing from a junction at the top of the engine room, ice advancing along the wall amidst shrieking clouds.

The noise was deafening. "Seal that coolant leak!" Franklin screamed.

Above him on the gangway, a terrified Morton rushed toward the leak as, twenty feet behind him, Newmyer tried to stabilise the core from a panel as it thundered below, brilliant blue, pressure beginning to rise. Morton arrived to a sight of destruction; all around him, sparks flew from exposed cables as his hands reached out, trying to stay under cables as he desperately tapped the panel to attempt to bypass the junction. The *Hordec* lurched from impacts, Morton trying to keep his footing amidst still more impacts, and suddenly Morton stood bolt upright, pain racking his body with cables collapsing onto the panel, electrifying it. Newmyer saw it all through the clouds of gas. "Morton!" he screamed, rushing toward him and almost reaching when… a deafening crash erupted, the wall exploding and taking Newmyer over the barrier with the debris. Appearing for a second in the wreckage, Newmyer screamed, his arms flailing as he watched the steel floor rush up to meet him.

Franklin heard the impact as Newmyer crumpled into the floor to his left, the engineer beside him looking on in horror before being snapped out of it by his shout over the noise. "Seal the breach!"

Two engineers by the core made for the gangway. When they were almost at the ladder, there was a blinding flash from plasma conduits blowing out in front of them, waves of green vapour spewing out. Instantly, they were under.

"Get out!!!" Franklin screamed.

Engineers raced for the already falling blast doors as a wave of plasma filled the room, two half-human monsters flailing hard and wrenching forward as one managed to rise, eyes seared white, screaming as his skin melted away to reveal the core behind him through sears in his face. Franklin felt the heat on his back as he dived for the falling blast door, hearing the slam as plasma swamped the other side behind him just as he got through.

On the clear side of the door, crews struggled to free a screaming Franklin, whose elbow had been crushed flat under the door. Shouts from panicked crew filled the air as searing steam began to rise from under the door.

"We gotta get outta here!"

"Where you gonna go to? The whole ship's coming apart!"

The two-man damage control team struggled into the torpedo room over a gangway above the loading arms that had collapsed, jamming as they'd been dropped to release the six torpedos which now sat uselessly at the top. Maine's voice came overhead: "Bridge to damage control, report!"

"Philips here; a beam's fallen into the loading arms and they're jammed at the front under the number-one torpedo."

"Can you free them?"

"We're trying," Philips replied as he tried to wrestle the beam free with Blair. Try as they might, the beam wouldn't budge; they were straining hopelessly as weapons slammed into the starboard side, sending them flying across the room. The Hearack passed over the nose above, visible through the guard field protecting them from space outside, as Philips struggled to his feet with Blair already running for the beam. Philips knew it was hopeless.

"Watch out!"

Blair turned to see Philips draw a Del 10 from his holster.

"Come on, get outta the way!" Philips shouted.

A stunned Blair looked on as Philips fired and held the beam. *He's crazy*, thought Blair as he watched the Del slowly turn, the beam molten, while resting on top of it was a type nine thoran torpedo!

"Philips, what's happening?" Maine's voice broke overhead.

"We're cutting through it!"

"How long?" Maine demanded.

The beam glowed red, beginning to melt away as, above it, the thorans' black paint began to blister. "A few more seconds!" shouted Philips.

The *Hordec* lurched violently as weapons slammed into her nose from the Hearack passing above, Blair's eyes widening as the Del beam wandered dangerously, striking the thoran and then falling back to the beam. He looked on in terror as the bottom of the thoran began to glow.

"Shields down to nine percent!" Brent shouted.

"We've got a hot torpedo—it's gonna blow!" Sanderson screamed, alerted by his panel.

"Damage control, what's going on?" Maine demanded.

As he did, the beam broke free, collapsing to the floor with a deafening grind of steel following it as the arms came down. Through the grind, Blair screamed as the arm behind him crashed down on his shoulder. Lost in their task, the danger forgotten now, the arm sent him screaming to the floor as the same arm narrowly missed Philips, who was now behind it. The crash as the arms locked down was overtaken by a thundering; Philips turned his head and immediately ducked in an involuntary impulse as a huge black shape narrowly missed him, brushing the tips of his hair as it passed, another deafening crash signalling six torpedos locking into place on the arms. Underneath, Philips and Blair were bathed in red light—the thorans arming lights engaging, their intent clear.

"We've got thorans!" Gray shouted.

Philips wrestled a screaming Blair to his feet, and overhead came Maine's voice. "Damage control, get clear!"

"We're almost out!" shouted Philips as, arm over arm, they struggled for the door.

"Brent, on my mark, round the bow of the *Holsadt* and head for the nebula!" Maine ordered.

"Damage control, are you clear? Report!"

"Almost!"

"Hearack approaching fast!" Sanderson shouted. "They're firing!"

A deafening crash sounded out, and Philips and Blair were thrown from their feet, the impact of the Hearack attack hurling them to the floor with debris raining down around them. Dazed, Philips grabbed Blair and hoisted him up; struggling forward, he looked up to meet a gut-wrenching sight… another gangway had collapsed, and the door was blocked.

Still screaming, Blair felt Philips release him. Unable to stand on his own, he fell to the floor. His back crashing against the wall, he looked up at Philips in angry confusion, but caught his expression and followed the gaze. He knew what the expression meant now; he had an identical expression of his own.

"Damage control!"

Philips looked down at Blair. The other man had stopped screaming; he just looked back in silence with the moment holding them still, no words to be said… none they had time for, anyway.

"Damage control, your final report!"

With the men's eyes still locked together, Maine's

call echoed around the room, Blair watching as Philips slowly reached for his communicator, his face tensing as he tapped it, the dropping hand leaving both of them looking on in quiet acceptance.

"We're clear," he said.

"Gray, we're gonna take these bastards head-on—wait till they're danger-close and hit one of them with everything you've got!" Maine ordered. "Brent, once they've detonated, pull up hard over them and floor it!"

"They've turned—they're on an attack run and coming straight at us!" Sanderson interrupted them.

On screen, the two Hearack ships loomed into view like great steel dragons, black against the nebula behind them.

"Alright, let's do it! Brent, engage!" Maine roared.

The *Hordec* lurched upwards and swung to port over the bow of the *Holsadt*, Philips and Blair watching as the stars rushed by behind the guard field of the torpedo doors like three raging locomotives, the ships baring down on each other.

"Eighteen thousand kilometres!" sounded out Sanderson.

"Fourteen thousand!"

"Steady," Maine growled.

"Ten thousand!"

Gray tensed over the weapons panel.

"Eight thousand!"

"Five thousand!"

"Fire!"

A brilliant flash came, and Philips and Blair were in agony—their screaming drowned out only by igniting thorans leaving the *Hordec*. The lead ship exploded in a fireball racing out toward the *Hordec*.

"Pull up hard!" Maine screamed.

Heaving upwards, the *Hordec* strained as it crested the inferno, the crew seeing the nebula beckoning behind the blaze. Through adrenaline, hope appeared for the first time with a feeling of… suddenly, a ghostly shape appeared in the fire below—a black dragon screaming out and unleashing hell, ions tearing under the *Hordec* so that the bridge erupted. Brent flew backward as his panel exploded, more ion fire tearing into the lower decks and exploding into space while Maine flew across the bridge, landing teeth-first against the side rail with the *Hordec* swinging round completely to see the dark angel sail into the distance.

Sanderson looked behind him to see a torn-faced corpse lying on the floor, and then he looked up at Gray… but Gray was gone.

"Report!" screamed a choking Maine, blood overflowing from his mouth.

Sanderson, shocked by the half-toothed Maine, spun around. "Engines offline, weapons are out, sensors have failed; our inertia's still carrying us toward the nebula!"

"Go to thrusters and bring the nose around to…."

A ghostly horror caught Sanderson's eye—it was looming out of the distance on screen as Maine struggled to his chair. "Captain, that bastard's still out there; he's comin' around… he's comin' straight for us!"

"Shields!"

Sanderson looked at the smashed helm panel, responding in a terrified whisper, "They're gone."

Maine grimaced, looking into the jaws of death approaching on screen; in an instant, red fury erupted from them and, like a raging animal, Maine roared in anger, louder and louder as death approached. It was deafening, compelling Sanderson to join him, both men facing death with pure rage. Weapons exploded in front of them, the men roaring through the blinding white light and their rage shallowing out as the two watched blinding explosions give way to shimmering blue as a gentle rocking motion passed through the *Hordec*. Sanderson turned, bemused, to Maine, the same look coming back to him, and then he looked to the helm to his right through a cracked glaze, to a flashing warning… *"Shield Failure"*. Sanderson looked back to Maine, shaking his head as Maine looked out over the shimmering blue, which had begun dissipating to reveal a black terror so close that Maine froze, his body unable to take anymore shocks. Suddenly, the *Hordec* was shrouded in shadow, a huge bow appearing overhead and bringing a soul-wrenching roar as a huge curtain of ions ran out of it, tearing the Hearack limb from limb in front of them ablast wave surging out in all directions.

Aboard the Rheinvar her extended shields rippled blue absorbing the impact…

"Transporter rooms, get them outta there!" Brenner demanded.

"Seven Hearack ships coming out of warp zero, one-zero-mark-three-nine," Hollin voiced.

"Mr Steiner," was all Aidin had to say.

"Aye!"

A barrage of thorans was loosed from the *Rheinvar*, the seven Hearack vessels arriving in a hail of weapons with two exploding instantly, the rest left reeling from the impact. By the time they'd regrouped, the *Rheinvar*'s transporter rooms had taken everybody and the brief flash of them leaving was soon eclipsed by the *Hordec*'s core collapsing, her last gasp shielding their escape.

Chapter 20

Reputation Preceding

Finally docked at 177, the injured were rushed off to the larger and more adequate station's medical infirmary. It took almost an hour—an hour of victims being brought off on anti-grav beds. It was sickening. Fuller and his men had been ordered off for debriefing along with the other Marines and most of the ship's crew, who'd left to find what little respite they could, leaving only a skeletal force. When Aidin finally walked through the airlock, he looked tired and grey.

"Captain Aidin," came a voice from further down the corridor.

Looking down the familiar grey decor with its neon blue accents, Aidin could see two men near the maglift. As he approached, he made out the still-bloodied uniform of Captain Maine. "Shouldn't you be in the infirmary?" he asked, knowing full well that the man wouldn't go till all his crew had been attended to, just as he wouldn't have left his ship without the same provision.

"I'm fine," replied Maine with a tired sigh. "Your boys fixed me up real good, and besides that, I had to thank you in person."

"No need; it was nothing—" Aidin was cut off suddenly.

"No, no, it was, eh... definitely something." Maine smiled wryly. "I've never seen ships torn apart so quickly." Maine stared intently, waiting for Aidin's answer.

Aidin sighed, himself staring at the ensign before answering, feeling Maine was due a real response. "The *Rheinvar* has had some experimental new increased yield thorans loaded onto it, aligned with a new modular weapons targeting array."

"Why haven't I heard of these new weapons?" Maine asked.

"They're not strictly legal," Aidin admitted.

"Meaning?" Maine asked.

"They're completely illegal they haven't been through any qualified testing procedures."

Maine stared at him.

"Meta-dense thorans based on base compounds from heavy elements in alloy wreckage from Hearack ships… synthisised, of course," came his answer.

Maine remained quiet, squinting.

"The elements don't have the radiological properties assosiated with the vessels," Aidin explained.

Maine looked relieved. "IN6?" he questioned.

Aidin paused, then answered, "Station 185."

"Ah!" Maine laughed, the effort paining him. "Seamus' place." He coughed, still laughing.

"Captain, you're sure you're alright?" Aidin asked.

"I'm fine." Maine waved his hand away.

He was lying through his teeth, those he had left, but Aidin didn't pursue it.

"Besides," continued Maine, "Ensign Davis here just informed me an old friend of mine wants to see us; he's waiting up on D1." Maine looked over at the ensign. "Alright, son, we'll be up in a minute."

The ensign left, boarding the maglift to continue his station duties elsewhere.

"Look," Maine went on as they boarded the next

maglift. "This guy's a nightmare of a control freak, connections on high; he'd step on anyone to get on, you know what I mean?"

"Who is he?" Aidin inquired.

"He was the commander of the Irachan escort fleet you were supposed to report to; goes by the name of Captain Ritter."

"Oh, I've heard some stories from Marines we've picked up from Aurin 2."

"Saved, you mean," Maine corrected him. "I heard you did a hell of a job, and that's twice in two days." Maine smiled with gratitude. "But you're not gonna get a medal from this guy—not even a thanks. Just wait till you meet him."

Just then, the maglift slowed to a halt, opening on deck D1.

"It seems a lot of people have a problem with him," Aidin commented.

"Yeah, anyone in the forces has," Maine answered. "He's a real asshole."

"What exactly—" An intruding voice came from above, the bustle of the crowd outside interrupting Aidin.

"Is that him? Has he arrived?" came a shrill voice from behind the crowd.

Maine recognised it even if Aidin didn't, and stiffened himself despite his injuries. Aidin squinted at him before following his gaze out of the maglift to the commotion developing amongst the crowd outside. Irritated utterings could be heard from the shrill voice as the crowd began to part, confusing Aidin as a captain's uniform broke through—carrying a scowl and trailing two lieutenants. The scowl marched forward, barging into the maglift and almost sealing the doors on the lieutenants behind him as they followed.

"Deck B1—" Aidin just managed to say.

"What the hell do you think you're doing?" screamed the scowling captain, turning red with the outburst.

"Captain Aidin, allow me to introduce Captain Ritter," Maine said calmly.

"Captain," began Aidin, "it's a pleasure to—"

"You turned my command out there into a circus! God knows who you could have injured, and you act like this is a Sunday lunch!" raged Ritter, ignoring Aidin's outstretched hand. "Who the hell do you think you are?"

"I'm the one who went back for those people you left to die!" Maine returned.

"That's right, you are, aren't you? You're the smartass who broke the banning orders on using molecular splice arrays to transport people while taking half an Irachan delegation to their graves!" screamed Ritter, pointing at him.

"And you're the one that used the *Holstadt* to secure your flank and then ran off like a chickenshit and left them!" Maine raged, stepping forward and throwing Ritter's hand out of the way.

Emotions exploded in the maglift as both men grabbed for one another, Ritter screaming. "I'll show you chickenshit!"

As fists raised, both men felt bodies jam in between them as Aidin and the lieutenants pulled them apart.

"There'll be another time!" Maine roared as Aidin wrestled him to one side of the maglift.

"Not for you!" screamed Ritter, trying to fight out from between the two lieutenants. "The Irachans we rescued are waiting on the main galleria between this lift and the bridge lift, and I'm sure they're gonna want to meet the man that got their delegation killed! And if they don't finish you, the IAF will when they get my report!"

"Come 'ere, you motherfu—" Maine began, trying to reach across the Maglift.

"No!" shouted Aidin, holding him back.

On the main galleria, the usual bustle was much quieter, and people turned in confusion to the maglift as it opened to show two captains at each other's throats. A few more expletives erupted, but the men steadied themselves with the help of their companions, restraining themselves and throwing their last blows in looks before filing out of the maglift to the sight of their bemused audience.

"Alright, step aside," Ritter growled, trying to make his way through as a commotion in front of them caught his attention. Shouts and cries were heard as, above the throng of people and a ways off, three figures towered above the rest of the crowd, roughly pushing people out of the way. Arriving first at Ritter, the crowd dispersed as he raised his hands, saying, "Now, look—"

Ritter was thrown aside as they descended on the wide-eyed lift occupants. Maine could only take hold of the massive arms as he was pulled forward into the chest of the lead Irachan, who roared down into his face. In the next instant, Maine felt his feet leave the ground as he was hoisted above the Irachan, who looked into his face as he roared up at him. A second of silence, a second of looking into the raging warrior's eyes, and then, a grin crept across his face and, with another roar, the Irachan was whirled round by the arm as another Irachan took hold of Maine's other side and he was hoisted onto their shoulders. Roaring with triumph, the Irachans carried him off through the scattering crowd to their waiting comrades, with cries of *KRAL IR DOR! KRAL IR DOR!* Sounding out.

Aidin watched as they made off with their captive into the deafening reception. *KRAL IR DOR*, he thought, roughly translated as "fearless one"—Maine was a bloody hero to them! Instead of waiting to kill him, they'd been waiting to honour him. To them, bravery was paramount, and Maine had led them into a battle of certain death. To them, in fact, he was more than a hero—he was revered, to be carried around the galleria aloft with Irachan warriors screaming up at him, arms outstretched, and this much at least was clear.

"He's lucky they believe in honour," said one of the relieved lieutenants, quietly watching from the maglift entrance.

"Yes, we all are," Aidin replied, looking over at Ritter, whose face was contorted as he watched the scene through clenched teeth, livid over Maine's good fortune and reception.

As Maine, smiling now, was turned again and again, he eventually caught Ritter's gaze and motioned for quiet with his hands as he tried to speak. Containing their excitement, Maine was brought to a halt near the middle of the galleria as his chaperons demanded quiet on his behalf.

Noise subsiding, Maine began to speak: "Thank you, all, it was an honour to fight alongside your brothers for what little time we had."

A roar of appreciation met his words before dying down at his gestures.

"But I can't take all the credit!" Maine continued, smiling at Ritter. "I was ordered to save those people by

Captain Ritter while he saved the rest of your delegation," Maine claimed, smiling gleefully and pointing at Ritter.

There was a slow rise in voices as people were again shoved aside, Ritter's teeth clenched and his face giving way to anxiousness as Irachan warriors broke through the crowd onto him. He raised his hands in front of himself and began to protest, but his hands were simply grabbed by gracious Irachans and he was hoisted aloft like Maine had been, to the cheers of Irachan warriors. A reluctant Ritter was circled around the room then, feigning smiles down to the mob of cheering warriors below him. Maine and Ritter were carried round the galleria like trophies, both coming to rest near the centre of the frenzied crowd.

Sitting atop the shoulders of the Irachan who'd initially picked him up, Maine smiled gleefully into the face of a glaring Ritter, smiling because he knew he had him; the IAF would never contest the claim he'd made, and Ritter would be made to agree to the report. For the Irachans, the lies would go down as a great Terran-Irachan battle bonding their cultures and securing their support. So, oh yes, he had him... and so he smiled all the more!

Chapter 21

Thin Veil

Rians hadn't been home in months; as the ship had approached this familiar world, Earth, he'd been like a child wanting a window seat. His eyes had set on a hundred others like it, but this one was different.... It was home.

The muffled crunch of steel vibrations through the shuttle indicated that they'd set down on the pad, and if anyone was still unsure, the whoops and cheers of Marines on board soon quelled any doubt. Soon, order had almost broken down as harnesses were unbuckled and people began fumbling overhead in lockers for their jump bags, barely able to see in the shuttle's cabin with its dark grey interior only slightly lit from the spill of green light coming from the cockpit that was now open.It wasn't long till they were out and finally through the terminal check gate; Rians had only just turned when a cry took his attention completely.

"Daddy! Daddy!" the words rang out, totally clear to Rians despite the thousands of people around him. The cries still coming from in front of him forced the homesick Marine to search, to try and see through the mass of people jammed into the terminal like sheep, but it was useless. Then, as if by magic, the crowd in front of him was moved aside, split apart not by some powerful force, but by a child—the most powerful force that Rians himself knew.

"Daddy! Daddy!" The screams loosened him up, slamming into him just before his daughter as he pulled her close, scooping her up while trying to keep his balance as he rose from his knees, winded by emotion. Being winded didn't matter—nothing did—as the crowd around him seemed to disappear along with everything else as he closed his eyes, listening to his daughter's joy. It seemed to go on forever from the place he was in at that moment, but it wasn't long enough, and soon he had to open his eyes. Meeting his daughter's eyes only made him more of an obstacle to the crowd around him as they filed past on each side, struggling since this man was lost in the nonsense babble of a father and daughter.

So much so that minutes must have passed, the disembarking crowd filtering out and dissipating in front of him while a solitary figure stood at its head, waiting in a summer dress—like the crowd, not interrupting. Still staring, listening to his daughter, Rians became aware of someone watching them, his eyes knowing who it was even though she wasn't in focus. Slowly turning just enough, his eyes met the floral dress with his daughter still running on in his ear. It was his wife, her face offering a small smile to meet his as he tried to hide his excitement; she looked different... tired, but that was alright, as so did he. Reaching down, he left his eyes on his wife as he picked up his jump bag with his daughter cradled against his shoulder on the other arm; with that, he started up toward her, that small smile still in place and his life complete once again.

The taxi back to the apartment didn't see much go on between Rians and his wife Carla—just occasional looks between them, neither minding the other's tiredness, small smiles making up for it while their daughter dominated all conversation.

The apartment door no sooner closed than his

daughter was off, scuttling away through the door on the left, determined to show her daddy this and that from her room—all of what he'd missed while away. The room falling quiet with her leaving, Rians was left with Carla. His more familiar setting of black suites and multi-toned grey carpeting of service quarters all unmissed as he took in his wife. With her back to him, the evening light gently filtering through the small window high in front of her and to her right leaving her a perfect silhouette for his eyes to enjoy as he watched her pour a glass of water over the sink of the small, open-plan adjoining kitchen. Finished, she turned, sensing the calm with their eyes meeting over the room.

"It's great to see you," Rians said, smiling—too excited to find better words.

Carla looked back, tired, the strain showing in her face, and yet she kept smiling through it, apparently trying not to let it show. "You, too," she replied, raising the glass to her mouth, her body taut like they'd just started dating again.

Rians smiled, about to say more when a flurry of activity coming through from the other rooms to Carla's left put a stop to that.

"Daddy, look at this, look!" his daughter's voice called out just before she came running into the room, brandishing crayon drawings and other fine artworks.

It was the same all through dinner in the front room, with Rians sitting in the black armchair with his back to the front door, revelling in his daughter's enthusiasm over his return, neither he nor Carla in the chair across the other side of the table able to get a word in edgewise. Food forgotten half-eaten, their daughter had taken the three-seat sofa on the left for herself and laid siege to the dining arrangements, ruthlessly bringing down anyone who dared speak.

All too soon, though, it was coming to an end, with Carla informing her daughter that it was time for bed, not realising the fight she was in for since her daughter wasn't yet willing to let her daddy go. It was madness, but madness Rians missed; he sat back in his seat, quietly watching the two people who meant most to him vie for his attention, all the time full of pride over them—the fight making him feel more welcome than ever.

"Look, Charlotte, no more arguing!" Carla said as she began to lose patience with her daughter. "It's time to go to bed and that's final."

"But—" her daughter began to panic, trying everything she could.

"No!" Carla cut her off, beginning to shout.

"But…" Charlotte tried again.

"No!" shouted Carla.

"But Michael would let me!" Charlotte blurted out.

The room fell silent. Charlotte looked into her mother's eyes to find a look she'd never seen before there—not anger and not rage or fear, but something which made her scared all the same. Lip trembling, Charlotte kept looking scared; scared, too, was her father to her right, but his trembling was of a different kind as he heard Carla try to send their daughter out of the room.

"Go to your room, Charlotte," her mother's voice requested, but her eyes had her daughter scared, pinned to the seat. "Go to your room, Charlotte."

"Who's Michael?" Rians asked, hoping for a simple answer, but feeling anxiety setting in all the same.

"Go to your room!" shouted Carla, pressured on two sides now.

Pressure for Charlotte, as well, as she was still unable to move; she felt the change in the atmosphere and saw the looks in her parents' eyes. She didn't know what to do, and soon she started to cry.

"Who's Michael?" Rians voice trembled, his stomach dropping with his wife's reluctance to respond. His mind raced as she continued to try to move Charlotte, his little girl crying all the louder. Trembling turned to fear and then to anger and back to fear. Carla shouted again.

"Charlotte, go to your room—go to your room now! Go to your—"

"Who's Michael?" Rians demanded, bursting up off the chair. Carla jolted at the outburst, turning to look up at her husband, and then it happened.

Rians was a soldier—he'd seen it all, looked into eyes that were dying and otherwise, and often he didn't need words—so at that moment, as theirs met, he knew.

"Who the fuck is Michael!" he screamed, stepping forward as the cries of a child filled the room, his wife sitting lost for words before him. "Who's fucking Michael?"

Carla looked up at him silently, speechless at the rage in his eyes and trembling at a sight that had never been in her home in the past, a sight she'd never seen before.

Trembling also was Charlotte, who was unable to understand what was happening, but feeling it was all her fault—all the time sitting helpless and crying in between her screaming parents.

"Who is he?" Rians took another step. "Who is he?" he screamed again, grabbing the table between them and hurling it right across the room so that Charlotte screamed in panic.

Carla looked across at her child screaming on the couch, about to use her plight against him, but she felt too scared to try in case he saw right through the ploy. "You're scaring her..." Carla uttered, trying to find some footing.

"Who is he?" Rians screamed, wrenching her up from her seat. "Who is he?" he screamed again, shaking Carla by the arms—enraged she'd try to use their daughter like that.

"You're scaring... her..." Carla tried to utter while attempting to pull herself from the wrenching grip. "My arms, you—"

"Who's fucking Michael?" Rians screamed into her face, the pleas wasted on him as she dropped her head, turning trying to hide behind her hair. It didn't work, though; it only enraged him all the more, bringing more shaking with her husband screaming uncontrollably, now determined to find out if what he suspected was true, and all the while Charlotte looked on, being traumatised over what she was seeing.

More shouts, more crying, more shaking...

"He's a guy I'm fucking!" Carla screamed back, cracking under the pressure.

A moment of calm and silence came.

Then, Rians' unintelligible scream was quickly followed by the thud of his wife's back on the chair; she'd been hoisted up by her arms and slammed down against it, her arms still held stiff as an animal raged over her, screaming down into her face.

Rians didn't even notice his daughter's anguish beside him, screams and jealous rage blocking all else. But she was screaming, too—screaming as she watched her mother subjected to everything but being hit by a monster she'd never seen before. It went on for what seemed like hours, the monster demanding to know where Michael lived before finally barging out of the house with no regard for anything else. No regard for the wailing occupants left behind, one on the sofa and scarred by a nightmare for a memory, the other on the floor with a life shattered by her own actions.

Chapter 22

Rage

If there was thinking on the way, Rians couldn't remember it afterward; there were no memories of downtowns's bright lights, the Plazean Towers, or the raised city ways. Nor could he remember running red stops or crossing half the city that night—all he remembered was a feeling, a rage, and this was remembered only because, when his memory did start…coming round that corner, it was the first thing in it.

Beforehand, awareness of his surroundings had been sporadic, like a dream, brief glimpses with the sound of tires spreading water along rain-soaked suburbs, the shower then coming overhead before dropping a last few drops on his windshield as he crept forward through the streets. The night was still, cars silent and witnesses staring blankly from either side of the streets, water dripping from their lights as one of their own, lights dimmed, crept past… turning, searching….

He was in the right area, he knew it. Edgemont Avenue, Edgemont Crescent… moving slowly through each roadway, amber glows from streetlights maddening against the rain-soaked windshield. Fine houses with kept grounds prepared for night, lights on in some and off in others, with whitened wooden finishes—all with porches and three bedrooms, wholly detached.

Detached as Rians, in fact… detached from reason or sense, detached from sanity as he rounded that corner, the house standing on it and offering its porch for view just as its owner had seen it when he made to leave.

The area was stable, affluent, well-off and dripping with success; it called for feelings of jealousy in the common man, yet despite all this, it hadn't been enough. Not satisfied, it had moved forward in its greed, moved into a man's life and taken what little he had… it wouldn't take any more.

The decision was no sooner cemented into Rians mind than he saw him, noticing him close and lock his door before moving over his porch.

Coming down his porch stairs, Michael saw the car—and he stood squinting at it confused as it pulled silently up behind his with its dimmed lights half-illuminating his champagne-coloured coupe. Inside the car, though, the driver had no confusion as he saw Michael step onto the path across the lawn. Breaking open the door, there was no thinking at all.

Michael slowed, pausing as the man came up his path, his vehicle left open with the engine still running, lights making him an approaching silhouette against the cars behind him.

"Can I help you?" Rians heard ring out, but he didn't hear words; he heard arrogance.

Michael froze solid as his quiet street was shattered by the roar of a madman answering the only way he had left to him—rage taking over and carrying him the last few steps at a charge.

Rians smashed into him, both men falling to the ground as two silhouettes leaping in the car light. Sounds of the struggle filled the street as they rolled off the path and onto the grass, Michael realising who it was while already suffering under a rain of blows as he tried to fight back. Roars and shouts continued, the men rolling one over the other on the lawn, the grass torn up and their knees slipping in the mud.

Dark sidewalks fell away, lights coming on in windows across the street with heads appearing as punches flew. The shouts continued as blood mixed with earth, faces watching on in shock as Rians was hurled to the ground, Michael being bigger by far—gym-sculpted and ready to answer each blow. Unable to remove the grip from his chest, blows now rained down on Rians, his returns merely glancing off of Michael unfelt with this stranger's rage joining Rians in the night. But he'd no idea what he was doing or the danger he was putting himself in, as each blow meant to break the other away only fed the anger beneath him. Rians felt the upper-class arrogance, sensing each superiority-laden strike with his blood spewing out and his eyes closing... till, finally, it happened. He was on a battlefield again. The howl welling up from Rians stunned Michael, who'd never before heard war, and suddenly he felt strength he couldn't understand—survival that was inhuman... primal!

In an instant, Rians blows turned to savage strikes as he jammed his finger deep into Michael's left eye. Screaming, Michael tried to pull back, but Rians was no longer in control as he curled his finger to the right in the socket, blood shooting out as he locked into his rage and training, severing the muscles behind Michael's eye as they were pulled right by those remaining on the other side. Still pulling back, screaming in terror, Rians went with him—one man falling to the ground as the other staggered up, now an animal with all reasoning long since gone.

On his knees, blood-soaked and in agony, Michael

was held up by a finger, his screams filling the street and heard by all except Rians, who was no longer even part of this world anymore. Rage, memory, training, and battle stress had taken Rians to a terrifying place… a place known only by soldiers, where barriers collapse and men become monsters. Monsters like the beast in the rain who was being watched by onlookers as it fell back on its instincts, pushing harder into the eye socket and forcing its screaming victim's head back for the final blow. Amber streetlights fought with shadows over the lawn, revealing Rians' free arm pulling back the palm and opening, lining up with Michael's nose, and the next step was so clear from his rage, impulses driving as he….

"*David!*"

The shriek stunned Rians, shattering the street, his arm jolting in indecision at the voice's familiar sound; his mind pulled as it wrestled between two worlds.

"David, don't do it!"

He'd missed everything—where he was, the screams of his victim, the cries of his neighbours, and even the car drawing up, its occupants now visible to his right. Rians' head clearing, he let Michael fall away as his grip loosened, blood spurting clear as his finger left the socket.

Rians watched the scene continue to unfold, rain dripping from his face as his wife, screaming, grabbed her face with her hands while running from the car as her father exited the driver's side.

"Oh… oh… what have you…?" Carla stammered, looking down and covering her mouth with her hands, trying to keep her balance over the wet grass, her steps taking her straight past Rians.

Through swollen eyes, he watched his wife step

straight past him, coming to a stop with her hand over her mouth above Michael.

"Michael, oh, Michael...." More stammering came from Carla, Rians watching in disbelief, her husband standing behind her, as the object of her concern writhed in agony beneath her.

"What do you mean, 'oh, Michael'!" Rians shouted, jolting Carla round, the rage from before still present in his voice.

"I...." Carla reached out gently, unsure of what to do.

"You what? You wanna make sure this bastard's alright! Huh! You wanna fuck him on the lawn right here? Well? Answer me, bitch!" Rians raged at Carla's actions, stepping toward her menacingly.

"David!"

The voice from behind him forced Rians to turn as it successfully competed for his anger, receiving it in full, complete with murderous expression. But it wasn't just the voice's owner that Rians' look fell on—his eyes signed in not just on Carla's father, but on his own daughter held by Carla's mother beside him. Dropping the expression immediately from his face, he still saw it was too late, as the look on his daughter's face was one of terror, fear... fear of her own father. Rians' horror turned to rage, which was thrown at Carla where she stood trembling beside him. "How could you do this to her?" he screamed, grabbing her arm even as she tried to pull away. "How could you let her see this?"

Anger returning, a groan from Michael below was all it took for Rians' fury to descend on him again, so that he began kicking wildly into his ribs—this man on the ground was the cause of it all!

"You go near her again, I'll kill you, you fucking prick! Do you hear me? I'll fucking kill you!" Rians screamed between kicks. "I'll kill you! I'll kill you!" he continued, not caring whether Michael heard or not, content inflicting pain as he fell finally to his knees, locking an arm round his victim's neck with Carla screaming behind him. "You come near my house or family again, I'll rip out your fuckin' throat!" Rians growled, blood running down his arms from the socket, groans of pain wasted on him as he choked Michael further. "You come near them again, I'll rip it out and spread it all over your prissy-assed street, you got that?" Rians' growl dropped to a sinister whisper, the promise evident in his voice as Michael choked his last breath for the moment, his vision going hazy. With Michael's body almost limp in his arms, Rians reluctantly let go, Michael collapsing directly—near paralysed. Rians stared down at his handiwork, rain running off his face as his stare drifted up to a shivering Carla, rain-soaked and terrified, her look saying it all as she stood leaning crumpled against the house front for support.

"What do you think you're doing!" came a gruff older voice, Carla's father stepping between them and shielding his daughter from the apparent threat.

"What am I doing?" roared Rians, stepping forward, his quick response startling Carla's father. "Your daughter turned into the whore of the south and you're asking what I'm doing!"

"Now, wait just a minute." Carla's father composed himself, not about to let his daughter's name be dragged through the mud in front of all the people now lining the street.

"Wait!" Rians glared at him. "Wait! Did you tell her

to wait before she moved him in? Huh? Well?"

"And what the fuck is she supposed to do!" Carla's father shouted back, embarrassed for his daughter and angry at her being laid bare in front of the crowd beginning to surround them. "What the fuck is she supposed to do while you're away for months, huh? Just stay here and rot?"

"So, what? It's alright for her to be whoring it out when I'm gone when she's supposed to be looking after our daughter?" Rians screamed, furious at the defence.

"Now, you listen," growled Carla's father, angry at the assault on his daughter and poking Rians in the chest as he spoke, raging at...

Rians suddenly winced in pain, his own rage no longer shielding him from the injuries he'd taken. It was the first time he'd been physically excessive since the plasma graze, and what met his eyes as he looked down horrified him. Blood and tissue oozed through his whole shirt... but from the inside, his chest torn open from his own movements. Worse was to come as Rians heard a wail from the sidewalk, and upon looking up, he realised it was coming from his daughter, who'd been brought closer by Carla's mother, determined to see what was going on.

But her determination had only brought Charlotte a new nightmare as she bore witness to her father's blood-soaked chest and gruesome appearance. Hearing her wail at the sight, Rians turned away, forced to turn away from his own daughter, from what meant most to him. Ashamed, he stood there all but paralysed, unsure of what to do with his own child crying behind him, terrified by his appearance. He just wished that... that...

"Please, son... just go home."

Carla's father's words were well-meant, pity in his voice as he watched where Rians was, suffering in front of his own. But they offered no comfort as Rians walked away, and no comfort as he drove off, unsure if there was anything left for him.

Chapter 23

Truce

They all looked up as he entered the bar, even Copeland, but Rians didn't look back at them for long, still raging from earlier. Rians came through the door and for a moment he seemed normal; then the light hit him, showing he was drunk. Passing through the tables with a scowl they'd never seen, they were sure he saw them, but he walked right by anyway—right to the bar.

Chatting to a customer, the barman looked over as Rians slammed his arms onto the bar.

"Hern!" demanded Rians, catching his glance.

The barman's face strained as he sized Rians up; deciding to save him embarrassment, he walked over. "Look, son, you're in pretty bad shape—"

"I didn't ask you what I look like," Rians growled, cutting him off. "I asked for Brandy."

"And I said you've had enough," said the barman, returning Rians' growl and glaring into his face with his experience dealing with drunks showing.

"Yeah, buddy, give the man a break; he's trying to do you a favour," came a voice from the other end of the bar.

Rians turned, blood already boiling, his eyes falling on two men at the other end. "What?" he demanded, glaring.

"I said, give him a break," repeated the nearest man in a less confident tone.

"Oh!" Rians shouted sarcastically. "I didn't know you two were so close; if I'd have known, I'd have had more respect for your little bitch wife!"

"Hey, you watch your mouth!" shouted the second man.

"Oh ho!" laughed Rians. "Threesome, is it? Well, I'll get right outta the way so you can dance."

"Dance on this, asshole!" screamed the second man, lunging forward and connecting. But connecting didn't matter, as Rians was used to being hit, and although drunk, he still sent the civilian clear over a table with a broken jaw for his troubles. Suddenly, arms grabbed round Rians' neck from behind and he was pulled back up onto the bar by the barman. Reaching back with his arms, Rians struggled, searching for his head when suddenly he felt a fist in his stomach. Screaming out through the headlock, he felt his skin begin to break, the first man having no pity as he landed another shot and then another. Bringing his hands back from the fourth and fifth, the man felt them to be wet and looked down on blood streaming off his knuckles to the floor. Confused, he looked at Rians' shirt; it was saturated with blood, his pained expression held fast by the barman, and the man was just about to speak when suddenly he had one of Rians' boots jamming itself into his crotch. Screaming out with his knees almost buckling, any pity fast turned to anger as he raised his fist again. But it was another that would connect, Fullers sending him sprawling to the ground clutching his groin.

It had been three days since they'd last seen him; three days since the brawl with Michael, and the drinking and the shouts were all about to start all over again as they tumbled outside into the night, Rians still as drunk and incoherent as they'd found him the first time.

"Look, just calm down—you're going through a…"

"Fuck you! You don't know what the fuck I'm going through!" Rians screamed, staggering to his feet. "My wife ran off with another guy, and everybody loves him! My chest won't heal, so I'm a freak! My daughter thinks I'm a fucking monster! You fuck, you've never known what it's like to lose everything!"

Silence fell around them as the two men looked at one another, Rians realising what he'd said and Fuller just looking back at him. After a time, Fuller drew breath, dropped his head, and pulled away, the loss of his own family now weighing on his mind exhausting his patience with the situation, "C'mon, guys. Leave him to it."

Rians watched after them as they walked up the incline, realising what he'd said in his drunken state, so that his shame felt all the more total. His whole world finished, it was all, all…. A couple of steps away from the bar, he collapsed as his breath quivered in the night and he tried to hold back. After a time, he lifted his head from the gravel, looking out across the nearby lake, between his hands to the moon shining down like a stairway across the lake. He took his head in his hands again and, on the point of despair, suddenly raged upward, screaming everything he had out across the lake. The anger felt good, better than the pity, but it didn't last; he flumped down on the pier, legs swinging freely, just looking out across the water.

He heard the footsteps, but didn't care; he just didn't. The person sat close beside him in the dark, nothing being said.

Minutes passed insilence.

"It's not easy, is it?" came the voice, which didn't really even register for him. "Everyone's just so full of advice, aren't they? Everyone knows what you should do…." Rians remained dazed. "Yeah, they all know…."

Silence descended again. Water gently lapped at the shore, moonlight flickering over the blackened surface.

"But they don't—no one does," came the voice again.

Rians' began to clear—the voice was familiar. Fulkes. It was that little bastard Fulkes. Who the fuck did he think he was, trying to give advise from the standpoint of his miserable existence? Rians spun round, moonlight lighting up his face and it taking everything he had not to explode again, glaring through the darkness at the figure obscured only feet away. Still glaring, he could just make out Fulkes' horrible little head staring out across the lake—and he kept talking!

"Yeah, I've been there. It's been a while, though."

Rians just kept scowling, amazed he could sit through his stare.

"I had all the answers once, was full of ideas and had it all figured out; eighteen, college in front of me, girls, beer… yeah, I was king of the world and nothing could spoil it. Nothing except my stepdad."

Rians had lost the malice of his gaze; he'd grown tired of holding the expression, but kept trying.

"Yeah…" Fulkes continued from the darkness, "he'd only been around eight months, and everyone thought he was the best thing that ever happened to Mom since Dad died. He was full of ideas of his own, you know, a real 'I'm right and you're wrong' kind a guy. Noone ever got to see that part except me. Well, I don't know what it was; maybe he had a harder time growing up, maybe he didn't have the chances I had, but eight months on from Mr nice guy showing up, everything had changed. Nothing I did was right and everything was criticised, put down. Oh, I stood my ground; we had our fights, but he was clever, you know, always twisted... it made me look bad. After a few months, members of my own family were talking, like, 'Come on, son, you gotta get it together and stop being such a pain in the ass!' Huh, my own family. Friends wouldn't come round no more, girls wouldn't phone... he had everything wound up so tight. A real authoritarian. One night before my friend Jimmie was leaving for college up north, we had a party on the beach; it was real fine, one of those nights that goes off without a hitch. Beer, women, old times, new times... it couldn't have been better, and I went home that night knowing everything was gonna work out just right. Soon as I got inside into the front room, I knew it wasn't; they were still up... that's how it started usually, all nice and family-like at first."

Rians looked at the outline in the darkness, his scowl almost gone; he'd become vaguely interested and hadn't even noticed.

"Yeah... it wasn't long before he started to pick, and I tried to just back away in each thing we talked about, knowing it was only a week till I was gone, but he wasn't gonna have that. Yeah, he pushed and pushed till finally we were arguing. 'You're disrespectful about this; what do you call that?' I pulled back like I always did, but that night, it wasn't gonna work. We'd never fought before, but he just kept pushing that night. Well, it was all over pretty quick as far as I remember. Front room was trashed and I was outside; he got the better of me drunk. Well, next morning, coming home from a friend's, I found I wasn't welcome. The bastard had twisted my own mother... I tried, for a week, for that last week. But he'd done it, and done it well…. I was the bad guy. No matter what I said, Mom, the family, everyone knew it. I left not long after for college. Friends were gone, girl was gone… and it didn't work out. I had this attitude, see; I'd never had it before, but I just couldn't get rid of it… felt I'd been shit on. Couldn't make friends, couldn't concentrate in class. Inside four months, my grades had went to shit and…. Well, it wasn't long before I was hauled up in front of the dean. He was full of all kinds of good words, but they kept slippin'. Year later, I was out on the street, finding work where I could, and six months later I was in jail, in and out of all kinds a shit. In one week, see, I'd lost my whole life. Guy inside got to talkin' about the army at chow time, how there was easy money, roof over your head, and women, even."

Rians looked through the darkness at the side of Fulkes' face, not able to be bothered shouting now and annoyed at his own interest growing for his story. He let out a sigh and slumped down, his feet hanging freely off the pier. Giving up, he just looked out over the water as Fulkes quietly rolled on.

"Money sounded good; would get me off the street, stop me… well, there was a few things I wanted to, eh… let go. But it wasn't that easy. Seemed my views weren't liked by commanders—they said I had an attitude, and shit, maybe I did. I was transferred from unit to unit and it all went downhill, just like outside; everyone seemed to turn on me, the whole fucking world, so I turned right back on it all. Almost ended up in the fucking stockade. Instead, I was transferred to this unit on Maires Drift for my last shot, and I fucked it up."

Rians was barely listening, vaguely interested in his little sob story.

"Not getting on too well with the latest bunch of pricks," Fulkes continued, "I got to feelin' real sorry for myself and got so drunk that night that the next day I fell asleep on watch."

Rians' interest suddenly perked up; he hadn't heard this part. He'd been on leave when Fulkes had gotten transferred in.

"Some lifer lieutenant prick found me asleep and started roughin' me up real bad; I did what I could, but I was screwed from the night before, and if Brice hadn't been comin' through that compound when he was, I'd have ended up in the infirmary, for sure. He fucked that lieutenant up real bad, real bad, and that felt good, to have somebody on my side. That was the first time I'd felt that in a long while. Oh, he chewed me out, and Fuller, too, and the lieutenant... shit, he went straight to the base commander. I was on a one-way ticket to another kind of compound, I was sure of it, standin' in that office that day. That lieutenant laid it on thick. Shoutin' down on me like some prick father, the base commander wanting to know it all, and I was about to try to explain when Fuller cut me off, too. He said the lieutenant had it in for me, that he'd been waitin' for this since I'd arrived. Cap called him out as a bare-faced liar, inventing some bullshit story right there. Man, the lieutenant couldn't believe it." Fulkes smiled, the expression all but unseen in the darkness. "There was all sorts of cussin' and shouts and screams, but Brice backed us right up and said he'd had to pull him off; that he'd tried to kill me. It was three against one. I don't know if the base commander believed us or not, but he threw the charges out anyway. They risked their careers—shit, prison time—for me. That changed something. Oh, I fucked up some more, but they never abandoned me. Some of the unit were real shitty to me, but they were always there. I'd never had that before. Right then, I straightened up some; didn't wanna lose what I had.... It's funny how, when you're at your lowest, you seem to find what's important in life.... Just wish I'd have found it sooner."

There was a long silence, peaceful, with Rians listening to the waves gently lapping the shore and Fulkes words running like a breeze through his mind. Seated in the darkness, they almost forgot about one another as the moon glazed over the lake hypnotically. After a time, Rians heard Fulkes get up; he didn't look up, remaining fixed on the lake as the sound of gravel underfoot in the distance grew quieter as Fulkes made off. The mist in his mind had cleared a bit, being less stressful now; he thought he still had something, something important to him that he hadn't seen over everything that had happened. And he was annoyed. Annoyed because he felt indebted now; he didn't like Fulkes being right, didn't actually like him at all, and Rians knew he'd been nothing but shitty to him all along, yet Fulkes had just helped him anyway, thought Rians... that little bastard.

Chapter 24

Rejected

Looking in the mirror was scary. Who was he? Who was that looking back? He didn't recognise him, though it was probably just as well.

Rians came gingerly into the room; he'd almost crept up through the lobby outside his own home and he'd felt the need for this, like it was him who'd done something wrong. He snapped himself out of it as he stood in their main room, the front door behind him.

Listening for signs of life, he found it was quiet, like no one was home, and he sighed upon taking in the room, finding the light grey carpet and those walls much the same. The black three-seater flanked by two singles dominated the centre of the spacc, light coming in through a high-set window next to a door that was back and to the left, leading to the other rooms. They were service quarters alright, rented cheap from the military, not much at all, and yet he'd dreamt of coming back here, the memories offering so much in lonely times, but now... now, he saw how drab they really were.

Uncomfortable with the prospect of what was going to happen with Carla, the talking they'd have to do and the fights they were certainly going to have, he decided to sit down and wait for his family to return. Making for the side of the three-seater nearest the window, he planned to think about what he was going to say, but he never got there.

"Daddy!" screamed his wide-eyed daughter, not even four feet tall. They'd entered quietly from the adjoining room, so Rians hadn't noticed, but he shared her wide-eyed happiness as she came bounding forward, arms outstretched for her waiting father's.

"Oh... ho, oh, Charlotte," Rians uttered as they squeezed the life out of each other. Happier than he'd been in days, Rians pried her from him while looking down at the one thing that meant more to him than anything else so happy she didn't seem frightened of him after what she'd seen, as she beamed back up at him, clutching his arms. "How've you been sweetheart, huh?"

"Fine, Daddy, where've you been?" replied a voice that was more music than words to Rians.

"Oh, Daddy was real busy, hun. Did you miss him?"

"Yes, Daddy," came the instant reply.

"Where's your mother?" Rians asked, still lost in the joy of being with his daughter.

"Mummy's in the garden, Daddy, but she said you were working. Are you going away again?" asked a concerned face—the one light in his life that always wanted him.

"No, honey, no," Rians assured her honestly, bending down on one knee so he could look into her eyes. "Daddy isn't going away anymore. He's staying right here."

"Forever!" Her expression had changed to one of joy.

"Forever, honey," Rians answered, overcome with joy as his daughter latched onto him, squeezing with glee.

Happy as he was, he remembered the night on the street; she couldn't understand and he didn't want a repeat of what had happened as he felt the pressure on his chest. "Careful, honey, don't squeeze Daddy's chest too hard," he said gently.

She suddenly sprang back with frightened eyes. "Did the monsters get you again, Daddy?" she asked with a scared tone.

"What?" Rians uttered, quickly realising she'd been frightened that night and that Carla must have tried to explain with some talk of monsters. "No, honey, the monsters didn't get me. Daddy's just a little sore, that's all."

"Mommy said you were fighting with the monsters when you were away, to stop them coming here," she said with a worried face.

"That's right, hun, Daddy did, but he's back now," he reassured her, running his hand through her hair, but the face looking back at him was still worried. "What is it, hun?" he asked her.

"Lori said her daddy was fighting with them, too, and that they were coming. They're not going to get us, Daddy, are they?"

"No." Rians almost laughed. "No, Daddy made them all go away, so don't you listen to Lori," he said, taking hold of her head and resting it on his shoulder.

"Are you sure?" came a frightened voice in his ear.

"Of course, hun, there's no monsters going to get you," he reassured her.

"Promise," came a voice that was a little less frightened.

Rians took his daughter by the arms, holding her out in front of him so she could see him. "I promise, honey, the monsters won't get you." His smile seemed to be contagious, as another one slowly spread across her face. "Come 'ere," he said, reassuring her, hugging her close.

All ready with a thousand questions on what she'd

been up to, he didn't get the chance to ask; his family was completed as Carla came into the room, a basket full of freshly dried clothes in her arms.

"Mummy, it's Daddy!" shouted Charlotte, clinging to him.

"I know, honey, I see him," replied Carla, trying hard to make a forced smile pass her daughter well enough not to spoil her happiness as she put the clothes down. "How are you?" she asked, the voice sounding genuine as she began lifting clothes out, not looking at her husband.

"Alright," replied Rians, his half-smile going unseen by her.

Charlotte remained quiet, and unusually so, not understanding but sensing the atmosphere between her parents. Seeing the look on her face, Rians smiled, nodding his head and trying to reassure her. Carla struggled, oblivious, her back to them as she reached down for more clothes, spreading them out over the kitchen island as she stood back up and prepared to fold them.

Nodding to Charlotte again, Rians slowly stood up, moving for the clothes on and talking as he went. "I bumped into the guys yesterday," he said as he lifted a sweater for her.

"Yeah," was all Carla could manage, unsure if she wanted him this close with her nerves fraying as she half-snatched up the sweater from him without looking.

"Yeah, they're, eh, looking well," Rians tried again, taking jeans from the hamper and holding them in his outstretched hand this time.

"That's nice for them," Carla said sarcastically.

Rians took the sarcasm in hand, knowing they both

had ground to make up as he lifted one of Carla's blouses. "Yeah, they... ah," he exclaimed quietly, the blouse catching round his fingers and jarring them awkwardly as Carla grabbed it.

Knowing she was raw, he backed away, saying nothing and instead still talking about nothing, trying to...

Suddenly, a wail came from Charlotte, her eyes wide with fear and her father's instinctual turn only making her scream as Carla followed her gaze, screaming as she dropped the clothes. "Oh, look at you!"

Rians' eyes fell on red streaks wetting through his shirt, these the result of Carla's grab. Half-covering himself with one arm, he reached out with the other. "Oh, honey, it's not..." But his reach met a squeal of anguish, his daughter pulling away from him and into Carla's grasp.

"The monsters have got Daddy! The monsters have got Daddy!"

Charlotte's cries jammed in her father's ears.

"Will you just get out!" screamed Carla, holding her bawling daughter. "Every time you appear, everything gets screwed up, so just get out!"

She was thinking of Charlotte; all she wanted to do was calm her down, and she didn't care about anything else—didn't care about her words at all. She just wanted what was frightening her daughter to go away.

Rians didn't see it that way, though he put a brave face on while leaving, then collapsing down the hallway wall, the door slamming behind him on the last thing he'd thought he could count on. It was the last straw, and crouched sobbing in the hallway, he felt the weight come crashing down along with his world, Carla, her parents, the forces, and now his daughter… it was all too much. He felt like the night at the lake when he'd thought he'd lost the guys, only worse. Six-foot-two and sobbing uncontrollably, he again heard Fulkes words, which were so clear to him; he understood them now. They'd all turned on him, all of them, except the guys… Fulkes was right.

Tears still streaming down, he forced himself up to march down the hallway, anger building with his thoughts. There was only one place for him now… and it wasn't here.

Rians caught a cab happy the driver didn't talk to him as they went…

Arriving at the shuttle dock, Rians' brush with emotion had passed during the twenty minute cab ride. Having nothing but his uniform, he passed through the shuttle gates and into the main complex, the guards on the door offering no challenge to his rank. It was a small dock, and he went passing through a door to the left of the reception so that he entered the main departure station, which was just one big massive room, white with a roof-length skylight overhead and black tiles over the floor. The room was full, bustling with Marines all the way up to the yellow holding line, which the desk jockeys defended with their lives if so much as a stray boot passed over it. He began to move through the hundreds of servicemen jostling in groups, all waiting for their turn to sign in at one of a dozen checkpoints. In rows of three, one row behind the other, the four lines of checkpoints stretched back to the end of the room where an open doorway was just visible on the left and revealed the start of a raised, metal-grated walkway. Glancing through the five massive floor-to-ceiling windows running the length of the room to his left, Rians caught sight of a huge steel fence in front of the walkway, it being designed to protect people from the engine blasts of the shuttles. Running a hundred yards down, the fence ended and a stub of walkway jutted out before taking a ninety-degree turn left and continuing parallel with the windows, running out of sight to the left. Attached to this parallel part was what Rians had come for… five more grated walkways spread out evenly and ran into the distance; at their ends loomed the raised docking platforms where five huge, whale-like shuttle craft sat patiently in the evening sun. Were they already on? Rians wondered, and with that thought, he suddenly remembered his jump bag sitting on the floor at home with his papers inside. In his wrecked state, he'd left without it. There wasn't time to get back to get them and return, and he didn't want to see her… she'd screamed her last at him. Rians began to fret as he looked at the shuttles—how would he get onto one without his papers, let alone get onto the ship waiting in orbit. Suddenly, for the first time in sixteen years, he felt marooned, trapped. Two years earlier, he'd have done anything to be left on Earth, but not now. Panicking at the thought, he began to push more desperately through the crowd, scanning the room and hoping to catch a glimpse of his unit, when suddenly….

"What?" screamed a familiar voice.

Rians pushed through the remainder of the crowd, arriving at the first row of checkpoints with Marines glaring at his intrusion.

"What do you mean, where's my papers?" screamed

the irate voice again.

Glancing behind him at the third row, Rians saw the cause of the commotion—a familiar sight in Fulkes and Brice.

"You mean I'm going up there to have my ass shot off so you little bitches can sit pretty down here, and you're bitchin' at me about a piece of paper?" Brice screamed, standing six-foot-four and almost the width of the desk while a fresh-faced cadet tried to be assertive.

"Look, Sergeant, without papers, I can't let you board. It's policy," replied the cadet from the other side of the desk, a little shaken by Brice's stare.

"C'mon, Sarge, it's probably near the top of your pack; let's just find it and get on—I'm sick off this place," Fulkes spoke up from Brice's left, trying to calm him as he turned his stare in his direction.

"Like I said, it's just policy, Sergeant, it's nothing—" the cadet didn't get to finish, as unlike Fulkes, he didn't know Brice; he hadn't served with him and didn't have the luxury of knowing about Brice's lack of restraint.

"Policy!" screamed Brice, slamming his sixty-pound pack on the desk and frightening the cadet up from his seat as the monitor in front of him almost shook to the floor. "Damn policy!" he muttered, tearing open the top of the pack and reaching inside. "Goin' up to die and you're carin' more about policy."

"We can't just let people board without papers! It's for your own safety!" the cadet began to rant. "Anyone could smuggle weapons on board, and they could be dangerous—"

"Do I look as if I could be dangerous to you?" Brice screamed lurching over the table, the wide-eyed cadet falling back a step under the man mountain.

"Come on, man," Fulkes cut in. "Hey, there it is!" he said, pulling out a crumpled page covered in signatures. "Maybe Momma should pack next time," he joked as he smiled, holding up the page.

Fulkes knew Brice wasn't in the mood for his wisecracks—he never was—so when Brice turned his way, snatching the paper from his hand, it never fazed him. Neither did the anger-filled stare nor the gritting teeth, as Fulkes just laughed through them all, sending him back to the cadet even angrier.

"There!" was all Brice could say as he slammed the paper down under his palm, trying to hold back more anger as the monitor was jarred again.

"How you guys, doin'?" Rians asked suddenly, his approach having gone unnoticed.

Brice turned, his rage dissipating as Fulkes behind him shared his confused look.

"Why are you—" Brice began.

"Things have changed," Rians cut him off before the cadet got wind that he was out on medical. "I'll tell you all about it on the shuttle," he said, staring the message through to them.

"Right," Brice caught on. "Well, we best get goin' since he's held us up long enough," he said, motioning at Fulkes.

"Ha, like you've never forgotten your pack before," Fulkes defended himself as they began to walk. "What about Rolis 3? You didn't get the—"

Rians listened to the latest squabble, following on and hoping the cadet didn't...

"Excuse me, sir!" the cadet spoke out behind him as they were making for the doorway. "I'll need to see your papers."

"Papers?" Rians asked, squinting and acting confused.

"Yes, sir," replied the cadet.

"I've already checked through twice today," Rians replied.

"I'm sorry, sir, it's policy; no papers, no boarding," said the cadet unflinchingly.

"Look," said Rians, growing angry and letting it show in his voice as he walked back to the front of the desk, the day's events heavy on his mind. "I don't have time to—"

"Without papers, you've missed it," the cadet cut in unhelpfully, his smart little expression placing him in more danger than Brice could ever have posed.

Rians' blood began to boil. He'd been through hell today, lost everything, and now a smart-mouthed, puberty-faced cadet was about to take all he had left. "Look, cadet, I don't have 'em because something happened, but I'm meant to be on that ship, so if you'll just put a call up to the captain—"

"I'd never get through," the cadet cut him off. "Besides, there's no time and we're too busy, so if you've—"

"Then check the crew manifest" Rians broke inwalking back, rapping a hand on top of the monitor in frustration.

"Look!" started the cadet sternly, looking down at his paperwork, "no papers, no boarding! Now, if you'll stand aside, we've got a lot of people to get through."

Rians glared down at the snivelling cadet who was staring down at his paperwork, hiding. He tried to find a way to reason with him, but the words didn't come out; instead, he just grabbed at the kid, raging and pulling him over the desk by the throat, choking him as he slammed him into the monitor, sending it crashing to the floor. With the whole desk now free for him to choke him, Rians squeezed with everything he had, sending the whole day into his throat as he gargled helplessly, eyes bulging as he flailed on the desk. After what felt like hours to Rians, another set of hands joined in, but they fought against him, and in his rage-filled state, Rians couldn't understand why they were prying him off, it was so clear what had to be done. Struggling backwards against a ferocious grip, the shouts and screams of the room began to filter through his red haze as shocked faces looked after him and Brice dragged him toward the door.

Suddenly, more faces, and cadet uniforms from the port authority, were everywhere, helping the choking checkpoint worker and descending on them before they could make their escape

"Hold it, asshole, you're not goin' anywhere!" said a lieutenant, grabbing at Rians' uniform.

The man was quickly brushed away by Brice, but Fulkes now got into the fray in front of them, trading shoves and insults with the port authority staff.

"You're stayin' right here till we get this sorted out!" shouted the lieutenant above the din of the room.

"Why? So he can grab my ass again?" Fulkes shouted.

"What?" demanded the lieutenant.

"Your little friend grabbed my ass!" screamed Fulkes, barging past him and pointing, making sure the hundreds of Marines heard him. "Your little port authority boy grabbed my ass and you want us to stay— what, so you can grab some more, girlfriend?"

Roars went up from the Marines, many of them already incensed by the long delays they'd been made to wait through and the attitude of the port authority staff, that anger now exploding, as the thought of one of the port authority grabbing one of their own like that demanded a response. As the crowd surged forward, Fulkes turned back, grabbing the lieutenant by the shoulder and shouting, "Hey, man, if you don't want a fucking massacre, you better get us on that shuttle!"

"You're not goin' anywhere, fucko!" returned the lieutenant.

"Alright then, try to go out like a man!" shouted Fulkes, gesturing with his head as the crowd surged through the first checkpoints, the first few port authority men being punched to the ground.

A few more seconds passed and the situation became clear to the lieutenant as he watched the crowd barrel into the third checkpoint. "Alright!" he screamed, glaring at Fulkes, "But you'll be back here some time, you fuck!"

"Sure, we will!" returned Fulkes, smiling back at the lieutenant as he jumped up on one of the checkpoints in the last line to use his rank to calm the crowd.

The lieutenant could only glare after his laughing counterpart as Brice dragged Fulkes through the doorway, smashing through the wire mesh gate just outside and on down the walkway with the sounds of metal grating under their feet masked by the roars coming from the crowd inside.

Back at Rians apartment…

Carla pulled the door shut quietly behind her. She'd

just got Charlotte to sleep. Her daughter had been crying for almost an hour after he'd left—how could he have let that happen again she thought thinking of Rians injury and their daughter seeing it? Coming into the main room, she sat down exhausted in one of the singles with the high window behind her. Her mind went through the last few days—the trouble, Michael, her husband, Charlotte, and all those who'd been involved. Everyone had something to say about it; her parents said this, her friends said that, and still others wouldn't speak to her at all. She'd thought she'd known what she was doing and that she could see a future with Michael, but he was gone and so had all her plans along with him. How could he do that to her? How could he just leave, she wondered… had it just been sex? Had she been a casual convenience for him? And what about all those things he'd said? Carla sighed, taking her head in her hands and resting her elbows on her knees; shc'd asked all these questions before and now felt the start of the headache that came with them. Try as she might, though, she couldn't stop asking them, and now he'd come back with the trouble following him, in the house less than five minutes and it had started again. What did he expect, leaving her for months at a time? How was she supposed to have a decent kind of life like all those around her? Drawing her hands further down her face, she peered over the top of them, the room silent around her. Still thinking about her relationships, her eyes picked up an object to the right of the front door; she'd been too busy to notice it lying on the floor earlier—it was his jump bag, and she new this was the day his unit was supposed to be shipping out, he'd walked out without it. Suddenly, she realised what he'd been trying to tell her, that he was leaving the forces and coming back to them for good. Carla breathed in again, still holding her head in her hands; she thought of all the good times they'd had before he'd gone away and, even in between his times away, all the happiness. Could it still work? Sitting there with the past filing through her mind, she began to think it could, and started seeing those sides of him she'd forgotten; they'd both made mistakes, but maybe they could fix that and try again. She smiled at the thought.

But she'd chased him out and said such horrible things that afternoon; the smile she wore faded, and she began to feel awful about the things said. She'd really cut deep this time. Well, that was going to change, she thought decidedly. When he came bac,k she was going to straighten it out, straighten them out. She half-smiled, still torn because of the guilt over the afternoon. But she'd fix that, for Charlotte's sake—for all their sakes, she'd fix everything.

Thinking on her plans was suddenly interrupted as the doorbell rang, making her start in the quiet. Staring at the door and thinking a little longer, she rose on the second ring, ready to try to listen, to make it work. Taking the handle in one hand, she quickly ran the other through her hair before opening the door with her best smile in service.

With the door opening, though, her smile fell away; it wasn't Rians standing there. Sean and Jools stood there, vibrant, and before any questions could be asked, Jools' arms were round her neck.

"Congratulations!" giggled Jools, bounding inside. "I always said you'd change him!" She laughed, pulling away and revealing her huge smile.

"Change who?" Carla asked, sending a confused

frown to both in turn.

"Rians!" Jools replied with a laugh, but she quickly calmed as Carla's expression didn't lift. "Where is he?" she asked, now looking similarly confused.

"We had a fight. He—" Carla began, still unsettled.

"Already!" Jools cut in, startled. "You two better not bring it to the party."

"What party?" Carla asked, becoming frustrated with them.

"*The* party! Didn't he tell you?" Jools demanded.

"No! What party? What are you talking about!" Carla demanded, angry now.

"He's out of the service!" Sean said.

"What?" Carla asked, her focus shifting to him.

"He's out! Didn't he tell you?" Sean asked, but he was already seeing the answer on her face. He continued, "He got a choice to leave on medical. The service wasn't happy he'd been reassigned; he was supposed to leave today, had his papers and everything, but they had to give him the choice when he got a second opinion from some doctor. As long as he doesn't turn up today, that's it— he's out," Sean explained, clearly confused as to why they weren't being greeted by celebrations. "Where is he?"

A moment of stunned silence was shattered by Carla's shriek as she realised what had likely happened. "Oh my God! Take me to the shuttle dock!"

"Wha—" Sean began.

"Take me to the shuttle dock!" screamed a hysterical Carla into his face, cutting him off.

Carla's shrieks barely subsided over the near twenty minute journey to the shuttle dock, Jools' efforts to calm her doing nothing. Hysteria had turned to outright panic after she'd found her husband's papers in his jump bag, which she'd grabbed from the floor as she'd passed with Charlotte in her arms. With her being so worked up into a frenzy, Sean hadn't even stopped the car fully when she'd broken out the door with Charlotte in her arms as she made for the entrance.

Troops now checked in, the front guards were gone, leaving only a bare staff on reception—whose protests went unnoticed as Carla barged past them and into the checkpoints. Voices behind her weren't even heard as, running through the room, she felt the ominous vibrations as her steps echoed on the marble with a dozen empty checkpoints looking on.

Passing through the exit, she heard the familiar rumble of shuttles' engines from behind the blast fence, heightening her panic as she battered her fist against the mesh gate while tearing down the walkway… but it was too late.

Arriving at the bend of the blast fence, she saw where it fell away to reveal the setting sun in the distance; exhausted, she fought for air, holding her daughter and realising the engine drone hadn't been coming from the lift-off pads, as the scene was now empty. Empty but for the thunder overhead that was growing fainter and fainter as she followed it up with her gaze, the shuttle's lights fading out through the clouds.

Chapter 25

The Message

It was busy, and staring out of the shuttle windows, Rians couldn't remember when he'd last seen it so busy. Held in a holding pattern, transports and armalites shuttled back and forth feeding a huge hull trapped in orbit around the planet with the docking station grappling onto its side. Personally, though, Rians felt weird; he was a husband, a father, but right now he didn't feel any of that… like he'd been cut free, disconnected. It was like being eighteen again, free and single, and he wasn't sure if he liked it or if he was supposed to, it had been so long.

A shuttle loaded with Marines wasn't the place to talk about emotional problems—who was he going to talk to anyway? Mr calm himself, Brice, or Mr sensitivity, Fulkes? Neither was much of an option, so he sat quietly trying to work it out for himself.

The shuttle was quiet, its stillness broken only by the occasional cough as two hundred-plus Marines sat in near darkness with only a faint green glow from the flight cabin creeping through the doorway left ajar. Staring out the window brought a sense of calm, like a dentist's waiting room—blue rail exhausts were moving back and forth as red proximity lights flashed intermittently above the ball-like curve of Earth off to the left. Looming in the distance, the black and grey silhouette of the station and a ship dancing over the planet's edge only added to the serenity. With the ship queued for over an hour now, Rians could have happily remained so for hours more, but soon the light thrust everyone felt in the back of their seats signalled the engines lighting up and the queuing coming to an end.

Engine smoke swarmed around their ankles as it always did in shuttle bays, and stepping out from under the shuttle's huge, hinged side door, they felt small as Marines from seven other shuttles did the same. Marching for the airlock, they were accosted by deafening noises as engineers in helmeted black sat with torque wrenches and welding torches under the bellies of shuttles, half-buried in smoke and with sparks flying in the dark environment, lit only by bursts of brilliant blue from torches.

Far better to be under the smoke-laden work than where he found himself three hours later, back where he'd begun all those years agomin basic training, wet-eared and trusting, no information on where they were going, just rumours swirling around like the smoke in the bays.

"I heard it from one of the ensigns off-duty," the private assured someone nearby. "Said they'd had a message from command; said we'd been reordered to some sector to take a look at something, eh... I don't remember what, but we're headin' elsewhere, brother. This might not be such a lame-assed milk run, after all— we might get to see some action!" He smiled, not knowing what the message might mean.

How could he? He was barely out of an academy, but Brice knew... he'd heard this before from other Marines, and he hoped he was wrong.

Aboard the Rheinvar Brenner brought a message Aidin...

"We've been ordered to exact radio silence, number one; whoever it is will have to wait," Aidin replied as he busied himself scanning through star charts.

"He's quite insistent, sir," Brenner said. "In the last half hour alone, we've had seven messages, all on secured channels."

"From where?" Aidin inquired, looking up with bemusement at the number of attempts.

"From Station 172, sir," Brenner answered.

Aidin's expression changed, and Brenner watched as Aidin fought with his orders, balancing this news against what he knew to be expected of them and feeling stressed with indecision before finally rising. "You have the bridge," was all he said as he made for his council room Darrant waiting on a secured channel.

"I figured that," Darrant said, his own voice stressed. "I just thought you oughtta know."

"Know what?" Aidin questioned, listening more to his stress than his words.

"Aidin, I know who's doing this," Darrant blurted out worriedly, his voice thickening.

"Yes, I've read the reports, and it seems—"Aidin never finished, as Darrant burst over the channels.

"Damn the reports, Aidin!" he hollered. "I interrogated the Vrail—it's Maral!"

Aidin started at the name, frozen for a moment as his mind raced through the implications."Maral is gone," Aidin answered assuredly, certain.

"No, he's not." Darrant's voice sounded defeated, but sure.

"How do you know?" Aidin finally asked quietly, as if fearing someone else would overhear them.

"Because there's not much left of the Vrail; in fact,

what's left is in a freezer four decks below me," Darrant answered.

Aidin didn't reply, listening to the hardship in the other man's voice and knowing what it must have been like for him to be the one doing the interrogating.

"Oh, and one more thing," Darrant said, almost offhandedly. "My Valraich trading post salesman on the station tells me there's been a Valraich reshuffle in command. Seems someone was turning a blind eye to ships running up and down the edge of their border just over from ours for months; says the new commanders aren't so blind, or not for now anyway. Darrant out."

Aidin sat back for a moment. It couldn't be true… Maral, a nightmare, was gone.

Aidins mind wandered to when this infamous Vrail commander arrived…

It was the third year of the war, and things almost seemed to be stabilizing; progress was even being made in some sectors with shipyards being pushed to their breaking point, but showing progress nevertheless. Then he came.

A change of command was how the captured files from a ship forced down on Elsa 3 put it. Unhappy with the way things were proceeding, the Dren command had removed the Vrail commanding their offensive forces in the western reaches of the IL 19 quadrant and replaced him with, as they put it, a seasoned veteran of the Norsigh Campaigns.

His arrival was heralded by blood hemorrhaging from every corner of the quadrant as defenceless outposts, ships, and people were slaughtered—out of range of rescue—simply in order to draw ships away, to break up the cohesion of the factions. And it worked.

Valraich and Irachan alike refused to listen, determined to protect their own and disgusted by the Alliance's apparent indecision, especially after finding out the circumstances in which victims had perished. Whole systems had been reduced to ruins, with loss of people, whole families, even, and the Dren seemed to thrive on their indifference to the suffering. Well-running fleets of attack ships were being cut to pieces in their efforts to fight back, traps set with blood along the Rennis line. Their attempts at rescue simply weakened the overall strength of the forces with ships now hopelessly far apart and losses mounting—all they had gained being lost.

By the time the new bloodshed unleashed had finished, the faction's suspicions had fallen back on the Alliance months of politique to try and quell the disputes almost failing with only a political saviour holding them together while generals versing and predicting Dren moves finally had success.

Communications with the settlements along the Rennis Line had ceased five months into the crisis, information on their status a mystery. That all changed eight months later when the Alliance Fleet finally pushed the front line back beyond the Rennis Line to reveal the true nature of the new commander. It was thought that the communications breakdown had been due to Dren dampening systems, a standard part of their procedure when invading, and that the settlers had been denied voice trans, but the settlers, it turned out, no longer existed.

Eighty-nine million gone, slaughtered needlessly by

the new Vrail master. For the Alliance arriving on his work the sights awaiting them were unimaginable; later, they would learn he had used them to hone the skills of his new troops out of lust for power, as well as sheer malice and cruelty. Both sides had taken massive losses fighting for the line, and prisoners on both sides lay in confinement, awaiting an uncertain future. Incredibly, though, a deal was reached with the Vrail commanders— all of them, save one. The Vrail were desperate for the retrieval of their captured commanders, for fear of information being gleaned from them and wanted to kill them themselves. The Dren code held that, after finding failure in his mission, a commander was to bring an end to himself, thus protecting any information he held, and failure to adhere to this demand guaranteed retribution. Knowing full well what would happen to them didn't matter to the Alliance, as any sympathy was long since gone, and so just under a dozen Alliance transports were sent out under computer control, all loaded with the soon-to-be victims.

At the same time, Dren transports left enemy-held territory with those who had survived their captivity, only three ships needed to carry them. The ships were headed for Shailin 1 with the Vrail and Hearack survivors set for the Crisilis system. Long-range scans of the ships showed life signs, although attempts at communication were met with silence. Ships soon intercepted the survivors, unwilling to wait and fearful of the Vrail turning back on the agreement, so they intercepted the convoy a parsec outside of the Shailin system. They had to dock with the ships manually, the people on board still not answering attempts at communication. When docking hatches were forced open it was clear why, but not how as it wasn't common knowledge yet with government secrecy worrying about panic and holding back discoveries about thirilian and the dangers it posed. Marines froze in shock as blackened, half-human monsters still raged, incandescent with anger and half crawling across decks with pain coming through their screams as they reached for the new arrivals. Bridges aboard boarding ships demanded explanations as sensors showed rapid power signatures, firing across every deck boarded, and with responses broken and panicked. Finally, the panic fading, most ships were fully neutralised, the thought of survivors being only a distant hope with what unit commanders reported back once control had been established.

Captains listened as the news came through, whole bridge crews' faces squinting as commanders announced the bodies were dead, and that the faces had stopped moving, but the worms were still alive and still twisting inside.

It had only taken two hours, the Marines falling back gladly with no casualties, but thankfully, the people on board had not been able to reach them, their legs gone and their states so deteriorated.

Airlocks sealing, confused captains gladly disconnected from the ships, not knowing they were about to learn firsthand what had happened on board, the thirilian still widly unknown and undetectable by scanners, and now gently filtering through their own ventilation systems.

That one parsec had saved the Shailin system and eight billion people from a nightmare. Communications failing on all channels, a brief cry for help finally came from the third ship in the rescue fleet. "They're everywhere—they've got the whole crew! The captain's gone! They're insane, resistant to weapons, but they still know how to operate the ship and how to… No! Noooooooooo!"

Heads fell as the screaming started the crewman's firing not enough, as the doors had opened behind him…

The fate befalling the Dren at Crisilis was better, their screams silenced in minutes as an armada of Dren attack ships loyal to the new Maral invaded the seemingly safe system deep in Alliance territory. The Vrail who had been awaiting the arrivals bent on their suffering were vaporised along with them, all ships coming to their rescue wiped out as Maral finally asserted his complete arrival, free now from any possible challengers and unleashed thousands of lightyears outside of anyone's control.

Maral had been sent by the Dren after they miscalculated, thinking he could be controlled and his talents wielded under the other Vrails. What else could they do from where they were, so far off and with only a few Vrail left in the IL19 quadrant? They had to accept it… but the few Vrail left didn't last long, what with accidents and missing ships, and the rest wisely disappearing into hiding themselves. Soon, only Maral remained, and the hell began.

Strangely, in some twisted way, Maral was loyal to the Dren and their cause, believing his own actions were for the Drens' greater good, for the future.

And so, three years of horror rolled on—three years of failed attempts by the Dren at replacement of their renegade commander each time ruthlessly cut down by Maral with still his unyielding servitude remaining to those trying to dispose of him, maddening, unexplainable.

It was finally the Alliance that finished their job for them; they finished it when Maral was finally captured, his luck running out at Grallen 4. But he was to slip the noose once more, the cries for his end held back while, in a twist of irony, negotiations with the few Vrail commanders that came out from hiding under orders from the Dren brought about an exchange of thousands of prisoners, Maral's end beginning right where it had started.

This time, no chances were taken; Alliance prisoners were delivered first before a small Dren frigate, granted docking privileges days earlier, was allowed to leave Station 196. Maral's fate lay in the hands of those who could deal with him from the beginning of his journey back to the Dren, his own kind whom he had wronged. People dreamed of the suffering he would endure—not to be reviled, not sick, but to be understood… understood for having lived through what he'd done. From the moment the frigate left, he was never heard from again. It had ended.

Chapter 26

Understanding

"Oh, I don't believe this!" Andrews said.

"What?" Captain Stanton asked.

"Take a look," Andrews replied, almost laughing.

Stanton stepped over, squinting at the con station bolted to the wall on these old ships instead of it having an independent unit like on the moderns. Gently laughing as he exhaled, he looked back to see Andrews joining him in gazing at the dimensions trailing across the screen. He and Andrews had never had the chance of most—not knowing important people and with no reputations to speak of, they had joined up almost thirty years prior, full of space battles and unknown this and that. Sadly, though, in the real world life, was less fulfilling than what dreams promised, and as for most others in their position, they'd felt brief spouts of hopeful recon throughout basic training, before being relegated out across the quadrant and tasked with menial escort duties, their training exercised to the full. Now, as usual, they were assigned another hugely important duty—piloting a wreck full of second-rate Marines to a garrison near the Fahraren Heights so that they could lead similar unmissable lives searching for a missing ship.

"Should I change course, sir?" Andrews asked, laughing at the readings of an eight-thousand-kilometer ship ahead, this latest scanner screw-up just like the others in being a running joke on the ship its antiquated systems providing ridiculous false readings and phantom anomolies as they failed with age,not unlike previous derelicts they'd been ordered to pilot before.

"Sure. Just be sure you don't run into that attack fleet we almost slammed into before," Stanton returned, referring to the earlier encounter they'd had in one of several disasters their latest decrepid ships sensors had assured them was about to happen.

Andrews laughed as he turned to the con mount, amazed by the depth of repair that the ship was in need of and smirking as he thought of how he'd tell the story later in the mess down on...

The explosion threw Andrews across the bridge. Stanton turned for his report only to see Andrews' head smash off the rear bulkhead as he went down. Making a grab for the con panel, Stanton was almost thrown, too, as the ship began cavitating, its engines straining against something nearby. The ship, relic that it was, had aged sensors that couldn't determine what the energy was which was surrounding the hull—only that it was held fast by the eight-thousand-kilometer sensor glitch that was now overhead and bearing down on them.

Below decks, men lay in a mass of wreckage and cargo, the ship's holds shaken apart by the unknown vessel so that it had trapped helpless bodies as they'd watched still others disappear in shrouds of energy, transported away to leave behind only those who were stuck in place. On the bridge, Stanton watched as his hand became see-through, the panel beneath it now visible with the touchscreen he would never hit, no distress signal being sent.

Those taken by the enemy vessel would never know help wasn't coming...

It had been a ridiculous mission, sending a barely functioning hulk to investigate the *Arnhem*'s disappearance; it was the only ship available, they' said. *Yeah, right*, thought Brice as he watched another crewman dragged from his cell with the others. He'd been screwed with the rest, sacrificed to try and find out what was happening. No doubt their ship had been watched by one of the long-range arrays, via telescopes like the Shairin array on Cal 2 or the Ferancs. He'd seen it during the war, too—send in a lone ship and watch where it got wasted and by how many, and then you'd know what you were up against. Except, this time it was different; this time,Alliance intelligence had seen nothing… they couldn't have since they'd just drifted into this ship, whatever it was and disappeared. Shit, he didn't even know what had happened. He'd been near the bridge when the stars had just vanished outside, and then there'd been the transporter beams and shit. If he didn't know what had happened, how could they?

The greenish light only pierced halfway down the corridor; at least, it felt that way, the darkness to the left hiding where it ended with the roof only seven feet above them. It added a claustrophobic feel to the misery etched onto the faces that were only barely visible ten feet across the way, slumped in their cells with the glint of blood and other fluids coming from them as such materials drained from cells into a central channel in the floor. On each side of the channel, cut into the floor, footsteps were slowly washed away, only to be made fresh by guards passing back and forth along the passage, sometimes in twos or more with a few minutes between them. Brice stared out through the bars hours later, waking with the rest of the men sitting at the back of the darkened cell, the scent of blood rank among them. Looking out at the next few prisoners being dragged away from their adjacent holdings, Brice and his unit with four more companions they didn't know watched them being dragged down the dimly lit corridor to the second door opposite the one they'd been through before, heard but unseen. The dim green hue halfway down the passage offered no clue as to where the corridor led, the only comfort those being dragged off would have before arriving on the hours they would spend wishing their journey there had been longer. The men being dragged off weren't long past having gotten through basic training—rookies, they had never seen the war or known anything about conditions like these, most of them remaining silent, uncertain like those looking after them, uncertain but for one thing, for those taken through the second door, noone had come back.

There wasn't any talking in the cells; guards patrolled along the decks and the cells ran the full length of the deck on each side. The prisoners peering through the bars as guards passed soon understood that those who stood out were taken sooner and more frequently, so there was silence. Silence broken only by the occasional coughing, with those few who were braver even letting out the occasional wince of pain that was quickly discouraged by their cell mates as they tried to avoid eye contact with the passing Hearack. It was maddening; there was no rest, the pressure constant and unwavering, so finally when their cells began to clank open again, it was almost a relief; at least now, there'd be no pretence, no games, their patience being gone. Even so, Brice felt his last reserves of self-preservation fire as they were dragged through the second door.

On the other side of the door, the contrast was immediate, as the green hue turned to darkness that was permeated only in places with deep green light, the Hearack visible in these patches at stations—but too infrequently placed for Brice or the others to gauge the size of this new place. Dragged ever further in, they couldn't figure out how far they'd gone or where the door back to the cells was, their disorientation made worse as they were twisted and turned by the occasional sharp hiss, the hairs on the exhausted men's necks still managing to jump. The strange hissing noise was like animals warning those getting too close, like a threat with the men being jarred in another direction; each time, it sounded, dull shapes only barely visible at times with the true nature of what they were hidden in the dark. Pushed further in, it grew cold—uncomfortably so—pained cries drifting over from places unseen their last suffering evidently ending for some, as they're cries came no more and others took their place.

Through the darkness ahead, a glow appeared—like the others, but larger this time and growing stronger as figures came into view. Hearack, lots of them, all standing fast as if on guard, their eyes meeting those of the prisoners as they approached. Passing by, their eyes followed as they moved sneering as long as they could before they'd move beyond them inside their circle. Relief was short-lived as another set of eyes met them upon entering… eyes with a face paler than white, seemingly welcoming and almost kind as the prisoners stopped. Recognition was fast, and it was obvious now why no one had come back through the second door.

"Hello, gentlemen," the voice came softly. "Do you know who I am?"

The answer was already there, written on their faces for Maral to see... fear finding what little energy they had left to shine through on their faces..

"Hmmph. Introductions not necessary then," he almost whispered, looking across them. "That should cut down on time."

A look to his guards, and they were ushered forward—forced into a line diagonally set ten feet from what appeared to be stations, each one's panel having symbols running across it all but indecipherably. But their attention was more focused on Maral standing midway between them and the panels. Maral looked back assuredly as sluggish footsteps approached, more figures appearing from the darkness behind them with one bloodied figure in particular being forced into their midst, pushed to their right and looking anything but assured. Silence lasted for a moment ,the new arrival breathing heavier than the rest with his head drooping with exhaustion as he stood by, his injuries hidden inside him.

"Gentlemen, might I introduce Lieutenant Preston, navigation officer of the late attack ship *Blerin*." Maral glared at him. "He has been most unhelpful ever since we met; in fact, he destroyed one of our two Drevauch class starships that were left over from the war by ramming his ship into one of its weapons bays. Thirilian energy transfers don't react well when the density fields needed to stabilise them during charging are breeched by uninvited guests," Maral hissed, his stare becoming ever angrier as he spoke in Preston's direction. "The subsequent explosion was magnified so much by the Thirilian, it also destroyed the other Drevauch behind it, and they are irreplaceable!" Maral growled, almost nose to nose with Preston now, his bloody head not lifting to the hate-filled eyes in front of him.

"His associates were far more helpful," Maral continued, his hiss returning as he moved off slowly down the line in front him, glaring into each man's eyes as he passed. "They were far easier... on the pallet." He came to a stop next to Fuller. "Updates, Mr Fuller, that's what I want: updates," Maral answered his questioning look. "Updates can avoid such setbacks," he continued, turning away toward the panels.

"I'm afraid we can't help you," Fuller answered, as if he were reading directions from a page.

"Hmmph." Maral laughed without turning. "Oh contraire, Mr Fuller, I think you can be most helpful." He turned staring squarely. "According to some of your cellmates, it seems you were dropped off to your new assignment straight from Aurin 2 aboard the Alliance fleet's replacement flagship. A relic... I hear it should have stayed dead on that planet where we left it," he growled. "In any case," he began again calmly, "there must have been conversations aboard it. Hmmm? Hints, perhaps, about future proceedings that were not sent across secure channels, rumours even...." Maral cocked his head questioningly.

"I'm afraid we can't help you," Fuller read from the proverbial page again.

"I see," Maral whispered in an accepting tone. "Well, if you won't help me, maybe you'll help him." Maral gestured toward the suffering Preston.

Moments later, a guard moved through and Preston underwent a savage beating, and the rest of them came under fire of it, too, as they moved to help, guards invading the space so that all of them were battered to the floor, the Hearacks' strength easily snapping ribs—the efforts of the captives to fight back becoming all but a waste. In a matter of seconds, they lay in need of serious medical attention, with attention of another kind being given, however, as they were hauled back to their feet, their needs ignored. The guards backed away slowly at Maral's look, his hand raising to stop the guard in front of Preston—this one guard's work not yet over.

Silence fell upon them as Maral looked on, a practised expression of regret on his face as the men fought down pain, groaning as they tried to maintain their dignity. They slowly began to lessen their complaints as seconds passed, almost used to the beatings now—but not so for Preston. He had no such luxuries as the rest looked on at his louder struggles, his body convulsing involuntarily with blood running from his mouth down his chin, betraying internal injuries.

"Isn't compassion the great virtue that separates you from us?" Maral looked at Fuller questioningly. "Or is this morality your species clings to only for those you deem worthy?" He looked at a shaking Preston as if with some regret.

"It's something you have to be born with," voiced Rians, sickened as he listened to Preston choking.

"I was born," Maral answered openly.

Fuller looked up, confused.

"Ah, you see," Maral spoke softly, "there is so much you can tell me, Captain, and I can tell you; so, the Vrail beginnings are still not understood by your intelligence divisions yet. Hmph. We have a birth," Maral explained happily. "The Vrail. that is," he went on. "Hearack genes may be cloned, replicated, but Vrail are quite different. For us, replication is impossible, but our abilities are so prized by the Dren that genetic modification within them is settled for.

"Modifications?" Rians asked.

"Intelligence, behavioural changes…" Maral began.

"Brainwashing, the arrestment of loyalty," finished Fuller.

"Yesss," Maral hissed, not taking well to the interruption.

"And your mother?" Rians questioned.

"Vrail parents do not survive the automated birthing process; in fact, I still bare a few scars myself, as the procedure is… basic." Maral turned on Rians' look of shock at the ease of his explanation. "Well, there is no need," he tried to explain, genuinely confused at the man's expression. "The mother's task for the Dren has already been completed."

"And them…" Fuller cocked his head at the ring of glaring Hearack, "they've gotta be artificial," he said in disgust. "No parent would bare that."

"Well." Maral's attention shifted to him. "If birth left them as weak as you, I'm glad they miss out on such a process."

"Not being born means you miss everything else that comes with it," Fuller added.

"Really!" Maral crowed condescendingly, looking at his Hearack guards. "Why bother with birth when you can clone perfection?" he challenged.

"What, you call that perfection?" Rians answered, looking at the nearest Hearack guard with disgust. "He may have strength, but he has no soul, no character."

"When you're as strong as he is, you don't need character." Maral glared back at the captive.

A sharp hiss echoed from the shadows, Maral's head

reacting to the sound—its source unclear in the darkness beyond the light, but animal-like and impatient. Straining their eyes from the line, the men could only pick up the faintest of movements, unseen before... lots, seemingly everywhere beyond the guards.

"Hmmph," Maral uttered as Fuller finally looked at him questioningly for an answer to what the menacing hissing sounds where in the shadows. "Strange isn't it, life? All that stands between you and them is us.... How does it feel to be under our protection?"

Fuller grimaced, raging at the prospect, wishing to reach out and grab...

Maral laughed gently, reading Fuller like a book. "I wouldn't," he hinted. "They're not a very friendly bunch." He raised his eyebrows refering to the dark shapes in the shadows. "In fact, they're really quite aggressive." Maral stared out past the guards into the darkness. "They conquer, well, consume every species they encounter," Maral explained quietly to Fuller, as if not wishing to agitate the unseen creatures further. "They take over—not with steel or fire, but with infection and hosting, burrowing inside anyone they find, quickly taking control in most and keeping the worst, the most aggressive, for their own ambitions mutating their traits with their own." Maral's voice rang with admiration, memories flooding forward. "The process is one of a most agonising manner." He smiled, his attention coming back to Fuller. "They come from quite far away," Maral continued. "Our meeting with them was accidental, you might say, and although our friendship was strained in the beginning, it turned out that we have quite similar goals in life, and death. After some very lengthy discussions, it was clear that we would be far better off complementing one another's endeavours."

"And what made you so special?" asked Fuller angrily.

"Why, our glorious rhirilian lineage, of course," Maral announced, gesturing to the Hearack as if proud of a family around him. "The small part of Dren code in all of us is what enables us to survive here." Maral stared back at Fuller's blank expression, his own becoming incredulous at what he viewed to be ignorance. "You mean to tell me that, over the entire war and afterward, you still haven't figured out the Dren beginnings?" He laughed, the Hearack going off with him.

"We haven't had the pleasure of meeting them," Fuller sneered through gritted teeth, thinking of what he'd do to the Vrail and Hearack overseers if he ever did.

"Oh, but you have!" Maral centred on him wryly, recognising his intent with his gritted teeth and showing his own in his eyes.

"I'm afraid I don't follow," Fuller answered almost sarcastically, tired of the games.

"You don't remember meeting their children?" He glared, as if angry that their presence had apparently never been sensed.

Fuller could only look back at their captor, as nothing Maral said was making sense.

"Thirilian is not just a weapon, Mr Fuller," the weapon's name instantly angering Fuller as he thought of his family. "No…." Maral stared as he pulled away, turning his back on him. "It brings not just death under its purview, but life!" he announced proudly, slowly moving across the space between the guards. "You have seen the Dren, Mr Fuller—their larvae anyway," Maral assured him. "Thirilian is not just radiation, but contains the Dren genetic code, spreading it to any genetic matter it comes into contact with; it's just that some…" he paused, "aren't strong enough to gestate the entire first cycle of larvae before death." Maral looked sullen, lost, as if feeling for the Dren and their young. "But not before they exact their revenge," he assured the men in front of him, straightening up and scowling at those standing before him. "For their weakness, those who cannot support gestation have their bodies ravaged all the same, everything being utilized, from the very strands of DNA to the tips of nerve endings—sanity and soul gone by the end!" Maral crowed, his scowl continuing.

"And this prevented you from being taken over by them," Rians concluded, staring into the darkness.

"They did try to take us as hosts," remembered Maral aloud. "Our bodies put up such a nervous reaction, they retreated out of us fairly quickly, unpalatable we were; still, there were some cases of heart failure among us."

"How terrible," Brice said sarcastically. "You could have been killed."

"Hmph, yes." Maral laughed forcibly, seeming to appreciate the candor. "It seems the Dren method of procreation leaves our immune systems able to detect and fight off such parasites."

"Takes one to know one, I guess," muttered Preston, beaten so badly now that he was past caring anymore, past being afraid.

Maral looked briefly over at him, then turning back to Fuller smirking.

"This thing is theirs?" Fuller asked, staring up into the blackness where a ceiling might be hidden.

"Yes," answered Maral, moving toward him. "A

most impressive carrier system, wouldn't you say? Perhaps if your pathetic race were not so consumed by your weaknesses and moralities, you would have finished me when you had the chance instead of trying to barter for a few thousand more worthless lives," he growled, now face to face with Fuller.

"But then, you never really finish things, do you?" Maral continued. "Always hesitating, mercy as your constant baggage," he growled, glaring at Fuller as if angry with a child unable to meet his expectations. "And that's your downfall… loose ends, I do so hate loose ends," Maral spoke quietly, circling Fuller and passing behind Rians and the rest to reach Preston. "How's the wound?" he whispered in his ear.

"It'll heal," Preston replied defiantly, straightening his shoulders.

"It won't…" Maral hissed as a scythe blade burst through Preston's chest, the others instantly reaching to offer him some aid, only to be savagely beaten down to the ground by the guards. Winded and bloody, they could only watch as Preston shook violently—now held up only by Maral via the blade through his back, his killer peering over his shoulder with sickening satisfaction. Preston's gasps for air became harder, louder, and were finally reduced to gargling as blood filled his lungs more completely with each involuntary effort for breath. Maral watched the life drain from his eyes as the panic mounted, the struggle to cling on paramount in him until the shaking slowly subsided and Preston struggled no more. With the sound of shredding tissue, the blade was sharply retracted and Preston's lifeless body collapsed to the floor.

Maral looked on innocently as the sickened men

were dragged back to their feet, his face turning to feigned regret as he looked down their number, stopping on Fuller. "One down," he whispered, looking along the line and back. "Ten to go."

"How can you act like this?" voiced a disgusted Rians, the guards glaring as he struggled to keep himself still.

Maral looked back at him, tilting his head and squinting. "Like what?" he asked, genuinely confused.

Rians was equally confused, gilded with shock. "Like this, how can you…?"

Maral looked down at what Rians was referring to— the mutilated remains of Preston with his blood flowing freely across the steel deck. "This?" Maral questioned, raising his head at Rians as if in disgust. "This is nothing. We will do whatever is demanded of us—"

"By the Dren, you mean," Rians cut in angrily as he watched the blood flowing.

"You have feelings over this…" Maral spoke questioningly.

Rians could only look back at their captor, his adrenalin ebbing and awareness of his precarious situation reasserting itself.

"What is it that you feel?" Maral asked with a look of genuine curiosity.

Rians could only stare back at him.

"Yes," Maral spoke softly. "It's not till you analyse it, is it? Think of what's holding you back…. And, by then, the chance is gone—and isn't that how you fail?" Maral asked.

Rians returned frown was unsure, confusion etched over his expression.

"You have a family, yes?" Maral questioned him.

Rians slowly nodded.

"And you wish to protect them?"

Rians nodded again.

"Against all that is out here?"

Maral's question brought no response. Rians only watched as Maral turned, his pale white face illuminated further in the light.

"It is simply an act of nature to institute desire, the desire to be the strongest, and with this strength, there comes pain. It is unavoidable, and so also will be the fact that one species, one kind…" Maral paused, looking at Rians, "will wield this pain above others."

Rians listened carefully, almost forgetting those around him as the monster seemed to show feeling, as if…

"Surely," Maral continued, his words soft, "the best way to protect a family against the worst that is out here is to be the worst."

Rians felt less threatened as he watched him approach, almost…

"Surely, this is the best thing you could do for them?"

Rians looked down at the lifeless and broken body on the floor.

"Yes…" Maral whispered, Rians' eyes turning back up to meet his. "The price." Maral stared gently back at his subject. "But wouldn't it be better? Better than the position you find yourself in now? The position you've left your family in, with your weakness?"

Rians watched, under the care of a sort of teacher standing over him.

"All your species holds dear is protected by what some would consider monsters." Maral stared at him.

"By you, their defence forces, who exist in this place inhabited by the same…. Don't you love your family?"

Rians stared at him, finally answering as Maral turned away. "Yes."

"Yes?" Maral questioned, only half-turning back as he stopped with his eyes on the floor.

"Yes," Rians confirmed, more resolute than before.

Maral turned, fully coming back to Rians and staring at him face to face, the comfortable space between them gone, holding an intensity that was almost unbearable as Rians waited to feel the blade that had just torn open Preston.

"I love mine, too," Maral spoke up, his tone honest and unthreatening, real…

"But they left you; tried to…." Rians stopped, seeing Maral's eyebrows raising and his face looking anything but friendly, now staring and waiting for him to finish. "After everything you've done for them, they turned on you and—" He never finished.

"No!" Maral screamed at him, the huge bellow making him start. "The Dren believed there were those stronger, those who would better serve them! But they were wrong… they just didn't know it at the time." Maral seemed to calm enough to think, and then continued, "We must be subject to all that they do, even their mistakes, which were after all made while trying to strengthen their interests. They thought there were others that could do more for them, a mistake, and when I finally bring them Quadrant IL 19, mistakes will be forgotten and we will go on… hand in hand, as before." Maral had been speaking softly, looking lost at the floor as if thinking of a parent he would impress. With his catching Rians' look of bewilderment, anger immediately returned. "We will do whatever our servitude to the Dren demands," he continued, glaring. "That is something you don't seem to be able to grasp, but we are the strongest force you will ever know, given power to do unspeakable things, but not by force or weapons or ships," Maral sneered. "No... but by servitude; for us, fear is no obstacle, death is no hindrance. Our power comes from what we are under the Dren, and it's not your pathetic loyalty or a group of rules or regulations; it's an allegiance... it is everything!" Maral looked down at Rians, sneering as if he were looking at some lower species. "I can't expect you to understand; you have no idea what it is to have such strength, as you value each other. You worry about feelings and the future. Your weaknesses are intolerable, and so it is not our power that will destroy you, but your inability to sacrifice yourselves for a superior way." Maral walked passed Rians in disgust, sneering, slowing as he went and turning his head. "In the grand scheme of things, when it comes to the point where everything is demanded of you, you will falter. You are not able to sacrifice all you hold dear; you are not able to because you have no allegiance."

In silence for a moment, the men began to feel weak, beaten. Fuller didn't like it, and he took a swipe on behalf of their pride. "Maybe we don't, but that didn't stop us last time and it won't this time, either."

Maral turned, stopping, surprised... but waiting for the explanation as he stood with his eyebrows raised in the eerie light.

"You don't stand a chance. Our ship was being tracked," Fuller spoke up defiantly as he looked hard at Maral. "Right now, people are sifting through data from long-range telescopes; your little game of hide and seek is over. By the time this crate arrives, they'll have pulled back from everywhere and be waiting."

Maral gave him a look of genuine amusement, a smile beginning to light up his face. "Don't you think I know that?" he asked, staring back at Fuller in disbelief. "I was part of the war for a little while, you know, so I've seen every laughable strategy you know!" He smirked. "And now, together and united, it'll be different… this time, we'll finish together what we almost did alone. Be waiting for us, yes—with only half your fleet, at best, with the bulk of its reserve garbage and your real firepower still entrenched lightyears away in Maires Drift. It'll be a slaughter!" he announced, staring round with glee at the Hearack guards, his back to the men as he revelled in his plot, the men listening as the Hearack jeered all around them, howling with laughter at the prospect he'd described. Eventually, the laughter faded, leaving Maral standing in front of them menacingly in the eerie light; slowly, he looked over his shoulder with his smile gone, evil in its place. "Like yours."

Suddenly, there was a muffled sound of explosions, alarms erupting and deafening the ship's occupants.

"What's going on?" Maral demanded, spinning round to his guards.

"We're under attack!" replied a guard. "An Alliance ship!"

"What?" Maral hissed as he thought feverishly. They were cloaked, so how could the ship have found them? It couldn't have, it was impossible… the only way was if something on board was… "Noooooooooooo!" he screamed, spinning round with his scythe blade in hand, slicing harmlessly through transporter beams and crashing into the wall behind the prisoners being transported out of the room.

Outside, the *Rheinvar* heaved up over the top of the sensor-gleaned image, invisible to the naked eye, but explosions from the thorans made impact, confirming there was something there. Pulling up over the ship's centre, well away from what appeared to be weapons stations underneath, they engaged the warp drive, tearing away before their unseen foe could return the favour.

Chapter 27

Witness from the Past

"You didn't think we were just going to leave you there, did you?" Aidin asked, smiling as Fuller walked onto the bridge, the maglift closing behind him.

Secrecy no longer an issue, Aidin spoke freely on the bridge over the next few minutes as crews busied themselves around the science stations, transferring sensor sweeps and other newly gleaned information into the ship's mainframe. Fuller listened as he found out how they'd been rescued—how their last, overgenerous meal aboard Station 185 had contained more than simple proteins and amino acids. Hidden inside the meals of the ill fated ships crew had been nano technology; it had been crawling with the stuff. Thousands of small machines, some designed simply to emit frequencies which Alliance sensors were attuned to pick up and others designed to leave the body and seek out a way into foreign systems. "That's how we were able to approach undetected," Aidin explained. "They jammed the ship's sensors before alerting us through their own communication system, disguising their signal as background radiation. I'm only sorry they took so long or we could have been there sooner." Fuller, like so many others, hadn't felt comfortable with their orders from the beginning, knowing damn well that something had been wrong. Anger welled up in him, but so did the realisation of the necessity of what had been done to them—and besides that, his attention was now focused elsewhere as he thought more about what he'd just been told.

Aidin trailed off, stopping as he caught Fuller's expression. "They're perfectly harmless," he assured the other man, Fuller looking up from his stomach with a frown. "In a few days, nature will take its course and they'll be gone."

His words had little effect on Fuller's uncomfortable expression. "Thousands?" Fuller asked, lifting a hand to his stomach.

"Well." Aidin smiled. "No one wants to be alone, do they?"

Aidin's smile wasn't joined, though, Fuller deciding at that moment never to take the Alliance up on its hospitality so trustingly again.

"But on another note," Aidin changed the subject, "the sensor data gleaned in the attack on your ship and our subsequent raid was sent to Command two hours ago. The dimensions of that vessel are startling—with no shields, the cloaking system must be taking up a staggering amount of space inside of it. They've sent preliminaries on the data; some of it still can't be uncoded since the language has the computers beat. We're awaiting orders on how to proceed, but given the size alone, there's very little we can do by ourselves. At least now, things are making sense; where the raids have been coming from, missing ships, strange sensor data… but one thing that doesn't add up is how they were able to get so far so fast. They've avoided sensor sweeps, patrols, every method of detection for months—nothing of that size could have done that unless they had complex insights into the internal running of the IAF."

"That part's easy. The Hearack on board were led by this…" Fuller was gently cut off, Aidin raising his hand.

"No," Aidin said, his voice lowering. "Not even at their deepest penetration into our services during the war would the Dren have obtained information like this. I tell you, Fuller, they would have to have read the very minds of IAF commanders at the highest of levels. Anything you can tell us which you haven't already during the debriefing could be invaluable, though… anything that's come back, no matter how small. You said there were other things on the ship, not Hearack and not Dren. Did you see them or discover anything of what they looked like?

Fuller thought on it, happy for something to take his mind off of his last meal; he thought of the inside of the ship, the noise, the smells… the pain. He began to speak aloud quietly, looking past Aidin to the floor as he dealt with the trauma of what had happened, the memory of screams from the holding cells bringing back involuntary expressions as the memories came back vividly, along with the cold, the darkness, and Preston.

"It was dark everywhere," Fuller recalled. "Dark green lighting lit some parts, but mostly there was just dark, dark everywhere; people were dragged away… It, eh…" he trailed off at the thoughts. "They took us to their Vrail…it was Maral."

Aidin started at the name he'd already read in Fuller's debriefing; even so, the thoughts attached to it brought disbelief, fear… almost jutting in he held back allowing Fuller to keep focused.

"He was in some sort of place… not a room just a space on the ship, controls all around him. And the questions, he asked so many questions… there was another guy there from some ship also, and he—" Fuller winced as he heard Maral hissing, and the blade…

"You've been through a lot, so perhaps—" Aidin stopped as Fuller raised a hand, clearly trying to concentrate.

"He said this time would be different," Fuller began.

"Maral?" Aidin asked.

Fuller nodded. "He said he didn't like loose ends, and that this time would be different that… *'We'll finish together what we almost did alone'*—that's exactly what he said," Fuller repeated Maral's words as he'd heard him shout them the stress of remembering etched across his face as he saw the room and the guards all over again. "It was as if he meant you'd met before… hissing, these things in the shadows kept circling just out of sight; they kept hissing as he spoke."

"We have met before," Aidin said. "But he's supposed to be dead; he's the sickest creature we've ever known, and it'll be different this time, all right… this time, we'll finish the job."

Fuller looked up, confused. "No, you don't get it. The way he was talking, it wasn't the Dren he was talking about… it was as if they'd met you before those things hissing in the shadows."

Aidin shared the confused look, unable to find anything in the past that even resembled the alien ship or what Fuller was telling him.

"Did you catch even a glimpse of what they looked like?" Aidin questioned as, behind him, crews began to download the data from Fuller's lost ship, now uncoded and sent by command into the *Rheinvar* computer core.

"No, no, it was dark, too dark; they were just shadows behind them at the backs of the rooms," Fuller explained. "Shadows and hissing."

"Hissing?" Aidin frowned.

"Yeah, weird, like an animal..." Fuller tried to explain. "It, eh... ahh, I'm sorry, you just couldn't see; it was too—"

Suddenly, the computer rang out a string of alarms as the signals from the cloaked ship downloaded. The men turned to see astonished crews staring at the screens as data flooded across them—torrents of data, mountains—but it wasn't the data or the amount that grabbed Aidin; it was something else. Standing quite still, he began to freeze as the signals rang out over the bridge, louder with each second in his mind as he saw the image displayed at the top right of the screen of a small creature, data flooding across beneath it. His expression, though initially unnoticed, was soon imitated by some who had also been there, those among the crew who'd been left from the....

And then he was gone, the captain's council doors sealing on his nerves—a privilege others wished they had.

Aidin's head hit hard on the back of the seat, but he barely noticed as he flicked on the table unit in front of him, the screen flickering into life with a blue glow gently illuminating the room, the lights forgotten on the way in. Lights, though, were the least of his worries as he thought of the implications of what he'd just seen; Aidin took hold of his chin, worriedly patching through to command. Bringing up a secured link, his hand became visible, gently lit from the screen as the channels were linked... but before they'd even been established, the memories had started.

It had been eight years earlier, exploration at its peak and the whole IL 19 quadrant enjoying an unparalleled time of peace, all sides prospering well under far-reaching treaties. Scout ships and long-range science missions had been extended in numbers unseen in recent times, missions even stretching deep into the Fahraren Heights, despite the risk. That was a section of space torn by energy believed to have come from the gravity wells of previous dying stars, their collapse just shy of the strength needed to form black holes. Instead, the swathes of energy had left plasma storms and un-navigable energy currents with shearing eddies, ships never making it very far and limping back damaged and shaken... until one ship, the *Taurwind*, had found luck on their side. For three weeks, they had charted the inside, new discoveries of rich mineral deposits and small planetoids deep within being duly reported back until contact with them had been lost. All attempts to raise them had failed, as had attempts at locating or rescue, all ships' efforts beaten back by the Heights. Considered lost, most likely drawn into the thermals, their efforts had finally been mourned, the general feeling being that they had pushed their luck too far, getting too confident and paying the price. Almost a month later, though, a hero's welcome had greeted the crew of a badly mauled ship as it had limped out of the Heights to be picked up days later by the Farancs Array before being helped to the nearest space station, the 190, by passing traders. Tales of harrowing piloting while trapped inside a deadly mix of thermals and currents had been told and retold as the surviving crew had spoken of their month dicing with death; over two thirds, though, hadn't made it back. Survivors had reported strange radiation effects, crewmen falling ill and succumbing to an unknown and bizarre set of ailments. That had explained the apparent high loading of their bodies with adrenalin levels, each person's physical health completely abnormal and giving rise to huge feats of physical strength, and a lack of appetite and need for sleep. The computers, though, could not be explained.

Vast tracks of memory had been lost, seemingly erased, the surviving crew putting it down to radiological effects with senior commanders being more than skeptical about they're claims. The skepticism hadn't lasted, though, with higher authorities coming round to their idea—seemingly persuaded to this way of thinking after having talks with various members of the crew as they reported in at stations and bases on route back to IAF Command.

It hadn't been till a minor skirmish with border pirates on the Valraich border that something all the more suspicious had been discovered. Injured during the engagement, the doctor on board had been found to have heightened adrenalin and hormone levels—dangerous levels, even. Nurses on board had been unable to bring them down, their drugs failing and instead bringing on nervous reactions and violent fits, all scans unable to find out why until, finally, a Toren scan had showed something that didn't belong there. At the base of the doctor's neck, inside his body, a frightening-looking parasite—spider-like and the size of a fist—had sat poised with its spined legs piercing into arteries and, worse, what seemed like thin fangs emersed in the spinal column. Efforts to remove it had been met with violent opposition, the creature forcing the doctor into heart failure several times before they'd finally given in, for fear of killing him otherwise, securing the patient in the brig to be quarantined from the rest of the crew. But he hadn't been the only one.

When a final brief message had broken through on all channels, it had briefly described what was happening, including communications sabotaged and repaired only to be brought down again, engine failures, crew disappearances, and finally mutiny. As the first officer had relayed the news about the discovery, the infirmary doors had been heard being forced open nearby, brief cries sounding out only to be drowned out by weapons fire before communications were swiftly severed. A final automatic relay from the ship had revealed that the first officer's codes had been entered into the ship's mainframe, forcing it to auto-destruct... and that hadn't been the last.

By the time Command had realised what was happening, even members of the government had vanished, others beginning to act strangely and becoming uncommunicative; by the time a way of scanning for the parasites outside of a lab had been found, panic had spread. Whole stations and settlements had been found to be infected, fleets of ships even raiding their own kind so that an all-out unofficial civil war had erupted and left to boil by the other factions standing idle as they'd watched the Alliance weaken. They'd stood by as families had been torn apart, infected loved ones torn from screaming figures' arms in the night, and stood by as whole cities had been "cleansed"—this being a euphemism for mass slaughter. They'd stood by—all but one. The Valraichs, back-stabbing as they were, had been able to see which way the wind was blowing. They'd even fought off infected Alliance ships trying to penetrate their own borders, so they'd known it was only a matter of time before one got through, and to lose their control was unbearable to them.

And so, the most unlikely of Alliances had been formed, Valraich ships tearing through Alliance space and assisting where they could, their zeal for—as they put it—"wiping out infected areas" being fairly disturbing. More disturbing had been the incidents with those who were uninfected, the Valraichs' natural paranoia bringing on cases of terrifying mistakes, so that at one point an entire station had almost been vaporised based on nothing more than suspicion. Something had needed to be done, and for the first time in history, Valraich representatives had been permitted on stations, their presence and intelligence relays intended to quell such incidents. It had worked, too, and apart from security breaches by prying Valraich and the protestats of the station commanders, the situation had been of benefit to the civil war. Eighteen months later, the panic had been over, all who remained declared safe, and the Alliance had assigned designated units to continue sweeping for sleeper cells, but none had ever been found. All steps to find the source of the parasites had failed, however, the incident in the Fahraren Heights becoming classified, buried, and any entry by ships into the area had been banned under the guise of it being too dangerous, stating that even salvage crews were being put in unnecessary risk when rescuing crippled ships. Suspicious minds had seen it differently, questioning the somewhat large deep-space re-deployment of Garrison 247 to the region and seeing it as a seemingly wasteful effort with the area being considered a non-event.

Progress with relations had kept small contingents of Valraich representatives and traders who were allowed to remain on stations only after thorough vetting procedures, much to the dismay of station commanders. It had been close, the highest echelons of Alliance Command brought under outside control and an insidious, invisible enemy almost taking over from the inside. They had been lucky, with the threat thought gone… until now.

"You're sure?" came Chelmski's nervous voice over the channels.

"Yes, Admiral, we're very sure," Aidin replied.

"How was this not picked up at Command?" he questioned, clearly hopeful for a mistake.

Aidin explained the news of the *Rheinvar Fs* discovery in Station 185's shipyard research facility. "She's very old for a starship, Admiral; her mainframe hasn't been updated in over a decade, so irrelevant and classified data wiped from other ships in services hasn't happened here… luckily."

Chelmski took a deep breath, his chin and lips resting on a closed fist with his eyes averting as he thought aloud. "I'll have to relay this to Command…. In the meantime, proceed on these orders until directed otherwise. I'll be in touch."

His exit was brief, spurned by worry, which Aidin understood as he thought over his next move.

Several decks below…

"They did what?" screamed Brice, grabbing his stomach instinctually just like Fuller had done.

"Don't worry; they're harmless. They'll be gone in a few days—" Fuller was cut off sharply as Brice launched into a tirade, the news not something someone of his disposition had needed to hear.

"I've got thousands of these little bastards crawlin' around inside me! Naw, naw, naw, this ain't happenin'— this ain't goin' on. I want these mother fuckers out now! Three days, my ass!" he protested, pacing around at speed with the thought of the nanites driving him mad.

"Look at it this way—they're the reason you're on this crate now and not in that cloaked hell hole. Those little guys saved our—"

"And for *that*, I am truly grateful," Brice cut in, still pacing but dropping his hands from his head. "But my stomach is not up for rent! I—"

"Brice!" Fuller shouted, trying to calm him before he went too far overboard. "Three days."

"Three days," Brice almost whimpered, turning to the other men. "They take us apart and put us back together with some machine; they stick robots in our stomachs. In three days, there'll be nothin' left but a set of clothes!" he cried out, his hands going back to his head as he turned away, pacing off to the back of the room.

Chapter 28

The Line

The meeting hadn't gone well—strain and pressure on commanders with politicians being ever-present, interference had sent tempers soaring and egos colliding as senior-this and long-serving-that had argued, or even raged at some points, with time ticking down on the meeting all the while. Resistance to shelving well thought-out plans had been rife as reputations and ranks had had to be pushed aside in order to acknowledge the new threat. It hadn't been easy, some attendees almost walking out, claiming the ideas ridiculous and that they might as well roll over and give in. But, things had been settled, the die now cast.

Eighteen hours had passed, the *Rheinvar* changing course upon finally receiving their orders along with notes of appreciation for the extra time their warning had given. The situation was clear now. They were to join what was literally an armada of Alliance might; every ship within range had been pulled back from borders, from everywhere, an absence of outside assistance being apparent as the other factions remained silent—as expected. The plan was crude, but it had to be with so many ships off in the Drift; they were racing back, but were too far out, Aidin thought as he mulled it over in his mind. All the computers and fancy strategist programs, all the centuries of technological evolution, and they were down to this... their efforts to advance over the centuries almost seeming like a waste of time. He ran it through his mind again; it was so, so...

unbelievable, but it would either work or it wouldn't, and if didn't, all the advancing wouldn't have mattered.

"On approaching, you'll see our second fleet," Aidin remembered Chelmski telling him as he mulled his orders over again. "Take position aft and come up under the Seren County at 382-mark-128; that'll bring you just off-centre right about three quarters deep inside the fleet. Our primary fleet is being held out of sight, as we believe the Hearack attack ships, invisible in the Drift, are what's been running silently down the Alliance-Valraich border," he'd continued, speaking of the intelligence that was so vitally provided by the Vrail on Darrant's station. Whoever they'd found to give them the access codes to the sensor grids along that area had to be of a senior stature. He'd gone on, "In any case, if we're right, that means they're still out there and we should expect them. Since they can't cloak, that means one of three things: they're either still over the border, which is doubtful with Valraich paranoia in full swing, or they've gone into the Fahraren Heights, or else they're hiding in some system, stationery behind interference. Whatever the case, we can't take them both at once, so it's either that ship or them, not both…"

"Shouldn't the primary fleet be first to—" Aidin was cut off sharply.

"That fleet is everything and it only works once; if it's found out or half its ships are lost, it's over, and we can't give them first strike at it. No one likes being the fall guy, Aidin; you're not alone in that."

Not being alone didn't help as Aidin remembered what had happened only a short time before; they had only lasted seconds when jarred by the monsters tractor assembly. If only the other captains had been told about that, they wouldn't be so compliant with…

"Captain!" the con sounded, startling him. "Picking up a massive contact on sensors."

"Well, they said they'd have the party started before we arrived," Aidin said to Brenner, smiling.

"How many are there?" Brenner asked.

"One, sir!" replied the con, clearly agitated.

"One?" Aidin repeated abruptly. "Where?" he asked, habit bringing his eyes up to the viewscreen in front of him.

"Behind us, sir, and it's massive; sometimes, it's there and then it just fades away into…" The con's voice tailed off, and then began again. "It's…"

"It's what?" Aidin prompted the con.

"It keeps altering dimensions, so I don't understand what's going on," the con replied, frustrated and wrestling with his panel, changing settings. "Sometimes, it's bigger, and then other times, it isn't. Then, sometimes it almost disappears—"

"Its cloaking is failing," Brenner cut in. "Its systems can't keep up with the changes across the cloak. I've seen it before; it happens to cloaked ships when they travel too fast. The computers can't make the changes fast enough, so they fail in places, relapse in others."

"We haven't seen it before, so why now?" Aidin asked.

"They must have increased speed dramatically; maybe hiding doesn't matter now that we know they're there," Brenner replied.

"Or maybe something has them spooked," replied Aidin, a sinking feeling running through him as he considered the possibility that the enemy's sensor array could see further than their own, their plans already discovered.

"Sir!" the con broke in.

"Yes?" Aidin looked up.

"Incoming communication—it's from them."

Aidin composed himself for a moment. "Put it through."

The screen opened up into life and, despite Aidin's preparation, he was immediately thrown by the presence of the pale white face with its eyes peacefully looking back at him. A peacefulness belying the horror they'd witnessed, the evil levied willfully against so many by their owner. It was an evil Aidin was all too aware of as he tried to compose himself in the figure's presence.

"Enjoying your scans, Captain?" came the voice.

Barely registering the face now because of what it represented, all Aidin could see rendered his own composition useless with his tightening face muscles giving away his nerves at the sight. The black surroundings on screen, with an eerie green gently permeating through them, only served to enhance the death-like white face now rolling its eyes gently around their bridge, causing similar effects to those Aidin was experiencing for each person they fell on.

"Lovely ship, very… comfortable looking." Maral smiled, his eyes falling back on Aidin, satisfied at his effect since it was etched onto their faces.

"You're supposed to be gone," Aidin said, fixing his stare against Maral though his voice was clearly tight.

"Dead, you mean," answered Maral, the peace leaving his eyes immediately as a wry smile appeared. "It's alright, Captain," Maral said mockingly, barely disguising his sarcasm and sensing Aidin's discomfort. "I've had worse welcomes."

"Station 196. You were transferred, and the prisoner exchange…." Aidin trailed off questioningly.

"Yes!" Maral laughed. "When you're in an organisation long enough, you come by a certain influence, don't you?"

Aidin felt confused at the line Maral was taking.

Maral squinted at Aidin's expression. "Certain loyalties, or at least desires for advancement in those below you, can be… useful." Maral smiled wider. "The ship didn't get very far before these loyalties surfaced; we had control in under three hours."

"But you were transferred to the Dren starship, and they released the shuttle when they had—"

"My body," Maral interrupted him. "I believe it was still warm on its arrival. Nice work, even if I do say so myself."

Aidin looked back at Maral.

"The Vrail…" Aidin began, unsure where to go from there.

Maral cocked his head at the look of confusion on Aidin's face and his slow start. "The one who picked me up, my replacement."

"But they must have seen him, identified him." Aidin stopped speaking as Maral broke into a huge smile—almost laughing, but holding it back.

"He put up quite a struggle when we got him onto the operating table! I could quite see why they thought him such a good replacement." Maral smiled as he remembered. "Still, he did complain a bit. Well, he did have to be alive for the surgery, as we needed the blood flow to be right through his face for the scanners, you know," Maral explained even through the horrified question of a look on Aidin's face. "And there simply wasn't time for anaesthetics," he announced gleefully to his audience, enjoying their discomfort. "In any case, there won't be any more exchanges from that little station, will there?" Maral gently pointed out, laughing suddenly after he did.

Faces of anger stared back at him as he swept the loss of life up in humour, as though some competition had been won.

"Oh, Captain, don't be mad," Maral spoke in a mockingly soft tone. "I had my reasons," he pointed out. "Have you ever been adrift, Captain? Watched your crew die one by one; thought you were going to follow them and drift away into obscurity? You see, that was the result of my transfer—the damage the ship took as we took control was quite serious. Guidance and engine failures meant that when we tried to hide our position from Alliance sensors in the Heights, we were pulled in, this time at the mercy of the currents inside. Three months," Maral answered the questioning look. "After a few weeks, the worrying set in—well, there were only so many of my replacement crew left, and Hearack can't survive on small meals. It had been three months and we were down to a dozen men when we were finally... rescued. It wasn't till we were only a handful left that our new-found allies realised we were more than just another species. It seems our goals in the past had been quite similar, each almost meeting success," Maral whispered threateningly.

"And your friends?" inquired Aidin. "Where do they come from?"

"Hmph. Your scanners not able to penetrate the systems in here? You'll know soon enough," answered Maral. "The mystery on the other side of the Heights finally explained to you… in the most dramatic of ways. Speaking of scans, your little con person can stop deftly trying to penetrate our weakened cloak," he said, centering his attention on Hollin, the affect apparent with his fingers ceasing to strike his panel. "Shortly, we'll be dropping it fully and you can get everything you want… everything you deserve." He smiled menacingly.

"Just wait till you get yours," Aidin hit back, angry at the effect he was having on his crew.

"Oh yes, your little friends," quipped Maral cheerfully. "They're a little over an eighth of a lightyear in front of you; it's quite a little display."

Aidin's expression changed, not happy his enemy was able to see beyond their range of scanning; he was ignored by Maral as he instead centered on Brenner's expression, his face changing and almost angry. "Yes, little man, well done—that was our reason for increasing speed and losing our cloak, but don't congratulate yourself too much. We're not worried, merely annoyed. They almost had you from the inside, and we almost had you from the outside; just imagine what we can do together."

"What happens if you pull it off?" Aidin demanded. "What then? Do you think your new friends will live quietly by your side, sharing power? They'll turn on you just like us."

"I doubt it, as we're far more valuable to them, what with our knowledge of Quadrant NM 15 and all. Besides, you assume they could," Maral replied. "Our bodies are far stronger than yours. Their means of infection, parasitic, is neutralised by our immune systems eventually if it doesn't leave. It's a shame you don't have that same ability, isn't it?"

"Then what?" Aidin asked. "Find a way to reopen the wormhole? To get home? To what? Do you think they'll really welcome you back after what you've done?"

"I think, when they see the strength of my toils, they'll come to realise my efforts were always for the good of the Dren, and they'll come round to my way of thinking... especially when introduced to our new... allies."

"And them," returned Aidin, "do you think they'll just sit by while you figure out a way to faze them out?"

"Captain, such suspicion! I can't imagine were you get it from." Maral smiled. "Wouldn't you trust this face?" he hissed, his eyes full of malice.

"What about the future?" Aidin pressed.

Maral's eyes slowly narrowed, his voice lowering to a hiss. "I am the future."

Aidin started as the communications suddenly cut out, stars gliding past the viewscreen serenely in such an abrupt contrast to what had just passed.

Chapter 29

Fake Left

They'd never looked so fine; that's the way the condemned looked before being drawn out at the end. Nothing had changed, either—Aidin ran through the plan again and again as people busied themselves around him. Their report on their communication with the now approaching juggernaut hadn't altered anything.

Ships still jockeyed for position, nerves forcing captains to alter and re-alter their positions relative to the rest of the fleet while their homes and everything they had ever known lay a few hundred thousand kilometres behind them, its green-blue glow missed as they stared out into the empty darkness in front of them. Ships manoeuvred as con officers on all vessels, both starship and attack, monitored everything, checking to make sure no collision was nearing with their attention off the viewscreens… an affliction that dormant members of the bridge crews wished they had. One hundred and thirty-eight ships were present, their magnetic flux trails spewing out from their rail exhausts and their manifolds invisible but for the sensors showing con officers great swathes of magnetic energy sailing back in unison from the fleet. Watching was hypnotic, the bright blue colours shown over the panels all-emersive when, for a moment, the hypnotism was broken with the swathes of energy seeming to jar suddenly. Con officers looked again, feeling it was nerves or exhaustion that… but no, there it came again, and this time the energy didn't come back to its uniform lines, instead skewing outward, each pattern thrown through the next and corkscrewing off into space with their fields becoming worse, erratic....

The con officer aboard the *Eslington* made to raise the alarm when suddenly the channels broke open from the Flagship *Lannan*. "Reading interference across all energy signatures; it can only be a massive power output—prepare yourselves, gentlemen, here they come!"

With everyone's awareness heightened, scanners peered out into space to no avail as the huge hex vessel reported by the *Rheinvar* slowed, its cloak now at full capacity and rendering it invisible. Not invisible were the magnetic fluxes of the Alliance ships now thrown to the four winds as, unseen, the alien ship descended on them from above, eyes looking forward and seeing nothing as it began decloaking.

Screaming sensors met with the con's fingers, all ships setting their viewscreens to the mass of alloy that was decloaking above them to see the first two starships lashed with tractor beams. Twenty-five halon green eyes glared down on them from above, descending in their hexes so that the darkness was momentarily blurred. Their captives exploded, their feeble attempts at defence merely glancing off of the huge vessel as it continued to bear downward.

Ships broke the lines in panic, Ritter's commands going unheard as his mass formation crumbled, tractors chasing them away. His force fatally weakened, Ritter tried to haul them back, but to no avail—the instinct for survival driving them off. Behind them, angling up on one side, the huge hex vessel heaved its underside toward the largest concentration of fleeing ships and opened fire. Nine shattered instantly under the jarring of the tractors, their flagship's fate relived as seven more strained to break free of the huge energy cascades holding them fast. The green hue in space around them was suddenly joined by crimson thunder as huge ion beams tore through, slicing ships apart with crews' screams sounding out over the channels only to be drowned out as their ships gave way in the darkness. Two… five… seven… eight ships exploded, their massive eruptions quickly fading into space as other ships fled to the sounds of tracking warnings, the hex vessel pursuing them. More warnings rang out as eleven more ships were snared, their fate only prolonged by their distance from the hex-monster behind them and their cries soon falling silent under the weight of its attack.

"Come to 187-mark-238!" demanded Ritter again, ships beginning to follow his command with their panic abating at their distance from the slower alien vessel. "Ritter to all ships: Maintain your distance perpendicular to the ship's top section. Do not stray near the underside of its hull!" he ordered as sensors showed the huge arms under it still angling to rain their tractors outward.

"Sir!" Ritter's con broke in over him.

"What?" came his response as he glared at the distance between his ships on the panel.

"Something strange with the alien vessel, sir. When it decloaked, its power readings were off the scale, but now they've dropped by eighty percent and…"

"And what?" Ritter gave the man his full attention.

"They're rising again," answered the con as his readings confirmed the conclusion. "It's like the ship is—"

"Recharging!" Ritter cut him off, no more

explanation necessary. "How long?"

"Several minutes, sir, but that's only an estimate."

"That's their weakness," Ritter spoke aloud. "Power consumption, and we've got seven minutes to figure out what to do with it." Ritter thought for a moment... if its power was weakened, then all weapons systems must not have the energy available, the strength to fight. "Send a message to all ships..." he began.

Like skulking dogs, the ships returned in twos and threes, spurred on by Ritter's orders and loosely taking up their positions overtop of the seemingly dormant alien vessel with its arms ceasing movement, its targets out of range. Ritter stared out at the fleet and began to make the decision which no commander ever wants—the decision he was famous for. Sacrifice. Ships' names flashed out on his display as he looked through the starships and attack ships for a vessel in a position that would allow it to move without unduly affecting the others formation his eyes falling on a vessel near the outer edge of the new formation. The *Nagoya*.

"Do you understand?" Ritter asked. "You are to engage at full rail under the hull, firing a broad spread and continuing out into space in a strafing arc to avoid taking fire." The Captain listened to Ritter's command, his heart sinking with those of the rest of his bridge.

"Yes, sir," came the answer, the delay tolerated by Ritter, his face grave and sorrowful though unseen by the *Nagoya* as it pulled off, similarly silent support from all ships going unheard as they watched its rail engines fire up and take it down out of sight.

"Any increased power readings from the alien ship?" Ritter asked, his brash tone gone as he lamented the descending blip on screen.

"No, sir," answered the con. "The enemy is not— wait," the con uttered as an energy transfer began to seethe throughout the hex vessel. "They've got them…"

Rounding the outer rim of the huge ship, the *Nagoya* broke right, avoiding the waiting hex face displayed on sensors with its tractors narrowly missing them as they shot underneath it and through waiting arms. Firing as they went, their small explosions did nothing as tractors from other arms shot across their path, only manoeuvres saving them as they tore out through the other side of the space beneath the arms and away. Behind them, though, a huge hex mount pulled round with its five eyes now tracking the fleeing ship. A rush of power and the green mist flew around the *Nagoya*, caught hard and shattering damage into it with the successful grab, its last manoeuvre breaking it free only for a moment before it was lost in a mist of its own, nothing remaining when the fireball cleared.

"How did they break free?" Ritter asked after the con relayed the news of their brief escape.

"The beam couldn't hold the ship, but the jolt of its grab on the *Nagoya* caused massive damage while the ship was pulling away at full rail—"

"Then we can break free," Ritter broke in over the con.

"The power of those beams is down to virtually five percent of what it was before, but they're still strong; the *Nagoya* only broke free because they were at full rail. An attack ship probably wouldn't from a standing start, but a starship might," reasoned the con.

"And the power readings now?" Ritter glared at the screen.

"We've got about four minutes left," came a nervous reply.

"Bring us to 155-mark-48," Ritter commanded. "Navigation, keep all ships in line single-file; give them nothing to fire on but the lead ships."

Banking in behind each other, both starships and attack ships thanked whoever was in front of them as, onscreen, they watched the sacrificed take the lead on the hex vessel's underside. Pulling hard under it, the lead ships unloaded every weapon before their point position forced them into panic firing as the great hex heads came into view. As if enraged by the insolence, five ships were ripped apart in a stroke, the tractors falling through the wreckage to land on more panicked vessels behind them—cries held back only by Ritter as the great beams fell on the next ship in line.

This time, however, there were no explosions. Straining hard, each starship pulled forward, breaking free and preparing to evade the massive ion surges ahead, though none came. A few kilometres further on, the beams reasserted themselves and the jarring motion tore decks apart inside of the affected ships, but again, the ships pulled through and kept going, now directly under the hex but with no ion beams falling.

"That last spread of tractors was the weakest yet!" shouted the con.

"They might be trying give us the impression they're weakened in order to draw us under and then fall on top of us with everything," cautioned Ritter's tactical officer.

"What's the power readings now?" Ritter shouted over him at the con.

"They've weakened further with that last spread;

they've cost themselves at least another sixty seconds."

"Order all ships to attack the hex heads now!" Ritter gambled, sensing this was as weak as the enemy would get.

A whole fleet of angered ships now began purling up under the alien vessel, all five hexes coming into view; assured of their weakness, crews watched thorans beginning to fly with the doubters among them joining in immediately, their yields detonating all around the alien alloy above. Unheard, the alien vessel's skin groaned under the massive weight of the weaponry, only to appear unscathed as the massive firestorm subsided. Scanners, though, revealed what the eye could not have hoped for, their findings spreading throughout the fleet as the second attack begun.

The mass of chemical fire blew out in a yield dwarfing its former eyes looking up from Alliance vessels below expecting to see a huge shattered hull but only a straining frequency on scanners emanated from their huge foes massive structure.

It was enough, though, and crews rallied forward with zeal, confidence winning out when suddenly alerts broke out across the Alliance fleet, a purging mass surging from the alien vessel above them and to the left, the fleet's scanners screaming.

"What the hell is that?" Ritter gasped as, onscreen, a blur in front of the huge alien vessel was met by a string of alarms on the *Lannan*. "Con!" Ritter demanded.

"Reading multiple signals; energy signatures… they're… they're ships," the con uttered, staring at his panel in disbelief.

In front of the hex vessel, ship after ship poured from a cavity near its top centre as Alliance crews kept looking on in horror.

"How many?" Ritter demanded.

"Forty-two, sir," answered the con.

"Now we know why we couldn't find them," Ritter uttered, staring at the long searched for phantom fleet pouring out in front of them.

Tearing right, the ships came out in a huge ark and veered in on the Alliance flank channels blaring to come round only to see the stream of vessels pull with everything they had through murderous fire to the Alliance left. Weapons exchanging fire, the Alliance broke formation, centring focus on their weakest ships and rendering all help available with still others releasing fire on the huge hull above them, only to be reordered to attend to the Hearack now pulling suicidal manoeuvres through the front of their lines.

"Come to order!" Ritter screamed over the channels as the Hearack, a third of their forces lost, heaved up onto the weakened right flank, four more of their ships exploding in the exposed arc. Four ships were nothing to them, though, as they slammed headlong inside the Alliance fleet, with the realisation setting in that they weren't expecting to come back, the first Alliance ship lighting up in confirmation as one of the Hearack sterred straight into them.

"*Narvik*, come around to 129 and seal that breach!" The order was heard for only seconds, the *Narvik* lost to a stream of weapons fire as she tried fighting her way out.

Offset now, the Alliance formation from the top numbered five starships holding on as four leaned out below them, attack ships shielding flanks with tens of vessels underneath and engaging in similar struggles as

Hearack took slices everywhere.

Ritter watched on his command panel vectoring wings of five attack ships apiece in on weakened areas as Hearack formed broke and reformed their attacks. On the far side of the formation, Ritter saw six Hearack ships come together and begin to descend unnoticed, heading for the weakened Alliance ships near the base of the line. Looking sharp for the nearest attack wing, Ritter's voice soon ordered the closest interceptors in—but in order to catch the Hearack, they'd need to descend through the minefield of engaging starships below.

The broad line of five attack ships offset to the left, one behind the other, suddenly broke off their target on orders, angling up behind the leader in a wide arc and pulling into a suicidal dive through the battered fleet. Crews fighting for their lives watched in horror as Ritter's latest order came tearing down between them— the *Renaud*, the *Sarenar*, and the *Briesan* all missed by feet as the five attack ships ripped down between them and their weapons fire. Steel screams passed with shattering explosions, the vessels held solid only by fate pushing for more as they followed their lead ship, pulling up hard and levelling out through two engaging starships as they fell on their dropping foe. In an instant, three Hearack barrelled through them in flames, one more damaged their own number minus four emerging on the other side.

Watched from overhead, the huge hexes had remained silent, sleeping, charging their efforts and restraining with their true focus now defenceless in their eyes. Thousands of miles of steel began moving off, leaving the battle raging behind it as it took in the calm and serene colours of the fragile planet in front of it—

this being its true target. Approaching faster, its engines began to overcome its inertia, the monsters on board watching transfixed as the colours grew more intense with their approach. Everything around them faded in importance as they viewed the culmination of their work, the very stars over it seeming to twinkle in welcome with a visual chorus to behold them all, random yet unified. The unification was the problem, though, their smiles fading as the stars over the planet became more than unified... not twinkling at all... as if...

Alarms!

Alarms everywhere, their computers ringing out as a fleet of Alliance ships left the magnetic shroud of the planet's pole, hidden no more with their two hundred twenty-odd number now visible ahead. Alarms rang clear as monitors showed a poorly armed mismatch of freighters and older ships, mere barges in truth and devoid of crews, controlled remotely from somewhere in the raging battle behind them—this being the last stand of a desperate people and hardly carrying enough firepower to raise an eyebrow aboard their colossal foe's vessel. This, though, only fuelled suspicion, scanners sent again and again to rake through the ships, searching for explosives, for weapons, for a trap... and they found nothing. Nothing but weight in numbers; mere flies to the steel windshield approaching. All the same, the ship came to full readiness, vibrating throughout as the five huge steel hexes underneath it were turned to meet them. Great red beams of energy pierced the darkness of space, showering the approaching ships in eerie light as scanners continued searching for a trap, paranoia fuelling the first ion attack over long-range and beyond the reach of tractors, the lead ships vaporised in seconds in the assault. The tiny explosions melting away were seized upon by scanners determined to find out their secrets, but none came—just the elements expected, with no volatile explosives or hidden materials. Neither did the rest suggest anything amiss as they came on one by one to be destroyed, some now being grabbed by tractors as the great ship became overrun, ships now held in queues for destruction as its huge weapons tried to keep pace with the swarm. Still uneasy, it moved forward, passing through the aftermath of its work and disturbing gravesite after gravesite, the remains of each last-ditch effort brushed aside as it came forward. With almost eighty ships gone, crews onboard the giant became focused on the ever-increasing brilliance of Earth, the deep rumblings of death from the weapons stations below hardly noticed as…

Suddenly, another piece of brilliance half-blinded all eyes onboard the giant as it was rocked by an almighty explosion.

Blurred eyes tried to focus on the blast through their panels, struggling to their feet only to be thrown again as another blast rocked the ship. Staring in disbelief, they listened as shrill screeches filled the ship from the shadows, the sound shaking the Hearack themselves as they looked at panels revealing huge cracks along the underside of their ship, only three hexes left intact. Looking on, they suddenly found out why as two ships held in tractors side by side on the third hex were destroyed, the first exploding harmlessly only for the second to set off a huge chain reaction in their wreckage, the contents of the ships cargoes combining to detonate a magnificent explosion. Blasting upwards, it blew out two weapons stations in the hex, the remaining having their targeting thrown off as still more ships now converged, all almost underneath them.

Like a wounded animal, the damaged monster raged in all directions with its tractors catching and tearing where it could as ions ripped and shredded at the ships, launching back in fury at the deception. All for nothing, though, these actions being mere death throws; even with its miles of exotic alloy, it was unable to withstand the punishment as ship after ship detonated under its hull, the force tearing open great swathes of steel and sending them clear into space. The ship torn open, more explosions forced their way inside so that great chemical fires began latching onto anything they could, whole decks going up in seconds as Command above still centered on hitting back. Beams of energy flew mercilessly as it launched back through the swarm of ships desperately, trying to destroy them at a distance as it attempted to heave back away at full power. The engines, though, had little effect reversing with all its might, its huge inertia dragging it ever closer to the swarm of ships now smashing against its hull. Explosions mixing with the wreckage of those gone before detonated huge bursts of energy, the enemies' hulls fracturing apart underneath it as it tried to heave back through the sea of wreckage it had easily ploughed through before. Now paying the price for its blindness, its scanners still registered no danger from the ships' different cargos as it heaved itself backward in desperation. How could they have spotted the danger, though? There wasn't any, apart, but now with the ships coming together all around the ship, great swirls of the elements kerrin and amalganite reacted everywhere.

Blasted from all sides, the ship groaned as it made

its desperate bid for free space, elements flowing through the cracked hull with decks filling underneath only to blast out into space as the two elements met up in fury within it. Hearack felt fear for the first time in their lives as aliens turned on them from the shadows, rage overcoming them as they watched their ship splinter apart, their very power systems now adding to the destruction inside of it. Huge swathes of energy now seared through the ship, unleashed from their holdings— their containment compromised by more and more explosions, massive sections of the ship now breaking off into space.

Ritter couldn't believe it, stammering over the news as his con officer Willis threw it up on screen—the great ship in front coming back toward them, tearing itself apart as it came.

"How much time do they have with—" Cut short, Ritter raised his hand with the rest of the crew as the viewscreen went almost blinding white; the monster came apart like a nova shattering itself in all directions.

Crews that had been staring in disbelief began whooping for joy as the searing remnants faded into the darkness, cries and laughter filling bridges as other crewmen slumped over panels, overcome by emotion and the pressure.

Aboard the *Lannan*, joy was short-lived with Ritter screaming over the crew: "Thirilian! Thirilian! Check for thirilian! Is it out there? Is it out there!"

"...No!" came a stammered reply. "N-no, it isn't, not a trace of it. It-it's not there!" Willis cried out, his nerves abating and joy streaming back as he scowered the wreckage. "It's not there!!!" he screamed out uncontrollably, the crew celebrating with him and Ritter unable to stop it this time.

Similar reports from other ships still involved in firefights confirmed the news as Ritter began smiling, smiling and almost laughing; his crew only encouraged the release, becoming ecstatic at the news.

"Sir!"

The voice's strike cut through the laughter, Ritter instantly losing his hard-won smile. "What is it?"

"A lot of interference from the elements, but I'm reading..." Willis trailed off as he wrestled with his fluctuating scanners. "Yes, definitely: ships, maybe half a dozen, they're braking right away from the—I've lost them again."

"Well, get them back," Ritter demanded, a face of concern staring out behind Willis. "Well?" he pressed a moment later.

"No, there's too much..." the con trailed off again.

"Too much what?" Ritter demanded with agitation from behind him.

"Interference from the... no, it can't be." The con's voice fell away.

"What? What can't it be?" Ritter's angry pacing came over from behind him.

"There's something else out there—big, beyond the wreckage and residual elements; it's...." The con desperately checked his results. "It's heading toward Earth!"

Though still battling a beaten foe, it became clear what the con's readings were soon enough—an entire hex had ripped free from the huge ship which had now been destroyed. Far too coincidental to be an accident, it quickly became clear what it was, exactly... readings indicated a huge amount of organic matter on board. Life signs—a doomsday weapon.

"If that thing gets to the planet, it'll release those things; this time, there's thousands and the infection will be unstoppable." The crew talked hurriedly, already briefed on the previously classified infection that lay years behind them. "Everyone down there will—"

"Enough talk!" Ritter broke in over the voices on his bridge. "The control barges—how many are left?"

"Five: two kerrin and three amalganite," answered Willis.

"Then patch in to them and get a kerrin headed for that thing!" Ritter ordered.

Connecting to one of the two kerrin-loaded barges left, Willis soon had it bearing down on what was left of the alien ship, but his actions hadn't gone unnoticed. Breaking out of the swarm of battles around them, three Hearack ships tore after it, one being lost to an explosion as it pushed through an amalganite and kerrin patch, another having its engine cores blown out by a pursuing Alliance ship. But the last was through. The unmanned barge lasted mere seconds as it came apart, its assailant pursued into the darkness by an Alliance ship.

"Damn it, I want that last Kerrin load escorted all the way in!" Ritter demanded. "Break off a dozen ships—I don't care what they're involved in!"

Objections from the ships involved elsewhere were soon quelled, as they now moved with the last kerrin barge. Fending off attacks, more were lost to the patches of free elements as they forced themselves through, mixing them as they went with Ritter gritting his teeth as he waited for the barge to have the same thing happen at any minute. Staring after them as the hex moved ever closer to Earth, he listened to reports as, out of sigh,t the barge smashed headlong into a cavity in the back of the hex, the cavity having been torn out when it had ripped free from the now lost monster it had come from.

"It's completely inside!" reported the captain of the *Ticondra*. "It's smashed into what seems to be decks in there, but it hasn't exploded."

Ritter now knew that all he had to do was bring in one of the amalganite barges, but so did the Hearack.

Abandoning their hard-won positions, they were soon streaming toward the barges. Orders flowed for a hastily constructed wall of ships to surround the barges, but it was too late for one of them as it vaporised between over twenty ships. The last two now nested precariously in a cloud of ships, seventy-two of them in all, split on both sides and now firing wildly at anything that came near.

Moving toward the slowly falling hex disaster befell one of the barges as its travels soon came to nothing not from enemy fire but from engine failure its help having to be abandoned as it drifted back out of the protective wall lost to the enemy behind. With one barge left, the waves of Hearack ships now increased in ferocity, each time coming closer and unloading before breaking off to re-arm and return in a game of brinkmanship that was anybody's and weakened both sides with every pass. The waves seemed to veer left, concentrating on only a half dozen ships, the Alliance manoeuvring to try and cover the rapidly weakening vessels. It was a mistake, as their manoeuvring only opened gaps far to the right—gaps that a few Hearack ships screamed off toward as the Alliance desperately tried to fight them off, throwing everything they had at them. Three enemy ships became no more than fire, hiding two more that were opening up with weapons behind them, but the last pushed through with sheer speed, not attempting to fire at all.

Aidin stared forward as, on screen, the lone ship that had broken through the lines was torn apart, ripped limb from limb by pursuing Alliance attack ships. But Aidin wasn't staring at the screen with everyone else; instead, he and Hollin watched the energy signatures that had momentarily emanated from the enemy ship that was now melting away.

There was a moment of calm—that moment when a man can pretend he didn't see something—but then it started. Alarms lit up across the con panel as scanners picked up new energy signatures, and multiple ones, moving and on board the barge.

Hails began to come across the channels—panicked, frantic, all directed at the flagship, at Ritter. The Hearack had never stood a chance of getting to the barge, but that had never been their intention; they had only wanted to get in close enough to use their version of a molecular splice inducer to transport troops on board, and that's what they had done!

"Destroy it and send in another ship!" called one frantic captain over the channels.

"There's no time to load another ship with that much amalganite; they—" another captain's counter was cut off, weapons fire heard crashing against his hull as his crew fought off another wave of the enemy.

From all over, the sound of fire flowed over the channels as ships tried to report in while fending off their determined enemy.

Ritter listened as each suggestion was countered as

giving way to more problems, each harder to solve than the last, but the one overriding factor that remained clear in his mind was time… time he didn't have. He looked after the barge as it gently drifted away, smaller in the distance and seemingly removed from the sounds of battle and frantic cries as he contemplated the price they'd pay if they failed to stop the alien vessel.

"Willis," Ritter spoke to the con sitting in front of him and to the right. No reply returned, his voice unheard since Willis was desperately consumed with trying to manage the ever-changing battle around him. "Willis!" Ritter barked.

The crewman turned in his seat at the sound of Ritter's voice, turning to see a tired look on his face—a look of exhaustion, as if all options had been used up.

"Willis, how much of a thoran yield do we think is needed to destroy that ship?" Ritter asked, a look of something near regret on his face.

"At least nineteen megs, sir—about eight thousand thoran torpedoes' worth," Willis replied, unsure why he'd asked.

"That's about the armament of forty ships," Ritter thought out loud, still looking at Willis. "And we've got seventy-two with weapons half-expended…" Ritter drifted off.

"There wouldn't be time, sir," Willis spoke up. "Not enough to load those onto a ship before that alien gets there, even if we could in this hailstorm."

"No, we can't do that," Ritter agreed, looking back, his expression unnerving Willis as he watched tectonic plates move in Ritter, the strain across his face being one of finality.

Ritter suddenly looked up at the still waiting con

officer. "I want you to send a message to all ships and set a course for the alien ship." Ritter paused at Willis' expression. "Tell them to prepare to go to warp on my mark."

Willis was hesitant, as if expecting another part to the instruction, another side to his decision—some way out—but none came. There were no more words… just stony silence from Ritter as he looked back.

"We're out of time, Willis," Ritter spoke softly, as if not wanting the rest of the bridge crew to hear.

Willis swallowed, looking back at him and knowing that there was only the order left for them. Blinking, breathing heavily, his head fell away as he nodded and offered a final look back before turning. All that was needed had been said already, and so he reached for the con panel.

Moments later, the channels were a flurry of objections and alternative suggestions coming in from all across the fleet as they battled still. So much so that Ritter, irate at his decisions being questioned, virtually banned any communications being relayed to him and instead patched his decision through to Command.

One though kept coming in, insistent and more frequent than the others… aggravating, threatening, doing whatever it had to be heard until finally… "Sir!" the con officer swung round to a stern look from Ritter. "One of the ships is insisting on communication; it—"

"I said no com traffic was to be relayed," Ritter almost growled.

"Yes, sir," the con officer responded. "But this one's different. It's threatening to brake from the lines after the alien ship."

Ritter's expression turned to one of indignation.

"Which... which one is it?" was all he could manage, this latest insubordination almost pushing him over.

"The *Rheinvar*, sir, captained by a Miles Aidin," replied the con.

Ritter stared off up at the viewscreen, drawing breath but hardly able to believe what was happening. "Put him through!" he forced out.

"It seems I've missed something," Ritter began almost calmly. "But lucky for me, I've got this super captain in the fleet who knows just what to do and—"

Channels open, Aidin ran right over him. "Ritter, we're close enough to that ship to put Marine detachments aboard; we've picked some up from—"

"I know where you picked them up from," Ritter growled, finding it hard not to begrudge the fact that a certain detachment had made it.

"Look, we've been working with the inducer over short-range and we think we can get to—" Aidin's plan only seemed to rile him.

"Have you got a problem with rules, Captain?" Ritter suddenly exploded at the suggestion. "Like the fact that this ship is the flagship! Like the fact that we have a chain of command! Like the fact that that thing those eggheads dreamed up is banned from transporting organic matter! Maybe you missed the report on their lab experiments with cattle, but four out of the ten came back an exotic species that their own mother wouldn't recognise!"

"It's been refined since then," Aidin countered.

"It's still banned!" shouted Ritter at his viewscreen.

"Ritter." Aidin gave up shouting, asking, "How long do you think the Alliance will last without ships around? Do you think the other factions in this quadrant will just let us lick our wounds and sit back while we rebuild the fleet?"

Ritter glared, unable to offer an answer; Aidin was right and they both knew it.

"You order us into that ship, it'll be destroyed, but so will any hope of the Alliance's survival. Just give us a chance, Ritter. Give us all a chance."

A long pause ensued, Ritter unable to let go, and then, finally, still determined to assert some control, he responded, "You picked up a few units; one of them is led by a certain Captain Etrick. However many units you send, his is in charge. Oh, and, Captain, you've got twelve minutes. After that, that sharp burning sensation you'll feel will be the rest of the fleet driving up your ass. Are we clear?"

"We're clear. *Rheinvar* out"

Chapter 30

Remember

Faces on the transporter plates had been so nervous that they had forgotten their petty squabbles, their revilement of one another, but as soon as they had arrived and the weird dots in their eyes had subsided, it was the first thing on their minds.

"My ass, it's down D2 corridor 71 and then the aft walkway," sneered Etrick as he brandished his scanner at Fuller. "Look, can't you see the signals?" he asked, referring to the mass of organic matter picked up on the scanner.

"Yeah," Fuller said, scowling back at him. "But there's nothing down there—they're wandering, trying to find engineering. It's two decks above them and they can't figure it out."

"And you can, Navy boy?" returned Etrick. "Our job is to neutralise them; it doesn't matter where they are."

"Look," Fuller growled, brandishing his own scanner. "There are other signals—weaker, not as many, spread out on decks above and below—scouts for the main force. They find engineering, they won't need the main group; they could do enough damage by themselves."

"We've got twelve minutes, and probably only eight before the nerosene gas starts pumping out of the vents and into the corridors; it'll affect us, as well!" Etrick shouted, referring to the ship's environmental system, already set by the fleet outside to begin flooding the ship soon after their arrival, that being a last-ditch effort to slow down the aliens. The thinking was that their movement from room to room could be brought to a crawl by using toxic methods known to eventually kill the parasites, that little factoid having been discovered during their previous encounter years before. Unfortunately, though the onset for the men would be slower, it would be fatal if prelonged exposure continued, the toxins flooded into the corridors would eventually seal their fate, humans resistantance though better with having lungs to filter, not leaving them invulnerable. The men had to find and neutralize the aliens if possible and failing that guard engineering till the gas began to concentrate enough across the decks to to kill them before making their own escape. "We're wiping out the main group," Etrick asserted, narrowing his eyes. "Then we'll deal with the stragglers after—"

"In twelve minutes," Fuller stated. "They're already wandering near engineering, and in twelve minutes, they could wreck the navigation, the computer core; they could blow the coolant tanks and the ship would—"

"I'm in command here!" Etrick stated. "And we go for the main group first."

"No, we don't! Dammit!" Fuller finally lost it. "You go and play soldier if it makes you wet, but we're heading for engineering!"

"You'll do as I—" Etrick stopped as he came nose to nose with Fuller, the other man's expression already answering back. "Ritter's gonna tear you apart," he said quietly, realising Fuller was giving him everything he wanted.

"I'll make sure he saves you some," growled back Fuller as he watched Etrick and his men move off.

"Yeah, the dick," quipped Fulkes, shattering the

seriousness. "We'll save him the dick; he likes the dick." He motioned at Etrick.

Turning back, Etrick cast a disparaging eye over the unorganised rabble behind him as his own men moved off in unison.

"Hmph." Etrick stared despairingly, shaking his head. "Trained Marines…." He looked over at Fuller. "Trained chimps," he said, Fuller looking like the comment got to him as he looked away, making off slowly down the corridor and going the opposite way from Etrick.

"Come 'ere, motherfucker." Brice grabbed Fulkes' aside out of earshot, forcing him against the wall. "Now you listen, you little prick! You better square up right now! Why you do this to this man? Why you make him look bad in there? Don't you remember when he was there for you? You can't go around expecting everybody else to clean up your shit, cause one day they're not gonna be here for you! You got that?" Brice glared down at Fulkes as he'd done so many times before, with the look of a chastised child coming back to him afterward. "Why we always havin' this damn conversation? Why don't you fuckin remember anything? Why you always gotta be fuckin' ignorin' me?"

"I'm not ignoring you," replied Fulkes, looking away from Brice's glare.

"Then why don't you fuckin' remember?" Brice demanded.

"I remember," replied Fulkes, still looking away.

"Do you? You remember his ass on the line and mine when you needed it, huh? Well, you better start fuckin' showin' it; you embarrassin' that man, embarrassin' me! Well?" demanded Brice, grabbing his arm and shaking him, forcing him to look him in the eyes.

Fulkes nodded, the point hitting him hard, low.

"Alright! Come on, you get back up there and you be done fuckin' around." Brice tried to fight back his anger.

"Yeah," uttered Fulkes, not looking at him.

"You understand?" Brice demanded again.

"Yeah," said Fulkes, nodding his head, still uncomfortable with this latest berating.

Brices' tone lowered. "He puts up with a lotta shit from you, brought on from you, and he doesn't have to."

Fulkes looked up, looking away to the right just as quickly.

"Come on," Brice said, pulling him from the wall and pushing him in front.

Two decks below, there was no pushing for the front, though, as an eerie silence drifted over Etrick's men, their marching reduced to a crawl. How could they all just disappear? Above, scanners had shown the deck to be infested with bio signs—moving, working their way everywhere—but now only they moved down here, nervously scanning everything as they crept forward.

Engineering was a different story, and rounds were flying as the second creature leapt against panels, the soldiers' shots shattering everything in the paths of their crosshairs in trying to follow them.

"Get it!" Fulkes panicked, firing as it streaked back further into the deck, their disciplined room entry now unprofessional with their weapons unloading near blindly after the huge beast as it took them into the heart of engineering. Rounds finding their mark, the men got their first real look at the huge black creature as it wheeled round, rearing up eight feet high in front of them before crashing down through panels to its right.

The ship jolted violently, the men losing their footing as, all around them, undamaged displays began flickering, their attention centering on the navigation stations. For a few frightening seconds, they watched the ship come off-course, only for the autopilot to begin pulling it back in an uneasy, jarring motion, as if fighting it all the way. With the ship almost back on course, the navigation displays flickered constantly, beginning to cascade before finally going blank.

"Was it on course?" Brice panicked.

"Yeah," answered Fuller. "The autopilot was bringing it back."

"Was," uttered Rians.

"Yeah, was," said Fuller, uneasy. "You saw it."

"But we didn't see it come back fully before the screens went down," said Rians, concern running across his face. "And that jolting motion it was doin' when it was comin' back stopped at the same time."

"What if there's damage?" Brice began to worry "What if—"

"Look," Fuller cut in, "it was coming back. Now, let's get back with the rest and help them down there; it took six of us to put these two down, and who knows how many are down there?"

"If any of these systems have been damaged outside of a few smashed panels—" worried Rians, looking around as Fuller cut in.

"They haven't been," he assured Rians.

"But how do you know?"

"I know the ship was coming back!" Fuller exclaimed. "And I know there's a moron below us taking his men into face a dozen more of these," he said, motioning at the monster, fluid slowly leaking from its dead mouth behind them. "You wanna worry about something, worry about that."

Heading out to try and warn Etrick, they left a pulsing mass eight feet in length with half a dozen muscle-clad legs laden with slime, lying amidst broken panels. In front of this, a slimy black exoskeleton lay five feet across, four spine-like protrusions off the top of each side tapering out to razor-like claws hinged at one end, like its massive head. The head drained darkened gel-like fluids that were now piling up to its mouth, where four-foot wrenching jaws held rows of serrated, bone-thick teeth. Above these, two huge, angled back slits on each side of the face hid eyes inside. Six men had unloaded two clips a piece, and it had still taken almost a minute to get both monsters down. They had good reason to be nervous below, though they just didn't know why yet.

Rounding the next corner, Etrick stopped them a short way down; he motioned to his lieutenant as the scanner showed waves of bio matter all around them, each silent pulse on the scanner not measuring up to the long empty corridor in front of them. Standing by confused, each man waited for instruction nervously, casting a look to the scanner held a short ways from them and then down the empty corridor, their attention fixed elsewhere… not noticing the creaking when it started. Like metal being torn slowly, ripped from a foundation, the noise began to echo down the corridor—getting louder with each passing second with faces looking anxiously for the source. Growing, it seemed to engulf the whole corridor around them, becoming louder and louder as feet began to gingerly pull the sound of steel tearing… Suddenly, the whole left wall caved into the corridor, steel debris flying everywhere as eyes closed to protect themselves, opening on huge-jawed creatures lurching out of the darkness, the first clamping down on the nearest man—his screams not even heard along the collapsing deck, blood flying from his abdomen as the rest of the men fired wildly on rows of teeth that were now surging round the first man, their actions bringing roars of anger as a second man was taken.

Falling back round the corner, they were showered with blood, the second victim's cries only heard for an instant as he was torn in two, still being carried forward by the creature with its roar joining the others and deafening the fleeing men. Firing everything they had on the first monstrous insect that came round the bend, they could do nothing as it descended on its terrified victim, his fate going unseen as the next horror came surging over its back. With it roaring toward them, the men for a second saw its eyes flexing in their sockets as it reached out razor-like claws and Etrick raised his weapon almost automatically, switching to an NME.

He pulled the trigger, sending it crashing through the creature's exoskeleton and into the tissue inside. He just hoped that… all thoughts were violently lost as it detonated right in front of them. Behind the creature, its insides burst out in a boiling mass flooding backwards down the corridor. Constrained inside the corridor, the pressure from the NME was magnified, wrenching open the ceiling above them along with Etrick's eardrums as he fell back to the floor, protected by the creature's carcass collapsing on top of him.

But it wasn't all going his own way, as he screamed out in pain with the creature's weight crushing his right leg, pinning him down and leaving him struggling in confusion as he heard his own cries, different and distant; he still hadn't realised the damage to his ears. Struggling to free himself, his body was wracked by pain, his hands being no help as he pushed hopelessly against the creature. Pain overwhelming him, he fell back flat to the floor, barely able to hear his own cries and reaching instinctively for his ears. Calming somewhat, he began to hear more inside than out—bones grinding in his leg accompanied by huge breaths of air in his lungs, the dull whine in his head noticed only for a moment as he felt the liquid trickling through his fingers from his ears.

Bringing his hands back, he felt things become clearer with realising his drums had gone, but they were forgotten almost instantly at the sight of Matheson lying to his right, his broken and lifeless body among the debris-strewn floor, open-mouthed and staring back at Etrick.

Etrick heard more dull, muffled sounds—the sounds of his own words, unrecognisable to his shattered ears as he reached for Matheson lying just out of his grasp, knowing full well that he was gone. Reaching out hopelessly, he fell back distraught, his friend dead by his own hand—the hand forced by this thing now pinning him down. Pain-drawn tears turned to anger his dirt-strewn face racking up in agony as he reared up in rage, jamming his hands against the creature with his roar coming out as a mix of anger and pain as he pushed desperately at the thing, trying to free himself. Roar subsiding, a red-faced Etrick fell back for a second time, still trapped and with the pain overwhelming him as he screamed out, reaching for his trapped leg, the motions jostling the broken bones inside. Soon, though, even that was too much as he fell back with his stomach muscles exhausted from his efforts, his shouts of agony still only a confused muffle to him.

But the respite from his pain was short-lived as a sound came down the corridor with no confusion attached to it at all, his struggles leaving him as the hairs on the back of his neck stood up to the menacing vibrations through the deck plates of something large approaching still unrecognised by his torn ears. Trapped, wide-eyed, Etrick stared over the carcass in front of him and those behind it, smoke rising from their charred remains and obscuring his view... but not enough to hide the movement at the end of the corridor, a dark form coming slowly round the corner. Instinctively, he looked for his weapon, his head spinning from side to side and his hands reaching for it as he caught sight of it behind him, wedged against the left wall. But it was out of reach; pinned, straining, he found that the weapon might as well have been a mile away, as it lay useless inches from his grasp. Suddenly, a huge vibration much closer spun Etrick's head—his eyes landing on a dark form among the steam; it was motionless, closer. His freezing didn't help the threatening stance towering over him only feet away, forcing him to panic so that his next move refused to come. Through his torn drums faint noise, the confusing sound of rising air was suddenly overtaken by a sudden shriek, Etrick's instinct to pull away from it useless as the creature came surging through the steam with its rows of teeth descending with outstretched claws, their eyes meeting for the first time as...

Suddenly, the corridor filled with echoes of weapons fire, rounds tearing into walls and the creature exploding inches from Etrick's face, blood instead of claws blinding Etrick as his head was flung back. Struggling, blinded, he noticed the overpowering stench of burnt flesh, his eyes stinging as muffled sounds of weapons were made maddening by his blood-soaked vision, flashes of red and orange coming in to disorientate him with voices screaming incoherently above.

The dull thuds on either side of his head panicked Etrick as he blindly fought off the creatures grabbing him. Trapped inside his nightmarish senses, he screamed wildly as he was dragged out from under the carcass, his bones wrenched apart in his leg and puncturing the skin. No punctures from the creatures, though; instead of tearing claws, he felt grasping hands pulling him back and lifting him up, his vision clearing enough to make out a screaming Brice and Copeland, Fulkes firing wildly down the corridor beyond them. Confused, his senses were jarred once again with more hands grabbing his clothing from above, his head falling back as he was lifted by his chest, Fuller and Rians looking down from one of the rips in the ceiling made by the NME's pressure wave. Dragged up, his back was torn across the serrated edges of the rip, his screams going unnoticed as he was hauled through into the next deck, agony continuing as he was passed to Carson and dragged back across the floor.

No time to listen to his pain, Carson dragged him back further as Fuller and Rians reached down through the rip in the ceiling with their arms outstretched, shouting for Copeland. Standing shoulder to shoulder with Brice and Fulkes below them, his face grimaced like theirs as they poured countless rounds down the corridor, the echoes ear-splitting in the confined space as they held back the leaping shadows at its end. The men's shouts from above finally getting through, Brice looked back, ordering Copeland to the hands while he and Fulkes continued to hold the monsters off, squeals from beyond the steaming carcasses mixing with weapons fire as rounds tore off wall panels and shadows fell behind them. Copeland was torn, too, his chest catching the edges of the rip on the way up and his pain evident as he hunched over against the wall behind Rians, clutching his wounds. The two men kneeling in front of him reached down once more into the echoes below.

The shadows at the corridor's end began to fade, deadly creatures turning to writhing wounded now that there were no more coming to support them. Rounds expelled, Fulkes hurried to reload, Brice's rifle falling silent soon after… just like the view ahead.

"Go!" shouted Brice, palming Fulkes' shoulder in front of him as Fulkes turned back, his magazine clicking in. "Go!" shouted Brice more loudly at the look of indecision. Fulkes backed off, hesitant, but slowly turning for the hands and passing his rifle up first, shouts breaking out between him and those above.

Brice was focused, though, watching the corridor and listening to the dying sounds of creatures filling the space, his rifle trained through the still steaming carcasses in front of him.

"Come on!" Fuller's shouts became louder, Brice's expression on turning matching the comical scene his eyes fell upon.

Just behind him and to his right, he stared in

disbelief upon seeing Fulkes reaching, half-jumping, a man inches too short who was trying to jump up yet again.

"Come on… damn it, Fulkes, try!" shouted Fuller, the inside of his arm being cut on the rip as he stretched further.

"I'm trying!" Fulkes struggled to reach, the embarrassment telling.

Brice stared, his face frowning in amazement at the pathetic sight.

"I can't…" uttered Fulkes, still stretching, but falling off-balance.

"Come 'ere, little man." Brice groaned upon moving over and grabbing Fulkes by the chest to hoist him up. Their expressions met as they stared awkwardly at one another, Fulkes' feet leaving the ground with his hands grasping and almost in reach of those grasping down for him, suddenly, though, Brice's expression changed, a sharp jolt separating them. Face reddening, Brice roared out in pain as, beneath him, Etrick's shot up alien carcass came to life ,with a claw knifing out to tear into his calft. As it latched on, tearing deeper, Brice cried out while looking down to see the grasping creature; his strength falling away from his arms, Fulkes slipping down from the reach of those above him with all eyes falling on the blood spewing from the scene below. Suddenly, eyes were turned to the corridor, the sharp hiss from its end accompanied by a dark form moving in slowly through the steam. A roar from Brice signalled the creature below him tightening his grip all the more, his agony only serving to fuel the form in the steam as it reared up, freezing, about to…

Cries of agony unrelenting, Brice violently regripped Fulkes, staring madly into his eyes before, with a roar, he hoisted him up and away from him into the waiting hands above, Fulkes screaming back but unable to hold onto Brice's jacket as he was pulled away. Over a screaming Fulkes, Brice's cries went unheard, his agony witnessed only through Fulkes' eyes, his hands still outstretched when a deafening screech came with a dark form slamming into the sergeant and tearing him away from view, his agony over.

On the deck above, Fulkes' feet had barely touched the floor and his protestations were about to go into full swing on behalf of Brice below, but he was shoved back by Fuller, his hand barely pulling away as a scything claw wheeled up between them, Copeland screaming out as it knifed through his shoulder—a monstrous creature bursting up behind it. Almost striking the ceiling as it came, it saw Copeland falling to the floor wide-eyed as it wheeled in mid-air, their eyes meeting as it drew its claws round to... But they weren't to meet, as the creature was thrown back under the weight of fire unloaded by Rians and Fuller, its screaming body narrowly missing Fulkes as it crashed to the floor, writhing its last movements as it slid.

Shocked expressions gave way to instinctual moving, Fuller helping Copeland away as the corridor filled with the sound of hissing echoing up from below. Rians covered them from the back as Fulkes took point, the other four struggling in between them and staggering down the corridor away from the rip and the noises underneath them. Fearful eyes in the group looked back with Rians, the noises unabating behind him and leaving Fulkes alone with his gaze forward as he approached the ninety-degree turn to the right ahead, his attention taken as he noticed the thickening air and his vision blurring when…

Shrieking as it came round the turn, it flailed past Fulkes and slammed into the left wall as he pulled back shouting, screaming and opening up uncontrollably with fire. Weapon finding its mark, the monster panicked, wrenching itself off the wall and squealing more as it lurched down the corridor away from the rounds. But they exploded in its back all the same, Fulkes' muzzle following and running dry as it lurched another few feet toward a wide-eyed Fuller before crumpling in a heap against the right wall, its legs giving way. Nerves gone, Carson and Etrick struggled away to the left, watching the huge, slime-ridden claws lurch and writhe on the floor, the heaving mass they were attached to fighting for air as it continued hissing and jerking, its movements taking time to recede. All wide-eyed, they froze, Fulkes stepping back as his search for another clip came up empty, each man expecting the creature to burst into life at any moment like so many times before, but nothing happened. Nothing more attacked as its breathing lessened—and theirs, too, thoughts coming through now enabled as emotions calmed down. Fuller began to listen as he held Copeland, glancing over his shoulder at the rip behind them, the sounds from below dying away.

A moment of confusion passed, and then it dawned on him as his eyes began to pick up what Fulkes had seen earlier, the air thickening in front of him. "It's the gas," said Fuller, almost whispering and with his nerves still high. "It's the gas!" he said louder, more reassuringly to the panicked group. "It's filtering through and thickening up; they can't take the mixture in the air because it's—"

"Yeeeeeeaaaaaaauuuuuuuuuccchhhhh!!!!!" came a fluid-soaked screech from the bleeding mass between the men, as if it were raging at Fuller's words, raging as it lay drowning in it its own fluids, Fulkes' work taking care of its insides. More screeching made the men jolt back and away from it, but that was all it was, screeching, a fake show being put on as they watched it slump further into breathlessness, its own weight now crushing it down and finishing off what the gas had started.

Nerves regained, Fuller lifted Copeland forward. "Come on, we gotta get outta here! The pod's not that far off—come on!" he shouted at the nerve-wrecked unit. "Fulkes!" he shouted, struggling by after Carson and Etrick. "Your sidearm!" He motioned with his head at the still-heaving beast. Fulkes looked down at his side as if surprised to see the weapon—a momentary lapse that soon faded as more memories returned... memories of a screaming sergeant, a friend shown no mercy who'd been torn away by these things. Dropping his rifle, he reached down to his hip, his face screwing up at the creature in front of him; he watched it in pain, fighting for breath as he unbuckled his holster. There'd be no mercy here, either.

But in his drawing of the weapon, something happened—witnessed by Rians as he turned from the rip to follow the others, his eyes landing on a surreal scene as Fulkes smiled gleefully, waving the weapon in the air while beginning to rant and rave, dancing toward the creature.

"Well, Mr Lucky, you've won!" Rians heard Fulkes say, confusion halting his step as he watched him continue to wave the weapon awkwardly. "Yes, damn it, you've won! Won the star prize for big-ass aliens everywhere!" Fulkes continued with Rians watching. But then his glee faded and his ranting changed; it turned angry as his face soured to a rage, his weapon finally opening up and his screams coming through between each shot to the monster's head.

"You've won! You've won! You've won, motherfucker!" screamed Fulkes, a madman as tissue burst from the head wounds, showering him in blood with each round going off inside the creature—it struggling no more. "You've won! Won, ha ha! Won! You've won the prize! You've won… you've… ha ha haaa…" Fulkes began to quiet, out of breath, confused as he stared down, only the clicking of his now emptied weapon sounding out as he stared on, as if lost.

The laughing had stopped now as Rians approached, and he reached out for Fulkes' arm, the man's hand still pulling the trigger on the empty weapon. His face full of concern, he aimed to help him, to try to talk him back from…

"Aaaaaaaaaaaarrrrrrrrrrrrrrrgggggghhhhh!" screamed Fulkes, turning to see a Hearack grabbing for his arm! Weapon lifting, he pulled the trigger again, screaming as the empty chamber clicked with the barrel pointed at its head, but it didn't work; it wasn't fazed at all and just kept coming at him, speaking some insane language as it grabbed for him! All of his rounds gone and his back against the wall, Fulkes launched at it, screaming in a frenzy and slamming the useless weapon off its face again and again, screaming as it…

Suddenly, there was blackness, a rifle butt the last thing he saw as he slumped to the floor, a panting Rians staring down at him, raging and torn-faced with blood running from fresh wounds. Fuller came back, panicked, running round the corner with his weapon focused on the rip, but instead only Rians was there to greet him… a confused and angry look on his face as he glared down at an unconscious Fulkes, seemingly lost in his anger.

"It's the gas!" shouted Fuller, Rians turning with a start at Fuller's appearance, which had gone unnoticed before. "Fuck knows what he's seeing! Help me get him up before we all end up the same!"

Wounds still streaming, Rians reluctantly helped Fulkes up—the reluctance uncharacteristic but unnoticed, like his head now feeling heavy, unnaturally so. Still angry, Rians struggled back with Fuller round the corner, down the blood-strewn walkway back to where Fuller had left a groaning Copeland bleeding against one side of the corridor.

"What happened?" Copeland uttered as they approached, dragging along Fulkes with his head down between them.

"Never mind—here, grab my arm!" Fuller shouted, hoisting Copeland from the wall and ignoring his struggles. "I got em, I got em!" shouted Fuller, motioning with his head for Rians to cover their exit, unnerved to have no eyes behind them as they struggled off, him between the two casualties and with the pod only a short distance away.

Chapter 31

Promise

They could hear the screaming as they moved toward the pod, Fulkes' struggles echoing down the corridor as he tried to fight off a Carson looking Hearack strapping him into his seat harness his heavy breathing from shock making him succumb to the gas even further his hallucinations intense and overpowering any reason. Fuller struggled with Copeland and Etrick, moving toward the door and all the time looking back for Rians, half-expecting an attack from some direction with his nerves shot as they approached their exit, simply wanting his men behind the closed door and safe from the things behind them. But Rians was slowing again, looking back as if for someone else "Rians! Rians!" Fuller half-shouted, unwilling to get any louder. "Come on, man!" He winced, gesturing with his head as Rians turned—an odd look on his face now, and barely moving forward. Fuller watched as he became hesitant, almost stopping and looking back again "Come on!" Fuller shouted more loudly, fearing the gas was affecting him, that he was about to turn like Fulkes. Rians looked back and then away again, his expression changing and troubled as if he was about to crack, Fuller just wanting him in the pod. They could deal with him there, where he couldn't run off.

But gas was only part of it, as Rians struggled in his mind; he struggled with a responsibility no one else had, and with responsibility that couldn't be ignored.

"Come on!!!" screamed Fuller, afraid and not

knowing what he was about to do, just anxious to get him in the pod.

Rians saw it in his face, and knew that if he got in the pod, that that would be it. He'd reason with Fuller, and try to tell him, but... but he wasn't listening even now, and Rians had to, to... Shuffling toward Fuller, he turned away once more to look down the corridor, almost at arm's length now as he turned back with Fuller about to reach for him when his rifle fell, slipping to the ground with his feet turning to follow and retrieve it.

"Leave it!" screamed Fuller, moving for him, exacerbated and frightened; he was on the verge of... "Arrrrgggghh!" was all Fuller got out as Rians boot suddenly crashed into his chest. Caught by surprise, Fuller reeled backwards—straight into the pod with his back slamming down on the steel floor and sliding further inside. In an instant, it was clear; the rest of the men were half into their harnesses, and looked down from their seats in confusion. But not Fuller as he tried to get to his feet, panic coming out in grunts and words not coming at all, he was so winded. Reaching his feet, he made for the door, but it was too late—a high-pitched rush of air was followed by a bang as Fuller slammed against the inside of the sealed door. Panic reigned as he lurched left for the door panel, but another sound was there first; dull thuds and small explosions teamed with muzzle flashes from outside so that Fuller's hand fell on a dead panel. Again and again, he punched at it, nerves tearing through him with his knowing full well what was happening. With the panel gone, he lurched right, still winded and groping for the steel lip around the pod's viewing port.

Panicked, he screamed through it at the sombre face

on the other side; he knew he was losing. Rians' look said it all, regardless of Fuller banging his fists frantically against the door. He didn't know that the decision was already made, and there was no way Rians could leave. It wasn't that the ship might not be on course, or that the threat might not be neutralised; it was much more than that, for at that moment, Rians finally understood what Maral had been telling him... he had found his Allegiance.

"Open the door!" Fuller screamed.

"I can't," Rians tried to explain.

"It's on course—open the door!"

"I can't take that chance... I—" Rians tried again.

"Open the door, and that's an order! Open this fucking door!"

No answer came, and a panicked Fuller's hands pressed against the door while he glared at Rians through the port as, head-bowed, the other man stood behind his side motionless, calm, as if....

Fuller watched as Rians slowly raised his head on the doomed side of the airlock to meet his gaze; his face looked through the glass at him holding an expression of despair, of resignation—a face trying to apologise in the last few seconds they had. *What was he thinking?* Fuller asked himself. What what was wrong that he'd done this?

Then he heard it—he heard why his friend wasn't leaving, and watched him speak from the other side, powerless to reach him.

"I told my daughter the monsters wouldn't get her. What kind of a father would I be if I can't keep my promises?"

Fuller looked back at him open-mouthed, both men

437

standing in silence, in pain, with only inches of glass for separation. Eyes looked back and forth, both men motionless, and then Rians' face tightened, his eyes saddening as he reached for the emergency crank.

"NO!" screamed Fuller. "DON'T YOU—"

An explosion of pressure shot out into space, the seal giving way between the ship and the pod, and between them through the white rush of freezing air, Fuller saw the ghostly face of Rians looking after them as they tumbled away.

Rians had watched Fuller screaming on the other side, but he'd already forgotten the sight of it as he made his way back up the corridor, his mind now hazy with the gas. But his feelings were instinctual—something the gas agent couldn't take away. There was no such luxury on the escape pod, though, with Fuller screaming hysterically with stars streaming past the viewing port as they tumbled, the others holding him steady as best they could from their seats.

Outside, too, there was no let-up, the pod not even noticed and looking like wreckage to scanners as both sides frantically tore at one another, ion beams ripping through space with vessels charging through the death shrouds of exploding ships. On either side of the amalganite barge, a wall of Alliance steel fought off waves of Hearack, their loss of contact with their allies on the vessel driving them into a frenzy of determination now to destroy the pursuing ship.

Struggling back up the corridor, Rians knew he had to get to the bridge eight decks above; he just felt—no, he knew—that the guidance had been damaged, and it wasn't paranoia or the chemical agent. He'd seen the creature strike the systems, and felt the ship lurch; he knew it hadn't come back before the guidance panels had failed. The turn to the maglift was just up ahead, and looking around as he went, his thoughts became flighty and harder to hold onto with the agent thickening in places, clearly visible as overheads pumped it in all around him. His breathing getting heavier, Rians felt a sudden stab in his head as he reached for the right wall to steady himself. Stopping, he grimaced, waiting for the pain to leave… it was happening—his body was filling with the agent. Struggling for breath, he noticed that the pain had almost gone, leaving a sickening feeling behind as if… laughter, familiar laughter, suddenly echoed down the corridor from in front of him. Rians looked up, following the sound, but it had gone. Confused, he tried to ease himself off the wall with the laughter ringing in his memory… and then, again it started, jarring his head up quickly through the thickening agent, and he saw her, his daughter. At the end of the corridor, he saw the small figure of his child run round the corner laughing, carefree, so happy… her voice bringing back memories, bringing smiles to Rians as she disappeared, leaving him thinking of the past, of the…. He suddenly snapped to with a start, an impact on the ship's hull cavitating through the ship and breaking his thoughts. He wasn't standing anymore—instead, he was half crouched against the wall in a near trance, sleepy as if he'd been ready to fall away… he got a hold of himself, angry. Angry at almost failing. Standing, he concentrated, struggling for breath and promising himself never to do that again, moving off from the wall and staggering forward with fear working now as his motivation; he realised time was running out.

The impacts Rians was feeling were the few lucky shots getting through the barge's protective barrier of ships on each side, its shields only suffering minor damage. But with so much amalganite on board, minor damage was enough to worry Aidin. Placed in command of the taskforce around the barge while Ritter tried to hold back the remaining Hearack behind them, he watched the hull integrity of the barge fluctuate on sensors. One wall of ships on either side of the barge, twenty-two in all, each one manoeuvring constantly with her trying to maintain her cover.

"Taskforce ships eighteen and twenty-five, close your gap with one another!" Aidin's voice came over the channels, concerned at how far the two were drifting apart. "Nine and four, target incoming waves on the port side."

Weapons soon blazed off the port quarter, the incoming wave checked and forced to veer off and try again under the weight of firepower.

Maglift whining to a halt, Rians moved as the doors opened, only for his knees to buckle as his hands just managed to close on the left-hand side of the lift, preventing him falling to the floor. His mind grew relaxed; thoughts were hard to hold onto now, his grip on the maglifts side leaving him comfortable his eyes beginning to close the sound of his breathing filling his head long, heavy, the bright lights on the other side of his eyelids seemingly soft inviting. It was taking him, just with him standing there, his bloodstream filling with the agent with each breath—the chemicals working deeper and deeper into him, taking control and beckoning him away from what had been so clear eight decks below. Suddenly, the laughter came again, and his eyes jarred open as it faded through the mist-laden deck in front of him; startled by the near miss, he steadied himself with a grimace—he just couldn't fall away. He was losing it, but he had to keep going… keep going before he turned into Fulkes, a madman on this ship and all alone.

Twenty yards clear of the mag, Rians didn't find the laughter haunting anymore, almost appreciating its occasional appearance since he'd started to find the sound comforting as he felt his way down the right wall, the agent now so thick that he had trouble seeing. Instead, he began to rely more on touch, the bright lights of the corridor overhead now striking the mist-like agent and reducing visibility to mere feet as he struggled on.

The struggle outside, too, was intensifying, the Hearack becoming suicidal and charging headlong into impossible firepower, but with every challenge, the taskforce became more rattled—cohesion weakening, ships drifting further apart as the enemy drew closer each time.

"Captain, the port side is becoming thin!" reported Brenner, watching his display from his seat with Aidin standing near the con station and turning at the statement. "Ships eight and ten are having engine trouble—they're falling behind! Ion arrays on one and five have malfunctioned—they're down to thorans only!"

Suddenly, the channels crackled from ship nineteen on the starboard side. "*Brunswick* to *Rheinvar*, were reading a course deviation on the barge; please confirm, over."

Concerned, Aidin turned to the con station display

and pulled up the barge's course, recently unchecked with their attention focused on the enemy ships.

Focusing his own attention was the one thing Rians was finding it harder and harder to do with each step; he was disorientated and unable to see the end of the corridor or where the bridge was, trusting the wall for direction. The laughter had stopped now, replaced by the gentle sound of the environmental overheads sending the agent flowing freely into the corridor, thickening in front of him. Inching forward, Rians had given up waving the dense air from his eyes—instead blindly moving forward over debris beneath his feet, feeling his way toward the bridge. Only up to his wrists were visible now as his hands searched in front of him, his feet stepping on debris unseen in the white shroud beneath him, and all the time, the relaxation beckoned, determined to take him away, to have him lie down and drift away.

It was irresistible. Eyes watering... his breathing began to grow shallow with willpower no longer being enough to fight the agent as it shut down more and more of his brain. His hands began to drop as he stumbled a few more steps, knees weakening again as he lost his thoughts, bewildered in the... his feet were striking against something beneath him, and Rians was incapable of balancing. Instead, he went over, tired and barely even reaching out for the floor, almost unaware of what was happening when suddenly there was a rush of air, dense clouds of agent swirling away behind him and his head jarring up off the deck to see a space clearing in front of him... brilliant white, a doorway opening at his approach, the bridge. The blast of air giving life to Rians' thoughts, he instinctively crawled towards it, his lungs filling with all the clean air from the bridge they could find. Struggling over the unseen debris on the floor, he was soon through the opening with a rush of air behind him signalling the closing of the doors. Coming to rest on the floor, Rians continued to breathe the fresh air he'd found the bridge having its own seperate environmental system for safety like all ships. The air was crisp and painful to breath his muscles gorging on it and ignoring the damage the gas had done to his throat and the cramp setting in, his head spinning as what little agent had come in with him was carried off by the overheads above. Jolted by an impact from outside, Rians struggled to his feet, wiping fluid from his eyes as the bridge slowly became clear to him.

Clarity also came from the readings on the *Rheinvar*'s con station, Evans reporting: "It's confirmed, sir—she's .013 out, heading off the alien ship and into open space. Her guidance computer must be damaged."

"Damaged from the creatures that got on," Aidin spoke out loud. "The Marine units couldn't have got to them," he continued quietly, fearing the worst for them.

"We can't hold them off if she strays into open space," Brenner voiced, sitting behind him and looking up from his panel as Aidin turned. "We'll never get more people on to turn her under these attacks, either; there just isn't time."

Aidin turned back, his eyes falling on the helm panel displays which Brenner's words had just confirmed; he saw the distance between the Earth and the alien ship dropping, their time now almost up. Silently, he surveyed the bridge crew as they worked feverishly in coordinating the taskforce, the gravity of the two men's exchange unnoticed. Aidin took a breath, Brenner's words so clear as he looked at the faces around him and then back to Brenner, staring for a moment. "We'll have to update the *Lannan*."

"You know what he's going to do." Brenner answered.

Their unseen conversation continuing, Aidin's expression didn't change, his eyes leaving words unnecessary.

"Mr Hollin!" Brenner commanded.

"Sir," he answered automatically, still embroiled in his displays and his head not rising.

"Inform the *Lannan* of our situation," he ordered.

Hollin's pause was soon shortened as the officers turned their faces to him, firm expressions showing understanding as he slowly turned to his helm panel, his reply soon following.

Only Evans beside him realised what was happening, the rest of the bridge crew being too focused on what they were doing, about to die and not even knowing why as Aidin turned to Brenner again, his face changed from one of command to one of friendship… and nodding.

"Mr Hollin," Brenner said loudly, maintaining his professionalism as he breathed in, "Open channe—"

"Sir! The barge is altering course!" Hollin shouted.

"Hold positions!" demanded Aidin, the rest of the crew jarred by the shouting and not knowing how close they'd just come to their ends as they watched their captain descend on the helm panel with Hollin.

"She's definitely turning, sir!" Hollin announced loudly, as if trying to convince him to change his mind, the two men staring intently at the helm display with

Brenner's face unseen behind them as he grabbed his panel—breathing deeper, nerves nearing collapse from the strain.

"Then the guidance computer…" Aidin almost whispered at the display, his nerves frayed like Brenner's although he showed a small smile growing more as he watched. "It's still functional, and it's guiding her into the cavity."

But it wasn't the guidance computer. Instead, a lone figure sat on the bridge, his fingers just leaving the control panel on the right of the captain's chair. On screen, stars meandered right as the barge's course altered to the left, bright flashes bathing her screen in light with ships fighting on either side of her. Soon, though, there were no stars, even the bright flashes falling away as a massive structure began crawling across the screen from left to right. A ravined steel surface, planet-like and jagged, menacing; a dark green form spliced with shadows and blocking out all behind it as Rians watched it appear with the green giving way to black as the barge finished its turn. The black was the leading edge of a great gouge in the craft made when it had been torn from its parent… the cavity.

The attacks became incessant now, almost panicked, the Hearack realising what was happening as the barge wheeled round, now back on course. Again and again, they hurled themselves at the taskforce as it veered back toward the alien ship, defenders on either side of the barge stretched to their limits.

Aboard the barge, though, there was calm for Rians, delirium setting in with hallucinations appearing and mixing with objects on screen as he sat quietly, the amount of agent he'd been exposed to now having its final effects. Inside him, there was anything but silence as he sat motionless, bearing witness to uncontrollable memories. His ears were alive with voices, the screen in front of him a black void with the cavity... but to Rians, the darkness was a vague outline with people from his past occupying its centre... walking, disappearing, and then returning, their faces staring intently at him and nodding their approval. And then there was the laughter. It returned louder than ever, eclipsing all else with her small image smiling out at him as the lead edge of the barge entered the cavity, the taskforce pulling off.

The barge struck the edge of the cavity as it moved in further, the vibrations going unnoticed by Rians with his mind lost in the screen, smiling back at his daughter as the ship began crashing through structures inside, huge gangways falling away. With the barge almost completely inside, steel mounting after mounting tore free till finally the barge hit the superstructure. The forward section of the barge buckled backwards, its steel weaker than the alien bulkheads but with its slow speed making no difference—its inertia crushed it against the steel ahead. Inside, whole decks of the barge buckled backwards with plasma conduits rupturing, explosions being forced backwards as, one by one, the front of each deck gave way to the next. Deck after deck, the far side gave way with all the straining quantum in the world still not able to give the barge's alloy the strength it needed to withstand the pressure as great buckles and warps began forming in the steel, the very fabric of material twisting and wrenched apart as the pressures became unbearable. Sounds of groaning and twisting finally resulted in cracks being torn open as the pressure forced its way through plasma fires, surging inside their light mixing with the agent, the deck becoming brilliant white as they moved. Each new space invaded by the fires was bathed in the brilliance of it all, the back wall of each new deck becoming a brilliant white before being engulfed in plasma, pressure forcing it apart and the fires moving through to the next.

The hull was now buckled a quarter way in, its massive bulk still forcing it against the alien vessel with explosions bursting out all around it as the hull began crushing up to the bridge. Inside, vibrations still went unnoticed with Rians lost in a brilliance of his own—his daughter being all he could see as the deck wall in front of him finally burst open. The viewscreen torn away with the wall, it was hurled away with plasma surging inside, and for an instant, Rians appeared brilliant white before being lost in the plasma, the bridge engulfed in flames.

Outside, warring ships were suddenly thrown apart with the alien ship exploding, the blast taking her and every ship nearby to the grave in a titanic death throw. Struggling crews were blinded by the explosion, soon struck by the blast wave with some exploding from damage and others hurled back even further. The rumbling dissipating, people began picking themselves up among coughs and confusion. But confusion wasn't to last long as eyes fell on viewscreens across the fleet to see a great, incandescent mass of burning elements casting shadows across the twisted wreckage of the alien ship tumbling away into darkness.

Through shocked emotions, small laughs and claps began joining system alerts till suddenly roars of joy burst forward, the strain releasing from crews with tears all around. As captains began to report in, whoops and cries in the background began to fill the channels, echoing across space from ships in every sector. The *Jutland*'s captain's arms were in the air, the *Keinbar*'s captain's arms thrown up so excitedly that he was hardly able to report as the *Dailis*'s captain reached forward for the screen while still screaming in joy.

Screaming came elsewhere, too, with other hands reached toward the slowly dissipating shroud outside, but not in joy... in despair as still others desperately held him back from the escape pod's viewing port, Fuller's cries turning to sobs as his hands fell, tears welling up also in the faces of those around him.

Further back from the explosion, a momentary calm faded away with sporadic battles breaking out, weapons fire appearing in distant positions as the remnants of the enemy went on with the only course they had left. But it was over; for the few that were left, it was just a matter of time, the taskforce breaking up and descending on the remaining enemy with the others. The *Rheinvar*, too, had been just about to join the fray, but a sudden report from the con had stalled their progress.

"You're sure!" Aidin asked excitedly.

"Yes, sir!" Hollin reported. "It's definitely from the barge; life signs inside. It must have passed unnoticed with all the activity before—initiate docking procedures, sir?"

"No, not a chance—we're not risking them being left out there any longer! Use the inducer and to hell with the protocols; materialise them directly onto the bridge, man!" Aidin's enthusiasm continued, his earlier fears falling away at the news.

There was a sudden sound behind the weapons station then, indescribable as an equally indescribable materialisation process began behind the tactical station, Steiner moving well clear as the process was not fully understood and banned for organic matter. But such rules were far from Aidin's mind, the whole book thrown out the window with this success as he bounded up the left gangway, degenerating into a teenager before the bridge crew's very eyes.

Chapter 32

Justice

"Well, Mr Rians!" Aidin spoke jubilantly as he bounded up the aft ramp to the new arrivals. "It seems I owe you that drink in—" Aidin stopped as he came to stand next to Steiner, finding a few exhausted men standing battered and bloody around a wounded creature knelt on the floor. It looked up at him with tears still evident. *Fuller.* Aidin's jubilance deserted him as, looking around, he could find no trace of Rians—his whereabouts only silently etched on the surviving faces. Aidin's mouth lay ajar, his face quickly joining the others. There were no words.

Forward at the stations, Evans And Hollin were still feverishly busy at their panels, unaware of the tragedy behind them.

"Captain, it seems our sensors were incorrect!" shouted Hollin. "The barge's computers could not have been so heavily damaged, as it made corrections right along its guidance axis…" Hollin began to spin round, still shouting enthusiastically. "It seems its course was—" His eyes fell on the scene behind him, the faces telling all in an instant and evaporating his enthusiasm, leaving his last word almost a whisper. "Perfect."

"Captain!" shouted Steiner. "There's a ship on an intercept course—it's a Hearack fighter!"

Hollin grabbed his panel as he spun round. "Weapons are tracking it, Captain, what do you want—"

The channels broke overhead, cutting Hollin off. It

was Ritter. "Aidin, there's a Hearack fighter heading toward you."

"We have it," Aidin assured him bitterly.

"Do not fire—I repeat, do not fire!" Ritter ordered him. "You are to escort it and its crew away to station 185."

"What?" Aidin retorted as he watched the fighter loom larger on the viewscreen, the top of Earth's curve behind it—the planet the approaching crew and their brethren had just tried to destroy.

"You are to escort their transport to station 185, and that's an order," commanded Ritter.

"You can't be serious!" Aidin said, standing side by side with Steiner now. "Why?" he growled.

"That doesn't matter," Ritter replied.

"It does if I'm to pull my crew up alongside the enemy—now, why?" Aidin demanded, his voice rising.

"It contains members of the enemy who IN6 wish to question; their information on the Dren could prove invaluable in the future, so their safe transport is essential," Ritter stressed.

"Which members?" Aidin asked suspiciously.

"That's none of your concern," Ritter retorted through clenched teeth at Aidin's obstinacy.

"Which members, damn it?" Aidin demanded.

"I told you that's none of your concern!" Ritter insisted. "Now, you will ensure their safe transport or I will have you relieved, do you understand?"

Aidin paused, squinting at the other ship that was now stationary, holding position in front of them. "Yes, sir."

"Ritter out!"

The gentle system alerts dominated the bridge as

they all stared suspiciously at the phantom vessel in front of them, all thinking the same thing—who was on it? Surely, that bastard wasn't about to slip the noose yet again, but their worst fear was about to be realised as a system alert went off on Steiner's panel.

"Captain," Steiner said, "we're being hailed."

"By whom?" asked Aidin, his face contorted.

Steiner looked up from his panel with a sickened expression. "By them," he said, motioning with his head toward the viewscreen.

Aidin looked at the screen again, seething with anger. "Put it through."

The screen broke to the incoming signal, and there…

"Captain!" Maral smiled with a voice of welcome but a face of contempt. "Are you alright? It's been quite a battle, wouldn't you say?"

"You're finished, Maral!" Aidin hissed, cutting off another speech.

"Oh contraire, I think you'll find I'm far from finished, Captain." Maral smiled, his chilling voice echoing over the channels. "You see, your people in IN6 seem to think I can be more than useful," he continued, surveying the bridge of the *Rheinvar* with mirth as if he were the victor.

His arrogance was overpowering, and the *Rheinvar*'s very walls strained under the crew's fury.

Watching their frustration, Maral smirked as he continued, "Don't be mad, Captain, it's not your fault… it's your culture. Despite everything I've done, despite all the misery and torment, it throws me yet another lifeline. It's simply… to die for."

Aidin couldn't help it. Watching the face and

listening, he just….

Steiner felt an arm shove his aside as a high-pitched acknowledgement came from the weapons panel beneath. A groaning rumble came from the bowels of the ship, it being a rumble they'd all heard before as a wave of thorans tore out from under the *Rheinvar*, their amber wrath charging for the other ship. Maral's eyes widened, his arrogant smirk leaving, to be replaced by his scream shrieking out over the channels. *"Noooooooooooooooooo!!!!!"*

The thorans descended with a rage on their target, and there were enough to crack open a starship; they smashed straight through the hull to a still-screaming Maral, bathing the ship's interior with fire before exploding outward and ripping the ship apart.

They watched on screen as the ship splintered in all directions, violence never looking so good and slowly dissipating into the darkness, leaving nothing but satisfaction behind.

They watched the emptiness in silence, awed and justified… before the channels broke open.

"Aidin! Aidin, what the fuck… what the fuck have you done!" screamed Ritter.

There was a long pause on their side, the bridge falling silent and still watching the fires melt away in front of them, before, finally, Aidin pushed the return and replied, "Escort complete."

Chapter 33

Homecoming

There wasn't any talking on the transport on the way down; with a skeleton crew left onboard, Aidin had joined the remainder of his crew along with Fuller's team and Etrick as they transported down to the surface. They had won, and they had beaten off annihilation. They'd live to see their loved ones and their families, and they should have been ecstatic. Should have been..

With a rush of dust, the transport landed on the docking pad, the sun dropping behind it and to the right with a send-off of golden warmth; it would have been a beautiful scene if not for all the medibeds being rushed back and forth.

The main door crashed down hard on the iron-grated pad, people beginning to disembark with relief, slowly at first but finally running—running to open-armed family members who waited, hoping, and among them Carla. She watched through the crowd, holding Charlotte's hand beside her. Nothing, nothing of her husband as she watched with a face of anguish growing worse with each passing moment and with each passing family reunion when there... yes! Fuller and Copeland and.... "Come on!" she demanded, beaming suddenly and grasping her daughter's hand, running with her down the gangway to her love. She came up against the crowds nearer the transport that were trying to leave, almost manic with joy as she tried to push through. Catching sight of them again, she began shouting over the noise. "Fuller! Fuller! Over here!" she screamed, bubbling over with joy as she tried to push through the crowd with Charlotte, finally arriving out of breath and grabbing Fuller to hug him, gasping for air and joy. She didn't notice him not hugging back or his statue-like posture. Still holding his arms and laughing with joy, she looked up at him, alive in front of her, with happiness. "Where is he?" she laughed. "Where is the son of a bitch?"

"Carla," Fuller tried to begin.

"Where is he?" she continued, looking behind him to the others, searching. "Where…."

"Carla," Fuller said again.

His expression hadn't changed, but with her mania subsiding, she began to notice his rock-hard stance, his…

Laughing it off suddenly, she looked around and back at Fuller. "Where is he?" She smiled again. "Where?"

Nothing, though. He just stood there, sombre and looking down at her. Then, feelings appeared, bad feelings.

"No," she said, still holding Fuller's arms but now shaking her head at him, her smile still trying to stay. She looked at Copeland and his eyes full of sorrow. "No, it can't…." Tears appeared as her eyes glazed over under Fuller's telling stare. "No… nooo…." she began to wail, going limp, and Fuller tried to steady her as she slid down him onto her knees, wailing on the grate.

The men fought back tears as Charlotte went to her mother's aid, lying her hands on her back and asking, "Mommy, what's wrong? Mommy?" It was all too much, and the scene went on for what seemed like a lifetime as similar scenes played out all over, witnessing this one, the men would rather have been back and fighting for their lives. With Carla wailing, Fulkes now started to lose it, the gas long since having worn off to leave the memories of Brice's final moments which assured him he'd never hear that angry kindness again. This was just… just unbearable.

Shouts came from the end of the gangway, voices angry and otherwise beginning to invade the sombre scene and approaching, unwelcome—at their centre, Ritter! Arriving on them with two ensigns at his side, there was no build-up. He just exploded on Aidin to Fuller's right, "What the fuck where you told?"

Aidin looked back, angered by his intrusion on such a scene, raising his head and narrowing his eyes on this man who he'd come to despise. He growled, "We had a malfunction."

"A malfunction!" Ritter shot back immediately. "A malfunction!"

"Yes," Aidin sneered, barely able to ungrate his teeth to reply. "A malfunction," he repeated, turning away in disgust and giving Ritter all the respect of an ensign.

"Yeah, your last!" returned Ritter, fuming at his attitude.

Unhappy with not getting his pound of flesh from Aidin or the rise out of him he'd wanted, Ritter turned his attention on Fuller.

"And you! I've had it!" Ritter screamed, pointing through the men at Fuller. "Your fucking name appears in every screw-up across the board—you're outta here!"

"Sir," Etrick tried with his head down, caught between loyalties.

"You abandon Etrick's team and go it alone, disobeying direct orders with the result of getting them killed!" continued Ritter unabated.

"Sir," Etrick tried again.

"They were going—" Fuller started.

"You shut up!" Ritter screamed. "You shut your mouth once and for all! You got a lot of good people killed up there, and when I'm through, you'll wish you were one of them! You fucki—"

The punch came from nowhere, and reeling back through the ensigns, Ritter collapsed with his head crashing onto the grating, his nose streaming. His pain brushed aside by anger, he tried to sit up. Drawing an arm across his face, he saw his hand strewn with blood and anger turned to shock and then to anger as, face grimacing, he looked up to confront his attacker, and found… it was Etrick!

Standing quietly beside Fuller and his men, Etrick looked down with disdain. and Ritter… Ritter looked back stunned, lost for words, the solidarity among them obvious. He felt small, and he also felt anger, rage. Grimacing, he screamed, "Ensign!"

One ensign drew a Del 10, raising it on…

The sound of steel bolts cocking rang out as, all around Etrick, rifles pointed out from behind him, the ensign's hand losing its steady grip as he heard the familiar whine and looked down at the laser sights gently weaving back and forth across his chest. Looking up, he tried to appear unshaken despite his panicked expression and unsteady hand. Greeting his glance were Fuller's men, armed to the teeth and stone cold staring over their rifle barrels.

In seconds, the tension could be tasted, and as the stand-off continued, it was broken only by a much quieter voice.

"…s-s-sstop…" came a weeping voice through the

silence. "What do you want…" the voice tried to push through the sobbing. "More blood? Why do you…" it degenerated back into sobbing and came no more, but it had been enough, the suffering their eyes fell upon dropping the men in a way that rounds couldn't.

Chapter 34

Vandalism

The IAF said they wanted to know what had happened, but most of the individuals didn't really; it was obvious and they weren't stupid. With everything that had happened, most didn't care and just wanted any answer for the records, but there were those who were sticklers for routine.

"So, Captain Aidin," the IAF inquiry council began. "It seems there was, aaah, ah, and I quote, 'a mishap' on your ship, and the council was wondering how often these mishaps occur. Could you tell us how many other ships have been so unfortunate around yours?"

Aidin stood there, the five members of the inquiry sitting high in front of him and some of their star witnesses behind tables on his left, none of them wanting to be there, save one.

"None, sir," Aidin answered.

"None," repeated the councilor. "Then this unfortunate incident was... bad luck, perhaps?"

"Yes, sir, quite bad luck."

"Indeed, and have you been able to ascertain just where this bad luck seems to have emanated from? It's just that we wouldn't want any similar cases of... bad luck to happen to any other unfortunate crew," added the councilor sarcastically.

"Well, sir," Aidin began, noticing a new face among the five councilors, this being a face he didn't recognise—not even with thirty-seven years service... a face that clearly didn't belong there, dressed in a general's uniform. "Unfortunately, during the battle, the *Rheinvar* sustained damage like many others," Aidin began again, his answer well-scripted. "And as a matter of course, sir, with life depending on us, there were certain oversights."

"Oversights?" repeated the councilor, highlighting his next line of attack.

"Yes, sir," Aidin answered, his same politeness now battling on the councilor's own ground. "Under attack, certain data from systems can seem unimportant at the time—"

"You're referring to the certain temperature data that flowed onto the ship's systems panels during your encounter with the alien ship which…" he paused, laughing and turning to the witness stand before proceeding, "highlighted a dangerous build-up of heat in the experimental weapons array targeting syst—"

"Yes," Aidin cut him off with a scowl, playing his own game. "When you have an N class attack ship pointing its entire weaponry array at you, enough to melt away half a city, your attention has a tendency to become occupied."

"Hmm, yes," continued the councilor with a similar sneer only barely hidden by a laugh. "And I suppose your systems had a similar lapse of attention, being that these log reports seem to be missing their time and date settings for the occasion, so tell me, Captain, is it normal for a computer to become worried?"

Aidin wrestled more and more with the councilor over the next twenty minutes as he questioned the evidence, trying to trip Aidin into admitting the truth, but it didn't matter. It didn't matter as Aidin sat there quietly seething, knowing full well that the only evidence that could help the councilor was being quietly destroyed two hundred and twenty miles above them as they spoke, Steiner And Danske just having entered the forward weapons bay twelve minutes before the shipyard inspection crew were due to arrive, the *Rheinvar*'s own crew all already sent on leave.

Danske's face, though, was another story as Steiner brought out a Del 10, Danske grimacing as he heard it begin to charge. Weeks earlier, he'd wanted to use one of these damn weapons on the modular array himself, and they'd given the ship's doctor as much of a headache as they themselves had had through stress, as the whole engineering staff had wrestled with the adjustments and calculations. It was perfect, aligned like a dream and transferring more power than anything else in the fleet… a one of a kind, and they were proud, given that they'd made work what the lab rats hadn't been able to manage.

The sudden energy burst jerked Danske's gaze from the floor, only for him to see Steiner step back out of the way with matrix shards shattering outward, falling still glowing to the floor. He hadn't even told him he was going to…

Steiner let out a grin, his latest feat of destruction complete and still sparking; it was a good job, looking like an overload… he'd even hit it at a good angle, leaving no scarring, he noticed as a look of satisfaction crept in across his face.

Turning, though, he came upon another look, a scowl like that of a spoilt child, Danske not able to find the words as he took a look at the remains which were still glowing, not one refractory matrix left intact and the whole unit shattered. Looking back at Steiner, there wasn't even a glimmer of understanding to be felt as he turned away, seething at his ease with the task.

Steiner never could understand Danske's almost unhealthy interest in machinery; it was weird, but as he watched him walk out the door, he did understand that he'd better stay clear of engineering… for a very long time.

Chapter 35

Sacrifice

His crew made it right on a hill overlooking the sea, the sun setting over wind-swept wheat fields. Carla would never know the significance her husband had made, and they'd never tell her, they just said it's what he talked about. But quiet it wasn't nobody dancing just thousands of onlookers on the hills determined on their respect Marines protecting the sight from those with too much good will.

Holding back tears during the ceremony, Aidin's mind was filled with the loss of it, all the weight crushing as he spoke aloud, "What's it all about, Number one?"

Brenner didn't answer, trying to hold in emotions of his own, but eventually subduing them enough, he stammered, "He seemed to think it was all about them."

Aidin looked at Brenner, following his gaze to Rians' daughter as she laid a rose on her father's coffin.

Watching through tear-filled eyes for Rians, his family, and the child he'd never have, he replied, "Of course."

A word about the author…

"We're all ships, sailing the seas of life, learning our lessons, but some of us, when we look up into the sky at night, know we should be sailing among the stars..."

Victor Salvatore